Summerland

Michael Chabon is the Pulitzer Prize-winning author of *The Amazing Adventures of Kavalier and Clay*. His other books include *Wonder Boys* and *Werewolves in their Youth*. He lives in Berkeley, California, with his wife and three children.

For more information on Michael Chabon visit www.4thestate.com/MichaelChabon

Also by Michael Chabon

Werewolves in Their Youth

Wonder Boys

The Amazing Adventures of Kavalier and Clay

A Model World and Other Stories

The Mysteries of Pittsburgh

MICHAEL CHABON

Summerland

FOURTH ESTATE • *London* and *New York*

First published in the USA by Miramax Books 2002
This edition published in Great Britain in 2003 by Fourth Estate
Fourth Estate
A Division of HarperCollins*Publishers* Ltd
77–85 Fulham Palace Road
London W6 8JB
www.4thestate.com

1 3 5 7 9 10 8 6 4 2

A catalogue record for this book is available from the British Library

ISBN 0-00-712712-X

Printed in Great Britain by
Clays Ltd, St Ives plc

To Sophie, Zeke, and Ida-Rose

CONTENTS

FIRST BASE

SECOND BASE

THIRD BASE

HOME

FIRST BASE

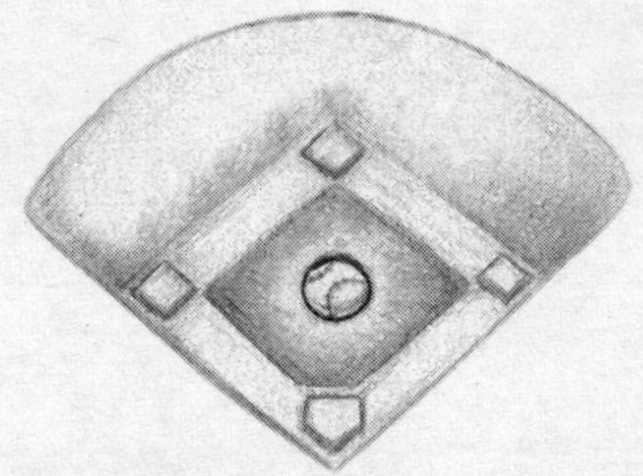

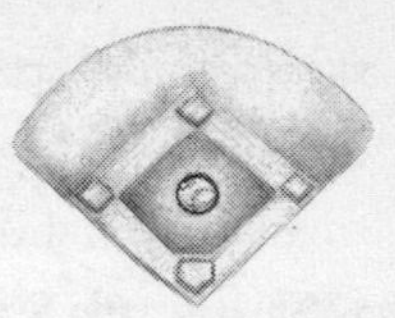

1

The Worst Ballplayer in the History of Clam Island, Washington

ETHAN SAID, "I hate baseball."

He said it as he followed his father out of the house, in his uniform and spikes. His jersey read ROOSTERS in curvy red script. On the back it said RUTH'S FLUFF 'N' FOLD.

"I hate it," he said again, knowing it was cruel. His father was a great lover of baseball.

But Mr. Feld didn't say anything in reply. He just locked the door, tried the knob, and then put his arm around Ethan's shoulders. They walked down the muddy path to the driveway and got into Mr. Feld's Saab station wagon. The car's name was Skidbladnir, but usually they just called her Skid. She was oranger than anything else within a five-hundred-mile radius of Clam Island, including traffic cones, U-Haul trailers, and a fair number of actual oranges. She was so old that, as she went along, she made squeaking and rattling noises that sounded more like the sounds of a horse buggy than of an automobile. Her gauges and knobs were all labelled in Swedish, which was not a language that either Mr. Feld or Ethan, or for that matter anyone in Ethan's family going back twenty generations on both sides, could speak. They rolled, squeaking and rattling, down from the little pink house where they lived, atop a small barren hill at the centre of the island, and headed west, towards Summerland.

"I made *three* errors in the last game," Ethan reminded his father, as they drove to pick up Jennifer T. Rideout, the Roosters' first baseman, who had called to say that she needed a ride. Ethan figured that his father was probably *not* going to let him out of playing in today's game against the Shopway Angels; but you never knew. Ethan felt that he could make a pretty good case for his staying home, and Mr. Feld was always willing to listen to a good argument, backed up with sound evidence. "Danny Desjardins said that I directly caused four runs to score."

"Plenty of good ballplayers have made three errors in a game," Mr. Feld said, turning onto the Clam Island Highway, which ran from one end of the island to the other, and was not, as far as Ethan was concerned, a highway at all. It was an ordinary two-lane road, lumpy and devoid of cars like every other road on the lumpy, empty little island. "It happens all the time."

Mr. Feld was a large, stout man with a short but unruly beard like tangled black wool. He was both a recent widower and a designer of lighter-than-air dirigibles, neither a class of person known for paying a lot of attention to clothes. Mr. Feld never wore anything in the summer but a clean T-shirt and a ragged pair of patched blue jeans. In the wintertime he added a heavy sweater, and that was it. But on game days, like today, he proudly wore a Ruth's Fluff 'n' Fold Roosters T-shirt, size XXL, that he had bought from

Ethan's coach, Mr. Perry Olafssen. None of the other Rooster fathers wore shirts that matched their sons'.

"I hate it that they even *count* errors," Ethan said, pressing on with his case. To show his father just how disgusted he was by the whole *idea* of counting errors, he threw his mitt against the dashboard of the car. It kicked up a cloud of infield dust. Ethan coughed energetically, hoping to suggest that the very atoms of dirt on which he would be standing when they got to Ian "Jock" MacDougal Regional Ball Field were noxious to him. "What kind of game is that? No other sport do they do that, Dad. There's no other sport where they put the errors on the freaking *scoreboard* for everybody to look at. They don't even *have* errors in other sports. They have *fouls*. They have *penalties*. Those are things that players could get on purpose, you know. But in baseball they keep track of how many *accidents* you have."

Mr. Feld smiled. Unlike Ethan, he was not a talkative fellow. But he always seemed to enjoy listening to his son rant and rave about one thing or another. His wife, the late Dr. Feld, had been prone to the same kind of verbal explosions. Mr. Feld didn't know that Ethan was only ever talkative around *him*.

"Ethan," Mr. Feld said, shaking his head in sorrow. He reached over to put a hand on Ethan's shoulder. Skid lurched wildly to the left, springs squealing, creaking like a buckboard in an old western movie. Her noticeable colour and Mr. Feld's distracted style of driving had, in the short time that the Feld men had been living on Clam Island, made the car a well-known local road hazard. "Errors... Well, they are a part of life, Ethan," he tried to explain.

"Fouls and penalties, generally speaking, are not. That's why baseball is more like life than other games. Sometimes I feel like that's all I do in life, keep track of my errors."

"But, Dad, you're a grown-up," Ethan reminded him. "A kid's life isn't supposed to be that way. Dad— look out!"

Ethan slammed his hands against the dashboard, as if that would stop the car. There was a small animal, no bigger than a cat, in the westbound lane of Clam Island Highway – they were headed right at it. In another instant they would mash it under their wheels. But the animal just seemed to be standing there, an alert little creature, rusty as a pile of leaves, sharp-eared, peering directly at Ethan with its big, round, staring black eyes.

"Stop!" Ethan yelled.

Mr. Feld hit the brakes, and the tires burped against the blacktop. The car shuddered, and then the engine stalled and died. Their seat belts were made of some kind of thick Swedish webbing material that could probably stop bullets, and the buckles were like a couple of iron padlocks. So the Felds were all right. But Ethan's mitt flew out of his lap and banged into the glove compartment door. A huge cloud of dust from the mitt filled the car. Maps of Seattle, Colorado Springs, Philadelphia, and a very old one of Göteborg, Sweden, came tumbling out of the glove compartment, along with a Band-Aid can filled with quarters, and a Rodrigo Buendía baseball card.

"What is it? What was it?" said Mr. Feld, looking wildly around. He wiped the inside of the windshield with his forearm and peered out. There was nothing in the road at all now, and nothing moving in the trees on either side. Ethan had never seen anything emptier than the Clam Island Highway at that moment. The silence in the car, broken only by the chiming of Mr. Feld's key ring against the ignition, was like the sound of that emptiness. "Ethan, what did you see?"

"A fox," Ethan said, though even as he said it he felt that he somehow had it wrong. The animal's head and snout had been like a fox's, and there had been the fat red brush of a tail, but somehow the, well, the *posture* of the animal hadn't been— *vulpine*, was the word. Not foxlike. The thing had seemed to be standing, hunched over, on its hind legs, like a monkey, with its front paws scraping the ground. "I think it was a fox. Actually, come to think of it, it might have been a lemur."

"A lemur," Mr. Feld said. He restarted the car, rubbing at his shoulder where the seat belt had dug in. Ethan's shoulder was feeling a little sore, too. "On Clam Island."

"Uh-huh. Or, no, actually I think it was a bushbaby."

"A bushbaby."

"Uh-huh. They live in Africa and feed on insects. They peel the bark from trees to find the tasty and nutritious gum underneath." Ethan had recently seen an entire programme devoted to bushbabies, on the Fauna Channel. "Maybe it escaped from a zoo. Maybe someone on the island keeps bushbabies."

"Could be," said Mr. Feld. "But it was probably a fox."

They rode past the V.F.W. hall, and the obelisk-shaped monument to the Clam Island pioneers. They drove alongside the cemetery where the ancestors and loved ones of almost everyone now living on Clam Island, except for Ethan and his father, were buried. Ethan's mother was buried in a cemetery in Colorado Springs, a thousand miles away. Ethan thought of that nearly every time they went past the Clam Island cemetery. He suspected that his father did, too. They always fell silent along this stretch of road.

"I really think it was a bushbaby," Ethan said at last.

"Ethan Feld, if you say the word 'bushbaby' one more time..."

"Dad, I'm sorry, I know you're mad at me, but I..." Ethan took a deep breath and held it for a few seconds. "I don't think I want to play baseball anymore."

Mr. Feld didn't say anything at first. He just drove, watching the side of the road for the turn-off to the Rideout place.

Then he said, "I'm very sorry to hear that."

As Ethan had heard many times, the first scientific experiment that Mr. Feld had ever performed in his whole life, back when he was eight years old, in Philadelphia, PA, was to see if he could turn himself into a left-handed pitcher. He had read that a kid who could throw left-handed had a better chance of making it to the big leagues. He hung an old tyre from a tree in his grandmother's backyard and every day for a whole summer tried to throw a baseball through the tyre a hundred times with his left arm. Then, when he could throw it straight and hard, he taught himself to throw a knuckleball, a slow pitch that travels without spinning, and makes its way towards the hitter like a butterfly over a bed of flowers, fluttering. It was not a very good knuckleball, though, and when he tried to throw it in real games, the other boys jumped all over it. Yet its crazy motion interested him, and Mr. Feld had begun to wonder about the shapes of things, and about the way air went over and around something that was round and moving very fast. In the end he had given up baseball for aerodynamics. But he had never forgotten, to this day, the way it felt to stand on the top of that small, neat hill of brown dirt, in the middle of a green field, holding on to a little piece of something that could fly.

"Dad?"

"*Ethan?*" said Mr. Feld. Now he sounded a little annoyed. "If you don't want to play anymore, then that's all right with me. Forget it. I understand. Nobody likes to lose every time."

The Ruth's Fluff 'n' Fold Roosters had, as a matter of fact, lost all of their first seven games that season. In the opinion of most of the Roosters, and of their coach, Mr. Perry Olafssen, the presence of Ethan Feld on the team went a long way to explaining their troubles on the field. It was agreed by nearly everyone who watched him take the field that Ethan Feld was the least gifted ballplayer that Clam Island had ever seen. It was hard to decide, really, why this should be so. Ethan was a boy of average height, a little stocky, you might have said, but healthy and alert. He was not a terrible klutz, and he could run pretty well, if something worth running from, such as a bee, was after him. Yet every time he put on his uniform and stepped out onto the dusty grey dirt of Jock MacDougal Field, something seemed to go dreadfully wrong.

"But I'm afraid, son," Mr. Feld continued, "you can't just not show up for today's game. The team is counting on you."

"Yeah, right."

"Mr. Olafssen is counting on you."

"Counting on me to make three errors."

They had reached the ramshackle assortment of roadside mailboxes that marked the entrance to the Rideout place. Ethan sensed that he was running out of time. Once Jennifer T. Rideout was in the car, there would be no hope of escape from today's game. Jennifer T. didn't have a whole lot of patience in general for listening to Ethan's arguments, however good they might be, or how solid his evidence. She just thought what she thought, and got on with it. But this was especially true when it came to baseball. Ethan was going to have to work fast.

"Baseball is a stupid game," he said, going for broke. "It's so *dull*."

"No, Ethan," his father said sadly, "it really, really isn't."

"I find it quite boring."

"Nothing is boring, son—" his father began.

"I know, I know," Ethan said. " 'Nothing is boring except to people who aren't really paying attention.' " This was something he had heard from his father many, many times. It was his father's motto. His mother's motto had been, "People could learn a lot from llamas." His mother was a veterinarian. When the Felds lived in Colorado Springs, she had specialised in caring for the vigilant, fierce, and intelligent guard llamas that Rocky Mountain sheep-herders use to protect their flocks from dogs and coyotes.

"That's right," his father said, nodding in agreement with his own familiar wisdom. He turned into the long, ruined gravel track that led to the tumbledown houses in the woods where all the Rideouts lived. "You have to pay attention, in life and in baseball."

"But nothing *happens*. It's so *slow*."

"Well, that's true," his father said. "Everything used to be slow. Now almost nothing is. But are we any happier, son?"

Ethan did not know how to answer this. When his father was at the controls of one of his big, slow sky-whales, sailing nowhere in particular at a top speed of thirty-five miles per hour, the smile never left his face. If he ever managed to sell the idea of the Zeppelina, the affordable family airship,* it would be on the basis of that smile.

Mr. Feld pulled into a wash of gravel-streaked mud in front of the house where Jennifer T. lived with her twin brothers Darrin and Dirk, her grandmother Billy Ann, her two great aunts, and her uncle Mo. Everybody in the house was either very old or very young. Jennifer T.'s father did not seem to live anywhere at all – he just showed up, from time to time – and her mother had gone to Alaska to work for a summer, not long after the twins were born, and never come back. Ethan wasn't too sure who was living in any of the three other houses scattered like dice in the green clearing. But they were all Rideouts, too. There had been Rideouts on Clam Island for a very long time. They claimed to be descended from the original Indian inhabitants of the island, though in school Ethan had learned that when the first white settlers arrived on Clam Island, in 1872, there was no one living there at all, Indian or otherwise. When Mrs. Clutch, the

*"The Darndest Way of Getting from Here to There" – slogan, Feld Airship, Inc.

social studies teacher, had informed them of this, Jennifer T. got so angry that she bit a pencil in half. Ethan had been very impressed by that. He was also impressed by Jennifer T.'s great-uncle Mo. Mo Rideout was the oldest man Ethan had ever seen. He was a full-blooded Salishan Indian, who, Jennifer T. said, had played in the Negro Leagues, and for three seasons with the Seattle Rainiers in the old Pacific Coast League, long, long ago.

Mr. Feld didn't need to honk; Jennifer T. was waiting for them on the sagging porch. She picked up her huge equipment bag and came down the porch steps, taking them two at a time. She could never seem to get away fast enough from her house. There had been times in Ethan's life – when his mother was dying inside it, for example – when Ethan had felt the same way about his own house.

As usual, Jennifer T.'s uniform was spotless. Her knit trousers, her jersey, her sanitary socks, were always somehow whiter than anybody else's. (Jennifer T., as Mr. Feld never tired of reminding Ethan, did all of her own washing.) She had tied her long blue-black hair in a ponytail that was pulled through the gap at the back of her ball cap, where you snapped the plastic strap.

She threw her bag onto the backseat and then climbed in beside it. She carried into the car the lingering stink of her grandmother's cigarettes and a strong odour of bubble gum – she chewed the shredded kind that pretended to be chewing tobacco in a pouch.

"Hey."

"Hey."

"Hello, Jennifer T.," Mr. Feld said. "Buckle up and let me tell you what my son has been attempting to convince me to let him do."

This was the moment that Ethan had been dreading.

"I saw a bushbaby," he said quickly. "An African bushbaby, at first I thought it was a fox, but it walked like a monkey, and I—"

"Ethan says he wants to quit the team," said Mr. Feld.

Jennifer T. snapped her gum a few times. She unzipped the ragged old equipment bag, patched with duct tape and stained by decades of grass and Gatorade. She took out her first-baseman's mitt, which she kept carefully oiled with a mysterious substance called neet's foot oil and wrapped in an Ace bandage, with a tennis ball tucked in the pocket to maintain its shape. The glove was much older than she was and had been printed with the signature of someone named Keith Hernandez. Jennifer T. unwound the bandage tenderly, filling the car with a pungent, farmyard kind of smell.

"I don't think so, Feld," she said. She gave her gum another loud snap. "Not going to happen."

And that was the end of the discussion.

CLAM ISLAND WAS a small, green, damp corner of the world. It was known, if at all, mostly for three things. First was its clams. Second was the collapse, in 1943, of the giant Clam Narrows Bridge. You might have seen an old film of that spectacular disaster, on TV: the long steel bridge-deck flapping and whipping around like a gigantic loose shoelace just before it falls to pieces and splashes into the chilly waters of Puget Sound. The Clam Islanders had never really taken to the bridge that connected them to the mainland, and they were not sorry to see it go. They went back to riding the Clam Island Ferry, which they greatly preferred. You could not get a cup of coffee or clam chowder, or hear all about your neighbour's sick cousin or chicken, on the Clam Narrows Bridge. From time to time, there would be talk of rebuilding the span, but a lot of people seemed to feel that maybe there just ought not to be a bridge connecting Clam Island to the mainland. Islands have always been strange and magical places; crossing the water to reach them ought to be, even in a small way, an adventure.

The last thing that Clam Island was known for, along with its excellent clams (if you liked clams) and its falling-down bridge, was its rain. Even in a part of the world where the people were accustomed to drizzles and downpours, Clam Island was considered uncommonly damp. It was said that at least once a day, on Clam Island, in winter or summer, it rained for at least twenty minutes. People said this about Clam Island on Orcas Island, and on San Juan Island, and down in Tacoma and Seattle. But the people of Clam Island knew that this saying was not entirely true. They knew – it was one of the first things they learned as children about their home – that at the westernmost tip of the island, in the summertime, it *never* rained. Not even for a minute and a half. A tiny, freak weather system ensured that this zone of the island, perhaps a square mile in all, knew a June, July, and August that were perfectly dry and sunshiny.

Clam Island, seen on a map, looked like a boar that was

running west. It had a big snout – called the West End – tipped with a single long jagged tusk. Most of the locals called this westernmost spit where it never rained in the summer the Boar Tooth, or the West Tooth, or just the Tooth; to others it was always known as Summerland. The Tooth was where the island's young people went to while away their long vacations, where the club picnics, league barbecues, and summer weddings were put on, and, above all, it was where the islanders went to play baseball.

They had been playing there since shortly after the arrival of the Clam Island pioneers in 1872. At the back of Hurley's Hardware, in town, there was a photograph of a bunch of tough-looking loggers and fishermen, in old-time flannels and moustaches, posing with their bats in the shade of a spreading madrona tree. The picture was captioned CLAM ISLAND NINE, SUMMERLAND, 1883.

For a long time – so long that men were born, grew up, and died in the arms of the game – baseball flourished on Clam Island. There were a dozen different leagues, made up of players of all ages, both male and female. Times had been better on Clam Island in those days. People were once more partial to eating raw shellfish than they are now. An ordinary American working man, not so long ago, thought nothing of tossing back three or four dozen salty, slippery bivalves at lunch. The Clam Boom and the universal love of baseball had gone hand in hand for many years. Now the clam beds had been mostly spoiled by plankton blooms and pollution, and as for the young people of Clam Island, even though some of them could hit, run, and catch the ball, the sad truth was that none of them really cared for baseball very much. Many preferred basketball, and others preferred riding dirt bicycles, and some just liked to watch sports on television. By the time of the season I want to tell you about, the Clam Island Mustang League was home to just four teams. There were the Shopway Angels, the Dick Helsing Realty Reds, the Bigfoot Tavern Bigfoots – and the Roosters, who had, as has already been mentioned, lost all of their first seven games. In the grand scheme of the universe, losing the first seven games of the season is nothing too grave, but to the Roosters it felt awful. Ethan was not the only one who had contemplated quitting the team.

"Now, listen, you kids," Mr. Olafssen said, that afternoon, gathering the Roosters around him before the game. Mr. Olafssen was a very tall, thin man with hair the colour of yellowed newspaper, and a sad expression. He'd had the expression even before the season began, so Ethan knew that it was not his fault that Mr. Olafssen looked so sad, but nevertheless whenever he looked at his coach, Ethan felt guilty. Kyle Olafssen, Mr. Olafssen's son, played third base, and he was also the Roosters' second-best pitcher after Danny Desjardins. He could throw pretty hard for a kid, but without much control, and since he was always in a bad mood the kids on the other teams were a little afraid of him. That was probably the best thing that Kyle had going for himself as a pitcher – he was a sourpuss, and wild.

"I know some of you left the last game feeling a little down," Mr. Olafssen continued. "And it was a tough loss." Ethan could feel, like a kind of magnetic force acting on the fillings of his teeth or something, how hard

Mr. Olafssen was trying not to look at him, and his three errors, with those sad pale eyes. Ethan was grateful to Mr. Olafssen – nothing made Ethan Feld happier than the knowledge that nobody was looking at him – but he blushed all the same. "Now, you look at our record, you see oh and seven, I know it's hard not to feel a little down. But what is a record? It's just some numbers on a piece of paper. It doesn't reflect who we are as people, and it doesn't reflect who we are as a team."

"Actually," said a deep voice, "if you had enough data, you could reduce every human being to a series of numbers and coordinates on a piece of paper."

The Roosters, who had been listening to Mr. Olafssen with a certain amount of trust, hope, and willingness to believe him, now burst into derisive laughter. Mr. Olafssen frowned as his point was spoiled. He turned, looking very annoyed, towards Thor Wignutt, who stood, as ever, just outside the circle of kids.

Though he was the same age as all of them, Thor towered over the other Roosters and was, in fact, the tallest eleven-year-old on Clam Island, as he had been the tallest nine-year-old, and the tallest five-year-old, and the tallest toddler, too. The top of Thor's head reached almost to the base of Mr. Olafssen's throat, and he was, if anything, broader in the shoulders. Thor was a kind of prodigy of growth in every way. He had a voice like stones rolling in a metal drum, and dark hair on his lips and cheek. He wore heavy black glasses and was generally regarded as smart, but unfortunately he was under the impression – most of the time – that he was a synthetic humanoid named TW03. TW03, as Thor never tired of explaining, was the most sophisticated and marvellous piece of machinery in the history of the universe. But of course like all synthetic humanoids, for some reason he wanted nothing more than to be human. Thinking of himself as somebody who was not human, but was trying very hard, as you might imagine, often got in the way of Thor's relations with other kids his age. With his big arms and shoulders, he looked like he would be a fabulous power hitter, but usually he was out on three pitches.

"Thor," Mr. Olafssen said. "What have I told you about interrupting me to make these ridiculous statements of yours without offering the slightest shred of evidence to back them up?"

During the last game, Thor had distracted everyone with his theory that there was an active underground volcano directly beneath the Tooth that was responsible for keeping the place dry in the summertime. He claimed to be able to detect seismic disturbances with his "logical sensor array." His constant reiteration of "one of these days that thing is going to blow this entire quadrant to atoms" had irritated Mr. Olafssen nearly as much as Ethan's poor play in the field.

"Can you prove it, Thor?" Mr. Olafssen wanted to know. "Have you *got* a piece of paper with *me* written on it?"

Thor blinked. He was standing right behind Jennifer T., who was the only person on the team, and perhaps on the entire island, who ever bothered to treat Thor like a more or less normal person. She had even been over to his house, where, it was said, Mrs. Wignutt, immensely fat, lived inside a clear plastic tent breathing air out of a tank. According to

Jennifer T., however, there had been no sign of any tent, or of Thor's gigantic mother, for that matter.

"It's true," Thor insisted finally. He was very stubborn in his ideas, which Ethan supposed was the case with synthetic humanoids, given the fact that they were, well, *programmed*. Ethan was probably the person, after Jennifer T., who was the friendliest with Thor, but he never treated Thor like a more or less normal person. It was clear to Ethan that Thor was not.

"Have you brought us any charts, Thor?" Mr. Olafssen pressed on. He seemed determined to beat Thor at his own game. "Do you have any proof at all?"

Thor hesitated, then shook his head.

"Then I'll thank you to keep your chipset occupied with solving calculations involving balls and bats."

"Yes, sir," Thor said.

"Now, then," Mr. Olafssen began, glancing across the field at the Angels, whose coach, Mr. Ganse, was passing out a pair of wristbands, in the Angels colours of red and blue, to each of the boys on his team. The Angels had told everyone about the wristbands that they would be receiving that afternoon, as their reward for having *won* all of their first seven games that season. They were each ornamented with a picture of the great Rodrigo Buendía, the star slugger for the big-league Angels, in Anaheim. "Here is what I would like us to do this afternoon. I want us to focus—"

"Dad?"

"Quiet, Kyle. Now. The focus for the game today is going to be on—"

"Dad!"

"Kyle, darn it, if you don't let me talk—"

"We just want to know something." Danny Desjardins and Tucker Corr, who were standing on either side of Kyle, looked at Ethan, who froze. He could feel the question that was coming like a trapdoor opening at the bottom of his stomach.

"What is it, Kyle?"

"Are you going to play Feld today?"

Mr. Olafssen could prevent it no longer. His sorry gaze wavered, then swung around and fastened, with a snap that you could almost hear, on Ethan. He ran the tip of his tongue around his lips. Ethan could feel all the other kids on the team watching him, hoping and praying with all of their might, that Ethan would be benched. And the worst of it was that Ethan too prayed that Mr. Olafssen would say *Well, no, he sort of thought maybe Ethan had better sit this one out*. Ethan hated himself for hoping for this. He glanced over to the bleachers, where his father sat, in his size XXL Roosters jersey, among the other fathers and mothers. Mr. Feld noticed Ethan looking at him, and raised one hand in a fist, as if to say *Go get 'em, Slugger*, or something doofusy like that, and smiled a great big, horrible, hopeful smile. Ethan looked away.

"I think you'd better shut your mouth, Kyle Olafssen," Mr. Olafssen finally said. "Before I bench your narrow behind."

The Angels took the field. The Roosters came together and built a tower of their hands, slapping them, one by one, into a pile. Then they yelled, all together,

"Break!" They did this before every game; Ethan had no idea why. But he figured that everybody else must know, and he was too embarrassed to ask. He had missed the first five minutes of the first day of practice and assumed that it had been explained then.

All the Roosters sat down, except for Jennifer T., who batted lead-off, and Kris Langenfelter, the shortstop, who was on deck. Ethan found a spot at the very end of the bench and waited, cap in his lap, to learn his fate.

Things got off to a good start, at least from his craven and shameful point of view, when the Roosters proved unable to score Jennifer T., who led off the game with a signature double, a seed that squirted off her bat over the shortstop's head and into left field. Then in the bottom of the first, the Angels got on the scoreboard right away with a pair of runs. Ethan relaxed a little, secure in the knowledge that Mr. Olafssen would never risk dropping further behind by putting him in. He sat back on the bench, folded his hands behind his head, and looked up at the blue Summerland sky. Over the rest of Clam Island the sky, as usual during the summer months, was more pearly than blue, grey but full of light, as though a thin cotton bandage had been stretched across the sun. Here in Summerland, however, the sky was cloudless and a rich, dark, blue, almost ultramarine. The air was fragrant with a beach smell of drying seaweed and the tang of the grey-green water that surrounded the Tooth on three sides. The sun felt warm on Ethan's cheeks. He half closed his eyes. Maybe, he thought, baseball was a sport best enjoyed from the bench.

"You better be ready, kid," said a voice just behind him. "Pretty soon now you going to get the call."

Ethan looked behind him. On the other side of the low chain-link fence that separated the ball field from the spectator area, leaned a dark little man with bright green eyes. He was an old man, with white hair pulled back into a ponytail and a big, intelligent nose. His skin was the colour of a well-oiled baseball glove. The expression on his face was half mocking and half annoyed, as if he had been disappointed to catch Ethan napping, but not surprised. There was something in his face that said he knew Ethan Feld.

"Do you know that guy?" Ethan asked Thor in a low voice.

"Negative."

"He's looking at me."

"He does appear to be observing you, Captain."

"Excuse me, sir?" Ethan said to the old man with the ponytail. "What did you just say?"

"I was merely observatin', young man, that sooner than you think you goin' to find yourself in the game."

Ethan decided that the old guy was joking, or thought that he was. An informal survey that Ethan had once conducted seemed to indicate that fully seventy-three per cent of the things that adults said to him in the course of a day were intended to be jokes. But there was something in the man's tone that worried him. So he adopted his usual strategy with adult humour, and pretended that he hadn't heard.

In the top of the fourth, Jennifer T. came up to bat again. She carried her slim blond bat over her shoulder like a fishing pole. She stepped up to home plate with her gaze at her shoetops. You could tell that she was thinking, and that what she was thinking about was getting a hit. Jennifer T. was the only member of the Roosters – maybe the only kid on the whole Island of Clam – who truly loved baseball. She loved to wear a bright smear of green grass on her uniform pants and to hear her bat ringing in her hands like a bell. She could hit for average and with power, turn a double play all by herself, stretch a base hit into a triple and a triple into an inside-the-park home run. She never bragged about how good she was, or did anything to try to make the other players look bad. She did, however, insist that you call her "Jennifer T.", and not just "Jennifer" or, worst of all, "Jenny".

Bobby Bladen, the Angels' pitcher, came in low and outside to Jennifer T. Jennifer T. had long arms, and she liked her pitches outside. She reached out with her slim bat and once again sent the ball slicing over the shortstop's head and into left field. The left fielder had a good arm, and he got the ball right in to the second baseman, but when the dust settled Jennifer T. was safe with another double.

"Here it come, kid," said the old man. "Get ready."

Ethan turned to give this annoying elderly person a dirty look, but to his surprise he found that there was nobody there. Then he heard the crack of a bat, and the Roosters and all their parents cheering. Sure enough, Jennifer T. had started something. Troy Knadel singled, scoring Jennifer T., and after that, as Mr. Feld later put it, the wheels came off Bobby Bladen. The Roosters batted all the way around the order. The next time that she came up that inning, Jennifer T. drew a walk and stole second. When Kyle Olafssen finally made the third out, the Roosters had taken a 7–2 lead.

"Mr. Wignutt," barked Mr. Olafssen. His face was all red and his pale eyes were just a little crazy looking. Five runs was the biggest lead the Roosters had had all season. "Take third."

"But, Dad," said Kyle Olafssen. "*I'm* third."

"You're third something, all right," said Mr. Olafssen. "Third *what*, I have no idea. Have a seat, son, you're out of the game. Wignutt, get your synthetic hiney out onto the field." He started to give Thor's shoulder a shove in the direction of third base but then glanced at Ethan, and hesitated. "Oh, and, uh, upload your, uh, your infielding software."

Thor leapt instantly to his feet. "Yes, *sir*."

Ethan's heart began to pound. What if the Roosters were able to hold the lead? What if they added a few more runs? If Mr. Olafssen felt comfortable putting Thor into the game with a five-run lead, how many runs would the Roosters need before he would consider putting Ethan in? Ethan had not the slightest doubt in his ability to erase a six-, seven-, even an eight-run lead, single-handedly.

Every time he looked over towards the bleachers and saw his father sitting there, squinting, with that big carnation of a smile wilting on his face, the feeling of dread grew stronger. Then, in their half of the fifth, the Roosters added two more runs, and Ethan really began to panic. Mr. Olafssen kept glancing his way, and there were only two innings left to go after this one. The Angels put in a new pitcher, and Jennifer T. came to the plate again. This time she hit a soft line drive deep into the grass of left-centre and lighted out for second. There were two men on: that made it 11–2. Ethan stole another look at his father and saw that the strange little old man had reappeared and was sitting right beside Mr. Feld now, and staring, not at the action on the field, like the normal people in the bleachers, but *right at Ethan*. The old man nodded, then fit his fists together as if they were stacked up on the handle of a bat, and swung. He pointed at Ethan, and grinned. Ethan looked away. His gaze travelled around the field, towards the parking lot, then out beyond that to the edge of the woods. There, atop a fallen birch, he caught a glimpse of something quick and ruddy, with a luxuriant tail.

That was when Ethan did something that surprised him. He got up from the bench, muttered something to no one in particular about needing to pee really bad. He didn't stop to think, and he didn't look back. He just took off into the woods after the bushbaby.

Jock MacDougal Field occupied only the lower portion of the Tooth – the part where it met the boar's jaw. The rest of the long, jagged spit was all forest, five hundred acres of tall white trees. These were paper birches, according to Mr. Feld. He had told Ethan that they were also called "canoe birches" because the Indians had once used the inner bark for boat building as they had used the outer bark, like a peeling pale wrapper, for writing and painting on. On a rainy day in winter, when the birches stood huddled, bare and ghostly, the birch forest at the very end of Clam Island could look extremely eerie and cold. Even on a bright summery afternoon, like today, when they were thick with green leaves, there was something mysterious about the tall, pale, whispering trees. They surrounded the ball field, and the parking lot, and the grassy slope with the flagpole where the wedding receptions were held. They stood, pressed together like spectators, just on the other side of the green outfield fence. Any ball hit into the birch wood was a home run, and lost forever.

Ethan ran across the parking lot and up over the log where he had caught a flash of bushy red tail. He found a clear trail leading away from there to the north side of the Tooth. At first he ran along the trail, hoping to catch sight of the bushbaby as it skittered through the woods. But, after a while, the dim heavy light filtering through the green leaves of the birch trees seemed to weigh him down, or tie him up in shadows. He slowed to a trot, and then just walked along the path, listening for something he kept thinking that he heard, a sound that was rhythmic and soft. He told himself that it was just the sound of his own breathing. Then he realised that it must be the waves, slapping against the beach at Summerland. That was where this particular trail headed: to Hotel Beach. Hotel Beach was popular with teenagers, mostly, but Ethan and his father had been there once. During the Clam Boom there had been some kind of resort, called the Summerland. You could still see the ruins of some cabins, a collapsed dance hall, the bones of an old pier.

Just now it seemed like an inviting kind of place to go and feel ashamed. He would sit there for a couple of hours, hating himself, and then by the time the police found him, his father would be so worried that he would have forgotten and forgiven Ethan's cowardice, and his failure as a ballplayer. He would see how upset and afraid Little League was making Ethan. "What was I thinking?" he would say.

"Of course you can quit the team, son. I only want what's best for you."

By the time Ethan reached Hotel Beach, he was feeling almost happy in his sadness, and had forgotten all about the bushbaby. He came out of the woods onto the sand and stood for a moment. Then he walked out onto the beach. The sand was dense and crunchy under his shoes. He sat down on the great gnarled log of driftwood where he and his father had sat to eat their lunch the day they visited. It was a real grandfather log, the wreck of some enormous old tree, spiked with snapped branches. He had just noticed the strange, cold sting of the wind, and the grey clouds that were blowing in from the Olympic range, when he heard voices nearby. He ducked back into the trees, listening. They were the voices of men, and there was a raucous note in them that struck Ethan as harsh and somehow hostile. Carefully, keeping low, he inched his way towards the ruined cabins.

A big Range Rover was parked in the clearing beside the dance hall. The words TRANSFORM PROPERTIES were written on the side of the car. Four men in suits stood around the front of the car, looking over some plans that they had unrolled across the hood. Although the day was perfectly dry, all four men were wearing bright yellow raincoats over their suits, and big rubberised leather rain boots, the kind that had steel toes. He did not know why – it was just four guys with neckties in raincoats – but he felt as if they had come here to do something very bad.

The men seemed to be disagreeing about something. One pointed at the ground, threw up his hands, and walked around to the back of the car. He opened the hatch and took out a heavy shovel. With a stern look at the three other men, he walked several paces up away from the beach, towards the dance hall that for the last forty years had been sinking back into the woods. The man pointed again at the ground, as if to suggest that whatever he found here was going to prove whatever point he had been trying to make. Then he raised his shovel, and the blade bit into the carpet of weeds and yellow flowers at his feet.

Someone at Ethan's elbow sighed. It was a bitter, long, weary sigh, the way someone sighs when the thing she has most dreaded finally comes to pass. It was right in his ear, unmistakable and clear. Ethan turned to see who had sighed, but there was nobody there. The hair on his arms and the back of his neck stood on end. The breeze was cold, and as sharp as the tooth of a shovel. Ethan shivered. Then the man with the shovel cried out. He reached up and slapped the back of his neck. Something – it looked like a little stone – went skipping off into the grass behind him. Ethan looked up and saw, in the branches of a nearby birch, the little red animal with the mocking eyes. It was much more like a fox, he saw, than a bushbaby. But it was not a fox, either. It had hands, for one thing, sharp-looking little raccoon hands, one of which was holding on to a forked slingshot. And apart from its pointed snout it had a human face, whiskered and long-eared and just now wrinkled in amused satisfaction. It saw Ethan, and seemed to raise the slingshot in a kind of salute. Then, solemn-faced again, it scurried straight down the tree and took off into the woods.

Ethan must have made some kind of a noise of surprise, because all four of the men looked up at him. He froze, and his heart kicked and thudded so hard he could hear it in his teeth. Their eyes were concealed by narrow sunglasses, and their mouths were thin and nearly lipless. They were going to come after him. He turned to run back into the woods, and immediately crashed into the old man with the Indian ponytail. For a little old guy he felt amazingly solid. Ethan fell backwards and landed on his behind. The old man just stood there, nodding his head.

"Told you," he said.

"Do I— is it my turn? Did they put me in the game?"

"They sure would like to," the old man said. "If you willin'."

Ethan just wanted to get away from the TransForm Properties men.

"I don't blame you for that," said the old man, and it is a measure of just how spooked Ethan was that it did not occur to him until much later that the old man had read his thoughts. "Come on, best get out of here."

"Who are they?" Ethan asked, following along behind the old man, who was dressed in a suit, too, but a baggy woollen one cut from a weird orange plaid that would not have looked out of place upholstering one of the old couches on the Rideouts' front porch.

"They the worst men in the world," the old man said. "My name is Chiron Brown, by the way. When I pitched for the Homestead Greys, they called me 'Ringfinger'. "

"Do you have a big ring finger?" Ethan reasoned.

"No," the old man said, raising his leathery right hand.

"I doesn't have no ring finger at all. You would not believe what kind of crazy motion I could put on a baseball without no ring finger."

"Did they send you to come get me?" Ethan said, as they approached the parking lot. He could already hear the shouting of parents, the shrill mocking voices of boys, the raspy pleading of Coach Olafssen.

"As a matter of fact, they did," said Ringfinger Brown. "A long time ago."

IT WAS THE strangest moment in what had so far been a fairly strange morning. When Ethan got back to the bench, nobody turned around, or even seemed to notice that he had ever left. But the very instant his butt touched the smooth pine surface of the bench, Mr. Olafssen looked over at him, and gave him a big fatal wink.

"All right, Ethan. Big Ethan. Let's get you in the game."

Things, it turned out, were no longer quite so rosy for the Roosters as when Ethan had left. The Angels had managed to come back with six more runs, and now the score was 11–8. But it was the top of the seventh and final inning, and Mr. Olafssen was pretty much obliged, by the laws of decency, fair play, and the Clam Island Mustang League, to play every able-bodied kid on the team for at least half an inning of every game. There were two out, two on, and no runs in, and it was going to be up to Ethan to pad the Roosters' lead.

"Get in there, now," Mr. Olafssen said, just the way he always did. "Get in there and take your hacks."

Ethan, however, did not want any hacks. Usually, when he came to the plate, Ethan Feld tried to swing his bat as little as possible. He just kept the bat on his shoulder, hoping for a walk. The truth is, he was afraid of trying to accomplish anything more, at the plate, than a walk. And he was afraid of being hit by the ball. But mostly he was mortally afraid of striking out swinging. Was there any worse kind of failure than that? *Striking out*. It was the way you described it when you failed at anything else in life, the symbol of every other kind of thing a person could possibly get wrong. Often enough, the opposing pitching was not too good in the Mustang League. Ethan's strategy of just standing there, waiting for four bad pitches to come across the plate before three good ones did, frequently worked. But it was a strategy that was not at all respected by the other players. Ethan's nickname in the Mustang League, in fact, was "Dog Boy," because of the way he was always hoping for a walk.

He trudged up to the plate, dragging his bat behind him like a caveman in the cartoons dragging his club. He hoisted the bat to his shoulder – it was still sore from when his father had stopped short to avoid hitting the little fox-monkey thing – and looked over at his father, who gave him a big thumbs-up. Then Ethan stared out at Per Davis, who had taken over the pitching for the Angels. Per looked almost sorry to see Ethan. He winced a little bit, then sighed, and went into his stretch. A moment later something troubled the air around Ethan's hands.

"Her-ite one!" cried out the umpire, Mr. Arch Brody of Brody's Drug. Mr. Brody prided himself on the authentic-sounding way he called the balls and strikes.

"Come on, Dog Boy," called Kyle. "Get that bat off your shoulder."

"Come on, Dog!" called the other boys.

Ethan let another blur colour the air between him and Per Davis.

"Her-ite TWO!" Mr. Arch Brody yelled.

Ethan heard the gravelly voice of Ringfinger Brown.

"When the time come," the old man said, "you best be ready to swing."

Ethan searched the crowd but could not find the old man anywhere, though the voice had sounded as if it were just at his elbow. But he saw that Jennifer T. was looking right at him.

"Breathe," she suggested, moving her lips without speaking. Ethan realised that he had been holding his breath from the moment Mr. Olafssen had looked his way.

He stepped out, took a breath, then stepped back in, resolved at last to take a hack. Playing the odds was one thing when the count was even at 0; with two strikes on him, maybe it made more sense to swing. When Per Davis reared back to let fly, Ethan wiggled his fingers on the shaft of the bat, and worked his shoulders up and down. Then, unfortunately, just before he swung the bat he did something kind of questionable. He closed his eyes.

"Her-ite her-REE!" shouted Mr. Brody, sealing Ethan's doom.

"That's all right," Jennifer T. told him as they walked out to the field. "We'll hold 'em. At least you took a hack."

"Yeah."

"It was a nice-looking swing."

"Yeah."

"Just a little early, is all."

"I shut my eyes," Ethan said.

Jennifer T. stopped at first base, which was hers. She shook her head, not bothering to conceal her exasperation with Ethan, and then turned towards home plate.

"Well, try to keep them open in the field, huh?"

In the field – Coach Olafssen always stuck Ethan out in right, a region of the diamond to which boys who prefer to remain invisible have been sent since baseball was invented – the situation was, if anything, even worse. Forget about catching the ball; Ethan never seemed to see it when it was headed towards him. Even after a fly ball landed in the grass, and went skipping happily along towards the outfield fence for a triple at least, Ethan often took quite a while to find it. And then, when, finding it at last, he threw the ball in! Oy! An entire row of fathers, watching from behind the backstop, would smack their foreheads in despair. Ethan never remembered to throw to the cut-off man, who stood waiting, halfway between Ethan and home, to relay the throw to the catcher. No, he just let loose, eyes screwed tight shut: a big, wild windmill of a throw that ended up nowhere near home plate, but in the parking lot behind third base, or, once, on the hindquarters of a sleeping Labrador retriever.

Ethan wandered into right, hoping with all his heart that nothing would happen while he stood there. His hand felt sweaty and numb inside his big, stiff new fielder's mitt. The chill wind he had felt at Hotel Beach was blowing across the ball field now, and clouds were covering the sun. The grey light made Ethan squint. It gave him a headache. An echo of the old man's voice lingered in his mind in a way that he found quite irritating. He puzzled for a while over the question of whether there was really any difference, as far as your brain was concerned, between hearing something and remembering how something sounded. Then he worked for a while on possible theories to account for the presence on Clam Island of a rare African primate. His thoughts, in other words, were far removed from baseball. He was dimly aware of the other players chattering, pounding their gloves, teasing or encouraging each other, but he felt very far away from it all. He felt like the one balloon at a birthday party that comes loose from a lawn chair and floats off into the sky.

A baseball landed nearby, and rolled away towards the fence at the edge of the field, as if it had some place important to get to.

Later it turned out that Ethan was supposed to have caught that ball. Four runs scored, making the final total Angels 12, Roosters 11. In other words, eight losses in a row. The Angel who hit the ball that Ethan was supposed to have caught, Tommy Bluefield, was angry at Ethan, because even though his hit had brought in all three baserunners and himself, it did not count as a grand slam home run, since Ethan had committed an error. He ought to have caught the ball.

"You stink," Tommy Bluefield told him.

The magnitude of Ethan's failure, the shame that he had brought down on himself, ought to have been the focus of everyone's thoughts, just then, as Ethan dragged his sorry self off the field to the bleachers, where his father was waiting with the crumpled flower of his smile. His teammates ought to have lined up on either side of him and beaten him with their mitts as he was made to run a gauntlet. They ought to have ripped the patch from his uniform shoulder, broken his bat, and uninvited him to come have post-game pizza in Clam Centre with everybody else. Instead they seemed quickly to lose interest in the shameful saga of Ethan Feld, and to turn their wondering faces to the sky. On Jock MacDougal Field, at the Tooth, where every summer for as long as white men could remember there had been an endless supply of blue sky and sunshine, it had started to rain.

2
A Hot Prospect

THE NEXT MORNING Ethan awoke from dreams of freakish versions of baseball where there were seven bases, two pitchers, and outfields beyond outfields reaching into infinity, to find the little red fox-monkey sitting on his chest. Its thick fur was neatly combed and braided, and the braids on its head were tied with bright blue ribbons. And it was smoking a pipe. Ethan opened his mouth to scream but no sound emerged. The creature weighed heavily on his chest, like a sack of nails. Whoever had bathed it and tied its hair in bows had also doused it in rosewater, but underneath the perfume it stank like a fox, a rank smell of meat and mud. Its snout quivered with intelligence and its gleaming black eyes peered curiously at Ethan. It looked a little dubious about what it saw. Ethan opened and closed his mouth, gasping like a fish on a dock, trying to cry out for his father.

"Calm, piglet," said the fox-monkey. "Breathe." Its voice was small and raspy. It sounded like an old recording, coming through a gramophone bell. "Yes, yes," it went on, soothingly. "Just take a breath and never be afraid of old Mr. C., for he isn't going to hurt not the tiniest hair of your poor hairless piglet self."

"What—?" Ethan managed. "What—?"

"My name is Cutbelly. I am a werefox. I am seven hundred and sixty-five years old. I have been sent to offer you everlasting fame and a fantastic destiny." He scratched with a black fingernail at an itch in the dazzling white fur of his chest. "Go ahead," he said. He pointed at Ethan with the stem of his pipe. "Take a few deep breaths."

"Sitting..." Ethan tried. "On... my... chest."

"Oh! Ha-ha!" The werefox tumbled backwards off of Ethan, exposing him to the startling sight of its private parts and furry behind. For Cutbelly was quite naked. This had not struck Ethan as odd when he was under the impression that he (Cutbelly was definitely a he) was an animal, but now Ethan sort of wished that Cutbelly would at least wear some pants. After completing his back flip, Cutbelly landed on his long bony back paws. The feet were much foxier than the quick black hands. "My apologies."

Ethan sat up and tried to catch his breath. He looked at the clock on his nightstand: 7:23 A.M. His father might walk in at any moment and find him talking to this smelly red-brown thing. His eyes strayed to the door of his bedroom, and Cutbelly noticed.

"Not to worry about your pa," he said. "The Neighbours worked me a sleeping grammer. Your pa would not hear the crack of Ragged Rock."

"Ragged Rock? Where is that?"

"It isn't a place," Cutbelly said, relighting his pipe. It had been worked from a piece of bone. Ethan thought: *Human bone.* On the bowl was carved the bearded likeness of Abraham Lincoln, of all things. "It's a *time*. A day, to be precise. A day to wake anybody who might be sleeping, including the dead themselves. But not your pa. No, even come Ragged Rock he will sleep, until you return safely from speaking with the Neighbours, and I tuck your little piglet self snug back into your bed."

In a book or a movie, when strange things begin to happen, somebody will often say, "I must be dreaming". But in dreams nothing is strange. Ethan thought that he might be dreaming not because a nude werefox had shown up making wild claims and smoking a pipe that was definitely not filled with tobacco, but because none of these things struck him as particularly unexpected or odd.

"What kind of a fantastic destiny?" he said. He did not know why, but he had a sudden flash that somehow it was going to involve baseball.

Cutbelly stood up and jammed his pipe between his teeth, looking very foxy.

"Aye, you'd like to know, wouldn't you?" he said. "It's a rare chance you're to be offered. A first-rate education."

"Tell me!" Ethan said.

"I will," Cutbelly said. "On the way through." He blew a long steady jet of foul smoke. It smelled like burning upholstery. Cutbelly sprang down from the bed and crept with his peculiar swaggering gait towards the window. He reached up with his long arms and dragged himself up onto the sill.

"Wear a sweater," he said. "Scampering is cold work."

"*Scampering?*"

"Along the Tree."

"The Tree?" Ethan said, grabbing a hooded sweatshirt from the back of his desk chair. "What Tree?"

"The Tree of Worlds," Cutbelly said impatiently. "Whatever do they teach you in school?"

WEREFOXES HAVE LONG been known for their teacherly natures. As they started down the drive from the Feld house, Cutbelly lectured Ethan on the true nature of the universe. It was one of his favourite subjects.

"Can you imagine an infinite tree?" Cutbelly said. They turned left at the mailbox that read Feld Airship, Inc., ducked under a wire fence, skirted the property line that separated the Felds from the Jungermans, and wandered west a little ways. "A tree whose roots snake down all the way to the bottomest bottom of everything? And whose outermost tippity fingers stretch as far as anything can possibly reach?"

"I can imagine anything," Ethan said, quoting Mr. Feld, "except having no imagination."

"Big talk. Well, then do so. Now, if you've ever looked at a tree, you've seen how its trunk divides into great limbs, which divide again into lesser limbs, which in turn divide into boughs, which divide yet again into branches, which divide into twigs, which divide into twiglings. The whole mess splaying out in all directions, jutting and twisting and zigzagging. At the tips of the tips you might have a million million tiny green shoots, scattered like the sparks of an exploding skyrocket. But if you followed your way back from the thousand billion green fingertips, down the twigs, to the branches, to the boughs, to the lesser limbs, you would arrive at a point – the technical term is the axil point

– where you would see that the whole lacy spreading mass was really only four great limbs, branching off from the main trunk."

"OK," Ethan said.

"Now, let's say the tree is invisible. Immaterial. You can't touch it."

"OK."

"The only part of it that's visible, that's the leaves."

"The leaves are visible."

"The leaves of this enormous tree, those are the million million places where life lives and things happen and stories and creatures come and go."

Ethan thought this over.

"So Clam Island is like a leaf?"

"It isn't *like* a leaf. It *is* a leaf. This tree is not some fancy metaphor, piglet. It's *real*. It's there. It's holding us all up right now, you and me and Bulgaria and Pluto and everything else. Just because something is invisible and immaterial doesn't mean it isn't really there."

"Sorry," Ethan said.

"Now. Those four limbs, the four great limbs, each with its great tangle of branches and leaves – those are the four Worlds."

"There are four Worlds."

"And all the twigs and boughs are the myriad ways among the leaves, the paths and roads, the rambles and routes among the stars. But there are some of us who can, you know, leap, from leaf to leaf, and branch to branch. Shadowtails, such creatures are called, and I myself am one of them. When you travel *along* a branch, that's called scampering. We're doing it right now. You can't go very far – it's too tiring – but you can go very *quickly*."

The werefox scrabbled up a low bank, in a spray of dead leaves and pebbles, then leapt through a blackberry bramble headfirst. Ethan had no choice but to follow. It was briefly very dark inside the bramble, and cold, too, a dank chill, as if they had leapt not through a blackberry bramble but into the mouth of a deep cave. There was a soft tinkling like the sound of the wind through icy pine needles. Then somehow or other he landed, without a scratch on him, at the edge of a familiar meadow, beyond which lay the white mystery of the birches.

"Hey. How'd we—? Is this—?"

They had been walking for a few minutes at most. Now, Ethan had done a fair amount of ranging alone through the woods and along the gravel roads of Clam Island. But he had never considered trying to walk all the way from his house to the Tooth. It was just too far. You would have to walk, he would have said, for more than an hour. And yet here they were, or seemed to be. The broad sunny meadow, the birch trees, the brackish green Sound that he could smell just beyond them.

"Now, there's one last thing I want you to imagine," Cutbelly said. "And it's that because of all the crazy bends and hairpin turns, because of all the zigs and zags in the limbs and boughs and branches of this Tree I'm telling you about, it so happens that two leaves can end up lying right beside each other, separated by what amounts, for a gifted shadowtail like myself, to a single bound. And yet, if you were to follow your way back along the twigs and branches, back to the trunk, you would find that these two leaves actually grow from two separate great limbs of the Tree. Though near neighbours, they lie in two totally different Worlds. Can you picture that, piglet? Can you see how the four Worlds are all tangled up in each other like the forking, twisting branches of a tree?"

"You're saying you can *scamper* from one world to another?"

"No, I can leap. And take you with me into the bargain," said the werefox. "And the name of this World is the Summerlands."

It was the Summerland Ethan knew; yet it was different, too. The plain metal bleachers and chain fences of Jock MacDougal Field at the far side of the meadow had been replaced with an elegant structure, at once sturdy and ornate, carved from a pale yellow, almost white substance that Ethan could not at first identify. It was a neat little box of a building, with long arched galleries through which he could see that it was open to the sky. It looked a little like the Taj Mahal, and a little like a big old Florida hotel, towers and grandstands and pavilions. There was an onion-shaped turret at each corner, and along the tops of the galleries rows of long snaky pennants snapped in the breeze.

"It's a ballpark," Ethan said. "A tiny one." It was no bigger than a Burger King restaurant.

"The Neighbours are not a large people," Cutbelly said. "As you will soon see."

"The Neighbours," Ethan said. "Are they human?"

"The Neighbours? No, sir. Not in the least. A separate creation, same as me."

"They aren't *aliens*?" Ethan was looking around for possible explanations for Cutbelly. It had occurred to him that his new friend might have evolved on some distant world of grass where it might behove you to work your way up from something like a fox.

"And what is an alien, tell me that?"

"A creature from another world. You know, from outer space."

"As I thought I had made clear, there are but four Worlds," Cutbelly said. "Though one of them, I should mention, is lost to us for ever. Sealed off by a trick of Coyote. Yours, including everything that you and your kind call 'the universe,' is just one of the three remaining ones, though if I may say, it's my personal favourite of the lot. Just now you and I are crossing into another one, the Summerlands. And this is where the Neighbours most definitely dwell. Now as I was saying, they are not very grand. In fact they are quite literally Little People."

"*Little People*?" Ethan said. "Wait. OK. The Neighbours. They are. Aren't they? They're fair—"

"Fair *Folk*!" Cutbelly cut him off. "Yes, indeed, that is an old name for them. *Ferishers* is the name they give themselves, or rather the name that they'll consent to have you call them."

"And they play baseball."

"Endlessly." With a roll of his eyes, Cutbelly threw himself down in the grass and weeds, of which he began gathering great handfuls and stuffing them into the bowl of his pipe.

"In that little building over there?"

"Thunderbird Park," Cutbelly said. "'The Jewel of the Chinook League'. When there was a league. It's a drafty old barracks, if you ask me."

"What is it… what is it, uh, made of?" Even as he said it the thought strayed once more into his mind: *human bones*.

"Ivory," Cutbelly said.

"Whale?"

"Not whale."

"Walrus?"

"Nor walrus, besides."

"*Elephant?*"

"And where would anyone get hold of that much elephant ivory around here? No, that ballpark, piglet, was carved from *giant's* ivory. From the bones of Skookum John, who made the mistake of trying to raid this neighbourhood one day back about 1743." He sighed, and took a contemplative puff on his pipe. "Ah, me," he said. "Might as well have a seat, piglet. They know we're here. A moment will bring them along."

Ethan sat down beside Cutbelly in the grassy meadow. The sun was high and the tall green grass was vibrant with bees. It might have been the loveliest summer day in the history of Ethan Feld. The birch forest was loud with birds. The smell of smoke from Cutbelly's pipe was pungent but not unpleasant. Ethan suddenly remembered a similar afternoon, bees and blue skies, long ago… somewhere… at the edge of a country road, beside a grassy bank that ran down to a stagnant pond. It must have been at his grandparents' house, in South Fallsburg, New York, which he had heard his mother speak of but, until now, never remembered. The country house had been sold when he was still a very little boy. His mother crouched down behind him, one slender hand on his shoulder. With the other she pointed to the murky black water of the pond. There, hovering just a few inches above the water, hung a tiny white woman, her hummingbird wings all a-whir.

"That was a pixie, actually," Cutbelly said, sounding more melancholy than ever. This time Ethan noticed that his thoughts had been read. "And you were lucky to see one. There aren't too many of them left. They got the grey crinkles worse than any of them."

"The grey crinkles?"

In the trees to their left there was a sudden flutter, like the rustle of a curtain or a flag. A huge crow took to the sky with a raucous laugh and what Ethan would have sworn was a backwards glance at him and Cutbelly.

"It's a great plague of the Summerlands," Cutbelly said, his bright black eyes watching the crow as it flew off. "More of Coyote's mischief. It's horrible to see."

Cutbelly puffed dourly on his pipe. It was clear that he didn't care to say anything more on the sad subject of the vanishing pixies and the dreadful plague that had carried them off.

As is so often the case when one is in the presence of a truly gifted teacher, Cutbelly's explanations had left Ethan with so many questions that he didn't know where to begin. What happened when you got the grey crinkles? What did coyotes have to do with it?

"What's the difference?" Ethan began. "I mean, between a pixie and a fair— a ferisher?"

Cutbelly clambered abruptly to his feet. The plug of charred weeds tumbled from the bowl of his shinbone pipe, and Ethan's nostrils were soon tinged by the smell of burning fur.

"See for yourself," Cutbelly said. "Hear for yourself, too."

They travelled, like the ball clubs of old, in buses – only these buses could fly. They came tearing out of the birch forest in ragged formation, seven of them, trying to keep abreast of one another but continually dashing ahead of or dropping behind. They were shaped more or less like the Greyhound coaches you saw in old movies, at once bulbous and sleek. But they were much smaller than an ordinary bus – no bigger than an old station wagon. They were made not of steel or aluminium, but of gold wire, striped fabric, some strange, pearly silver glass, and all kinds of other substances and objects – clamshells and feathers, marbles and pennies and pencils. They were *wild* buses, somehow, the small, savage cousins of their domesticated kin. They dipped and rolled and swooped along the grass, bearing down on Ethan and Cutbelly. As they drew nearer, Ethan could hear the sound of laughter and curses and shouts. They were having a race, flying across the great sunny meadow in their ramshackle golden buses.

"Everything is a race or a contest, with the Neighbours," Cutbelly said, sounding fairly fed up with them. "Somebody always has to lose, or they aren't happy."

At last one of the buses broke free of the pack for good. It shot across the diminishing space between it and Ethan's head and then came, with a terrific screech of tyres against thin air, to a stop. There was a loud cheer from within, and then the other buses came squealing up. Immediately six or seven dozen very small people piled out of the doors and began shouting and arguing and trying to drown each other out. They snatched leather purses from their belts and waved them around. After a moment great stacks of gold coins began to change hands. At last most of them looked pleased or at least satisfied with the outcome of the race, and turned to Cutbelly and Ethan, jostling and elbowing one another to get a better look at the intruder.

Ethan stared back. They looked like a bunch of tiny Indians out of some old film or museum diorama. They were dressed in trousers and dresses of skin, dyed and beaded. They were laden with shells and feathers and glinting bits of gold. Their skins were the colour of cherry wood. Some were armed with bows and quivers of arrows. The idea of a lost tribe of pygmy Indians living in the woods of Clam Island made a brief appearance in Ethan's mind before being laughed right out again. These creatures could never be mistaken for human. For one thing, though they were clearly adults, women with breasts, men with beards and moustaches, none stood much taller than a human infant. Their eyes were the colour of cider and beer, the pupils rectangular black slits like the pupils of goats. But it was more than their size or the strangeness of their pale gold eyes. Looking at them – just *looking* at them – raised the hair on the back of Ethan's neck. On this dazzling summer day, he shuddered, from the inside out, as if he had a fever. His jaw trembled and he heard his teeth clicking against each other. His toes in his sneakers curled and uncurled.

"You'll get used to seeing them in time," Cutbelly whispered.

One of the ferishers, a little taller than the others, broke away from the troop. He was dressed in a pair of feathered trousers, a shirt of hide with horn buttons, and a green jacket with long orchestra-leader tails. On his head there was a high-crowned baseball cap, red with a black bill and a big silver O on the crown, and on his feet a tiny pair of black spikes, the old-fashioned kind such as you might have seen on the feet of Ty Cobb in an old photograph. He was as handsome as the king on a playing card, with the same unimpressed expression.

"A eleven-year-old boy," he said, peering up at Ethan. "These is shrunken times indeed."

"He goin' to do fine," said a familiar voice, creaky and scuffed-up as an old leather mitt. Ethan turned to find old Ringfinger Brown standing behind him. Today the old man's suit was a three-piece, as pink as lipstick, except for the vest, which was exactly the colour of the Felds' station wagon.

"He'll hafta," said the ferisher. "The Rade has come, just like Johnny Speakwater done foretold. An' they brought their pruning shears, if ya know what I mean."

"Yeah, we saw 'em, din't we, boy?" Ringfinger said to Ethan. "Comin' in with their shovels and their trucks and their steel-toe boots to do their rotten work."

"I'm Cinquefoil," the ferisher told Ethan. "Chief o' this mob. And starting first baseman."

Ethan noticed now that there was some murmuring among the ferishers. He looked inquiringly at Mr. Brown, who gestured towards the ground with his fingers. Ethan didn't understand.

"You in the presence of royalty, son," Mr. Brown said. "You ought to bow down when you meetin' a chief, or a king, or some other type of top man or potentate. Not to mention the Home Run King of three worlds, Cinquefoil of the Boar Tooth mob."

"Oh, my gosh," Ethan said. He was very embarrassed, and felt that a simple bow would somehow not be enough to make up for his rudeness. So he got down on one knee, and lowered his head. If he had been wearing a hat, he would have doffed it. It was one of those things that you have seen done in movies a hundred times, but rarely get the chance to try. He must have looked pretty silly. The ferishers all burst out laughing, Cinquefoil loudest of all.

"That's the way, little reuben," he said.

Ethan waited for what he hoped was a respectful amount of time. Then he got back to his feet.

"How many home runs did you hit?" he asked.

Cinquefoil shrugged modestly. "Seventy-two thousand nine hundred and fifty-four," he said. "Hit that very number just last night." He pounded his mitt, which was about the size and colour of a Nilla wafer. "Catch."

A small white sphere, stitched in red but no bigger than a gumball, came at Ethan. The air seemed to waver around it and it came faster than he expected. He got his hands up, just, and clutched hopefully at the air in front of his face. The ball stung him on the shoulder and then dropped with an embarrassing plop to the grass. All the ferishers let out their breath at once in a long deflated hiss. The ball rolled back towards Cinquefoil's black spikes. He looked at it, then up at Ethan. Then with a sigh he bent down and flicked it back into his mitt.

"A hot prospect indeed," said Cinquefoil to Ringfinger Brown. This time Mr. Brown didn't try to stick up for Ethan. "Well, we got no choice, an' that's a fact. The Rade has showed up, years before we ever done expected them, and yer about ten years shy o' half-cooked, but we got no choice. There ain't no time ta go looking for another champion. I guess ya'll hafta do."

"But what do you need me for?" Ethan said.

"What do ya think? To save us. To save the Birchwood."

"What's the Birchwood?"

The little chief rubbed slowly at chin with one tiny brown hand. It seemed to be a gesture of annoyance.

"This is the Birchwood. These trees – ain't ya ever noticed them? They're birch trees. Birch*wood*. These woods is our home. We live here."

"And, excuse me, I'm sorry, ha, but, uh, save it from *what*, now?"

Cinquefoil gave Ringfinger Brown a hard look.

"Ta think that we done paid ya half our treasure fer this," he said bitterly.

Ringfinger suddenly noticed a bit of fuzz on his lapel.

The ferisher chief turned to Ethan.

"From Coyote, o' course," he said. "Now that he done found us, he's going ta try ta lop our gall. He does that, that's the end o' the Birchwood. And that's the end o' my mob."

Ethan was lost, and embarrassed, too. If there was one thing he hated more than anything else in the world, it was being taken for stupid. His natural tendency in such situations was to pretend that he understood for as long as was necessary until he *did* understand. But whatever the ferisher was talking about – *lop* our *gall*? – it sounded too important for Ethan to fake. So he turned for help to Cutbelly.

"Who is Johnny Speakwater?" he said miserably.

"Johnny Speakwater is the local oracle in this part of the Western Summerlands," the werefox said. "About ten years ago, he predicted that Coyote, or the Changer as he is also known, was going to find his way to the Birchwood. Listen, now, you remember I was telling you about the Tree – the Lodgepole, as these people call it."

At these words, a groan went up from the assembled ferishers.

"He don't even know about the *Lodgepole*!" Cinquefoil cried.

"Stop givin' me the fisheye," Ringfinger Brown snapped. "I done told you they was slim pickin's."

"Shrunken times, indeed," the chief repeated, and all his mob nodded their heads. Ethan could see they were already very disappointed in him, and he hadn't even done anything yet.

"Every so often," Cutbelly went on patiently, "two branches of a tree will rub right up against each other. Have you ever seen that? Every time there's a stiff enough wind. They do it so long, and so furious, that a raw place, a kind of wound, opens up in the bark on each limb where it's been rubbing. And then, over time, the wound heals over with new bark, only now, the two limbs are joined together. Into one limb. That joining or weaving together of two parts of a tree is called *pleaching*. And the place where they are joined is called a *gall*."

"I've seen that," Ethan said. "I saw a tree in Florida one time that was like that."

"Well, with a tree as old and as tangled-up as the Lodgepole, and with the Winds of Time blowing as stiff as they like to blow, you are bound to have some pleaching, here and there. By now it's been going on so long that these galls are all over the place. Galls mark the spots where two worlds flow into each other. And they tend to be magical places. Sacred groves, haunted pools, and so forth. Your Summerland is just such a place."

"So, OK, Summerland is in my world *and* this one," Ethan said, to Cinquefoil as much as to Cutbelly, hoping to demonstrate that he was not *totally* hopeless. "At the same time. And that's why it never rains there?"

"Never can tell what's going to happen around a gall," Cutbelly said. "All kinds of wonderful things. A dry sunny patch of green in a land of endless grey and drizzle is just one of the possibilities."

"And now this Coyote wants to cut the worlds apart again?"

Cutbelly nodded.

"But why?" Ethan said.

"Because that's what Coyote does, among a thousand other mad behaviours. He wanders around the Tree, with his Rade of followers, and wherever he finds the worlds pleached together he lops them right apart. But this local gall is tucked away in such a remote corner of the Worlds that he's missed it until now."

"OK," Ethan said. "I get it. I mean, I sort of get it. But, I mean, you know, I sort of agree with the whole idea of how I'm a, well, a *kid*. Like, I don't know how to use a, what, like a sword, or even ride a horse, or any of that stuff, if that's what I'm supposed to do."

Nobody said anything for a long time. It was as if they had all been hoping in spite of themselves that Ethan was going to rise to the occasion and come up with a plan for saving Summerland. Now that hope was gone. Then, from the edge of the meadow, there was a scornful laugh. They all turned in time to see a crow – the same great black bird, Ethan would have sworn, that he and Cutbelly had seen earlier – take to the sky. Some of the ferishers unslung their bows. They nocked arrows to their bowstrings and let fly. The arrows whistled into the sky. The black bird took no notice of them. Its wings beat slowly, lazily, with a kind of insolence, as if it thought it had all the time in the world. Its rough laughter caught the breeze and trailed behind it like a mocking streamer.

"Enough o' this," the chief said, at last, his face grim and his tone gruff and commanding. He tossed the tiny baseball to Ethan again. This time Ethan just managed to hold on to it as it came stinging into his palm. "Let's go talk ta that crazy old clam."

THEY TROOPED ACROSS the meadow, past the gleaming white ballpark, and down to the beach. Here in the Summerlands, in the Birchwood, there was no ruined hotel, no collapsed dance hall or pier. There was just the long dark stretch of muddy sand, with the ghostly trees on one side of it and the endless dark green water stretching away on the other. And, in the middle of it all, that big grey log of ancient driftwood, spiky and half-buried, on which he and his father had once sat and shared a lunch of chicken sandwiches and hot chicken soup from the thermos. Was it the same log, Ethan wondered? Could something really exist in two different worlds at the same time?

"That bristly old chunk of wood is the gall, some say," Cutbelly told him. "The place where the worlds are jointed fast."

They seemed in fact to be headed right towards it.

"But I thought you said the Tree was invisible, and untouchable," Ethan said. "Immaterial."

"Can you see love? Can you *touch* it?"

"Well," Ethan said, hoping it was not a trick question. "No, love is invisible and untouchable, too."

"And when your pap puts on that big Roosters jersey of his, and sits there watching you in the bleachers with the smile never leaving his face? And slaps palms with you after a game even though you struck out four times looking?"

"Huh," Ethan said.

"Some things that are invisible and untouchable can nevertheless be seen and felt."

They had reached the driftwood log. At a gesture from Cinquefoil a dozen or more ferishers got down on their knees and began, slowly and with a strange tenderness, to dig in the sand underneath it. They were digging separately, but all of them stayed in the area shadowed by the upraised, snaggled roots of the log. They slipped their small hands into the sand with a hiss and then brought them out, cupped, with a soft, sucking *pop*. The sand they removed in this way they drizzled through their fingers, writing intricate squiggles on the smooth surface of the beach. The driblets of sand made daisies and cloverleaves and suns. At last one of the ferishers cried out, pointing at the pattern her wet handful of sand had formed, like a pair of crossed lightning bolts. The other diggers gathered around her, then, and with vigour, they began to dig all together at the spot. Before long they had dug a hole that was three times taller than any of them, and twice as wide. Then there was another cry, followed by what sounded to Ethan like a loud, rude belch. Everyone laughed, and the diggers came clambering up out of the hole.

The last three struggled out under the shared burden of the largest clam that Ethan had ever seen. It was easily as big as a large watermelon, and looked even bigger in the ferishers' small arms as they staggered up onto the beach with it. Its shell was lumpy and rugged as broken concrete. The rippled lip dripped with green water and some kind of brown slime. The ferishers set it down on the beach and then the rest of the mob circled around it. Ringfinger Brown gave Ethan a gentle push at the small of his back.

"Go on, boy," he said. "Listen to what Johnny Speakwater gots to say."

Ethan stepped forward – he could almost have stepped right over the ferishers, but he felt instinctively that this would be rude. He arrived at the innermost edge of the circle just as the ferisher chief was going down on one knee in front of the clam.

"Hey, Johnny," Cinquefoil said in a low, soft voice, calling to the clam like a man trying to wake a friend on the morning of some long-awaited exploit – a fishing trip or camp-out. "Whoa, Johnny Speakwater. All right now. Open up. We need a word with ya."

There was a deep rumble from inside the clam, and Ethan's heart began to beat faster as he saw the briny lips of the shell part. Water came pouring out and vanished into the sand under the clam. Little by little, with an audible creak, the upper half of the clamshell lifted an inch or so off of the lower half. As it opened Ethan could see the greyish-pink glistening muscle of the thing, wet and slurping around in its pale lower jaw.

"Burdleburbleslurpleslurpleburbleburdleslurp," said the clam, more or less.

Cinquefoil nodded, and pointed to a pair of ferishers standing nearby. One of them reached into a leather tube, a kind of quiver that hung at his back, and pulled out a rolled sheet of what looked like parchment. The other took hold of one end, and then they stepped apart from each other, unrolling the scroll. It was a sheet of pale hide, like their clothing, a rectangle of deerskin marked all around with mysterious characters of an alphabet that Ethan didn't know. It was something like a Ouija board, only the letters had been painted by hand. The ferishers knelt down in front of the clam, and held the unfurled scroll out in front of him.

Cinquefoil laid a hand on the top of the clam's shell, and stroked it softly, without seeming to notice what he was doing. He was lost in thought. Ethan supposed he was trying to come up with the right question for the oracle. Oracles were tricky, as Ethan knew from his reading of mythology. Often they answered the question you *ought* to have asked, or the one you didn't realise you were even asking. Ethan wondered what question he himself would pose to an oracular clam, given a chance.

"Johnny," the chief said finally. "Ya done warned us that Coyote was coming. And ya was right. Ya said we ought ta fetch us a champion, and we done tried. And spent up half our dear treasury in the bargain. But look at this one, Johnny." Cinquefoil made a dismissive wave in Ethan's direction. "He's just a puppy. He ain't up ta the deal. We been watching him for a while now, and we had our hopes, but Coyote's done come sooner than ever we thought. So now, Johnny, I'm asking ya one more time. What are we ta do now? How can we stop Coyote? Where can we turn?"

There was a pause, during which Johnny Speakwater emitted a series of fizzings and burps and irritable teakettle whistlings. The letter-scroll trembled in the ferishers' hands. From somewhere nearby came the disrespectful cackling of a crow. Then there was a deep *splorp* from inside Johnny Speakwater, and a jet of clear, shining water shot from between the lips of his shell. It lanced across the foot or so of air that separated the clam and the letter-scroll, and hit with a loud, thick splat against a letter that looked something like a curly U with a cross in the centre of it.

"Ah!" cried all the ferishers. Cinquefoil scratched the U-and-cross into the sand.

One letter at a time, slowly, with deadly accuracy, Johnny Speakwater spat out his prophecy. As each wad of thick clam saliva hit the parchment, the letter affected was copied into the sand by Cinquefoil, and then wiped clean. The clam spat more quickly as he went along and then, when he had hawked up about forty-five blasts, he stopped. A faint, clammy sigh escaped him, and then his shell creaked shut again. Ferishers gathered around the inscription, many of them murmuring the words. Then one by one they turned to look at Ethan with renewed interest.

"What does it say?" Ethan said. "Why are you all looking at me?"

Ringfinger Brown went over to take a look at the prophecy in the sand. He rubbed at the bald place on the back of his grey head, then held out his hand to Cinquefoil. The chief handed him the stick, and the old scout scratched two fresh sentences under the strange ferisher marks.

"That about right?" he asked the chief.

Cinquefoil nodded.

"What did I *tell* you, then," Ringfinger said. "What did I *say*?"

Ethan leaned forward to see how the old man had translated the words of the oracular clam.

FELD IS THE WANTED ONE
FELD HAS THE STUFF HE NEEDS

When he read these words, Ethan felt a strange warmth fill his belly. *He* was the wanted one – the champion. He had the stuff. He turned back to look at Johnny Speakwater, flush with gratitude towards the clam for having such faith in him when no one else did. What he saw, when he turned, made him cry out in horror.

"*The crow!*" he said. "He has Johnny!"

In all the excitement over the words of the prophecy, the prophet had been forgotten.

"It ain't a crow," Cinquefoil said. "It's a raven. I'd lay even money it's Coyote himself."

When their backs were turned, the great black bird must have swooped down from the trees. Now it was lurching his way skyward with the clam clutched in both talons. Its wings beat fitfully against the air. It was a huge and powerful bird, but the enormous clam was giving it problems. It dipped and staggered and listed to one side. Ethan could hear the clam whistling and burbling in desperation as it was carried away.

Something came over Ethan then. Perhaps he was feeling charged from the vote of confidence Johnny Speakwater had given him. Or perhaps he was just angered, as any of us would be, by seeing an outrage perpetrated on an innocent clam. He had seen birds on the Fauna Channel making meals out of bivalves. He had a vision of Johnny Speakwater being dropped from the sky onto some rocks, the great stony shell shattered and lying in shards. He saw the sharp yellow beak of the raven ripping into the featureless, soft greyish-pink flesh that was all Johnny Speakwater had for a body. In any case he took off down the beach, after the raven, shouting, "Hey! You come back here! Hey!"

The raven was not making good time under all that weight. The nearer he got to the robber bird, the angrier Ethan got. Now he was just underneath the struggling pair of wings, right at the edge of the trees. A few seconds more and he would have run out of beach. The whistling of the clam was more piteous than ever. Ethan wanted to do something to help Johnny Speakwater, to justify its faith in him, to prove to the ferishers that he was not just a raw and unformed puppy.

There was something in Ethan's hand, round and hard and cool as a sound argument. He looked down. It was the ferisher baseball. Without considering questions of air resistance or trajectory, he heaved the ball skyward in the direction of the raven. It arced skyward and struck the bird with neat precision on the head. There was a sickening *crack*. The bird squawked, and fluttered, and let go of Johnny Speakwater. A moment later something heavy as a boulder and rough as a brick smacked Ethan in the chest, and he felt a blast of something warm and marine splash across his face, and then he felt his legs go out from under him. The last thing he heard before he lost consciousness was the voice of the ferisher chief, Cinquefoil.

"Sign that kid up," he said.

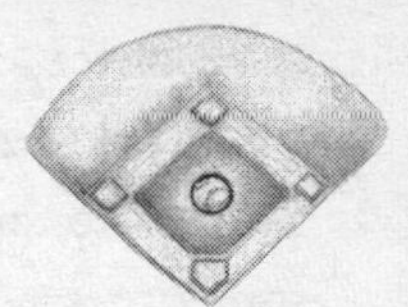

3
A Whistled-up Wind

ETHAN OPENED HIS eyes. He was lying in his bed, in his bedroom, in the pink house on top of the hill. From the singing of the birds and the softness of the grey light at the window, he guessed that it was morning. He sat up and took his wristwatch from the nightstand beside his bed. His father had designed and assembled the watch for him, using parts from a store down in Tacoma called Geek World. The face of the watch was covered in buttons – it was like a little keyboard – and there was a liquid-crystal screen. Mr. Feld had loaded the watch with all kinds of interesting and possibly useful functions, but Ethan could never figure out how to do anything with it but tell the time and the day. Which was 7:24 A.M., Saturday the ninth. Only a little more than a minute, then, since a foul-smelling werefox who called himself Cutbelly had appeared, squatting on Ethan's chest, to extend an invitation from another world. He heard the familiar Saturday sound of his father banging around down in the kitchen.

If this were a work of fiction, the author would now be obliged to have Ethan waste a few moments wondering if he had dreamed the events of the past few hours. Since, however, every word of this account is true, the reader will not be surprised to learn that Ethan had no doubt whatsoever that in the company of a shadowtail he had leaped from one hidden branch of the Tree of Worlds to another – to the realm that in books was sometimes called Faerie – for the second time in his life. He knew perfectly well that he really had met a sort of fairy king, there, and seen a ballpark made from a giant's bones, and rescued an oracular clam with one lucky toss of a ball. Ethan could tell the difference between the nonsensical business of a dream and the wondrous logic of a true adventure. But if Ethan had needed further proof of his having passed a few hours in the Summerlands, he need have looked no further than the book that was lying on his pillow, just beside the dent where his slumbering head had been.

It was small – of course – about the size of book of matches, bound in dark green leather. On the spine was stamped, in ant-high golden letters, *How to Catch Lightning and Smoke*, and on the title page the author's name was given as one E. Peavine. The print inside was almost too small for Ethan to make out. He could tell from the diagrams, though, that the book concerned baseball – specifically, the position of catcher. Of all the positions in the game, this was the one, with its mysterious mask and armour, to which Ethan had always felt the most drawn. But the fact that to play catcher you really had to understand the rules of the game had always scared him away.

He got up and went over to his desk. At the back of a drawer, under the detritus of several fine hobbies that had never quite taken, among them stamp collecting, rock collecting, and the weaving of pot holders from coloured elastic bands, Ethan found a magnifying glass his father had given him for his eleventh birthday. Mr. Feld was a passionate collector of both stamps and rocks. (He also wove a pretty decent pot holder.) Ethan climbed back into bed, pulled the blanket up over himself, and, with the help of the glass, began to read the introduction.

"The first and last duty of the lover of the game of baseball," Peavine's book began,

> whether in the stands or on the field, is the same as that of the lover of life itself: to pay attention to it. When it comes to the position of catcher, as all but fools and shortstops will freely acknowledge, this solemn requirement is doubled.

Peavine, Ethan learned, was a ferisher from a region of the Summerlands that, as Peavine put it, "brushed up to" Troy, New York. He had learned the fundamentals of his position during the summers of 1880, '81, and '82 by secretly observing the play of a catcher for the Troy Trojans, a human ("reuben", was Peavine's term) named William "Buck" Ewing. "These summers spent at the shoulder of the cool and elegant Buck," Peavine wrote, "as fine a reuben as I have ever encountered, in the dusty green bowl of Trojan Field, remain among the happiest memories of all my long, long life." When an outbreak of the grey crinkles devastated Peavine's native mob, he had wandered west and taken up the mask, mitt, and chest protector for a mob of ferishers living at a place called Snake Island "an easy leap from Coeur d'Alene, Idaho." It was here, playing for the

Snake Island Wapatos amid the cottonwoods and wildflower glades of the seventy-two-team Flathead League, that he had first begun, in his words, "to grasp the fundamental truth: a baseball game is nothing but a great slow contraption for getting you to pay attention to the cadence of a summer day."

"Eth?"

There was a knock at the door to Ethan's bedroom. He slid the book under his pillow and sat up as his father opened the door and poked his head into the room.

"Breakfast is..." He frowned, looking puzzled. "Ready."

Ethan saw that he had neglected to dispose of the magnifying glass. He was clutching it in his left hand, with absolutely nothing around him that he might plausibly have been using it to examine. Lamely Ethan held it up to the window next to his bed.

"Spider," he said. "Really tiny one."

"A spider!" said his father. "Let me see." He came over to the bed and Ethan passed him the magnifying glass. "Where?"

Ethan pointed; his father leaned in. A circle of empty air wavered in the watery lens. Then, to Ethan's surprise, a face emerged, grinning a yellow-toothed grin. A grey face, with a grey mosquito-stinger of a nose, equipped with a twitching black set of wings. Ethan's tongue seemed to swell in his mouth; he could not utter a sound. He watched in horror as the creature *winked at him*, waiting for his father's cry of alarm.

"I don't see any spider," Mr. Feld said mildly. He stood up again and the horrible grin vanished; there was nothing at the window but misty Clam Island morning.

"The wind must have blown it away," Ethan said.

He climbed out of bed, pulled on a pair of underpants under the extra-large Hellboy T-shirt he slept in, and followed his father out to the kitchen, to confront the weekly sadness of flannel cakes.

His father set a tall stack in front of him and then sat down with a stack of his own. They were enormous things, Mr. Feld's flannel cakes, each nearly the size of the plate itself, and there were invariably five or six of them that Ethan was expected to eat. During the week Ethan fixed his own breakfast – cold cereal, or an English muffin spread with peanut butter. This was necessary because Mr. Feld stayed up till all hours in his workshop. This in turn was because the night-time was when Mr. Feld felt the most inventive. Or so he said. Sometimes Ethan suspected that his father simply didn't like to see the light of day. When Ethan got ready for school or, now that school was out, for a morning walk in the woods or a bike ride over to Jennifer T.'s, Mr. Feld was usually asleep. But on Saturday mornings, no matter how late he had worked, Mr. Feld always woke up, or stayed up, as the case might be, to cook a pancake breakfast for him and Ethan. Pancakes – she called them flannel cakes – had been a specialty of Dr. Feld's, and the Saturday breakfast was a Feld family tradition. Unfortunately, Mr. Feld was a terrible cook, and his own flannel cakes never failed to live up to their rather unappetising name.

"Well," Mr. Feld said, tipping the bottle of maple syrup onto his stack. "Let's see how I did this week."

"Did you remember the baking powder?" Ethan said, with a shudder. He was still feeling unnerved by the memory of the ugly grey face, with the pointed nose and wicked grin, swimming in the lens of the magnifying glass. "The eggs?"

His father nodded, allowing a large puddle of syrup to form. One of the unspoken but necessary ground rules for eating Mr. Feld's flannel cakes was that you could use as much syrup as you needed to help you get them down.

"And the vanilla?" Ethan said, pouring his own syrup. He preferred Karo; he had seen a movie once of men in fur hats driving long, sharp steel taps into the tender hearts of Canadian maples, and ever since then had felt too sorry for the trees to eat maple syrup.

Mr. Feld nodded again. He cut himself a fat wedge, pale yellow pinstriped with dark brown, and popped it, looking optimistic, into his mouth. Ethan quickly did the same. They chewed, watching each other carefully. Then they both stared down at their plates.

"If only she had written down the recipe," Mr. Feld said at last.

They ate in silence broken only by the clink of their forks, by the hum of the electric clock over the stove and by the steady liquid muttering of their old refrigerator. To Ethan it was like the tedious soundtrack of their lives. He and his father lived in this little house, alone; his father working sixteen hours a day and more perfecting the Zeppelina, the personal family dirigible that was someday going to revolutionise transportation, while Ethan tried not to disturb him, not to disturb anyone, not to disturb the world. Entire days went by without either of them exchanging more than a few words. They had few friends on the island. Nobody came to visit, and they received no invitations. And then, on Saturday mornings, this wordless attempt to maintain a tradition whose purpose, whose point, and whose animating spirit – Ethan's mother – seemed to be lost forever.

After a few minutes the humming of the clock began to drive Ethan out of his mind. The silence lay upon him like a dense pile of flannel cakes, gummed with syrup. He pushed back in his chair and sprang to his feet.

"Dad?" Ethan said, when they were most of the way through the ordeal. "Hey, Dad?"

His father was half dozing, chewing and chewing on a mouthful of pancakes with one eye shut. His thick black hair stood up in wild coils from his head, and his eyelids were purple with lack of sleep.

Mr. Feld sat up, and took a long swallow of coffee. He winced. He disliked the taste of the coffee he brewed almost as much as he hated his pancakes.

"What, son?" he said.

"Do you think I would ever make a good catcher?"

Mr. Feld stared at him, wide awake now, unable to conceal his disbelief. "You mean… you mean a *baseball* catcher?"

"Like Buck Ewing."

"*Buck Ewing?*" Mr. Feld said. "That's going back a ways." But he smiled. "Well, Ethan, I think it's a very intriguing idea."

"I was just sort of thinking… maybe it's time for us— for me— to try something different."

"You mean, like waffles?" Mr. Feld pushed his plate away, sticking out his tongue, and smoothed down his wild hair. "Come," he said. "I think I may have an old catcher's mitt, out in the workshop."

THE PINK HOUSE on the hill had once belonged to a family named Okawa. They had dug clams, kept chickens, and raised strawberries on a good-sized patch that ran alongside the Clam Island Highway for nearly a quarter of a mile in the direction of Clam Centre. After the attack on Pearl Harbor, the Okawas were put onto a school bus with the three or four other Japanese families living on Clam Island at the time. They were taken to the mainland, to a government internment camp outside of Spokane. The Okawa farm was sold to the Jungermans, who had neglected it. In the end it was the island itself, and not the Okawas – they never returned – that claimed the property. The strawberry patch was still there, badly overgrown, a thick black and green tangle of shadow and thorn in which, during the summer, you could sometimes catch, like a hidden gem, the glimpse of a bright strawberry.

When Ethan and his father had arrived on Clam Island, they had chosen this house, knowing nothing about its sad history, mostly because Ethan's dad had been so taken with the glass and cinder-block hulk of the old Okawa Farm strawberry packing shed. It had wide, tall doors, a high ceiling of aluminium and glass, and ample space for all of Mr. Feld's tools and equipment and for the various components of his airships, not to mention his large collection of cardboard boxes.

"It's got to be in one of these," said Mr. Feld. "I know I would never have thrown it away."

Ethan stood beside his father, watching him root around

in a box that had long ago held twelve bottles of Gilbey's gin. It was not one of the boxes left over from their move to Clam Island, which were all stamped MAYFLOWER, with a picture of the Pilgrims' ship. There were plenty of those still standing around, in stacks, up at the house, corners crisp, sealed with neat strips of tape. Ethan tried never to notice them. They reminded him, painfully, of how excited he had been at the time of the move; how glad to be leaving Colorado Springs, even though it meant leaving his mother behind forever. He had been charmed, at first, by the sight of the little pink house, and it was enchanting to imagine the marvellous blimp that was going to be born in the hulking old packing shed. He and his father had rebuilt the shed almost entirely themselves, that first summer, with some occasional help from Jennifer T.'s father, Albert. For a while the change of light, and the feeling of activity, of real work to be accomplished, had given Ethan reason to believe that everything was going to be all right again.

It was Albert Rideout who had told Ethan, one afternoon, about the Okawas. The son, Albert said, had been one of the best shortstops in the history of Clam Island, graceful and tall, surefooted and quick-handed. To improve his balance he would run up and down the narrow lanes between the rows of strawberry plants, as fast as he could, without crushing a single red berry or stepping on a single green shoot. After the Okawas were interned, the son was so eager to prove how loyal he and his family were to the United States that he had enlisted in the Army. He was killed, fighting against Germany, in France. It was just a story Albert Rideout was telling, as they put a final coat of paint of the cement floor of the workshop, punctuating it with his dry little laugh that was almost a cough. But from that moment on, especially when Ethan looked out at the ruins of the strawberry patch, the sky over the old Okawa Farm had seemed to hang lower, heavier, and greyer than it had on their arrival. That was when the silence had begun to gather and thicken in the house.

"It's really a softball mitt," Mr. Feld was saying. "I played a little catcher in college, on an intramural team… hello!" From the box he was digging around in, he had already pulled the eyepiece of a microscope, a peanut can filled with Canadian coins, and a small cellophane packet full of flaky grey dust and bearing the alarming label SHAVED FISH. Like the others in the workshop, this box was tattered and dented, and had been taped and retaped many times. Sometimes Mr. Feld said that these boxes contained his entire life up to the time of his marriage; other times he said it was all a lot of junk. No matter how many times he went to rummage in them, Mr. Feld never seemed to find exactly what he was looking for, and everything that he did find seemed to surprise him. Now, for the first time that Ethan could remember, he had managed to retrieve what he sought.

"Wow," he said, gazing down at his old mitt with a tender expression. "The old pie plate."

It was bigger than any catcher's mitt that Ethan had ever seen before, thicker and more padded, even bulbous, a rich dark colour like the Irish beer his father drank sometimes on a rainy winter afternoon. Partly folded in on itself along the pocket, it reminded Ethan of nothing so much as a tiny, overstuffed leather armchair.

"Here you go, son," Mr. Feld said.

As Ethan took the mitt from his father, it fell open in his outspread hands, and a baseball rolled out; and the air was suddenly filled with an odour, half salt and half wildflower, that reminded Ethan at once of the air in the Summerlands. Ethan caught the ball before it hit the ground, and stuffed into the flap pocket of his shorts.

"Try it on," Mr. Feld said.

Ethan placed his hand into the mitt. It was clammy inside, but in a pleasant way, like the feel of cool mud between the toes on a hot summer day. Whenever Ethan put on his own glove, there was always a momentary struggle with the finger holes. His third finger would end up jammed in alongside his pinky, or his index finger would protrude painfully out the opening at the back. But when he put on his father's old catcher's mitt, his fingers slid into the proper slots without any trouble at all. Ethan raised his left hand and gave the mitt a few exploratory flexes, pinching his fingers towards his thumb. It was heavy, much heavier than his fielder's glove, but somehow balanced, weighing no more on one part of his hand than on any other. Ethan felt a shiver run through him, like the one that had come over him when he had first seen Cinquefoil and the rest of the wild Boar Tooth mob of ferishers.

"How does it feel?" said Mr. Feld.

"Good," Ethan said. "I think it feels good."

"When we get to the field, I'll have a talk with Mr. Olafssen, about having you start practising with the pitchers next week. In the meantime, you and I could start working on your skills a little bit. I'm sure Jennifer T. would be willing to help you, too. We can work on your crouch, start having you throw from your knees a little bit, and—" Mr. Feld stopped, and his face turned red. It was a long speech, for him, and he seemed to worry that maybe he was getting a little carried away. He patted down the tangled yarn basket of his hair. "That is, I mean— if you'd like to."

"Sure, Dad," Ethan said. "I really think I would."

For the first time that Ethan could remember in what felt to him like years, Mr. Feld grinned, one of his old, enormous grins, revealing the lower incisor that was chipped from some long-ago collision at home plate.

"Great!" he said.

Ethan looked at his watch. A series of numbers was pulsing across the liquid crystal display. He must have accidentally pushed one of the mysterious buttons. He held it out to show his father, who frowned at the screen.

"It's your heart rate," Mr. Feld said, pushing a few of the buttons under the display. "Seems slightly elevated. Ah. Hmm. Nearly eleven. We'd better get going."

"The game's not until twelve-thirty," Ethan reminded him.

"I know it," Mr. Feld said. "But I thought we could take *Victoria Jean*."

ONE WINTER MORNING about three months after the death of his wife, Mr. Feld had informed Ethan that he was quitting his job at Aileron Aeronautics, selling their house in a suburb of Colorado Springs, and moving them to an island in Puget Sound, so that he could build the airship of his dreams. He had been dreaming of airships all his life, in a way – studying them, admiring them, learning their checkered history. Airships were one of his many hobbies. But after his wife's death he had actually *dreamed* of them. It was the same dream every night. Dr. Feld, smiling, her hair tied back in a cheery plaid band that matched her summer dress, stood in a green, sunny square of grass, waving to him. Although in his dream Mr. Feld could see his wife and her happy smile very plainly, she was also somehow very far away. Huge mountains and great forests lay between them. So he built an airship – assembled it quickly and easily out of the simplest of materials, inflated its trim silver envelope with the merest touch of a button – and flew north. As he rose gently into the sky, the mountains dwindled until they were a flat brown stain beneath him, and the forests became blots of pale green ink. He was flying over a map, now, an ever-shrinking AAA map of the western United States, towards a tidy, trim bit of tan in the shape of a running boar, surrounded by blue. At the westernmost tip of this little island, in a patch of green, stood his smiling, beautiful wife, waving. It was Ethan who had eventually gone to the atlas and located Clam Island. Less than a month later, the big Mayflower van full of boxes pulled into the drive between the pink house and the ruined strawberry packing shed. Since then the shining little *Victoria Jean*, Mr. Feld's prototype Zeppelina, had become a familiar sight over the island, puttering her lazy way across the sky. Her creamy-white fibreglass gondola, about the size and shape of a small cabin cruiser, could fit easily in the average garage.

Her long, slender envelope of silvery picofibre composite mesh could be inflated at the touch of a button, and fully deflated in ten minutes. When all the gas was out of it you could stuff the envelope like a sleeping bag into an ordinary lawn-and-leaf trash bag. The tough, flexible, strong picofibre envelope was Mr. Feld's pride. He held seventeen U.S. patents on the envelope technology alone.

Mr. Arch Brody had arrived early at Ian "Jock" MacDougal Regional Ball Field to see to the condition of the turf, and he was the first person to hear the whuffle and hum of the Zeppelina's small motor, a heavily modified Mitsubishi boat engine. He stood up – he had been dusting the pitcher's rubber with his little whisk broom – and frowned at the sky. Sure enough, here came that Feld – no more or less of a fool than most off-islanders, though that wasn't saying much – in his floating flivver. As the ship drew nearer, at a fairly good clip, Mr. Arch Brody could see that the gondola's convertible top was down, and that the Feld boy was riding beside his father. They were headed directly towards the Tooth. Mr. Brody was not a smiling man, but he could not help himself. He had seen Mr. Feld tooling around over the island many times, making test flights in his blimp. It had never occurred to him that the crazy thing could actually be used to get someplace.

"I'll be darned," said Perry Olafssen, coming up behind Mr. Brody. The players and their parents had started to arrive for today's game between the Ruth's Fluff 'n' Fold Roosters and the Dick Helsing Realty Reds. The boys dropped their equipment bags and ran to the outfield to watch the *Victoria Jean* make her approach.

"I don't know if I'd want to be flitting around in that thing today," Mr. Brody said, resuming his usual gloom. "Not with this sky."

It was true. The hundred-year spell of perfect summer weather that had made the Tooth so beloved and useful to the islanders, seemed, to the astonishment of everyone, to have mysteriously been broken. If anything the clouds were thicker over Summerland than over the rest of the island, as if years of storms were venting their pent-up resentment on the spot that had eluded them for so long. It had been raining, on and off, since yesterday, and while the rain had stopped for now, the sky hung low and threatening again. In fact Mr. Brody had arrived at Jock MacDougal that day prepared to execute a solemn duty which no Clam Island umpire, in living memory and beyond, had ever been obliged to perform: to call a baseball game on account of rain.

"I bet that thing's what's makin' it rain," said a voice behind them, muttering and dark. "God only knows what that shiny stuff on the balloon part is."

Everyone turned. Mr. Brody felt his heart sink; he knew the voice well enough. Everyone on Clam Island did.

"That man's been messing with our *sky*," said Albert Rideout, sounding, as usual, absolutely sure of his latest ridiculous theory. He had turned up again two nights earlier, bound for someplace else, come from who knew where, with seven ugly stitches in his cheek.

"What do you know about it?" said Jennifer T. to her father. "Are you an aeronautical engineer who studied at M.I.T., like Mr. Feld? Maybe you'd like to explain to us about the Bernoulli principle?"

Albert glowered at her. His battered, pocked cheeks darkened, and he raised his hand as if to give his daughter a swat. Jennifer T. looked up at him without ducking or flinching or showing any emotion at all.

"I wish you would," she said. "I'd get your butt thrown off this island once and for all. Deputy sheriff said you're down to your last chance."

Albert lowered his hand, slowly, and looked around at the other parents, who were watching him to see what he was going to do. They had an idea that he was probably not going to do anything, but with Albert Rideout, you never knew. The fresh scar on his face was testimony to that. They had known Albert since they were all children together, and some of them still remembered what a sweet and fearless boy he had once been, a tricky pitcher with a big, slow curveball, a party to every adventure, and still the best helper Mr. Brody had ever had around the drugstore. Mr. Brody had even cherished a hope that Albert might someday follow in his footsteps and go to pharmacy school. The thought nearly brought a tear to his eye, but he cried even more rarely than he smiled.

"I ain't afraid of the deputy sheriff," Albert said at last. "And I sure as hell ain't afraid of you, you little brat."

But Jennifer T. wasn't listening to her father anymore. She had taken off at top speed across the field to catch hold of the mooring line as Mr. Feld tossed it down to the grasping, leaping hands of the children. Before anyone had any idea of what she was doing, or could have begun to try to stop her, she tugged herself up onto the rope, twisting the end of it around her right leg.

The *Victoria Jean* rolled slightly towards the ground on that side, then righted herself, thanks to her Feld Gyrotronic Pitch-Cancellation (patent pending). Going hand over hand, steadying herself with her right leg, Jennifer T. pulled herself quickly up to the gleaming chrome rail of the black gondola. Mr. Feld and Ethan took hold of her and dragged her aboard. They were both too amazed by her appearance to criticise her for being reckless, or even to say hello.

"Hey," Ethan managed finally. "Your dad's here?"

Jennifer T. ignored Ethan. She turned to Mr. Feld.

"Can I bring her in?" she asked him.

Mr. Feld looked down and saw Albert Rideout, red in the face, standing with his arms folded across his chest looking daggers at them. He turned to Jennifer T. and nodded, and stepped to one side. Jennifer T. took the wheel in both hands, as he had taught her to do.

"I was going to set her down by the picnic tables," Dr. Feld said. "Jennifer T.?"

Jennifer T. didn't answer him. She had brought the tail of *Victoria Jean* around, so that they were facing southeast, towards Seattle and the jagged dark jaw of the Cascade Mountains beyond. There was a funny look in her eye, one that Ethan had seen before, especially whenever her dad came around.

"Do we have to?" she said at last. "Couldn't we just keep on going?"

IT WAS A weird game.

The rain came soon after play began, with the Roosters as the home team taking the field in a kind of stiff mist, not quite a drizzle. The Reds' pitcher, Andy Dienstag, got into trouble early, loading the bases on three straight walks and then walking in a run. The Reds' pitching seemed to get worse as the rain grew harder, and by the fifth inning, when they halted play, the score was 7–1 in favour of Mr. Olafssen's Roosters. Then came a strange, tedious half hour during which they all sat around under their jackets and a couple of tarps fetched from the backs of people's pickups, and waited to see what the weather and Mr. Arch Brody wanted to do. Mr. Olafssen still had not put Ethan in the game. For the first time this was not a source of relief to Ethan. He was not sure why. Mr. Olafssen had met Mr. Feld's announcement that Ethan wanted to learn to play catcher with a thin smile and a promise to "kick the idea around a little". And it was not as if this were the kind of long, slow, blazing green summer afternoon that, according to Peavine, baseball had been invented to help you understand. It was miserable, grey, and dank. But for some reason he wanted to play today.

"I have been accessing my historical database," Thor said. He was sitting between Jennifer T. and Ethan, holding up the tarp over all of their heads. He had been holding it like that for twenty minutes, straight up in the air, without any sign that his arms were getting tired. Sometimes Ethan wondered if he really *were* an android. "The last reported precipitation at these coordinates was in 1822."

"Is that so?" said Jennifer T. "And what does all this rain do to your big undersea volcano theory?"

"Huh," said Thor.

"Maybe," Jennifer T. suggested, "you're experiencing the emotion we humans like to call 'being full of it'." She clambered out from under the tarp and stood up. "Shoot!" she said. "I want to play!"

But the rain went on, and on, and after a while the tiny spark of interest in the game that Ethan had felt kindle in him that morning, reading Peavine's book, had all but been extinguished by the dampness of the day. He saw Mr. Brody check his watch, and puff out his cheeks, blowing a long disappointed breath. This was it; he was going to call the game. Do it, Ethan thought. Just get it over with.

Suddenly Jennifer T. turned and looked towards the canoe birch forest. "What was that?" she said.

"What was what?" Ethan said, though he heard it too. It sounded like whistling, like a whole bunch of people all whistling the same tune at once. It was far away and yet unmistakable, the tune lonely and sweet and eerie, like the passing of a distant ship way up the Sound. Jennifer T. and Ethan looked at each other, then at the other kids on the bench. They were all watching Mr. Brody as he poked a finger into the grass, measuring its wetness. Nobody but Jennifer T. and Ethan seemed to have heard the strange whistling. Jennifer T. sniffed the air.

"Hey," she said. "I smell..." She stopped. She wasn't sure what she had smelled, only a difference in the air.

"The wind," said Albert Rideout. "Comin' from the east now."

Sure enough, the wind had turned, blowing in crisp and piney from over the eastern Sound, and carrying away with it, as it flowed over the field at Summerland, all the piled-up tangle of grey clouds. For the first time in days the sun reappeared, strong and warm. Curls of steam began to rise from the grass.

"Play ball!" cried Mr. Brody.

"Feld," said Mr. Olafssen. "You're in the game. Take left." He stopped Ethan as he trotted past. "At Monday practice maybe we can put you behind the plate for a little while, all right? See how it goes."

"OK," said Ethan. Running out to left, feeling almost ready to catch a fly ball, he looked up as the last low scraps of cloud were carried west by the softly whistling breeze. He was sure that it was the ferishers he had heard whistling. They were near; they were watching him; they wanted to see him play, to see if he was willing to follow in the footsteps of Peavine and apprentice himself to the game. They wanted to see him play. So they had whistled the rain away.

ETHAN CAME UP to bat in the bottom of the seventh, the final inning, with the Reds ahead 8–7. The change in the weather had proven more helpful to the Reds than to the Roosters – Kyle Olafssen, who was on the mound as six of the last seven Red runs came in, said the sun was in his eyes. Ethan walked over to the pile of bats and started to pick up the bright-red aluminium Easton that he normally used, because it was the one Mr. Olafssen had told him to use, back on the first day of practice. He could feel the eyes of all his team-mates on him. Jennifer T. was on first base, Tucker

Corr on second, and there were two outs. All he had to do was connect, just get the ball out of the infield, and Tucker, who was fast, would be able to make it around to home. The game would be sent into extra innings, at least. If there was an error on the play, as was certainly not out of the question, then Jennifer T. would be able to score, too. And the Roosters would win. And Ethan would be the hero. He let go of the red bat and stood up for a moment, looking towards the birch wood. He took a deep breath. The thought of being the hero of a game had never occurred to him before. It made him a little nervous.

He bent down again and this time, without knowing why, chose a wooden bat that Jennifer T. used sometimes. It had been Albert's, and before that it had belonged to old Mo Rideout. It was dark, stained almost black in places, and it bore the burned-in signature of Mickey Cochrane. A catcher, Ethan thought. He was not sure how he knew this.

"You sure about that, Feld?" Mr. Olafssen called as Ethan walked to the plate, carrying the old Louisville slugger over his shoulder, the way Jennifer T. did.

"Hey, Ethan?" called his father. Ethan tried not to notice the tone of doubt in his voice.

Ethan stepped up to the plate and waved the bat around in the air a few times. He looked out at Nicky Marten, the Reds' new pitcher. Nicky wasn't that hot a pitcher. In fact he was sort of the Ethan Feld of his team.

"Breathe," called Jennifer T. from first base. Ethan breathed. "And keep your eyes open," she added.

He did. Nicky reared back and then brought his arm forwards, his motion choppy, the ball plain and fat and slow rolling out of his stubby little hand. Ethan squeezed the bat handle, and then the next thing he knew it was throbbing in his hand and there was a nice meaty *bok!* and something that looked very much like a baseball went streaking past Nicky Marten, headed for short left field.

"Run!" cried Mr. Feld from the bench.

"Run!" cried all the Roosters, and all of their parents, and Mr. Olafssen, and Mr. Arch Brody too.

Ethan took off for first base. He could hear the rhythmic grunting of Jennifer T. as she headed towards second, the scuffle of a glove, a smack, and then, a moment later, another smack. One smack was a ball hitting a glove, and the other was a foot hitting a base, but he would never afterwards be able to say which had been which. He couldn't see anything at all, either because he had now closed his eyes, or because they were so filled with the miraculous vision of his hit, his very first hit, that there was no room in them for anything else.

"Yer OUT!" Mr. Brody yelled, and then, as if to forestall any protest from the Rooster bench, "I saw the whole thing clear."

Out. He was out. He opened his eyes and found himself standing on first base, alone. The Reds' first baseman had already trotted in and was exchanging high fives with his teammates.

"Nice hit, son!"

Mr. Feld was running towards Ethan, his arms spread wide. He started to hug Ethan, but Ethan pulled away.

"It wasn't a hit," he said.

"What do you mean?" his father said. "Sure it was. A

nice clean hit. If Jennifer T. hadn't stumbled on her way to second, you would have *both* been safe."

"Jennifer T.?" Ethan said. "Jennifer *T*. got out?" His father nodded. "Not me?"

Before Mr. Feld could reply, there was the sound of raised voices, men shouting and cursing. They looked towards home plate and saw that Albert Rideout had decided to give Mr. Brody a hard time about calling Jennifer T. out at second.

"You are blind as a bat, Brody!" he was saying. "Always have been! Wandering around half blind in that drugstore, it's a wonder you ain't given rat poison to some poor kid with asthma! How can you say the girl's out when anybody with half an eyeball could see she had it beat by a mile?"

"She stumbled, Albert," Mr. Brody said, his voice a little more controlled than Albert's. But just a little. The two men were standing with their faces less than a foot apart.

"Forget you!" Albert said. "Man, forget you! You are worse than blind, you're stupid!"

Albert Rideout's voice was rising to a higher pitch with every second. His jacket was falling off his shoulders, and the fly of his dirty old chinos was unbuttoned, as if he were so angry that he was bursting out of his pants. Mr. Brody was backing away from him now. Albert followed, lurching a little, nearly losing his balance. He might have been drunk. Some of the other fathers took a couple of steps towards Albert, and he cursed them. He reached down and picked up an armful of baseball bats, tossed them at the other men. Then he fell over. The bats clattered and rang against the dirt.

"Yo!" Albert cried, catching sight of Ethan as he picked himself up. "Ethan Feld! That was a *hit*, man! A solid *hit*! You going to let this idiot tell you the first hit you ever got wasn't nothing but a fielder's choice?"

All the boys, Roosters and Reds, turned to look at Ethan, as if wondering what tie or connection could possibly link Dog Boy to crazy, drunken, angry, wild old Albert Rideout.

It was too much for Ethan. He didn't want to be a hero. He had no idea how to answer Albert Rideout. He was just a kid; he couldn't argue with an umpire; he couldn't fight against ravens and Coyotes and horrid little grey men with twitching black wings. So he ran. He ran as fast as he could, towards the picnic grounds on the other side of the peeling white pavilion where people sometimes got married. As he ran, he told himself that he was leaving a ball field for the last time – he didn't care what his father loved or hoped for. Baseball just wasn't any fun, not for anyone. He cut through the wedding pavilion, and as he did his foot slipped on a patch of wet wood, and he went sprawling onto his belly. He thought he could hear the other kids laughing at him as he fell. He crawled out of the pavilion on all fours, and found his way to the picnic tables. He had hidden underneath picnic tables before. They were pretty good places to hide.

A few minutes later, there was a crunch of gravel. Ethan peered out between the seat-bench and the tabletop and saw his father approaching. The wind had shifted again – there was no more whistling. Once again it was raining on Summerland. Ethan tried to ignore his father, who stood there, just breathing. His feet in their socks and sandals looked impossibly reasonable.

"What?" Ethan said at last.

"Come on, Ethan. We calmed Albert down. He's all right."

"So what?"

"Well. I thought you might want to help Jennifer T. She ran off. I guess she was upset about her dad and the way he was behaving. Or maybe, I don't know, maybe she was just mad about getting called out. I was kind of hoping—"

"Excuse me? Mr. Feld? Are you Bruce Feld?"

Ethan poked his head out from under the table. A young man with longish hair was standing behind the car. He had on shorts, a flannel shirt, and sporty new hiking boots, but he was carrying a leather briefcase. His hair, swept back behind his ears, was so blond that it was white. He wore a pair of fancy skier's sunglasses, white plastic with teardrop-shaped lenses that were at once black and iridescent.

"Yes?" Mr. Feld said.

"Oh, hey. Heh-heh. How's it going? My name is Rob. Rob Padfoot? My company is called Brain + Storm Aerostatics, we're into developing alternative and emerging dirigible technologies?"

Wow, Ethan thought. This was exactly the kind of person his father had been waiting to have show up. A guy with long hair and a briefcase. Somebody with money and enthusiasm who was also a little bit of a nut. It seemed to Ethan that in the past he had even heard his father use the phrase "alternative and emerging dirigible technologies".

"Yes," Dr. Feld repeated, looking a little impatient.

"Oh, well, I heard about your little prototype, there. Sweet. And I've read your papers on picofibre-envelope sheathing. So I thought I'd come up here and see if I could, heh-heh, catch a glimpse of the fabled beast, you know? And then, like, I'm driving around this gorgeous island and I look up in the sky and… and…"

"Look, Mr. Padfoot, I'm sorry, but I'm talking to my son right now."

"Oh, uh, OK. Sure." An expression of confusion crossed Rob Padfoot's face. Ethan saw that his hair wasn't blond at all but actually white. Ethan had read in books about young people whose hair went white. He wondered what unspeakable tragedy Rob Padfoot might have undergone to leach the colour from his hair. "Hey, but, heh, listen, let me give you my card. Call me, or e-mail. When you have the time."

Ethan's father took the card and stuck it in his pocket without looking at it. For an instant Rob Padfoot looked incredibly angry, almost as if he wanted to hit Mr. Feld. Then it was gone, and Ethan wasn't sure if he had seen it at all.

"Dad?" he said, as Padfoot went slouching off, swinging his briefcase at his side.

"Forget it," Mr. Feld said. He crouched down in the gravel beside the picnic table. "Now, come on. We have to find Jennifer T. I have a pretty good idea that you might know where she went."

Ethan sat for a moment, then climbed out from under the table into the steady grey rain.

"Yeah," he said. "Actually I sort of probably do."

JENNIFER T. RIDEOUT had spent more time amid the ruins of the Summerland Hotel than any other child of her generation. It was a thirty-seven-minute hike, through woods, fields and the parking lot of the county dump, from the Rideout place to the beach. There was no road you could take to get you there; there had never been a road to the hotel. That was something she had always liked about the place. In the old days, her uncle Mo had told her, everything came to the hotel by steamship: food, linens, fine ladies and gentlemen, mail, musicians, fireworks on the Fourth of July. Though nowadays it was a popular spot for teenagers in the summer, on grey winter afternoons Hotel Beach could be pretty forlorn. As if in payment for the miracle of its summer sunshine, in the winter it was tormented by rain and fog, hailstorms, icy rain. Green stuff grew all over everything, this weird cross between algae and fungus and slime that settled like snow over the piles of drift and anything else that was made out of wood. On a damp, chilly winter afternoon she often found herself to be the only human being on the whole Tooth.

Another thing she liked, besides the solitude, were the stories. A boy from up by Kiwanis Beach wandered into one of the abandoned beach cabins at dusk and came out stark raving mad, having seen something he could never afterwards describe. Ghosts of the hotel dead, ghostly orchestras playing, phantoms doing the Lindy Hop in the light of the full moon. Sometimes people felt someone touching their cheek, pinching their arm, even giving them a kick in the seat of the pants. Girls had their skirts lifted, or found their hair tied in intractable knots. Jennifer T. didn't necessarily believe these legends. But they gave Hotel Beach an atmosphere that she enjoyed. Jennifer T. Rideout believed in magic, maybe even more than Ethan did – otherwise she could not have been a part of this story. But she also believed that she had been born a hundred years too late to get even the faintest taste of it. Long ago there had been animals that talked, and strange little Indians who haunted the birch wood, while other Indians lived in villages on the bottom of the Sound. Now that world had all but vanished. Except on the ball field of Summerland, that is, and here at Hotel Beach.

So when Albert made an ass of himself in front of her team-mates, that was where she ran. But she saw, as soon as she got there, that something terrible had happened, and that all of the magic of the place was gone.

The clearing along the beach was crowded with bulldozers and earthmovers. They were carefully parked in three rows of three, next to a foreman's trailer. She wondered how they could possibly have gotten there – by helicopter? Affixed to the side of the trailer was a large white sign that said TRANSFORM PROPERTIES and under this KEEP OUT. There were signs that said KEEP OUT everywhere, actually, as well as KEEP OFF, NO TRESPASSING, PRIVATE PROPERTY, and NO GATHERING MUSHROOMS. The cabins – there had been seven of them, in a shade of faded blue – were all gone. Now there were just seven rectangular dents in the ground. The tumbled remains of the great fieldstone porch of the hotel, the fortress, galleon and prison house of a million children's games, had been packed up and carted off – somehow or other – leaving not a stone. And, God, they had cut down so many of the trees! The slim pale trunks of a hundred birch trees lay stacked in an orderly pile, like the contents of a giant box of pencils. The ends of each log had been flagged with strips of red plastic, ready to follow the porch and the cabins and the last ghosts of the Summerland Hotel into oblivion. With so many trees gone, you could see clear through to the dull grey glint of Tooth Inlet.

Jennifer T. sat down on the big driftwood log that was her favourite perch. The desire to cry was like a balloon being slowly inflated inside her, pressing outward on her throat and lungs. She resisted it. She didn't want to cry. She didn't enjoy crying. But then whenever she closed her eyes she would see Albert running around, waving his arms, spitting when he talked, cursing, with his zipper undone.

She heard a scrape, someone's laboured breathing, a rattle of leaves, and then Ethan Feld emerged from the trees that still screened Hotel Beach from the ball field.

"Hey," he said.

"Hey." She was very glad she wasn't crying. If there was one person she did not want feeling sorry for her, it was Ethan Feld. "What's going on? Did the police come?"

"I don't know. My dad said— Oh, my God."

Ethan was looking now the devastation of Hotel Beach. He stared at the bulldozers and backhoes, the neat depressions where the cabins had stood. And then for some reason he gazed up at the sky. Jennifer T. looked, too. Here and there ragged flags of blue still flew, holding out against the surge of black clouds.

"It's raining at Summerland in June," Jennifer T. said. "What's *that* about?"

"Yeah," Ethan said. "Weird." He seemed to want to say something else. "Yeah. A lot of… weird stuff… is happening."

He sat down beside her on the driftwood log. His spikes still looked almost brand-new. Hers, like all the furnishings of her life, were stained, scarred, scratched, their laces tattered.

"So I hate my dad," said Jennifer T.

"Yeah," Ethan. She could feel Ethan trying to think of something to add to this, and not finding anything. He just sat there playing with the strap of his big ugly watch, while the rain came down on them, pattering around them, digging little pits in the sand. "Well, he was always, I don't know, nice to me and my dad."

That was when the balloon of sadness inside Jennifer T. finally popped. Because of course while she *did* hate her father, she also, somehow, managed to love him. She knew that, when he was in the mood, he could be surprisingly nice, but she had always assumed she was alone in that knowledge. She tried to cry very quietly, hoping that Ethan didn't notice. Ethan reached into his uniform pocket and took out one of those miniature packages of Kleenex that he carried around because of his allergies. He was allergic to pecans, eggplant, dogs, tomatoes, and spelt. She wasn't really sure what spelt was.

The plastic crinkled as he took out a tissue and passed it to her.

"Can I ask you a question?" he said.

"About Albert?"

"No."

"OK, then."

"Do you believe in, well, in the, uh, the 'little people'? You know."

" 'The little people', " Jennifer T. said. It was not the question she had been expecting. "You mean... you mean like elves? Brownies?"

Ethan nodded.

"Not really," she said, though as we know this was not strictly true. She believed there *had been* elves, over in Switzerland or Sweden or wherever it was, and a tribe of foot-high Indians living in the trees of Clam Island. Once upon a time. "Do you?"

"Yeah," Ethan said. "I've seen them."

"You've seen elves."

"No, I haven't seen any elves. But I saw a pixie when I was like, two. And I've seen fer... some other ones. They live right around here."

Jennifer T. moved a little bit away from him on their log, to get a better look at his face. He seemed to be perfectly serious. The chill wind blowing in from the west again raised gooseflesh on her damp arms, and she caught the faint echo of the whistling she had heard before, coming from somewhere off beyond the trees.

"I'm sceptical," she said at last.

"You can believe the boy," said a voice behind them. Jennifer T. jumped up from the log and spun around to find a small, stout black man standing there. He wore a suit of dark purple velvet, with a ruffled shirt, and the cuff links in his shirt-cuffs were shaped like tiny baseballs. His ponytail was white and his beard was white and there was a kind of white fuzz on the rims of his ears. "You do believe him. You know he ain't lying to you."

There was something familiar about the man's smooth, dark face, his wide green eyes, the missing third finger of his right hand. She recognised him, in spite of the passage of many, many years, from a grainy, washed-out photograph in the pages of one of her favourite books, *Only the Ball Was White*, a history of the old Negro leagues.

"Chiron 'Ringfinger' Brown," she said.

"Jennifer Theodora Rideout."

"Your middle name is Theodora?" Ethan said.

"Shut up," said Jennifer T.

"I thought you said it didn't stand for anything."

"Are you really him?"

Mr. Brown nodded.

"But aren't you, like, a hundred years old by now?"

"This here body is one hundred and nine," he said, in an offhand way. He was eyeing her carefully, with a strange look in his eye. "Jennifer T. Rideout," he said, frowning, giving his head a shake. "I must be gettin' old." He took a little notebook from his breast pocket and wrote in it for a moment. "I don't know how," he said. "But somehow or other I done missed you, girl. You ever pitch?"

Jennifer T. shook her head. Her father had been a pitcher; he claimed to have been scouted by the Kansas City Royals, and blamed all his problems in life on the sudden and surprising failure of his right arm when he was nineteen years old. He was always threatening to show her "how to really 'bring it'" one of these days. She supposed she ought to welcome his attempts to share with her the game she loved most in the world. But she didn't; she hated them. She especially hated when he used baseball lingo like "bring it".

"I don't want to be a pitcher," she declared.

"Well, you sure look like a pitcher to me."

"Missed her for what?" Ethan said. "I mean, uh, well, who are you, anyway? Like, OK, I know you were in the Negro Leagues, or whatever. . . ."

"Most career victories in the history of the Negro Leagues," Jennifer T. said. "One book I have said it was three forty-two. Another one says three sixty."

"It was three hundred an' seventy-eight, matter of fact," said Mr. Brown. "But to answer your question, Mr. Feld, for the last forty-odd years I've been travellin' up and down the coast. You know. Lookin' for talent. Lookin' for somebody who got the gif'. Idaho. Nevada." He eyed Ethan. "Colorado, too." He took something from his hip pocket. It was an old baseball, stained and scuffed. "Here," he said, handing it to Jennifer T., "you try throwin' with this little pill sometime, see how it go." Jennifer T. took the ball from him. It felt warm from his pocket, hard as a meteorite and yellow as an old man's teeth. "I done used it to strike out Mr. Joseph DiMaggio *three times*, in a exhibition game at old Seals Stadium, down in Frisco, away back in 1934."

"You mean you're a *scout*?" Ethan said. "Who do you scout for?"

"Right now I'm workin' for those little folks you met,

Mr. Feld. The Boar Tooth mob. Only I don't scout ballplayers. Or at least, not only."

"What do you scout?" Jennifer T. said.

"Heroes," Mr. Brown said. He reached into his breast pocket again and took out his wallet. He handed Ethan and Jennifer T. each a business card.

PELION SCOUTING
MR. CHIRON BROWN, OWNER-OPERATOR
champions found – recruited – trained
for over seven eons

"A hero scout," Ethan said. It was the second time the word *hero* had passed through his mind in the last hour. It did not sound as strange to him as it had at first.

"Or," Jennifer T. said, "you could just be some kind of weird guy following us around."

But she knew as she said it that there was no mistaking this man, from the intent, wide, slightly popeyed gaze to the fabled missing finger on the pitching hand. He really was Ringfinger Brown, ace pitcher of the long-vanished Homestead Greys.

"Mr. Brown," Ethan said. "Do you know what they're doing here? What it is they're building?"

"What they buildin'?" As if for the first time, Ringfinger Brown turned to study the devastation of Hotel Beach. His bulging eyes were filmed over with age or tears or the sting of the cold west wind. He sighed, scratching idly at the back of his head with the four fingers of his right hand. "They buildin' theirself the end of the world."

Ethan said something then, in a soft voice, almost an undertone, that Jennifer T. didn't understand. He said, "Ragged Rock."

"That's right," Mr. Brown said. "One at a time, cutting apart all them magic places where the Tree done growed back onto itself."

"And you really scouted me?" Ethan stood up and began backing towards the woods. "When I lived in Colorado Springs?"

"Before that, even."

"And the ferishers put all those dreams into my dad's head, about the airships and my mom?"

"That's right."

Jennifer T. heard voices coming through the trees, and recognised one of them, at least, as that of Mr. Feld.

"Because of *me*?" Ethan said. "What do I have to do with the end of the world?"

"Maybe nothin'," Mr. Brown said. "That is, if my conjure eye" – here he touched a trembling old finger to the lower lid of his left eye – "done finally gone bad on me." The milky film that was covering the eye, like the clouds of a planet, seemed momentarily to clear as he looked at Ethan. Then he turned towards the sound of men approaching. "Or maybe, if I still know my bidness, you goin' to be the one to help put off that dark day for just a little bit longer."

Jennifer T. was not following the conversation too well, but before she had a chance to ask them what in the name of Satchel Paige they were talking about, Mr. Feld emerged from the trees, along with Coach Olafssen, Mr. Brody, and a sheriff's deputy named Branley who had arrested her father three times that she knew about.

"Ethan? Jennifer T.? Are you all right?" Mr. Feld slipped on a slick pile of leaves as he approached them, and lost his footing. Deputy Branley caught him and hauled him to his feet. "What are you kids doing?"

"Nothing," Ethan said. "We were just standing around talking to—" Ethan raised a hand as if to introduce Ringfinger Brown to the men. But Ringfinger Brown was not there anymore; he had vanished completely. Jennifer T. wondered if such a very old man could possibly have gotten himself hidden behind one of the earthmovers so quickly, and if so, why he should want to run and hide. Hiding didn't seem in character for him, somehow.

"Huh," said Ethan. His face went blank. "To each other."

"Come on." Mr. Feld put an arm around Ethan's shoulders, and then draped the other across Jennifer T.'s. "Let's go home."

As she pressed into the warmth of Mr. Feld's embrace, a shudder racked Jennifer T.'s entire body, and she realised for the first time that she was soaked to the skin and freezing. Mr. Feld started to lead them back towards the ball field, but then he stopped. He looked at the heavy equipment, the stacked corpses of the trees, the empty, torn-up patch of earth on which, a hundred years ago, there had once stood a great hotel with tall pointed towers.

"What the hell are they doing here?" he said.

"They're putting out thc last little candles, one by one," Ethan said, and even he looked surprised as the words came out of his mouth.

4
The Middling

AN UNEXPECTED RESULT of Ethan Feld's determination to become a catcher was the discovery, by Jennifer T. Rideout, of a native gift for pitching. The two friends met, on the morning after the loss to the Reds, at the ball field behind Clam Island Middle School, which was closer to either of their houses than Jock MacDougal Field. Ethan brought his father's old mitt and, in the pocket of his hooded sweatshirt, Peavine's book on catching. Jennifer T. brought an infielder's glove that she had turned up someplace, and the baseball that Ringfinger Brown had given her. When Jennifer T. rocked back and let it fly, it came whistling and fizzing towards Ethan's mitt as if it were powered by steam.

"Ouch!" cried Ethan, the first time the ancient baseball slapped against the heel of his mitt, sending a crackle all the way up his arm to his shoulder. It hurt so much that he did not at first notice that he had held on to the ball. "Hey. You can throw."

"Huh," said Jennifer T., looking at her left hand with new interest.

"That was a fastball."

"Was it?"

"I'm pretty sure."

She nodded. "Cool." She waved her glove at him and he half rose, and arced the ball back to her. His throw was a little high but close enough. She caught it, fingered the ball, then concealed it once more inside her glove.

"So, catcher," she said. "Call the pitch."

"Can you throw the slider?"

"I'd like to see if I can," said Jennifer T. "I know how to put my fingers. I saw it on *Tom Seaver's Total Baseball Video*." She checked an imaginary runner on first, then turned back to Ethan. He put two fingers down, extending them in an inverted V towards the ground. He was calling for the slider. Jennifer T. nodded, her black ponytail flickering behind her. Her wide, dark eyes were unblinking, and she narrowed them in concentration. She reared back again, her right leg lifting and flexing in a high jabbing kick, then stepped down onto her right foot, bringing her whole body forwards and lifting her back leg until it stuck straight out behind her and hung there, wavering. Ethan saw the snap of her hand on the hinge of her wrist. Her fingers blossomed outward and the ball flew towards him in a long, straight line. At the very last second it broke abruptly downward, and he just barely got his glove down and under it in time. By the time you got your bat, if you had been the batter, to the spot at which you hoped your bat would meet it, the ball would have long since dropped away.

"Nasty," Ethan said. He had a sudden protective feeling towards Jennifer T., an urge to encourage and reassure her. This was not because she was a girl, or his friend, or the child of a scattered and troubled family with a father who was in jail yet again, but because he was a catcher, and she was his pitcher, and it was his job to ease her along. "The bottom fell right out of it."

"You caught it real nice," said Jennifer T. "And you had your eyes open all the way."

Ethan felt a flush of warmth fill his chest, but it was short lived, for in the next instant there was a sharp snapping in the blackberry brambles that made the edge of near right field such a terrifying place to find yourself during a game of kickball or softball. Cutbelly appeared, stumbling onto the field. He limped towards Ethan and Jennifer T., dragging a leg behind him. His coat was matted and filthy, and his sharp little face bled from three different cuts around the cheeks and throat. On his snout and on the tips of his ears there lay a dusting of what looked to Ethan like frost. The glint of mockery was all but extinguished from his eyes.

"Ho, piglets," he said, his voice hardly more than a whisper. "I'm very thirsty. Thirsty. Thirsty and cold." He shivered, and hugged himself, then brushed the powdery ice from his ears. "I scampered here much too quickly."

Ethan dug a half-empty squeeze bottle out of his knapsack and passed it to the werefox. Then he took off his sweatshirt and draped it over Cutbelly's furry shoulders. Jennifer T. had not moved from the pitcher's mound. Her glove dangled by her side. Her mouth hung open. Cutbelly tipped back the squeeze bottle and drained it in a single draught. He wiped his mouth on the back of his bloodied arm.

"Thank you," he said. "And now, perhaps it may be for the last time, I'm to ask you to hurry along with me. You're needed."

"What can I do?" Ethan said. "I can't fight. I can't play baseball. I can't do squat."

Cutbelly sagged, and sank to the dirt of the infield. He buried his face in his hands. "I know it," he said, rubbing at his long snout. "I told them as much my own self. But we have something less than a choice. It may be too late already as it is." He held out a tiny paw to Ethan, who pulled him to his feet. "We must cross over, now. The other piglet, too, it's unfortunate she saw me, but there's no helping it now."

For the first time since Cutbelly's appearance, Ethan remembered Jennifer T. She was still standing on the pitcher's mound, a little behind the rubber now, as if to keep something between her and Cutbelly. Her mouth was twisted into a strange half-smile but her eyes were wide and empty. Ethan saw that she was afraid.

"It's OK," Ethan said, using his newfound catcher's voice. "He's a friend of mine. I tried to tell you yesterday, but—"

"Little people," Jennifer T. said, in a thick voice.

"—but you didn't believe me."

"She believed you," Cutbelly said. "Come on, girl. See what you'll see."

THEY LEAPED ACROSS to the Summerlands through deeper shadows than Ethan remembered, the frost of the crossing streaking their hair and dusting the brims of their caps. The darkness was only partial but thick and deep. It reminded him of the false night that had fallen on Colorado Springs during a solar eclipse, one winter day back when he was in the first grade. Cutbelly hurried along as quickly as he could on his wounded leg, looking all around him as they went, his bright orange eyes darting from left to right. From time to time he would stop, and motion for the children to do the same with a curt gesture, and stand motionless, his long ears quavering, studying the air for a sound they alone could detect. Though Ethan was filled with questions, Cutbelly refused to listen to them, or to reply. He would not say how he had been injured, or what was happening in the Birchwood.

"Two thirds of all the shadows you are seeing around you are not real shadows at all," was all he would say, in a low whisper. "Try to keep that in mind, piglets."

They looked around; the shadows twisted like smoke, billowed like curtains, dangled like Spanish moss from the limbs of birch trees; then they looked again and all was still. Jennifer T. bumped up against Ethan and they walked that way for a while, shoulder to shoulder, holding each other up as they lumbered after the werefox through the silent woods. Great slow wheels of crows turned in the grey skies overhead. Rain was falling all around. And then they stepped out of the trees, into the clearing where Ethan had met Cinquefoil and the other Clam Island ferishers, to find that the final lines of the first paragraph of the last chapter in the history of the world had already been written.

"Too late!" Cutbelly cried. "Too late!"

The clearing was filled with grey smoke and hissing jets of steam. The turf was trodden and torn. And the Birchwood itself was gone; all the trees had been cut down and apparently hauled away. All that was left of the great mass of tall white trees were splintered stumps and tall piles of stripped branches. The beautiful little ballpark, made from the bones of a giant, lay in ruins, the towers torn down and scattered, the stands collapsed in on themselves. In the midst of the field that had once surrounded the ballpark, churned up in a muddy tumult of earth, lay an overturned vehicle of some kind, a twisted hulk of black iron with heavy leather treads, cruelly spiked. Here and there around this ruined hulk lay a number of small bodies. They might have been children, or even ferishers, but for their pale grey skin.

In all this expanse of waste and wreckage nothing was moving but the twisting curls of steam. Except—

"Hey," Ethan said. "What's that?"

Down on the beach, where the ferishers had gone to consult Johnny Speakwater, one final skirmish was taking place. A ferisher stood on top of the great driftwood log, while around him crowded half a dozen winged creatures that Ethan recognised, even from a distance, as the same one that had grinned at him through his bedroom window.

Cutbelly cried out. "That's Cinquefoil! The skrikers are on him!"

"Skrikers," Ethan said. "What are they?"

"Ferishers changed by the Changer," Cutbelly said. "They hate what they are and even worse what they once were. Help him, piglet!"

"What should I do?" Ethan said. "Just tell me."

Cutbelly turned to him, his black-tipped snout quivering, his eyes wide and lit with what looked to Ethan like a surprising glimmer of hope.

"Search your heart, piglet!" he said. "You were dug up by old Chiron himself! The wight that scouted up Achilles! Arthur! Toussaint and Crazy Horse! You've got to have the stuff in you somewhere, piglet or no!"

Ethan felt something catch inside him at Cutbelly's words, like the scrape of a match against the rough black stripe of a matchbook. He looked around, something bright and dense and hot kindling inside him. He started, trotting at first, towards the beach.

"Ethan!" Jennifer T. said.

He looked back at her. She was standing behind Cutbelly. Her gaze was as blank and strange as before, but now the crooked half-smile was gone.

"What are you going to do?"

Ethan shrugged. "I guess I'm supposed to save him," he said. He didn't really believe that he could do it, in spite of Cutbelly's words. But he felt he ought to try. After all, it was just a question of saving one ferisher, not a whole tribe. Maybe he could do something to draw them off, and give the ferisher a chance to recoup his strength. He was clearly an excellent fighter, much better than Ethan could ever hope to be.

Ethan ran towards the driftwood log. Cinquefoil leapt and ducked, thrust and slashed, hacking at a swarm of the bat-things with a long, wicked knife. His hair blew back from his head and his knife arm lashed and flailed and held steady. The sight was inspiring. That was a hero. That was how you did it. Ethan ran up, yelling and screaming, hoping to distract the skrikers for a moment. Cinquefoil turned, and smiled faintly, and then three of the skrikers looked Ethan's way. They grinned yellow grins, and the bridges of their sharp little noses wrinkled with a rank pleasure that snuffed out the little flame of purpose which Cutbelly's words had kindled in Ethan. They flew at Ethan, scattering themselves around him, their wings jerking and spasming. Ethan saw that the wings were not a part of them but queer machines, affixed to their backs by means of brass-red screws. Ethan ran past them, ducking underneath their spindly legs, and then when he turned they were on him.

He looked around for something to use to defend himself, but all he could see were the spiky stumps of broken limbs that jutted from the driftwood log. Most of them were much too short to be of any use, but there was one that was longer, and nearly perfectly straight. He clambered up onto the log and grabbed hold of the limb, and pulled. It made a dry, cracking sound, but held firm.

"Glad you could make it," Cinquefoil said, and then there was a muffled explosion, and the ferisher cried out and tumbled from the log. One of the skrikers, Ethan noticed, seemed to have lost its head, and was wheeling crazily around in the air. Cinquefoil must have decapitated it just before he himself fell. The skrikers hovered over his motionless body, now, poking and prodding it with their steel-tipped toes. Ethan threw his weight against the limb, putting his whole shoulder into it. With a great crunching snap it broke loose, and came away free in his hand.

It was about the size and length of a baseball bat, more

or less straight, but knotty and weathered grey. He lifted it, and hefted it, and gripped it at one end in both hands. It felt good and solid. He swung it over his shoulder and came after the skrikers that were molesting the dead ferisher. One of them reached up and took hold of its own ears, one in each hand. Its grin grew wider and yellower. Ethan saw that its teeth were made from jagged shards of what looked like quartz. There was a series of ratcheting clicks, a nasty wet sound of ripping. And then the face with the dirty crystal grin was no longer atop the neck at all. It perched on the skriker's left hand like an old grey mouldy peach. The skriker had removed its own head, and was cackling at him now from this weird vantage. The severed neck was tipped with a black ball that gleamed like a bead of wet ink. Ethan recoiled, and then the bat-thing reared back and tossed its head at him. Without thinking he swung his big stick at the head as it spun towards him.

"Breathe!" he heard Jennifer T. call.

He kept his eyes open, too: and connected. There was a burst of white flame, a *whoomp* shot through with a crackle, and a sweet, unpleasant smell like burnt cheese. Another head came spinning at him, and he swung, and there was another sharp blazing whoomp. He fought off three more of the head-bombs, swinging wild and hard, and then, it seemed, there was a power failure in Ethan's head somewhere.

RED AND BLACK. Blood and sky. Jennifer T. was looking down at him, with the heavy sky spread out behind her, a nasty cut on her cheek. Then a gamy, butcher-shop smell: Cutbelly. And finally, something jabbing at his cheek: Cutbelly, again, poking him and poking him with one of his sharp little fingers.

"Wake up, piglet!"

Ethan lay on his back, in the doomed green grass of the Summerlands.

"I'm awake," he declared, sitting up.

"Come," Cutbelly said. "The Rade has carried away the Boar Tooth mob. They have felled all the trees on either side of the gall. We have only a short while to leap through or be forced to find another route back. That could take a while. Come! Failed or not, we must get out of here."

Failed. The word resounded in his mind. He had struck out, swinging. Some kind of marvellous opportunity had been granted to him, and before he could even begin to understand what was happening to him, he had blown his chance. He could already taste the regret of the lost moment, how it would haunt him for the rest of his life.

"Will they— are they all dead?" he said. "What about Cinquefoil?"

"I'm all right," said a gruff voice behind him. "You get back to the Middling now. No telling what Coyote's up to there."

Ethan rolled over and saw the little chief crouching on the ground beside him. He was filthy, and his hair dripped pale streaks down his grimy cheeks. The coat of rough mail he wore over his buckskin had been slashed through and through. It hung in tinkling strips from his shoulders. His tan leggings sagged, his feathered cap sat askew, its savage green feather snapped in two. And his quiver of arrows was empty.

"I'm in yer debt," the ferisher said, sounding unhappy about it. "Nice work with that stick o' yers."

"You were amazing."

"I weren't nothing. I done nothing. I saved nothing and no one and all was lost."

"Did he get your… your family?"

"Those in the mob what aren't my sister or my brother are my child, my mother, or my aunt," he said. His voice broke with sorrow. "And all o' them ta be changed. Twisted inta the things ya saw, them skrikers."

"Greylings, too," the werefox pointed out, in a morose tone. That must be the name of those horrible little grey children whose bodies littered the field.

"And greylings." Cinquefoil shuddered. "And then sent back, no doubt, ta take their revenge on the chief that failed ta keep 'em whole."

There was that word again: *failed*.

"I wish I could have done more," Ethan said. "We were too late."

"There weren't nothing ya coulda done. Coyote and the Rade, they grown stronger and swifter in the last one thousand years, as we have grown scattereder and few."

"Did he get them all? Everyone?"

"I don't know, but I fear it's so. Go, g'wan back. I mean to take off after them a ways, see if some got left behind."

"We'll come with you," said Jennifer T. "We'll help you find them if they're there."

But the ferisher shook his head.

"Go," he said. "Ya heard Cutbelly. There ain't much timc."

So they said goodbye to the little chief, and he turned and wandered through the charred ruin of the Birchwood off into the green fields beyond. Ethan could see that the fields were rutted with deep muddy tracks, as if some kind of heavy vehicles had passed that way. The farther away he got, the faster his pace became, and he was soon lost to view in the dim green haze of the Summerlands.

"Come on," Cutbelly said. They turned back towards the ordinary forest of firs and pines through which they had come. Ethan followed after Jennifer T., who followed the scurrying shadowtail. They had not been walking long when Ethan became aware of a low, steady rustling in the trees around them.

"What's that noise?" Jennifer T. said.

Cutbelly's earlier warning, about the shadows' not being shadows, had made little sense to Ethan at the time. Now he understood. The thick shadows that filled the woods with the half-night of an eclipse had detached themselves from the trees and hollows. They were following him and Jennifer T. and Cutbelly. They fluttered in great gauzy sheets, now drifting like a piece of rubbish caught by the wind, now flapping steadily with great vulture wingbeats. They passed through the limbs and trunks of trees, some weird cross between fishnet and smoke. And though Cutbelly was leading them as fast as his short legs could go, scurrying back to the world where such things were not, the false shadows were gaining on them.

They ran for home, so fast that snowdust began to drift and swirl around them in glittering white gusts. Cold burned the inside of Ethan's nose. The air in his ears tinkled like ice. Ethan saw Jennifer T. trip over a root, and go flying forwards. He stopped and reached down to grab her hand. As he did so he heard a soft flutter of drapery, a curtain parting, and looked up to see one of the false shadows settle down over him and Jennifer T. Burning cold, a smell like rust on a cold iron skillet. Ethan reached up to fight it off and saw that he was still holding his stick. It caught on something inside the shadow, something at once springy and hard, and when he yanked it out there was a sickening wet sound. The shadow faded at once and was gone. Jennifer T. was back on her feet by now. She grabbed Ethan by the elbow and pulled him along the path they had been following. There was no sign of Cutbelly ahead, and Ethan looked back and saw, to his horror, that one of the false shadows had taken, lazily, to the sky. From its shifting silk depths there protruded the white tip of a bushy red tail.

There was silence, and Ethan thought, *They got him.* Then there was the rumble of an engine in the near distance.

"Harley," said Jennifer T. "Big one."

They were standing at the edge of the Clam Island Highway. They were home. The motorcycle roared downhill and then pulled onto the line for the Bellingham ferry.

"How'd we get here?" Jennifer T. said.

There was Zorro's Mexican restaurant, the ferry dock, and the long green smudge of the mainland. Somehow they had come out of the Summerlands at the southern tip of

Clam Island. The Harley-Davidson growled on down the hill to the lanes where you waited for the next ferry. A moment later they heard another engine, and a car appeared, a big, old, finned monster, peppermint white with red roof and trim. It slowed as it passed by Ethan and Jennifer T., then stopped.

Mr. Chiron Brown rolled down his window. He looked surprised but not, Ethan would have said, happy to see the children. He shook his head.

"Well," he said. His eyes were shining and for a moment Ethan thought he might be about to cry. "Let this be a lesson. Don't never listen to a crazy old man when the old Coyote be workin' one of his thangs." A tear rolled down his cheek. "I let them poor creatures down."

No, Ethan thought. *I* let them down. "I struck out," he said.

"Nah," Mr. Brown said. "Don't blame yourself. It's like you said. You too young. In the old days, not so long ago, we used to be able to afford to bring 'em along a little bit. Season 'em up. Hell, it took U. S. Grant most of his natural *life* to finally find his stroke."

"Hey, where are you going?" Jennifer T. said. A pickup truck appeared at the top of Ferrydock Hill and came down towards them, slowing as it neared the white Cadillac. "Are you leaving?"

Ringfinger admitted that he was headed for home.

"Where is your home?" Ethan said.

"Oh, I doesn't have no fixed abode, not here in the Middlin'. But lately I've been livin' down in Tacoma."

"What's the Middling?" Jennifer T. said.

"The Middlin'? You standin' in it. It's everythin'. All this here local world you livin' in."

The pickup had settled in behind Mr. Brown's car. Its driver tried to be patient for a few seconds, then began irritably to honk. Mr. Brown ignored or seemed not to hear. Another car rolled in from the top of the hill, with a third right behind it.

"So is it… is it all over?" Ethan said.

"Well, I ain't as up on my mundology as I ought to be, which is a word signifyin' the study of the Worlds. I ain't sure how many galls we started out with, back before Coyote's mischief commenced. And I couldn't say how many we got left now. But there wasn't never very many, even in the glory times. And Coyote been hackin' and choppin' on 'em for a long, long time now."

"And so now, what? Now the whole universe is going to come to an end?"

"It always was goin' to," Mr. Brown said. "Now it's just happenin' a little bit sooner."

"Ethan? Jennifer T.?" The driver of the second car, behind the pickup truck, had rolled down *her* window now. "You kids all right?"

"Yeah," said Ethan and Jennifer T. Ethan saw how they must look to Mrs. Baldwin, one of the secretaries in the office at school, hanging around the southend ferry dock, talking to some weird old guy in a Cadillac.

"Well," Mr. Brown said, rolling his window up most of the way. "Look like I'm holdin' things up." He put the car in gear with a lurch. The big engine coughed and roared. "You kids enjoy the rest of your summer."

"Wait!" Ethan said, as the drivers, angry now, swerved around Mr. Brown's car and took off one after the other down the hill. "Isn't there anything we can do— I can do— to stop it?"

"You doesn't know magic. You doesn't know baseball." Mr. Brown looked at Jennifer T. "You knows a little about both of them, I reckon, but not much besides." He shook his head. "Plus, you *children*. Tell me how you going to stop Ragged Rock?"

Ethan and Jennifer T. had no reply to this. Mr. Brown rolled his window all the way and drove off. Ethan and Jennifer T. started the long walk back to her house, which was closer to Southend than Ethan's. For a long time they didn't say anything. What can you say, after all, about the end of the world? Ethan was deeply disturbed by the memory of the ruined Birchwood, and by the thought of all those ferishers carted off to be made into horrible little grey bat things. And every time he closed his eyes, he saw the tip of a little red tail, disappearing into a world of shadows. But he could not help being cheered by the fact that when asked, Mr. Brown had not said, *There is nothing to be done*. Merely that he didn't think there was anything Ethan and Jennifer T. could do.

Ethan tried to imagine how the conversation would go when he tried to explain to his father about the ferishers, and Ragged Rock. Few things made Mr. Feld truly angry, but one thing that did was when people insisted that there was more to the world than what you could see, hear, touch, or otherwise investigate with tools and your five good senses. That there was a world behind the world, or beyond it. An afterlife, say. Mr. Feld felt that people who believed in other worlds were simply not paying enough attention to this one. He had been insistent with Ethan that Dr. Feld was gone forever, that all of her, everything that had made her so uniquely and wonderfully her, was in the ground, where it would all return to the elements and minerals it was made of. This satisfied Mr. Feld, or so he said. He would not look kindly on tales of fairies and skrikers and shadows that could come to life and carry off werefoxes into the sky. And yet Ethan could think of no one else to go to for help. He decided he was going to have to tell his father some version of the truth. And then Mr. Feld would call Nan Finkel, the therapist that Ethan had been seeing on and off since their arrival on Clam Island, and Nan Finkel, with her two thick braids that were so long she could sit on them, would have him put in a hospital for disturbed children, and that would be that.

"Jennifer T.," he said. They had been walking for half an hour in silence, and were nearly to the Rideout place. "Nobody is going to believe us."

"I was thinking that."

"You know it's true, right?"

"Everything is true." Jennifer T. spat on the ground. Her spitting was as professional in quality as the rest of her game. "That's what Albert always says."

"I know. I've heard him say it."

They had reached the gap in the trees where a teetering old mailbox, perforated with bullet and BB holes, was painted with Jennifer T.'s last name. One of the dogs came tearing towards them, a big black mutt with his pink tongue flying like a flag. There was a little green parakeet riding on his shoulder.

"We can tell the old ladies," Jennifer T. said. "They believe a lot of even crazier stuff than this."

THE HOUSE WHERE Jennifer T. lived had two bedrooms. In one slept Jennifer T. and the little twins, Darrin and Dirk. In the other slept Gran Billy Ann and her sisters, Beatrice and Shambleau. The toilet was attached to the house and had a roof over it, but it was outside. You had to go out the back door to get to it. There were seven to nine dogs, and from time to time the cats became an island scandal. You came in through the living room, where there were three immense reclining chairs, so large that they left barely enough room for a small television set. One chair was red plaid, one was green plaid, and one was white leather. They vibrated when you pushed a certain button. The old ladies sat around vibrating and reading romance novels. They were big ladies, and they needed big chairs. They had a collection of over seven thousand five hundred romance novels. They had every novel Barbara Cartland ever wrote, all of the Harlequin romances, all the Silhouette and Zebra and HeartQuest books. The paperbacks were piled in stacks that reached almost to the ceiling. They blocked windows and killed houseplants and regularly collapsed on visitors. Island people who knew of the Rideout girls' taste in fiction would come by in the dead of night and dump grocery bags and liquor boxes full of romances in the driveway. The old ladies despised other people's charity, but the free books they seemed to accept as a tribute: they were the oldest women on Clam Island,

and entitled to a certain amount of respect. They happily read the abandoned books. If they had already read them before, they read them again. If there was one thing in life that didn't trouble them, it was having heard the same story before.

"The Little Tribe," said Gran Billy Ann. She was sprawled in her chair, the red plaid one, her feet up in a pair of big black orthopaedic shoes, vibrating away. "How about that! I remember Pap had stories about them. One time when he was a boy they stole a silver pin right out of his sister's hair. Over at Hotel Beach that was. Before it was a hotel there. But I never heard of this Ragged Rock thing." Gran Billy Ann lit a cigarette. She was not supposed to smoke. She was not supposed to drink, either, but she was drinking a can of Olympia beer. That kind of thing was all right if you were one of the three oldest women on Clam Island. "I don't like the sound of that."

"Ragged Rock," Aunt Beatrice said. "Ragged Rock. I don't remember Pap having anything to say on that score."

"I saw one of them, once," said Aunt Shambleau, in a low voice, almost to herself. "It was in the summertime. A beautiful little man. Naked as a fish. He was lying on his back in the sun."

The other two ladies turned to her.

"You never told me!" Aunt Beatrice said.

"She's lying," said Gran Billy Ann. She scowled at her sister, then turned her scowl on Jennifer T. and Ethan. "You don't want to lie about seeing the Little Tribe. They'll come at night and pinch you till you're black and blue."

"Come over here, girl," said Aunt Shambleau. Though

Gran Billy Ann was the biggest grump of the three, Shambleau was the aunt that Ethan feared the most. She had a quiet way of talking and she wore her big, black, wraparound space-warrior cataract-patient sunglasses in the house, for reasons that Ethan was afraid to inquire about. She was the oldest of the sisters, and sometimes when she was lying in her bed you could hear her talking to herself in a strange throaty language of which, though Ethan realised it only much later, she was the last living speaker on the face of the earth. Now she took hold of Jennifer's arm and pulled her close. She studied the girl's face through the impenetrable lenses of her cataract sunglasses. "She ain't lying, Billy Ann. This girl has seen the Little Tribe."

Jennifer T. jerked her arm loose.

"Get off me!" she said. "Old witch. Of course I ain't lying!"

Shambleau laughed delightedly. Her sisters joined in. They always seemed to get a good laugh out of making Jennifer T. mad.

"It's true," Ethan said. He didn't think this was really the time to be laughing. "Ragged Rock is the end of the world."

"What is this I'm hearing?" said a gravel-bottomed voice. Uncle Mo. He was standing in the doorway to the kitchen, with a beer of his own. He was not supposed to be drinking, either. "Who is talking all this crazy talk?"

"Uncle Mo, Uncle Mo," Jennifer T. said. "I was throwing today. Ethan said my fastball was nasty."

"It really was," Ethan said, momentarily forgetting the end of the world. Mo Rideout would know what to do. He had travelled. After his arm gave out he had served in the Navy, and then in the merchant marine after the war. He had been to Alaska, to Japan, to the Caspian Sea. Though he looked and talked and cursed like an old sailor, he had shown Ethan his diploma from Lutheran College, earned by means of a special correspondence programme for seamen. Plus, he was a ballplayer, and an Indian, too. "It had bite."

Uncle Mo, it turned out, knew more than they had ever imagined.

"Ragged Rock," he said, sadly, after Ethan and Jennifer T. told their tale again, this time with help from Mo's big sisters. Jennifer T. brought a chair in from the kitchen and he sat down. "Ragged, Ragged Rock. I can't believe it's true. I gave up thinking about all that business a long time ago."

"Pap never said anything about any raggedy old rock," Gran Billy Ann insisted.

"Not to you," snapped Uncle Mo. "Some things were not meant to be said to girls or women." He looked at Ethan. "Or to white people."

Ethan blushed. "It's like— I mean, it's the, well, the end of the world," he said. "What we want to know is, well. How you stop it. We think it can be stopped. Cutbelly believed that somebody could stop it. Even if it wasn't us."

"A mortal champion," Uncle Mo said, his voice softer. "That's right. A man of the Middling."

"Or a woman of the Middling," Jennifer T. said. "Mr. Brown said I had champion stuff, too."

"Mr. Chiron C. Brown." Uncle Mo's eyes misted over now. "How about that? And this is the day he always worried about, come to happen."

"So you know Ringfinger Brown?" Ethan said. They must have played ball together; Uncle Mo had played a season or two in the Negro Leagues. "Did he tell you what to do?"

"Many times," said Uncle Mo. "Yes. Bear in mind it has been a long, long time and many empty bottles since then." As if to emphasize this point, he took a long swallow of beer. "Ragged Rock is a day, the last day. The last day of the last year. The last out in the bottom of the ninth." He smacked his lips. "The day when the Story finally ends."

"What story?" Ethan said.

"The Story. All stories. All the stories, all of them that anybody ever lived or told or experienced or heard about. All these long years, Coyote's been working to make that day come. See, there are these… *spots*, along the branches of the Lodgepole. Places where the Worlds got stuck together."

"Galls," Ethan said.

Uncle Mo fixed him with a sharp look. "I believe that's the term," he said. "Wherever you have one of these gall things, that's a place where the great adventures begin. The worlds flow together, and travellers tumble through and come out the other side. And they get into all kinds of yarns and escapades. Voyages and misfortunes. So for a long, long time, now, Coyote's been going around *cutting* these knots. Trying to bring all the little stories to a stop so that he can put a stop to the one great Story, the one about you and me and all the creatures that ever lived. He's tired of things the way they are. He's been tired of them almost since they first got this way, which they only did thanks to him."

"What lodgepole?" Jennifer T. said.

"*The* Lodgepole. The mother Tree. The Tree of the whole wide everything. I forget the right name of it just this minute. That holds up all the different worlds. Keeps everything in its proper place."

"There used to be four worlds," Ethan said. "But now there are only three."

"That's— well, that's right, Mr. Feld," Uncle Mo said, looking a little surprised. "How did you know?"

"What happened to the other one?" It was Aunt Shambleau. The other ladies were listening to but not, it seemed to Ethan, quite following their brother's words.

"It was the world of the big *Tahmahnawis*," he said. Aunt Shambleau nodded as if she understood what this meant. "The spirit tribe, I guess you could say, the spirit nation. The other worlds are the Summerlands, the Winterlands, and this one. The Middling. The Lodgepole – what's its name – it holds the worlds in its branches. And then there is a Well, I forget the name of it, if I ever knew. It waters the Tree. That's right."

"A Well," said Aunt Shambleau. "Boiling cold and blue as night. I remember. Pap told me about it."

"Did he?" Uncle Mo said. "I don't remember him ever saying anything about it. It was from Mr. Brown that I heard all this."

"No," Aunt Shambleau said. "You're right. It was in my dream last night that Pap was telling me all this stuff."

"We should listen to him," Ethan said, taking himself and everyone else by surprise. They stared at him. Jennifer T. looked the most surprised of all.

"Should we, now?" said Gran Billy Ann, one eyebrow raised. Her eyebrows were just painted-on lines of brown makeup and therefore looked extra sceptical.

"When the ferishers wanted to get me here to Clam Island," Ethan said, "they sent dreams to my father. To put the idea of Clam Island in his head. Mr. Brown told me they did. So maybe someone or something sent that dream to you, Aunt Shambleau."

"Interesting theory," Uncle Mo said. "So what would this someone or something be trying to say."

"I remember the dream now!" cried Aunt Shambleau. "There was that pool, like I told you, all boiling cold. And then Pap and me was watching, and he said, look at that, here comes Coyote. And there was a coyote, and it was going along. It saw the pool, and all at once it gets this guilty face on it, like it's having a good, mean idea. And then right while Pap and me are watching, it goes over to the water and then just lifts its leg and has itself a big old whiz right into that pretty blue water. I was so mad!" She shook her head in disgust, remembering. Then she pointed at her grand-niece. "You got to get yourself to that Well, girl. Before that Coyote gets there." Her voice rose to a shout. "Don't let him get there first." The soft-looking brown flesh of her arm trembled as she jabbed at the air. "Don't let him spoil that water!"

Ethan and Jennifer T. looked at the old man, who was looking at his sister and shaking his head.

"You frighten me, Shambleau," he said. "You always have."

"Is that right, Uncle Mo?" said Jennifer T. "Do we have to go to that Well thing?"

"I don't remember anything about that. I'm racking what little there is left of this brain to rack. All I know is about Coyote cutting those knots in the worlds. Sorry, kids." He reached for one of Billy Ann's cigarettes. As you might imagine, he was not supposed to smoke anymore, either. "I don't have the faintest idea how you would get to that Well. I was only over to the Summerlands one time."

"What in the heck are you talking about, Morris?" Gran Billy Ann said. "You spent every summer of the first twenty years of your life over to Summerland."

"Not that Summerland, Billy Ann. That Summerland is just a shadow of the real Summerlands."

"This is getting too deep for me," said Gran Billy Ann. With a good deal of grunting and moaning, and some help from Ethan, she managed to creak forwards in her red recliner and to get herself up onto her big feet. Then she headed for the kitchen. "You better have left me some of that pie, Beatrice Casper."

Aunt Beatrice bunched up her mouth and tried to look innocent. "I ain't saying anything," she said. "I plead the Fifth."

"As I recall, it takes a special kind of creature to guide you from one world to another," Uncle Mo said. "A regular person just can't manage the trick."

"A shadowtail," Ethan said.

"It's something neither fish nor fowl, you know. A little bit of this, a little of that. Always half in this world and half in the other to begin with."

"Like a werefox."

"Like Thor Wignutt," said Jennifer T.

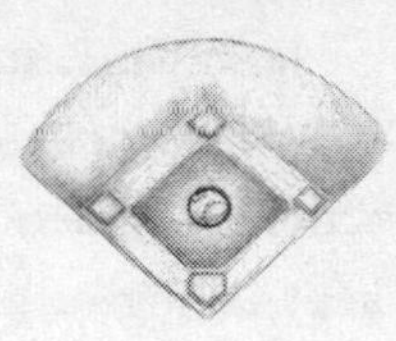

5
Escape

THEY AGREED TO split up. Jennifer T. would go recruit Thor Wignutt to the cause, while Ethan went home to ask his father to help them find a way to stop Coyote from bringing an end to the Story of the universe, if necessary by venturing into the Summerlands themselves. Jennifer T. had been to Thor's house twice, two times more often than any other child on the island who had lived to tell the tale. (Mrs. Wignutt, as has been mentioned, was herself a figure of island lore.) In the meantime, Aunt Shambleau and Uncle Mo were going to pack camping gear, lunchmeat, flashlights, fishing tackle, and anything else they could think of that would not unduly weigh the children down. It was five o'clock now. Ethan promised to return at seven, having made his arguments to his father. What Coyote was trying to do sounded an awful lot like maximum entropy, the heat death of the universe, and other grim ideas from physics that his father had told him about over the years. Maybe if he put it more that way, he had explained to Jennifer T., he could help his father take an interest in the project. And if the worst happened, and Mr. Feld could not be moved? In that case, Ethan would wait until his father went to bed, whenever that was, even at the crack of dawn. Then he would sneak out of the house.

Jennifer T. took off on her bicycle, and Ethan on an old Schwinn that had belonged to a whole bunch of different Rideouts over the years. It had a bad chain that kept falling off, and between that and riding one handed because of his big stick, it took Ethan nearly an hour to reach home.

When he turned into the gravel drive his heart lurched, and his nerve failed him: he saw the orange station wagon. Skid was like a droll, slightly battered symbol of sensible Mr. Feld himself, the colour of a warning sign: *Stop, Ethan. You have gone too far.*

What was he *thinking*? There was no way in the *world* that Mr. Feld was going to believe any of it: baseball-playing fairies, bat-winged goblins that hurled their own exploding heads, Ragged Rock. To convince his father of something, as Ethan well knew, you needed to offer proof. What proof of Summerland's existence did Ethan have, beyond a weathered grey tree-branch and a tiny book that claimed to have been printed at a place called Duyvilburg, in the Summerlands, in the year 1320th Hoptoad? *How to Catch Lightning and Smoke* was something – it was pretty hard to explain away – but Ethan doubted it would be enough.

He dropped the old Schwinn in the drive and walked up to the house. It was dark, though the back door was unlocked. His father must still be sleeping; sometimes he didn't wake until dusk. Ethan walked through from the kitchen to the front door, checking his father's bedroom.

"Dad?" he said. His voice sounded thin and lost and he

switched on a light. There was a scrap of paper in the middle of the table, a white business card that read

ROB PADFOOT

BRAIN + STORM AERONAUTICS

with a Seattle address and telephone number, and the e-mail address padfoot@changer.com, and the fancy white ski-bum sunglasses. His father must have finally gotten around to calling back that Padfoot guy. Perhaps something the man said over the phone had fired Mr. Feld's imagination, and he had wanted to get an early start on his work. Ethan picked up the sunglasses and tucked them into the back pocket of his jeans. Then he walked out the back door again, headed for the packing shed, his heart sinking. Now it was going to be even tougher to persuade his father to leave the island. If he were caught up in his work, hoping to impress a possible investor, leaving would be the last thing Mr. Feld would want to do.

As soon as Ethan saw that the workshop, too, was dark, he knew that something was wrong. The high glass doors were shut but, like the house doors, unlocked. Mr. Feld never left for any length of time without locking up the workshop. It contained, as he often said, his life's savings. It would seem, then, Mr. Feld had wandered away from the house sometime, expecting to return very soon, and had not yet returned. Mr. Feld had never done anything like that before, but you never knew. No, that was untrue. You knew. You knew how it felt to come home and have everything feel somehow wrong. Too quiet. Too neat. And a smell in the air that was no smell at all, yet somehow not the proper smell of your home.

"Dad?" Ethan called again, the fine hair rising on the back of his neck. Outside the shed, the shadows had gathered, and were pressing against the windows, blotting out the world beyond. In the windowpanes Ethan could see only his own small, staring reflection. "Oh, my God."

Victoria Jean was gone. Ethan had been so focused on looking for his dad that he had failed to notice it before. In the place where the creamy white gondola usually rested there was only bare cement floor, mottled with oil and dust. The fuel cell unit was still there, but the envelope, tethers, and moorings were all gone, too. As he took this in, two certainties occurred to Ethan, one hard on the heels of the other. The first thing he knew for certain was that Rob Padfoot was responsible. The young man with the briefcase and long brown hair had come to the island again – had perhaps never left – and this time taken both his father and *Victoria Jean* away. The second certainty – he felt this one in the pit of his stomach – was that Padfoot and Brain + Storm were nothing but guises or operatives of Coyote. He remembered the way Padfoot had gone out of his way to praise the picodermal fibres of his father's envelope. Was that just a ploy? Or did Coyote really *want* Mr. Feld's ultrastable, nonconducting envelope material, for some reason? For the very reason, whatever it might be, that he wanted Mr. Feld, too? If any last doubt – of his own sanity, or the wisdom of his plan – had remained in the heart of Ethan Feld, it now fled. Everything, as Albert Rideout always said, was true.

Ethan heard a faint rattle of leaves. Something was moving in the ivy just outside the doors of the packing shed. He turned, wishing he had his stick, but he had left it leaning against the bicycle. There was a low moan, the clatter of steel. And then Cinquefoil stepped into the shed. He seemed to be hiding something behind his back. There was an orange gash on his forehead, thick orange streaks on his cheeks and throat. It was the orange of apricot jam, deep and shining. There was a spreading sticky circle on his buckskin shirt. The haste of his flight across the gap between Branches had left a thick rime of ice on his shoulders and the tips of his ears. He drew himself up to his full height of perhaps sixteen inches, swept the cap from his head, and bowed low to Ethan.

"At yer service," he said. From behind his back he produced the old catcher's mitt that Ethan's father had dug out of a box that morning. "I believe this might be yers."

Then he pitched forwards and fell flat on his face.

Ethan picked up the ferisher – he weighed as much as a big cat, and his body felt like a slumbering cat's in Ethan's arms – dense and loose at the same time. He carried him over to an old couch in the corner where Mr. Feld often abandoned his researches to a few hours' sleep, and laid him gently down on the cushions. Then he stood back, and wondered if he was about to watch the beautiful, battered little creature die.

"Not yet," Cinquefoil said, without opening his eyes. "Not this side a the Winterlands."

"The Winterlands," Ethan said. "Is that where he lives?"

"The Changer? He don't live anywhere. He's got no home. No home would have him, and there's none that'd suit him fer longer than a day. But he's fond a the Winterlands, they say, and all that crew of shaggurts and stormbangers and frost giants. They say his wife is a great grey shaggurt named Angry Betty. It won't surprise me none ta go looking and find him there, camped with all his Rade around him, his contraptions and contrivances, his hags and harridans and hobgoblins." Cinquefoil opened his eyes. "But I don't know fer sure; I've never set foot in the Winterlands my ownself, nor ventured inta the circle o' his wagons when he halts in his wandering fer a night. Nor has anyone I know that ever returned ta tell of it. Not in any form that I cared ta know them." He closed his eyes again.

"Did you… did you find any of your…" Ethan didn't bother to finish his question. If Cinquefoil had found anyone alive, surely they would have come back with him. The ferisher said nothing. He just slowly shook his head.

Ethan went to the sink in the corner and filled a pail with warm water, feeling honoured to have the Home Run King of three worlds in his care. The ferisher's blood seemed thicker than human blood and it had a distinctive smell that reminded Ethan of the smell of spring mud, of the first baseball practice of the season. It cleaned up easily enough, and the cuts and slashes themselves seemed to Ethan already to be healing as he dabbed at them with the damp towel. Cinquefoil sat up. He took the sponge from Ethan and tended to the rest of his wounds himself.

"Thanks, again," he said in a soft voice. Part of his beard had been singed off, and he patted at the bald spot. "It were a helluva leap. The gap between the branches is sadly wide now, where once they was jointed t'gether like lips in a kiss.

And likes o' you and me weren't never meant ta leap alone."

"Did they come after you? Skrikers? Greylings?"

Cinquefoil shook his head. "A quickgloom," he said. "Like a living shadow that—"

"I know," Ethan said. "They came after us, too. They got Cutbelly."

"That's bitter news," the ferisher said.

"And they also got my dad, Cinquefoil. I know they did. Somebody named Rob Padfoot came and took him away, and he took the Zeppelina, too."

"*Padfoot*?" said Cinquefoil. "There ain't no doubt about it. Coyote has your father."

Ethan remembered the sunglasses. He took them out of his back pocket and turned them over in his hand. The iridescent black lenses were like two pools of spilt oil. The white stuff they were made from, a kind of stiff rubber or vinyl, soft to the touch, was shot through with thin veins of wire in a crackly pattern. The rubber or whatever it was – some modern polymer his father was no doubt familiar with – held the warmth of Ethan's pocket.

"You know this Padfoot guy?" he said, slipping on the dark glasses. They were *warmer* than his pocket, somehow. As warm as if heated from within.

"I know him," Cinquefoil said. "More's the pity. He sits at Coyote's table. Shares in his mischief and trouble. Breaks his slaves and tempts his victims and rewards his stooges and darlings. A nasty, nasty character."

Ethan nearly took the sunglasses off, then, as though the nastiness of Rob Padfoot might be clinging to them like a sticky residue. But it was too late; the lenses covered his eyes.

When you look through a pair of glasses, even dark glasses, you expect to see *through* them. You expect, that is, to perceive – more clearly, or with less glare – the world that lies directly before your eyes. This expectation is rooted so deep that it took Ethan's brain a moment – a strange, nauseating moment – to realise that the signals it was getting from Ethan's optic nerves had nothing at all to do with the workshop, the old couch in the corner, or the wounded ferisher chieftain. It was another moment more before his baffled brain was able to form a definite impression from the mass of greyish and whitish and bluish blobs his eyes were claiming they saw.

"I see him!" he shouted, gripping the earpieces tightly in his fingers. "Oh, my God, I see him!"

"Padfoot?"

"No," Ethan said. "My father!"

He saw him dimly, as through a layer of thin black oil, and the image was oddly jerky, swooping back and forth and up and down. Mr. Feld was lying on a square mattress or pad, with a blank wall behind him. He was lying on his side, with a couple of inches of his belly showing at the waist of his jeans. Only his chest was moving, expanding and contracting with his breath, and he might have been asleep. It was impossible to say for sure, because the entire upper half of his face was covered in a blindfold. But that was his father's furry belly, there was no doubt about it. And that was Mr. Feld's big old chunky wristwatch. Though his father appeared to be at peace, there was something about the blindfold and the barren mattress that terrified Ethan. His father was a prisoner, a hostage. Maybe he was even being tortured. The image in the glasses had that awful shuddering quality you saw in footage taken by terrorists and kidnappers.

"I'm going to get my dad," he said, tentatively, realising his plan and testing it aloud at the same time. He took off the sunglasses and returned them to his pocket. "I'm going to get my dad," he repeated, more firmly. He didn't care, all at once, about the end of the universe. He didn't care about being a hero, about Johnny Speakwater's prophecy or the things there might be inside of him that had led Ringfinger Brown to single him out as a hot prospect. All he wanted to do was get his poor, blindfolded father back. He had lost one of his parents already in his short life. If he needed to save the universe to get the other one back, then he would. "Can you, like, guide me? Help me out?"

Cinquefoil rubbed his hands over his broad impassive face and sighed. "By the Starboard Arm, I'm tired, little reuben." Now that he had recovered somewhat from his wounds and the strain of crossing, the loss that he and his tribe had suffered seemed to settle on him all at once. "Tired and beaten and old."

"If Coyote took my father, it might have something to do with Ragged Rock. I think he wanted this stuff my father has figured out how to make. You can't burn it or tear it or cut it. It's pretty cool stuff and— Oh. Wait."

"What?" said the ferisher. "What is it?"

"*Stuff*," Ethan said, feeling the bottom fall out of his stomach. "I think we... I think there's been a mistake."

"What are ya talking about?" Cinquefoil said.

" '*Feld* is the wanted one'," Ethan quoted. " 'Feld has the stuff he needs', It wasn't me. It was my *dad*. My dad has the *stuff*

– his picodermal fibres. And the 'he' is Coyote! See? All along, Johnny Speakwater wasn't talking about *me* Feld. He was talking about Feld, my father. My father has the stuff Coyote needs. And what he needs it for is to poison the Well!"

"Yer getting too far ahead of me," the ferisher said, a hand to his brow. "Slow it down."

"You know my friend? Jennifer T. Rideout? Well, her aunt had this dream, see, about a magic Well that feeds the Tree? And in the dream a coyote was, you know. Peeing in the water. Ruining it. Poisoning it."

"Murmury," said the ferisher.

"What did you say?"

"Murmury Well. It's in the Greenmelt. The part of the Winterlands that lies nearest to the heart of the worlds. Yes, if he can figger a way ta foul those waters, the Tree is doomed and that's fer sure. And then comes Ragged Rock, in a Mole year, just like the old folks always said it would. And we're the ones what put yer pap in the Coyote's way. *We* brung him up this way, with those airship dreams. *We* parked him right next ta a gall, where Coyote was bound ta take notice someday." His voice went soft and frayed at the edges. "It's all our fault."

They said nothing for a long time. Ethan felt the last sparkling residue of being a prophesied hero drain away. But as it departed he found he was left with a strange kind of thoroughly unmagical resolve. He was not the wanted one. Well, that was fine. He might not be the one to save the universe. But he was going to save his father. That was something that had nothing to do with the vision of an oracular clam.

"So," he said, at last. "How are we going to do this?"

The ferisher sighed. Every ounce and inch and atom of him seemed to be rebelling against the idea of ever doing anything again but lie on this old couch. And yet he had come here, of all the places he might have gone after his search for his tribesmen failed. Ethan was beginning to get the feeling of some kind of force at work, some purpose that was driving things to happen in a certain way.

"We don't have a shadowtail. And I've just leaped my last leap without the help of a shadowtail, that's fer damn sure." He shuddered, and gave the left side of his head a sharp whack. "I done lost all the hearing in this ear."

"Well, we know this kid named Thor Wignutt?"

"Thor Wignutt," Cinquefoil said, looking doubtful. He seemed to know just who Ethan was talking about.

"To leap across. We think Thor might be—"

"Aye," Cinquefoil said. "That one will do quite well." He climbed down from the couch and started pacing back and forth, thinking things out. "We'll need a ship or vee-hickle o' some sort," he said. "Coyote has all type o' fleet wagons and swift beasts, and turrible contrivances that travel ten times faster than ever we could afoot. We've no hope o' catching him without a ship. And should we end up after all headed inta the Winterlands, well, in all the tales I've ever heard, no hero or adventurer ever got there on the leather o' his shoes."

"A ship," Ethan said. "Yeah, OK. Man, too bad they stole *Victoria Jean*. What about one of those flying buses of yours?"

"Alas, the greylings burned 'em all. The big sky bladders o' yer pap, there was only the one? Didn't he craft none to spare?"

"Huh," Ethan said.

A few pieces of an idea began to arrange themselves in Ethan's mind. Key elements were still missing, but he felt somehow that Cinquefoil might be able to help work them out. He went to one of the big storage lockers and worked the combination, which was set, like all of Mr. Feld's locks, to 21-10-80, the day on which the Philadelphia Phillies had won the World Scrics for the first time in the seventy-seven years of its existence. He found a handsewn polycarbon picofibre envelope, carried it outside, and laid it on the grass, turning it over and over, checking it for tears or weak patches. It was the first that Mr. Feld had had manufactured, a prototype, which he had never actually used to make an ascent. Ethan carried the untested envelope and all the wire tackle he could find down to the driveway.

Cinquefoil dragged himself from the couch and trudged down the hill to watch as Ethan spent most of the next hour threading cables, setting clasps, and double-checking all his connections. He helped Ethan wrestle a gas regulator unit onto a dolly and wheel it down to the driveway, too, along with a big tank of helium. Ethan connected the regulator to the rubberised valve on the envelope. Then he pushed a button on the regulator, and with a loud metallic *whoosh* the gas flew through the hose. The gas bag lurched, rumbled, and then with a crinkling sound expanded, all at once, billowing out at either end, bobbing and thrumming, rising into the air to the limits of the stay cables and then beyond.

Gently, gracefully, the orange Saab station wagon rose three and a half feet off the ground. Cinquefoil clapped his hands, losing his sorrowful mien for a moment in the simple delight of seeing something extremely heavy floating easily as a bit of dandelion fluff.

"Yeah. Neat. There's only one problem," Ethan said. "It's a dummy."

Cinquefoil looked puzzled.

"I mean, it floats all right. But there's no propulsion. You know? And there's no tiller. I mean, I could turn on the engine, and spin the steering wheel, but they're not— you know. They're for a *car*."

Cinquefoil's smile had returned. "There isn't no problem, then."

"There isn't?"

"What da ya think makes a ferisher bus go forwards, or left, or right? Racks and pinions? Gasoline?"

"Right," Ethan said.

"Go get what ya'll need from the house," Cinquefoil said. "I'll start working the grammer."

Ethan went into the house and changed into clean, warm clothes. He put on thermal underwear and packed two more sets in his duffel, along with several sweaters, three pairs of clean underpants, and lots of socks. It could get awfully cold up in the sky. He packed Peavine's book, and a toothbrush. Then he went into his father's bedroom. Mr. Feld was a naturally sloppy man, but Ethan's mom had been a neatnik, and in the days of their marriage it was her way that had prevailed. Now that she was dead Ethan's dad had pretty much relapsed to his old messy ways, but he still kept the bedroom tidy. His penknife, pocket change, and wallet lay on the dresser, the coins neatly stacked. The bed was made, its coverlet pulled tight and smooth as the skin of a drum, and to Ethan it looked astoundingly empty. *I am never going to see him again*, he thought, and with a shudder tried to force the thought down. He took the dark glasses out of his pocket again and put them on. Again there was the strange warmth in the earpieces, like a pair of long fingers laid against his temples.

This time he understood right away what he was seeing. It was a bowl, and this bowl contained some kind of dark and glistening brownish mass, a stew or soup of some kind, in which darker chunks of something swam. The bowl rose up in the direction of Ethan's face – it was the strangest sensation – and then tipped towards him. Ethan jumped back, as if hot soup were about to pour into his lap. But of course nothing of the sort occurred. The soup, and the person eating it, were somewhere far away. The view through the lenses shifted abruptly, then, slid to the left, and there was Mr. Feld again. He was still lying on the square of foam, but he had rolled over and it was impossible to see his face at all. That was when Ethan understood that when he put on Rob Padfoot's dark glasses, he could see what Rob Padfoot was seeing, way off in the Winterlands or wherever they had taken his dad. Rob Padfoot was keeping watch over Mr. Feld, in that barren room, sitting down to a meal of something glistening and foul. It was as if the dark glasses were a lost piece of Padfoot himself, still keeping in contact with the eyes and brain from which they had been parted.

Taking off the glasses, Ethan turned them over in his hands, feeling a faint pulse in the thin wire that veined them. He went over to his father's dresser and rummaged around in the top drawer until he found a thin black case. In it lay a pair of gold-wire granny glasses that had belonged to the late Dr. Feld. He took them tenderly out and laid them on the dresser, and replaced them with Rob Padfoot's dark glasses, which just fit. He snapped the case shut and started out of the bedroom, with something nagging at his conscience. He turned around and looked back at the deserted bedroom. The wallet. Mr. Feld, Ethan knew, hated going anywhere without his wallet in his back pocket. It was not the cash or the credit cards or the photos it contained, nor the wallet itself, a battered hunk of sweat-darkened cowhide. Actually, Ethan was not really sure what the big deal about the wallet was. But many times his father had delayed their departure from the house, for the most urgent appointments or a simple walk in the woods, until he tracked it down. "I just feel kind of naked without it," he would explain. Ethan went back and stuffed the wallet into his duffel. Then he went back down to his homemade zeppelin. It floated above the driveway, tethered by the inflation hose (something Mr. Feld hated to see – it damaged the hose) just about where he had left it. Cinquefoil was nowhere to be seen.

There was a low bubbling sound, followed by a soft, sweet twittering. It was almost like the sound of one of those novelty whistles, shaped like a bird on a branch, that you fill with water. And then the makeshift airship eased forwards a few feet and came to a stop. A moment later Cinquefoil's head appeared in the driver's window.

"Ya'll have ta test it," he said. "I can't reach the pedal and the wheel at the same time. What's more I'm a might—

uneasy— in the midsta all this steel. Steel ain't a stuff we ferishers are all that partial ta."

Ethan found an empty wooden cable spool and used it to climb up into the car. He tossed in his duffel bag. Just before he climbed in along with it, he remembered his stick. He didn't think it was such a hot idea, somehow, to travel without it. It was not much of a weapon, really. But it had served him well once. He got down from the spool.

"Where ya going?" Cinquefoil said.

Ethan went over to the old Schwinn and grabbed the stick, and once again found that there was a strange comfort in holding it. He showed it to Cinquefoil, who looked at it carefully, with his little head tilted to one side.

"Ah," he said. "Yer bit o' woundwood."

"Woundwood?"

"Woundwood is the stuff that forms around a gall," Cinquefoil said. "That's a splinter o' the Lodgepole itself, rube. That's a rare thing ta have, a real piece o' the Lodgepole. Ya'll wanta hold onta that. They don't come loose too easy. You might almost say woundwood is *choosy* about who it lets get a piece o' itself." He looked at Ethan, and scratched his head. "Mebbe there's something in ya after all."

"I don't know why," Ethan said, "but when I hold it— it feels— just really holdable."

"It might make ya a fine bat someday."

"A bat," Ethan said, turning the stick over in his hand. Though scarred and knotted, it was perfectly straight. It had never before occurred to Ethan that a baseball bat started out as a piece of some tree.

"The Lodgepole is a ash tree," Cinquefoil explained. "It's thc Ash o' Ashes."

"And baseball bats are— is that right?— made of ashwood?"

"Always. From the start o' the game until now. And why would that be, da ya imagine?"

"Why," Ethan repeated, uncertain.

"Yes, why. Don't ya *ever* wonder why, little reuben?" Cinquefoil sank back into the interior of the car, then reappeared. "Don't forget yer mitt, neither."

"My mitt?"

"It's a long journey we're contemplating. There'll be ample time along the way ta work on yer catching game."

Ethan retrieved the mitt, and then, carrying it and the unborn bat, he climbed up once more onto the wooden spool and pulled himself into thc station wagon. He put his hands on the wheel. Cinquefoil stood on the passenger's seat and held onto the dashboard, looking eager as a dog.

"Touch the pedal," Cinquefoil said.

Ethan reached out with his right foot. There was nothing there.

"I can't reach the pedals," he said.

"Move the seat forward."

Ethan shifted his seat until his chest nearly touched the steering wheel. Now he could hit the gas with his right toes.

With the same watery chirping they glided forwards twenty feet or so, maybe a little too quickly.

"Can ya see through the foreglass, there?"

"Yeah."

"Then ya must know we're about ta hit the glass barn."

Ethan moved his foot to the brake, hoping that it too was under a grammer. The car came shuddering to a stop when the front bumper was three inches from smashing into a corner of the packing shed.

"Oops," Ethan said. "Sorry."

"Just… what are the words? 'Back her up'."

"Back her up."

"Put the machine inta *ree*-verse."

Ethan found the red R on the shift knob and tried to drag the gearshift over, right, and towards the back of the car. It wouldn't go.

"The *clutch*," Cinquefoil said. "Ferisher machines don't even have such things. But fer some reason I thought ya'd find it simpler."

"I'm only eleven," Ethan said.

"Don't remind me," said Cinquefoil.

Ethan got it into reverse, and gave the wheel a spin. Skid backed around to the right, and then with another twist, and a shift into first gear, lurched forwards and down the driveway to the road. They were still only a few feet above the ground.

"I need loft," Ethan said.

"The radio."

Ethan switched on the radio. He touched the volume knob and looked at Cinquefoil, who nodded. Slowly he twisted the knob, clockwise, and Skid ascended, creaking and shuddering, into the sky.

"OK," Ethan said. "We're up."

"We seem ta be," Cinquefoil remarked.

Ethan took her up until he was twice as high as the

highest trees. Then he turned towards the Rideout place. The ferisher drive burbled and rang like rain in the gutters. A breeze filled Ethan's ears.

"We call her Skidbladnir," he said. "My dad and me. It's a Scandinavian name."

"What does it mean?" Cinquefoil said. " 'Ugly as a greyling's hind parts?' "

"It was a flying ship that belonged to the god Frey," Ethan said. "In Norse mythology. A huge, beautiful ship, so cleverly made that you could fold it up and stick it in your pocket."

"A jesting name, then," Cinquefoil said. "Like calling a bald man Curly."

"I guess so. Actually mostly we just call her Skid."

Cinquefoil nodded. "If I were ta give this craft a name, it would definitely be—" and then he uttered a series of weird syllables, full of k's and g's and x's. Something like *Karggruxragakkurgorok*.

"What language is that?"

"Old Fatidic."

"What's it mean?"

"It means, 'Ugly as a greyling's hind parts'. "

Ten minutes after leaving the house on the hill, they were hovering over the Rideout compound. Jennifer T. and Thor Wignutt were waiting for him in the dusk, next to a small mountain of gear.

"What the heck is that thing?" she called up to Ethan.

"I made it," said Ethan. "Shut up."

He dialled down the radio volume, and eased the car onto a large bald patch in the centre of the Rideouts' ragged yard. As they were landing, the twins, Darrin and Dirk, came running out of one of the side houses, along with some of their young cousins. They stood gaping at the airship, except for Dirk, who tried to hit it with a brick. His shot went wide, and then his older sister gave him a smack on the back of the head. After that Dirk just stood there gaping, too. Uncle Mo and Aunt Shambleau came out onto their porch to see. But their eyes were not on the aged Swedish automobile that was descending from the heavens onto their weeds. They were looking at the ferisher.

"Can they see you?" Ethan asked Cinquefoil in a whisper.

"I didn't see no point in wasting a grammer on them," Cinquefoil said. "No one ever believes a Rideout. Rideouts don't even believe their own selves."

"Can everybody see you? I mean, if you don't work a grammer on them?"

Cinquefoil smacked him on the thigh. "Don't ya read? Don't children *read* anymore?"

"I read!"

"And ya mean, ya don't know who we let see us and who we never, ever do?"

"You only let people see you who believe in you already," Ethan said.

"That's the very one!" cried Aunt Shambleau. "Naked as a fish!"

"Naked as a fish!" said little Dirk Rideout, and his brother said, "Naked! Naked!"

"You kids get back in the house and look at television," Aunt Shambleau said. The twins and their cousins just stood there. Aunt Shambleau reached for her cataract glasses and made as if to take them off. The little cousins took a step backwards. She started to slide the big wraparounds slowly down the bridge of her nose. The Rideout cousins all ran, screaming and yelling, back into the cabin they'd come out of. Nobody actually knew what would happen next if Aunt Shambleau ever took off her glasses. But clearly it would not be something good.

Ethan got out of the car and Jennifer T. brought Thor over.

"They got my dad," Ethan said. "Coyote did. This guy Rob Padfoot came and took him. Here." He crouched down and unzipped the duffel, taking out the glasses case. He took out Padfoot's glasses and passed them to Jennifer T. "Put these on."

Jennifer T. slipped on Padfoot's glasses. She started, and ducked her head. Her mouth opened.

"Huh," she said.

"What is it? What do you see?" Thor said.

"I see Mr. Feld," Jennifer T. said. "He's wearing a blindfold. He's sitting up."

"He's sitting up?" Ethan said. He wanted to see that.

"He's talking. He's doing that pointing thing he does when he's explaining stuff."

Ethan wondered what his father could possibly be explaining to his captors. He took the glasses back from Jennifer T. and put them on. She was right; Padfoot was clearly on the receiving end of a lecture from Mr. Feld, who was pointing at electrons or air molecules or whatever invisibly fine thing was the subject of his talk. It made

Ethan's heart ache to see his dad patiently trying to enlighten Rob Padfoot on some score.

"Why did he— why would Coyote take your *dad*?" Jennifer T. said.

"Maybe he's going to make an airship?"

"Oh, Coyote *loves* contrivances," Cinquefoil said. "He made the very first one."

"The net," Thor said. It was his turn with the dark glasses; he had taken off his own horn-rims to try them out.

"That's right." Cinquefoil studied him, frowning.

"How did you know *that*, Thor?" Ethan said. "Did Jennifer T. explain this to you?"

"I tried," she said. "It turned out that I don't actually understand what's going on."

"But do you get it about all this 'scampering' and 'leaping' stuff, Thor?"

"Of course," Thor said, in his most reasonable TW03 voice, still peering into the lenses of Padfoot's glasses. "There is an underlying structure to the universe. This structure takes the form of a quantum indeterminacy tree. Apparently there are certain individuals who know how to locate the underlying structural elements and follow them for short distances. When it's done within a single dimension of reality, it's called *scampering*. When the travel is interdimensional, it's a *leap*."

It was hard to know what to say to this. Nobody spoke for a moment. Thor took off the dark glasses and passed them back to Ethan, who returned them to their case.

"He's talking about you," Thor said.

"Huh? How can you tell?"

"I read his lips. He said, 'Ethan'. He said, 'my son'."

Tears burned Ethan's eyes. He brushed them away.

"Thor," Ethan said. "Do you think you can do it? Get us over from here to the Winterlands, or wherever this Coyote guy has taken my dad?"

Thor didn't answer right away. He looked at Ethan, his tiny brown eyes blinking furiously between the lenses of his glasses. He scratched his right calf with the toe of his left foot. For the first time Ethan noticed that Thor was wearing only his pyjamas and a pair of track shoes. They were the kind of pyjamas that Ethan's father wore, with a top that buttoned like a shirt, patterned with old-fashioned ballplayers in knickers. The silence went on for an uncomfortably long time. It was one of those moments when Thor seemed to realise that at the bottom of it all he was just a little kid and not a synthetic human. Such moments didn't happen very often, and usually just as he was about to carry something a little too far.

"It sounds like something I ought to be able to do," he said at last. "Doesn't it?"

They got to work loading what they could into the back of the station wagon. The rest had to go under their feet and on the backseat. They took three sleeping bags and a small tent, a cooler filled with sandwiches (mostly liverwurst, alas), two jugs of water, a camp stove, several flashlights, some rope, Jennifer T.'s baseball glove, and a small duffel stuffed with Jennifer T.'s clothes. She took along three Roosters jerseys and three caps, since Ethan had forgotten his, and Thor had only the pyjamas and running shoes.

"Were you asleep?" Ethan asked him as they jammed the

sleeping bags in around the gas regulator in the trunk. "Why are you wearing pyjamas?"

"My mother makes me go to bed at six-thirty," he said. "Five-thirty in the wintertime."

"I'm sorry," Jennifer T. said. "I forgot to tell him to pack a bag. I was kind of freaking out about his mother hearing us."

"She would have come after us with the Big Strap," Thor said. "I would rather live in my pyjamas."

Mo Rideout pitched in with the loading, but Aunt Shambleau seemed unable to move. She just sat on the top step of the porch, watching Cinquefoil as he stood, on Skid's front bumper, trying to work a grammer that would make the engine disappear, so they could use the space up front for cargo. He mumbled and muttered, waving his arms around, then cursed loudly and stomped his foot. Each time he stomped it the car creaked loudly. It was hard to believe a little foot like that could stomp so hard.

"It ain't no use," he said, giving up. "I was trying ta work a housekeeping grammer. It's a kind o' vanishing spell, so I hoped... but you aren't supposed ta twist a grammer so hard. Not to mention with that old grey she-reuben staring a pair o' holes in my head..."

"It's all right," Ethan said. "We might want to actually *drive* it at some point."

When everything was loaded, Uncle Mo came over and stood by the children.

"I'd like to come with you," he said. "There ought to be an adult present. I have valuable skills to offer."

Cinquefoil shook his head.

"Ya wunnit survive the crossing."

"Too old?"

"The Maker gave ya a fine physique, Morris 'Chief' Rideout. If ya had treated it more kindly, maybe it still, even at yer age, could carry ya through. I know the dearest wish o' your heart since ya was a young reuben has been ta see the Summerlands again. And at one time, we had high hopes o' seeing ya there, not ta mention that poor, fine Okawa reuben. Now, that boy had the hero stuff."

Uncle Mo nodded. Tears stood in his eyes. He rummaged in the hip pocket of his shiny blue blazer. Then he handed his grandniece a small, fat book, about the size of a pocket dictionary, maybe a little bigger. It was covered in thick cardboard with a matte-silk finish, cracked and torn at the corners. The page edges had been rubbed by use and reuse until they were soft and mossy to the touch. The spine was badly buckled. On the front a group of red-cheeked boys sat at the feet of a tall, ghostly man in a feathered headdress.

"*The Wa-He-Ta Brave's Official Tribe Handbook*," Ethan read. "What's a Wa-He-Ta Brave?"

"It was an outfit they used to have, sorta like the Boy Scouts," Uncle Mo said. "Mostly on the West Coast. It folded years ago."

Ethan came to look at it over Jennifer T.'s shoulder as he flipped through the pages. Across the tops of the pages ran chapter titles such as "Wa-He-Ta Fieldcraft", "Wa-He-Ta Tribal Spirit", and "The Law of Wa-He-Ta".

"What's Wa-He-Ta mean?" Jennifer T. said.

Uncle Mo looked embarrassed. "Oh," he said. "They made up a bogus Indian language. There's a glossary at the back. The whole thing was bogus. They just made up all that Wa-He-Ta stuff in there, there never was such a tribe. Anyway, in the little alphabet they cooked up, it works out to W-H-T or Wonder, Hopefulness, and Trust. The Threefold Lore, they called it. All that's nonsense, like I say. But there's a lot of actual woods lore in that book, things I learned about fishing and firebuilding and tracking an animal that I still use from time to time today. Also engine repair, radio craft, even shooting firearms. I just thought you might need it."

"Thanks, Uncle Mo," said Jennifer T. When she got into the car, she put the book into Skid's glove compartment, then took hold of the wheel. She was the best choice for pilot, since she had not only flown *Victoria Jean* but had also secretly driven her father's car. Ethan started to climb in alongside her.

"I'm the Home Run King o' Three Worlds," Cinquefoil said. "I don't take the rear seat ta nobody." So Ethan got into the back with Thor. As Thor squeezed in behind the passenger seat, which Cinquefoil was holding aside, Ethan thought he saw the ferisher chief flinch slightly. Ethan wondered if Thor gave off some smell that the ferisher found objectionable. Human beings had certainly made the same complaint about Thor from time to time.

At the last instant Aunt Shambleau seemed to shake off her funk. She came lumbering over to the car and peered in at Cinquefoil.

"I love you," she told him. "I've loved you all my life from the moment I saw you, on the third day of August, 1944."

Cinquefoil gazed levelly at her, listening, his ageless face expressionless, his gaze hooded.

"I used to dream about you," she went on. "Every night for a long, long time."

Now Cinquefoil's expression softened, and he reached up to touch her wrinkled cheek with one of his small, rough hands. He lifted her black glasses. The eyes behind were large, brown, and surprisingly tender.

"They wasn't all dreams, my dear," Cinquefoil said.

Aunt Shambleau stared a moment, then blushed. The glasses fell back into place on her nose and she pulled away from the car.

"Goodbye, children," Uncle Mo said.

Then Jennifer T. switched on the radio and took them up.

SECOND BASE

6

Thor's Crossing

"OK," THOR WIGNUTT said, as they left behind the lights of Butler Beach, at the eastern tip of Clam Island, and headed out over the shining black waters of the Sound. "I'm ready."

"Great," Ethan said.

"I just have one question."

"What's that?"

"Where are we going?"

Ethan turned from Thor to Cinquefoil, still standing in the front passenger seat with his ruddy hands on the dash.

"That's hard ta say," said the little chief. "Ya can't never predict what old Coyote will do. Just about everything that could turn out two ways or more was invented by him, back when he Changed the world the first time. Before that, as ya may or may not know, everything could only turn out one way. There weren't no crossroads, fer instance. Only straight paths that didn't bend. Toss a coin, it always came up heads. And nobody died. That's one o' the things Coyote changed. He brought the *wobble* inta the world. Everything that turns out one way but could just as easy turn out the other. Good or bad. Dead or alive. Hungry or with yer belly nice and full."

"So you're saying... what are you saying?" Ethan was having a hard time getting a handle on this Changer person, this Coyote who had taken his father. Was he only evil? Did he *really* want to destroy the Worlds? Why, in spite of the dreadful creatures and terrible machines, the Padfoots and skrikers and greylings in his army, the horror that his human agents had wrought at Hotel Beach, why was there always the tiniest glint of *appreciation* in Cinquefoil's eyes whenever he talked about Coyote?

"I'm saying, I don't like ta try ta outguess Coyote, fer it can't be done but badly, and what's more it gives me a pain in the head. But I'm thinking we ought ta head inta the Summerlands after all. If Coyote changes his mind, which he loves ta do, or if he ain't really headed ta Murmury Well at all, then we sure as moose scat don't want ta be hanging around the Winterlands fer no good reason. And if he is headed ta Murmury Well, then we don't need ta go by the Winterlands at all. There are other ways o' getting ta the Greenmelt that surrounds Murmury. With luck and a talented shadowtail, we might be able ta make it by way o' the Summerlands. In the meantime we might find answers there. Help. Weapons. A grammer book or two. A map. P'raps some tricks ta trick the trickster. Even a few stout arms."

"Sounds like a plan," said Jennifer T. "I'm not sure I'm ready for the Winterlands yet. The Summerlands were weird enough for me."

Cinquefoil looked back at Ethan. "Well, hero?"

Ethan nodded.

"OK," Thor said. "The Summerlands it is."

"Take us forward, then," Cinquefoil said to Jennifer T. "If I remember my Tree lore there's a spot up ahead where a branch o' the Summerlands hangs close enough ta leap it. It's a old Thunderbird Trail."

Jennifer T. sent them careening ahead for about half a mile, and then Cinquefoil said, simply, "Here."

Thor closed his eyes, and settled against the backseat of the Saab. Jennifer T. let go of the wheel with one hand and twisted around to see what he was doing. Thor's face relaxed. The furrow of bafflement, like a letter V, that was always there, over his nose, went smooth. His hands lay open and palm up on the seat beside him. Ethan hugged himself, awaiting the inevitable cold breath of a leap between branches. Thor opened his eyes.

"I have absolutely no idea what I'm doing," he said. Ethan had never heard him say anything of the sort before. But he said it in the same unflappable humanoid voice as ever. "I hope the crew all realise that."

"Just feel yer way along the branch," Cinquefoil said. "Until ya sense the shadow falling over ya. The shadow of a leaf, like. Then ya know yer right under the spot."

"But I don't know what the Summerlands look like," Thor said. "There's nothing." He tapped the side of his head. He meant, Ethan knew, that there was nothing about the Summerlands in his *database*.

"That's not true," Ethan said. "You've gone there a thousand times."

"Wull, yeah, *that* Summerland. But not the real one."

"But our Summerland is part of the real Summerlands, somehow. Or was. Stuck in the middle of the Middling."

"Yer Summerland wasn't no part of the Birchwood," Cinquefoil said. "They was two sides o' the *same* place. Like twin brothers on either end of a great endless bear hug."

"Then shouldn't we have scampered over from there?" Thor said.

"We could've, yesterday, maybe," Cinquefoil said. "But not today. Barely made it over myself, the parting was so wide. An' I could feel it getting wider by the minute. It's a gap that no shadowtail will ever leap across again."

"That's terrible," Ethan said. Summerland, that enchanted island of blue sky in the grey sea of a Clam Island summer, was gone forever. "Picture it," he told Thor. "Just try to see Summerland in your mind."

"Picture the ball field," Jennifer T. suggested. "On a sunny afternoon."

"Green," Thor said.

"And the water at Hotel Beach, and the leaves of the birch trees."

"Green, with some grey in it. Flashing green."

"The blackberry brambles," Ethan suggested.

"Green, with all these dark green shadows. OK. Huh."

On the island, they had crossed from birch wood to Birchwood, with no apparent gap in the fabric of the worlds. What would it look like as they glided across the sky from one world to the next? Would they go from night to day? From seacoast to forest? Ethan peered out the rear windows of the station wagon. At first the darkness around them seemed no different from before. Below, the straggling lights of some coastal town. Above them, the stars, pale and distant. Then the temperature plunged, and abruptly the stars went out. The lights of Coos Bay or whatever town lay beneath them winked and were gone.

"Hey," said Jennifer T. She started twisting knobs on the dashboard. "Is there any heat in this hunk of junk?"

"Fascinating," said Thor. "My climate sensors indicate a temperature drop of over ten degrees in the last nine seconds."

"He's doing it," Ethan said. "Chief, he's doing it, isn't he?"

"He seems to be. But whether he's crossing us to the Summerlands or no..."

A great shudder racked Ethan, and he zipped his fleece to the collar. He had never felt anything so cold before.

"We're losing altitude," Jennifer T. said. "The gas in the envelope is shrinking or what's it called. Contracting."

"Ice," Thor muttered. He reached up to wipe at the lenses of his heavy-rimmed eyeglasses.

Jennifer turned up the radio dial while Ethan looked out the window again.

"Losing altitude over *what*?" he said. "It looks like there's nothing down there. No fog. No clouds."

"Yer right," Cinquefoil said. "It's Nothing. The Nothing that lies among the leaves and branches o' the Tree. The mightiest Nothing there is."

Thor rubbed some more at the lenses of his glasses with his sleeve.

"Ice," he said again. He was snuffling a lot, and his nose was running, and he looked pretty miserable.

Cinquefoil gave him a poke with the tip of his boot.

"Take care," he said. "It sounds ta me yer thinking overmuch about—"

"Ice!" cried Jennifer T. There was a sudden opening of light, like a great blazing flower bursting into bloom, so bright that Ethan had to shut his eyes against it. It was like popping up out of a cardboard box into a brilliant afternoon; the nerves of his eyes were so baffled that even with his eyelids clamped shut they were busy turning everything red and blue and the luminous green of a beetle. When Ethan dared to open his eyes again, what he saw made so little sense that they might as well have remained closed.

Outside the windows of the car, all below them, there stretched a limitless expanse of ice, a hundred or a thousand or ten-thousand miles of jagged ice teeth and shining ice prairies, under a sky that was the blue-black colour of a scorched steel pot. Though the sky over the ice was dark, it also shone, frothing with stars, great swirling jets and eddies of blazing snowdust. And then there was the radiance of the ice itself. The ice mountains, the ice pillars, the jagged broken staircases of tumbling glacier flow, all seemed to blaze from within, as if they were made not from mere water but from some compound of the radiance shed by the stars overhead: frozen starlight. The ice lit the sky; the sky lit the ice.

Ethan turned around and looked out the rear window of the hatch; it was filled with the starless empty darkness they had just come sailing through.

"Brother!" cried Cinquefoil to Thor Wignutt. "Oh, little brother! Where have ya brought us? This ain't the Summerlands, not at all."

"I'm sorry!" Thor said miserably. "There was— it was— I had ice— on my glasses."

"We're still going down!" Jennifer T. said. She grabbed at the volume dial, so calmly labelled LJUDVOLYM, and twisted it all the way up. Their course was angled towards the ice only slightly, but enough so that if they continued to drop they would eventually come down.

Ethan clung so tightly to the strap of his shoulder belt that the thick edge of it dug into his fingers. "What—what's—"

"You're lying on your back, on that little hill behind the picnic tables," Jennifer T. suggested urgently to Thor.

"Yeah?" Thor said. He didn't sound too convinced.

"Looking up at the dark green shade of that tree, the big one that gets those little helicoptery things. Do it!"

"OK, OK!" Thor shouted. "I know the tree you mean— yeah. OK."

All at once the windows began to stream with water, bright droplets chasing one another across the glass. The ice was melting; the sky all around them was blue. Ethan shielded his eyes against the sudden brilliance of the sun. They rolled down their windows, and the car filled with a delicious sharp smell of evergreens. The colour returned to Cinquefoil's face. His eyelids fluttered, opened, and then he smiled, and rolled down his own window. He stood up on the seat and hung his head out the window.

"The Summerlands," he said. "Ya did it, boy."

Jennifer T. stuck her head out her window and into the blindingly blue sky. She peered down. Beneath Skidbladnir's useless wheels stretched an immense forest, shadowy and cool. The spiky carpet of evergreens below was ripe with the vibrant green of a summer afternoon. At its farthest limits rose a range of smoky blue mountains. They didn't look like the Cascades; they looked older, lower, as if far more worn away by the passage of time.

"Where are we?" Ethan said, looking down. "Is it any place you know?"

"I might be mistook in this," Cinquefoil said. He was looking very hard at Thor. "But I believe ya just crossed us ta the heart o' the Far Territories."

"Was that wrong?" Thor said.

"Nah, nah, it was very well done." Still he stared, tugging at the curly tip of his playing-card-king beard. "Also impossible."

"Compared to what?" Jennifer T. said. "This whole thing is impossible."

"See here," Cinquefoil said. "It just ain't *right*, leaping from a branch o' the Middling ta one in the Winterlands and then over ta a branch in the Summerlands lickety-split like a sharp-turned double-play. *Nobody* can do that. It's like... that's like passing from one room in yer house ta another, then going back through the door again an' finding yerself in a third room on a whole nuther floor."

"But I just did what you all said to do," Thor protested. "I thought of sunshine, and blue sky, and some kind of green that was almost like black, it was so green."

"It's all right," Cinquefoil broke in. "No harm done, ta the contrary, ya done brought us ta a part o' this world where even Coyote don't much like ta set his foot. The Far Territories. Hard by the Raucous Mountains, by the look of it. It's still a wild place, the wildest in all the Worlds, not excepting the most shaggurt-infested corner a the

Winterlands. An' what's more, if we can just get ourselfs over those mountains, we ought ta be able ta find our way ta the Greenmelt."

"I thought the Greenmelt was in the *Winterlands*," said Jennifer T.

"So it is. But beyond the Far Territories, see, over the Raucous Mountains, down through the Lost Camps, and way across the Big River, there's a spot called Applelawn. Beyond it lies Diamond Green, where the four limbs of the Tree rise from the trunk."

"The axil point," Ethan said.

"So I've heard it styled. It's where Old Mr. Wood was standin' when he tossed the first fireball o' creation. The same and very spot where Coyote laid down the lines fer the first inning a baseball ever ta be played. Now, the part of the Winterlands called the Greenmelt, well, it lies just across Diamond Green from Applelawn in the Summerlands. We need only step across Diamond Green to reach it. Come at Murmury Well from the back door, so ta speak, and if we can, beat Coyote to it. Yeah, this was well done, indeed, Thor Wignutt." His eyes narrowed and his normally placid gaze turned sharp. "Almost like you *knew* where you were leaping."

Ethan's attention was diverted by a creaking rumble like some heavy old piece of furniture being slid across a wooden floor. He turned to see a massive shaggy thing, part polar bear, part enormous starfish, appear from beneath the car, right there in the middle of the sky. It wiggled its pink-skinned, white-furred tendrils in front of them, its bones cracking audibly.

"Chief? Hey, Chief? Oh, my gosh!" Ethan shouted, pointing.

A moment later the thing was joined by its twin. Each long-haired pale creature was at least twice the size of Skid herself.

"What are those things?" Jennifer T. said. It was a natural question and Ethan would have asked it himself, but he suddenly found that he could not open his mouth to speak. "They look like giant *hands*."

"Those are *giant's* hands," said Cinquefoil, just before they were snatched from the sky.

7

The Eighteenth Giant Brother

THE GIANT HAD to go up on tiptoe to get hold of them, reaching for them like a right fielder robbing a batter of a home run at the wall. Though of course there was no altimeter in Skid's dashboard control panel, Ethan had been up in *Victoria Jean* enough times to be able to estimate their altitude as somewhere around thirty metres. As high, that is, as fifteen extremely tall men standing one atop the shoulders of the next. The envelope of the airship was capable of lifting two tons but offered no resistance to the giant's great creaking arms. It plucked them down from the sky carefully, even tenderly, like someone with a lightbulb that has to be changed. The wind whistled through the open windows of the car as they made their captive fall towards the trees. About a third of the way down their progress abruptly stopped. An enormous eye, the iris blood-red, the white pink-veined, blinked in at them through the windows on Ethan's side. The lashes were palest yellow, like the fur on the great pink hands. It was an albino giant, then. Somehow that made it even more frightening.

"*It's looking at me,*" Ethan said finally, his voice emerging in a faint, strangled whisper.

The giant's red eye was veiled in a heavy mist, which each flapping of its pale blond eyelashes sent whirling and eddying away. Then a moment later the mist would return, dense and stinking something terrible of fish and rancid meat. It was, Ethan realised, the giant's breath.

"It's his job to look at ya," Cinquefoil said. "That is Mooseknuckle John."

"You— you *know* him?" Jennifer T. said, peering out through the screen of her fingers.

"He and his seventeen brothers, Johns all, done wandered inta our parts from time ta time over the years," Cinquefoil said, returning the giant's bloody gaze with an expression of polite uninterest. "Raising a considerable portion o' hell. For which we done paid 'em back handsomely, often enough as not."

"Is he going to *eat* us?" said Thor. That positronic brain had a way of cutting right to the core of any complicated problem.

"If he has the taste fer little reubens," Cinquefoil said, "and it's likely he does. Most o' them boys do. In the old days they used ta eat human children by the fistful."

"OK, I would like to be somewhere else right now," Jennifer T. said. "I—"

"PRETTY TOY!"

The voice of the giant, when he finally spoke, was not something they heard as much as felt, in every joint and soft part of their bodies. It shook the bolts of Skid's chassis and made the glass in her windows hum. The car was suddenly drenched in a stink of dead fish and sweet rotten flesh. Ethan felt as if he might have to vomit. It would certainly not have been the first time he had vomited in Skid. The memory of a summer night after thc Colorado State Fair at Pueblo came to him, when his stomach, scrambled by the Tilt-A-Whirl and tilted by the Scrambler, had brought up the corn dog, fried dough, cotton candy, snow cone, and caramel apple that he had consumed, all over Skid's backseat. His mother had so calmly, so patiently, so dutifully comforted him, wiped him with paper napkins dampened with ice, changed him into some clean sweatpants that were in the back of the car, given him a piece of Juicy Fruit to take the bad taste away.

The eye narrowed and seemed to focus in on Ethan alone for a moment.

"ONE IS LOST," said Mooseknuckle John. "ONE IS ANGRY. ONE DREADS. AND ONE IS BROKENHEARTED."

The four passengers of Skidbladnir looked at one another. It was not immediately apparent to any of them which was which.

"Giants have sharp eyes," Cinquefoil said dryly.

"And bad breath," whispered Jennifer T.

The ferisher chief clambered across from his seat and climbed right up onto Jennifer T.'s lap, without a word of excuse or pardon. Awake and active, there was yet something catlike about him. He perched on Jennifer T.'s knees, but as when a cat comes to visit your lap, he did not quite settle there. He stuck his fierce head out her window.

"Now, Mooseknuckle John," he said in his soft, clear voice. "We're bound ta urgent bidness, and awful far from home. Do us the kindness ta let us alone, just this once, won't ya, now?"

"WANT THE TOY, MORSEL," said Mooseknuckle John. He let go of Skid with one hand and with an enormous index finger flicked the taut gas envelope, as you might thump a melon to hear if it is ripe. It throbbed like a drum. "LIKE IT."

"Thing is, John, we'd be happy ta make it a present ta ya, if only we didn't need it so urgentlike."

"DON'T NEED IT NO MORE, DO YOU, MORSEL?" The giant's voice was not a growl so much as a deep sonorous ringing, as of an enormous bell. He was extremely ugly, his face at once smashed-looking and bug-eyed, but Ethan supposed that was how it was with giants.

"True," Cinquefoil said in a low voice. "Each one's uglier than t'other. And ta answer yer question, little brother," he said to Thor, catching him by surprise in mid-thought, "he knows English because he is thirty thousand years old, at least. He's had more ta do with reubens than I'm sure he cares ta recall. He knows Sumerian, Urdu, Masoretic, and San. He knows all the dead languages o' the Middling and the living ones, too. Of course he speaks my tongue, but I thought ya might want to know what I'm saying."

"I don't like the way he keeps calling you 'morsel', " Jennifer T. said. "It sounds like he's planning to eat us."

"He would never eat me," Cinquefoil said. "I wouldn't agree with him one bit. Ya saw that yella sap bleeding outta this old jar o' mine, little reuben?" He pointed to his head; the wounds had by now completely healed. Ethan nodded. "It's like poison fer 'em. They'd as soon eat stones or tree bark. No, it's *children* they like, children and sheep. If ya only read more true stories ya'd know that."

The children looked at each other, their eyes wide. They had never been troubled much by the ancient fear of being eaten. They lived in a world devoid not only of giants and ogres but of wolves, bears, and lions, too. And yet Ethan, like many children who are not otherwise vegetarian, had always felt a strange unwillingness to eat the young of animals. Lamb, veal, suckling pig – the idea of eating baby *anythings* had always repelled him. Now he understood why. It would be a kind of cannibalism. It would imply that he, little, defenseless Ethan Feld, might himself quite easily be eaten.

Cinquefoil poked his head back out the window.

"Look here, John, stop yer nonsense and send us on our way. There's considerable trouble afoot just now. Coyote is making fer Murmury Well. We believe he aims ta spoil it. Waylay us and ya might just be bringing down Ragged Rock itself. I wager that's somethin' ya'd regret sore enough."

"LOSE YOUR BET, THEN," replied the giant. "COMES RAGGED ROCK, WON'T HAVE MUCH USE FOR REGRET." He cupped his hands around Skid, tightly, leaving them in darkness. Thor cried out.

"Gah!" He was afraid, Ethan knew, of small spaces and dark corners.

The giant's voice was muffled now, but still booming. "MIGHT AS WELL HAVE ME A SNACK."

"Isn't there anything you can do?" Ethan said Cinquefoil. "Some kind of grammer or something?"

"Too big a job," Cinquefoil said. "Even fer a chief. I mebbe could confuse his thoughts a little. Mebbe fill one a his eyes with smoke too thick ta see through." But he looked doubtful.

Ethan tried to think of something, to remember what he might have read about giants in the fairy tales which it still felt odd to think of, in spite of all that had happened in the last week, as true.

"They're gamblers," he said at last. "Giants. Isn't that right?"

"Crazy big gamblers." The voice of the little chief, in the darkness, took on a certain edge. "They'd bet their own eyeballs on a snowflake's falling or not. If we only had something ta wager with, mebbe we... *John*!" he shouted, right in Ethan's ear. "Ho, *Mooseknuckle John*!" His light voice took on a ragged crow's-caw huskiness. "He can't hear us."

They all began to shout and cry out the giant's name, until their throats were raw. But there was no reply from outside the prison of his cupped fists. Ethan could feel them swinging back and forth as the giant walked, each footfall on the ground sending a deep rumbling shudder through them. The interior of the car rattled and creaked. They gave up calling. They were going to be roasted on a giant's cookfire.

"YAIIIIIYAH!"

The great shout of the giant came blasting into the car, along with a flood of light, as, on Jennifer T.'s side, he lifted the hand that gripped Skid. Jennifer T. grinned. She was holding a Swiss Army knife, its blade open and bright with blood. In the meaty pleats of the giant's palm was a tiny red speck.

"He heard *that*," she said.

"EAT THE GIRL FIRST!" roared Mooseknuckle John. "BEFORE SHE'S COOKED HALF THROUGH!"

"We was trying ta get yer attention!" Cinquefoil explained. "We was wondering if ya'd care ta take a more *sporting* interest in yer meal."

The giant stopped. They were nearly to the slope of a great mountain of boulders, an enormous cairn with a dark maw that was as high as Mooseknuckle John himself. Outside the great gash of a doorway there was a smaller mound that seemed to be made up entirely of bones. Many of the skulls looked disturbingly human, and small.

"A WAGER?" He grinned. The idea was clearly appealing to him. "BUT WHAT CAN YOU WAGER, APART FROM LIVES THAT ALREADY BELONG TO ME?"

He raised the car once again to his bone-and-blood eye and, batting the envelope out of the way, peered in, regarding Jennifer T. with greater wariness than before. He tilted the car this way and that, tumbling them into one another and making a shambles of the gear they had packed into the back of the car.

"NOTHING JOHN WANTS. LOT OF RUBBISH. DON'T SEE— AH. TO WHICH IS THE PIE PLATE?"

"Pie plate?" Thor said. "I didn't know we brought a—"

"It's mine," Ethan said. "Actually it's my father's. He's an engineer, see, and Coyote—"

"YOU CATCH, MORSEL?"

"Well, I just sort of took it up the other day. I'm not—"

"THIS IS THE GAME, THEN. JOHN THROWS A TERRIBLE, TERRIBLE FASTBALL. BREAKS DOWN THE SIDES OF GREAT FORTRESSES. BURNS HOLES IN THE HEARTS OF MIGHTY OAKS." His pink eyes gleamed and his face collapsed with the deep, ancient gigantic pleasure of boasting. "BLEW IT PAST SKOOKUM JOHN THREE TIMES IN A ROW. STRUCK HIM OUT LOOKING."

"Giants play baseball, too?" Ethan said.

"Not with any style," said Cinquefoil. "But old Skookum John was a slugger, all right, before Sees Canoes brought him down."

"Sees Canoes?" said Jennifer T.

"A great reubenish giant killer o' some years back. Indian fella. Scouted by Mr. Brown, it seems ta me."

"I've heard of him!" Jennifer T. said. "Uncle Mo talked about him one time. He was a Salishan. I think he was like my great-great-grandsomething or whatever."

"Ya might want to keep that ta yerself," Cinquefoil said.

"YOU CATCH THE MOOSEKNUCKLE JOHN FASTBALL, THREE TIMES, IN THAT SHREW'S-BUTTON MITT OF YOURN. MOOSEKNUCKLE JOHN DON'T ONLY LET YOU GO, HE GIVES YOU A LITTLE PUSH! YOU DROP IT, YOU LET IT GO PAST, HE SUCKS THE JUICES OUT THROUGH THE HOLES IN THE TOP OF YOUR HEAD."

"Uck," Jennifer T. said.

"Catch one of *your* pitches? How big is the *ball*?"

"BIG BALL!" the giant said. "NICE BIG ONE! BIG

LITTLE REUBEN, TOO! FAIR AND SQUARE! UNIVERSAL RULES!"

The giant waited, happily, for Ethan's reply. His rank breath billowed and curled around the car.

"What are Universal Rules?" Jennifer T. said.

"The rules for interworld play," Thor said. He tilted his head to one side and gave it a thump with the heel of his hand as if to reseat a loose circuit board. "How did I know that?"

Cinquefoil eyed him carefully. "That's right," he said. "When creatures o' different size engage in play on the diamond, they play at the scale o' whoever's the home team. The shape-shifting grammers are usually worked right inta the pattern o' the diamond itself."

"You mean *I'll* be a giant?" Ethan said.

"Only so long as yer standin on his turf, and yer conduct is sportsmanlike. Try ta sneak up behind him and, say, brain him with a oak tree, the grammer's undone and yer a pipsqueak all over again. And then it's snacktime fer sure."

Cinquefoil climbed into the backseat, then over into the wayback of the car. He dragged out the old leather mitt and handed it to Ethan.

"Well," he said.

"I can barely hold on to one of Jennifer T.'s," said Ethan. "Even if I'm his size, how am I going to catch a fastball from a full-grown giant?"

"Why don't ya look in yer book?" Cinquefoil said.

8

Taffy

ETHAN HAD FORGOTTEN all about *How to Catch Lightning and Smoke*. Now, as the party warmed themselves beside the giant's huge cookfire, trying to banish thoughts of how that fire might very soon be put to awful use, he searched the index for anything there might be about making up a battery with a giant.

The giant's lodge was a kind of immense igloo of rocks, a stony dome formed from huge chunks and jags of granite, puzzled together like stones in an old wall. You entered through an arched notch – right beside that pile of bones, which they had all tried not to look at too closely. Then you proceeded inward along a steep-walled corridor that wound in on itself, until you got to the centremost chamber of the spiral. Here the dome was high enough for Mooseknuckle John to enter without ducking, and wide enough for him to stretch out to his full length on the floor in his fur cap and boots. To Ethan, creeping in with his friends huddled close around him, it seemed vast, filled with echoes and shadows and hints of all kind of unpleasant odors. The floor was covered from end to end in thick furs and skins, some of which seemed to be those of bears, grey and brown, of wolves and moose and elk; others, Ethan would have sworn, were the lush, silvery-black pelts of gorillas. The only opening, here at the centre of the giant's lodge, was a wide triangular notch cut in the roof to let out the smoke from the towering bonfire over which he cooked his grisly food. Apart from the furs there was no furniture of any kind. From three stout leathern ropes worked into the joints of the walls hung an iron pot as big as a garage, a dipper as deep as a bathtub, and a spoon whose bowl was as wide as a trash-can lid. And, on one side of the room, stood an iron cage, bigger than Ethan's bedroom at home, empty but for a heap of bones and old fur blankets in one corner.

"Anything?" Jennifer T. said. She had picked up one of the furs from the floor and come to stand beside him, draping the soft, thick, rank-smelling brown mantle over their shoulders. In spite of the fire, it was not exactly warm inside the lodge. "Does Peavine have anything to say about giants?"

"It's hard to tell," Ethan said, paging with the tip of his little finger through the latter sections of the book. "The words are all so *small*."

He had, of course, neglected to pack his magnifying glass. And though he stood close to the light of the fire, it was still pretty dim. Cinquefoil knew the book well, and might have been able to provide some guidance about relevant chapters. But as soon as Moose-knuckle John had ushered them into this vast echoing room, the ferisher, exhausted and weak from his injuries and from the grammers he had worked, curled up under a bearskin and went to sleep.

"It's only a matter of minutes until that giant comes back, Captain," Thor said. The giant had gone back outside again to raid his root cellar for some turnips or whatever it was that he planned to use to garnish his little-kid stew. "I advise you to make haste."

"Noted, TW03," Ethan said, captainishly. He looked at his watch, which he had not bothered to consult since leaving the Middling behind.

"Huh," he said. "Check this out."

Thor and Jennifer T. leaned in to take a look at the marvellous bit of hardware that the genius of Mr. Feld and the sale bins of Geek World had produced.

The liquid crystal display had changed. Across the top, where it had once read SUN MON TUE WED THU FRI SAT, with a digital mark over the proper day, it now read SUN CAT TOD RAT DOG PIG and MOO (for Moonday, as Ethan would later learn). Ethan pressed FUNCTION and 1, which normally gave the month and day, and found that while the month was still given as "4," in place of the old Gregorian year it now read "1519 Mole."

"So this is a Mole year," Thor said.

"Is that bad? Cinquefoil told me that the old people always said the end of the world would come in a Mole year."

Thor scratched at his right temple for a moment, then shook his head. He shrugged.

"That sounds right," he said.

In the lower right corner of the calendar screen, Ethan saw, where there had never been anything before, there was now a numeral one, and beside it a small triangular arrow pointing down. He pressed the buttons a few times, scrolling back through the functions he knew about, but every time he returned to the calendar screen, the little number one was still there. He could not get rid of it. He wondered if the strain of leaping across worlds was overloading its circuits somehow.

"Come on," Jennifer T. said. "Stop fooling around with the watch, E."

Ethan nodded, and returned his attention to Peavine's book, squinting at the pages as he flipped through them.

"What was that?" Jennifer T. said, grabbing hold of Ethan's wrist before he could turn another page. "What was that chapter called?"

"Hey," Ethan said. "Good eye. 'Barnstorming… the Far… Territories.' Huh. It…" He moved the book back and forth, and tilted it towards the fire. He simply couldn't make out the words. "Man!"

"Perhaps these will be of some assistance, Captain," Thor said. He took off his glasses. "As you know, my photo-optic sensor array is equipped with these adapter-lenses."

Ethan held the glasses up to his eyes. Of course they were, unlike Padfoot's, only an ordinary pair of eyeglasses with no special powers whatever. Thor's pale, serious face swam in and out of focus, and Ethan saw that the lenses of his glasses were different from those of Mr. Feld's. Ethan's father was nearsighted, and when you looked through his glasses everything seemed to bend inward, shrinking the world down to a miniature replica of itself. But Thor must be farsighted; in the lenses of his spectacles everything loomed and swelled to twice its normal size.

Ethan held the glasses to the first page of the chapter Jennifer T. had found. The words swelled to a readable size as he passed the left lens across them, reading aloud for the benefit of his friends. In the years reckoned, in the Summerlands, as 1319th Adder, 1319th Hoptoad, and 1319th Otter, he learned, a team known as Peavine's Travelling Ferisher All-Stars had made what the author called "a mad tour of the Far Territories, taking on giants, kobolds, adlets, and all that vast and motley crew of eldritch characters who still revere the great and glorious Game." A good number of these games had been played against nines of giants.

"What does 'eldritch' mean?" Jennifer T. said.

"I think it means magical," Ethan said.

"*Eldritch*," said a dark, unhappy voice not very far away, "is the term used by some to designate a world where the Rule of Enchantment remains in force."

The children looked at each other. None of them had spoken. Ethan grabbed Jennifer T.'s arms and they froze, listening. They looked at Thor. He shook his head, looking young and frightened without his glasses. The glum voice spoke up again.

"Once, yours was also ranked among the eldritch worlds," it said. "But it has been some time since then."

"There's a ghost," Jennifer T. said, clinging now to Ethan in return.

"It's coming from that *cage*!" Thor said, pointing, his outstretched arm trembling in a very unandroidlike way.

Ethan slid Peavine's book back into the muff pocket of his sweatshirt and, still holding tight to Jennifer T.'s arm, crept across the giant's hall to the black iron cage. As he drew nearer he saw that what he had taken at a distance for heap of old pelts amid a scattering of bones was gazing right at him with a pair of yellow eyes. The eyes were large, intelligent, and held a sad expression. They were set into a dark face, heavy-browed, in a ruff or mane of thick, black fur.

"There's nothing special about catching a giant," the creature said. Its voice was at once so glum and so reasonable that it was hard for Ethan to feel afraid. It stood, slowly, and the heap of furs seemed to gather and twist. The fur was thick, glinting with silver – like those, scattered across the floor of the giant's lodge, which Ethan had taken for a gorilla. But this unfortunate creature in the iron cage was no gorilla. It stood fully erect, like a man, though its long powerful arms reached below its knees. It had breasts like a woman, dangling and heavy, black as coals, and only partly covered in fur. And it was at least nine feet tall. "It's just like catching a man, or a fairy, or even, I imagine, a bloodsucking white adlet, though I never played against a team from the Utternorth. You just put down the sign, and call for the pitch."

There was a strange sound just behind him, a strangled cry. Ethan turned. The sound had come from Thor Wignutt. He was gazing at the furry prisoner with a look that was somewhere between horror and delight.

"A Sasquatch," he said.

"True enough, alas," said the Sasquatch. "A She-Sasquatch, to be precise. And believe me, it's a hard, hard fate."

"Do they have a taste for Sasquatches, too?" asked Jennifer T. "Giants, I mean."

A faint smile briefly haunted the Sasquatch's bitter face. "No. Though I could dearly wish that the great stinking ill-tempered old heap would make an end to me, even if it was between the grindstones of his rotten old molars. Like you reubens, a giant will eat anything – whale dung, boiled wendigo hoof – but they're also like you humans in one curious respect: they never eat their pets."

"You're a *pet*?" Ethan said.

The Sasquatch nodded, her eyes brimming over with tears. "It's fashionable among giants to keep one of my race in the house, and feed us from the scraps and leavings of their horrid tables. Before that they used to hunt us for our pelts. I don't doubt that you're wearing a close relative of mine."

"So what do you, well, *do*?" Jennifer T. said, letting the soft black Sasquatch fur slide to the ground. "What does he do with you?"

"Yeah," Thor said. "Does he, like, take you out and walk you?"

The Sasquatch looked offended. She gave her head a vehement shake. Then she said something, too softly for them to hear.

"What?" Ethan said.

"I said, 'I sing', " the Sasquatch said. "I have a fine contralto voice."

Before they could ask her to demonstrate, however, the floor beneath their feet began to tremble and jolt, and a moment later Mooseknuckle John emerged from the mouth of the spiral corridor. He was carrying an armload of huge turnips, parsnips, carrots, and potatoes. The vegetables tumbled to the floor with a terrific rumbling and booming, like an armload of boulders. One of the potatoes rolled lumbering towards the children, and they just barely managed to scamper out of its way before it slammed against the iron cage with a horrible clang, sending the Sasquatch flying backwards, and splitting in two with a great gusty whiff of potato.

"Blubber-stinking clumsy son of a dungheap!" muttered the Sasquatch, rising shakily to her feet.

"HA HA HA!" Mooseknuckle John doubled over with laughter. "IS SHE ALL RIGHT, TAFFY? IS TAFFY NOT HURT?"

He clumped over towards the cage and bent down to look inside, an expression on his ugly face of amused but genuine concern.

"IS SHE ALL RIGHT, MY ITTLE BIT OF SASSY-QUATCHY FURRY-WURRY? IS SHE, PRETTY LITTLE TAFFY LITTLE BIGFOOT?" He stood up again, to his full height, and gazed down at Ethan, Jennifer T., and Thor. His face was serious now. "COME," he said to Ethan. "TIME FOR ME TO DRILL A MOUSEHOLE IN THAT MITT OF YOURN."

9

A Game of Catch

OUTSIDE, IN THE mellow glow and soft air of a Summerlands afternoon, they assembled on the Gigantic ball field to settle the wager between Ethan Feld and the Mooseknuckle John. The infield had been hastily raked and the outfield was patchy and weedy. It was on this very spot, the giant claimed, that Peavine's barnstorming ferishers had played a series of eighty-one games against him and his seventeen brothers (forming two squads, the Gnashers and the Thumpers, of nine giants apiece), in a great yard built from the bones of leviathans and other elder beasts, that could accommodate ten thousand stomping, whooping beastmen and wood-haints and fair folk. According to the Universal Rules – the details were all in *How to Catch Lightning and Smoke* – powerful grammers had been worked to grow the ferishers until they were of a size with the home nines. The dimensions of the field were appropriately vast. From the pitcher's mound to home plate, Ethan reckoned now, it must be about a thousand feet.

"GIANTS *WON* THAT SERIES, TOO," Mooseknuckle John said, as he trudged off to take his place. "FORTY-ONE TO FORTY. DON'T BELIEVE ALL YOU READ IN THAT BOOK OF FERISHER LIES."

Ethan looked inquiringly at Cinquefoil, who shook his head.

"It went down hard with the Johns, that loss," the ferisher said.

"Stay focused, Ethan," Jennifer T. said. "Just bear down."

"And keep your eye on the ball," Thor offered.

Jennifer T. gave Thor a look. They were both sitting on what was left of the ruined bleachers of once-mighty Eighteen Johns Field.

"What was wrong with what I said?" Thor said.

" 'Keep your eye on the ball', " said Jennifer T. She spat.

As Ethan stepped, cautiously, onto the field, he was aware of a burning sensation in his legs. It quickly spread upward, through his hips, up the side of his body, and down his shoulders to the tips of his arm. It was a muscular kind of burn such as you get when you hold your arms over your head for too long. At the same time there was a bizarre crackling, as if the bones of his skull were starring, like a windshield hit by a pebble. His stomach lurched, and his heart swelled and flopped in his chest, and he had a strange taste in his mouth of the interior parts of his face, as you do when somebody punches you in the nose. The wind rushed in his ears, and the trees all around him shrank, and the earth fell away, until Skidbladnir lay at his heels like a toy.

"Whoo-hoo!" shouted Jennifer T. her voice thin and chirpy. "Look at Big Ethan Feld!"

Ethan could feel the enormous grin on his face. He was a giant! He could have lifted up his friends and tucked them into the muff pocket of his sweatshirt!

The thought of his pocket reminded him of Peavine's

book, and he reached in, hoping it had grown with him, or else reading it was going to be like trying to prize open a stubborn pistachio. There it was, grown now to a still small, just-legible size, about as big as a king-size bed.

The giant had taken his place on the mound, and stared in, flat-footed, hands dangling at his sides, at Ethan, and Ethan saw that Mooseknuckle John still looked very, very big indeed. The shapeshifting grammer seemed to have increased Ethan's size *proportionately*. So it was going to be like catching an adult – a hard-throwing and hungry adult.

"Ready?" the giant called, his voice no longer quite so thunderous to Ethan's ears.

Ethan consulted Peavine. On page 18 there was a series of illustrations of the catcher's proper stance and glove positioning. They were tough to make out without a magnifying glass, but he remembered them well enough, and found himself assuming his position with surprising ease. As he pounded the heel of his glove, he felt a surprising surge of confidence in his ability. They had left behind, far behind, the world in which a kid who had picked up a catcher's mitt for the first time in his life two days earlier could never possibly hope to accomplish what Ethan was now trying to do. There were, for example, no hundred-foot, flame-throwing, albino giants back there in the Middling. Other rules were in force here, in this world, in the Summerlands. Perhaps being a catcher was something he would simply be able, magically, to do. Back there in the Middling, his father's softball mitt was only an old hunk of sewn hide and knotted thongs. Here, perhaps – he was aware of the warmth of his hand inside it – it was a magic glove, like that one the god Thor wore in the Viking myths, so that he could catch the smoke and lightning of his magic hammer, Mjolnir. Perhaps nothing would be required of Ethan at all, really, but to keep his eyes open and stick out his mitt and wait for the ball to find it three times in a row.

And if not? Then he and his friends would be tossed like lobsters into a giant black kettle and boiled up with onions and turnips. (Lobster was another food Ethan had never been able to bring himself to eat. He was certain that a lobster felt agonizing pain as it was tossed into a bubbling pot.) And then his father would languish in the grip of Coyote. And maybe someday the painful news would come to him, far away in some frozen corner of the Winterlands, of Ethan's final disaster on a baseball diamond. Quickly he slipped on the dark glasses for a glimpse of his father. Mr. Feld was now sitting up against the wall behind him, his head slumped forwards, tapping his foot. Singing to himself, it appeared. Of course there was no way for Ethan to hear the song, but he was certain that it must be "Kiss Him Goodbye" by Steam. The song had gotten lodged like a small stone in Mr. Feld's brain sometime around 1973 and had yet to work itself loose. Whenever he was tense, nervous, or troubled Mr. Feld could go through hundreds of choruses of

Na na na na
Na na na na
Hey hey hey
Goodbye

There was a sound like bricks tumbling in a clothes dryer; the giant was clearing his throat. Ethan whipped off the glasses, racked with the ache of seeing his father and of imagining his ragged lonely voice whispering "Goodbye" over and over in that dark, faraway room. Ethan put the dark glasses away.

Mooseknuckle John seemed to be waiting for some kind of signal to begin. Ethan, swallowing hard, pounded his right hand into his mitt, and finally, slowly, nodded. The giant nodded back. Then, tossing his great shaggy blond head, he staggered backwards, with a crazy style that reminded Ethan somehow of Albert Rideout. Furiously he cranked his windmill arms. Then there was a sizzling sound, like cold water dashed onto a hot skillet, and then Ethan's left hand seemed to explode. He could feel it taking leave of his wrist. His palm collapsed in on itself, his fingers flew off and shot out in all directions, and the old leather mitt itself caught fire and flared up in a sudden blaze that stank of burning hair. The pain shot up his arm, jagged as lightning, to his shoulder, where it forked and shot down along his rib cage, shattering each rib like an icicle, and straight up to the top of his skull, which cracked in several places and dropped in steaming pieces to the ground at his feet.

A thousand years later, lying at the bottom of a deep dark well of pain, Ethan seemed to hear the tiny voice of Jennifer T. Rideout, someone he vaguely recalled having once known, back in the days when his body still included a functioning head.

"*Way to go, Feld!*" she said inexplicably.

Ethan opened his eyes. All of his body parts seemed

somehow to have reattached themselves, and the tide of pain was subsiding. He turned the mitt and peered into the webbing. There, hissing like a fresh-fallen asteroid, lay the ball.

"I caught it," he said to himself and his friends and everyone in the Lodge of Worlds.

Cinquefoil pointed to the ball that Ethan held up to the clouds.

"See that, ya great pale pile!" he squeaked across the infield to Mooseknuckle John.

The giant ignored him; Ethan tossed the ball back, a little wide, pulling the giant off the mound.

"Just do what ya did again," Cinquefoil advised, stepping away from the plate, and Thor and Jennifer T. both chimed in with the same sentiment, as if that would be the easiest thing in the world. Only Ethan knew how close he had just come to shattering like a boy made of ice under the impact of the pitch. He didn't know if he could stand a second one, let alone a third. Though having your body explode all at once was slightly preferable, if you had to choose, to having your vital juices sucked out of your head.

A little more shakily, he settled down into the rocking, alert crouch prescribed by the great Peavine in his book. The palm of his left hand was still throbbing. Again Mooseknuckle John hesitated before going into his windup, studying Ethan across the distance that separated them as if for some information that might help him to drill a deeper, cleaner hole in his hand. Again, less steadily this time, Ethan nodded, and again Mooseknuckle John reared back, tumbling backwards on one leg as if about to fall over, then lurched forwards, landing on his front foot with a thunderous *whomp*.

This time the sound was like a basket of frozen potatoes being lowered into bubbling hot fat, and then the next instant every single molecule in Ethan's body began to vibrate furiously, as if he were a bell that had just been struck, and his poor left arm was the clapper. The molecules vibrated so swiftly that they finally vanished with a hiss of steam, and in their place, where once there had been a boy named Ethan Feld, there was only a shimmering red cloud of pure, screaming pain.

For some reason this horrible transformation seemed to please a number of disembodied entities in the immediate vicinity of the cloud of pain.

"Yes!"

Gradually the cloud condensed, the vibrations slowed, and like a tuning fork falling silent the blur of pain was stilled. Ethan opened his eyes. There in the mitt lay the second of the giant's fastballs.

"One more," Cinquefoil said. His manner was less exuberant this time. He seemed to be able to tell how close to failure Ethan had just come. "One more and it's on our way to yer father."

"I can't do it," Ethan said. "Chief, there's just no way. That giant is throwing some serious cheese."

"Ya *can* do it," Cinquefoil said. "And ya *will* do it."

"I can do it," Ethan said, and it sounded as hollow as a lie can possibly sound.

This time the pain lingered, growing deeper and angrier. His left hand seemed to be buzzing, loud enough for him to hear it. And, staring out across the green distance at the giant, Ethan knew in his heart that he would never, not in a million years, be able to catch another of Mooseknuckle John's fastballs. What could he do? He fished *How to Catch Lightning and Smoke* out of his sweatshirt pocket and desperately paged through it, hoping his eye would light on some secret technique for catching the pitches of giants. But of course Peavine hads never caught a *giant's* pitches, only those of his own ferisher teammates, swollen by magic, like himself, to six hundred times normal size. How wrong Sasquatch had been – catching a giant *was* different from catching ordinary itches. What had she said? *You must put down the sign and call for the pitch.* That was laughable. How could he think – but this was odd. Just as he recalled the advice of Taffy the Sasquatch, his scrabbling fingers happened to turn to a page in *How to Catch Lightning and Smoke* that diagrammed the various finger-signs that a catcher could use to call for a particular pitch from his pitcher.

Ethan squinted, and blinked, and squinted some more.

"Time out!" he cried. The giant nodded.

Ethans stepped back from the plate and studied the diagram. There was one finger for the fastball, two for the breaking ball, and three for the change-up, a pitch that looked just like a fastball coming out of the pitcher's hand, but which travelled far more slowly, fooling the batter into swinging at it too soon.

"Remember," wrote Peavine,

> the pitch is the pigment, the pitching arm the brush, and the pitcher himself is the mind and hand of the artist,

directing the movements of paintbrush and colour; but you, the catcher, are the artist's eye that clearly sees what must be painted. You are in charge of the pitching game; you call for the pitch. Do not be swayed by the passions of your battery-mate, in particular if he is a fireballer; above all, *don't let that rascal shake you off.*

"Thanks, Peavine," Ethan said.

"What are you going to do?" Jennifer T. called up to him.

"I'm going to call for the change-up," Ethan said.

He took his position once more, squatting on his haunches. Mooseknuckle John climbed up onto the hill again and looked in at Ethan, as he had twice before without Ethan's understanding why. This time, however, instead of merely nodding, Ethan held out the first three fingers of his right hand, pointed them at the ground, and waggled them back and forth.

Mooseknuckle John stood perfectly still. His mouth hung open as if he couldn't believe what he was seeing. Then he smiled a sour smile and gave his great head a firm shake. He started to rear back. Ethan jammed his fingers downward, stabbing again and again at the air with them. The giant stopped again, and again shook off the sign. He wanted to throw a fastball; the potatoes and the parsnips were waiting. Ethan held his breath, and flexed his hand a few times, and then put down the sign for the change-up one more time.

"Don't you shake me off," he called out to Mooseknuckle John, and his voice sounded surprisingly large and authoritative. "What are you, a rookie?"

The giant started to say something. Then he closed his mouth and reared back one last time. His arm swung out from his side and his hand turned over and the ball came tumbling and screaming across the sky towards Ethan's mitt. It landed with a sharp meaty crack, and Ethan clapped his bare hand around it; Mooseknuckle John had thrown the change-up.

"It worked," Ethan said, once he had stepped off the field again and the grammer had drained him like sand from the top of an hourglass, down to his usual size. "He didn't shake me off."

"He couldn't," said Cinquefoil. He took Peavine's book, opened to the page on pitch calling, and pointed with a finger at the bottom of the page.

There was a footnote to the passage that Ethan had been reading. It said:

> **N.B. In the Middling these ancient Signs have not the eldritch power that they once possessed.*

"It's powerful stuff," he said. "Putting down the Signs."

THE TANTRUMS OF giants, are, of course, quite literally the stuff of legend. How many of the world's volcanoes, maelstroms, and boiling geysers, how many of its hurricane winds and earthquakes, have been attributed to the ill-tempered fumings and poor sportsmanship of giants! In the days before the giant-killers flourished, when the waycrosses of the Middling were thick with *Homo giganticus*, terrible and sad were the lengths to which humans would go to appease the wrath of a massive, hungry neighbour in the hills. Their fattest calves, their juiciest hogs, even, as you must know, their own sons and daughters, were offered up to still the eruptions and blusterings of a giant in the grip of a rage. When Mooseknuckle John realised that some scrap of a little reuben he-puppy had somehow managed not only to hold on to a pair of his nastiest fastballs, but then, at the last moment, to work the powerful magic of the Signs on him, obliging him to bring to the plate only a skiddering slow change-up, he was, to say the least, exceedingly irritated.

First he stood, with a foot on either side of the mound, knees bent, arms flung out to either side of him, fists raised to the sky. He threw back his head, opened his throat, and roared. It was not the roar of a lion or a bear, but a horribly human-sounding roar, at once low and screeching. It was so loud that it made the air over his head tremble in a high, shivering blue column, and shook the needles from the trees, and opened several long jagged cracks in the stone walls of his lodge. The wind from his lungs set Skid's envelope trembling and shuddering like a sail. Then, as the children and the ferisher threw themselves to the frozen ground and covered their ears, the giant left off roaring and began to leap and caper about the field, cursing and stomping, kicking up great clots of dust and turf. In the process he injured several toes, which only made him angrier. At last he flung himself headlong across the outfield on his belly, and began like an enormous toddler to kick and beat with his fists. The ground shook as if it were about to split open. The children were thrown against one another; a portion of the lodge fell in with a sound like a crate full of bottles rolling down iron stairs.

He sputtered and raged; he snorted and choked on his own saliva. He threatened punishments and uttered oaths so heinous and foul that even to summarize them here in the mildest of terms would curl the very pages of the book you are holding and make your hands and fingertips hum as if they were swarming with bees. But there was nothing that Mooseknuckle John could say, no curse he could utter or horrible punishment impose, because he and Ethan had struck a bargain, and in the two remaining eldritch worlds, as here in the Middling once upon a time, the stuff of a sworn bargain is a metal less yielding than iron. He was bound, in the end, to send the party on its way, and to give them, what was more, a helpful shove in the right direction.

And in the end, as is so often the case with tantrums, this one ended up costing the giant even more than he had originally bargained to lose. For while Ethan and Thor rode out the ranting winds and trembling earth of the gigantic fit huddled, terrified, under the behemoth-bone planks of the bleachers, Jennifer T. struck out across the grass towards the giant's lodge. She was intent on freeing herself from a hard ball of pity that had lodged in her chest and would not go away.

She ran along the spiral corridor, across the carpeting made from the hides of five hundred poor, peeled animals, and over to the big black iron cage. The Sasquatch lay asleep, a great miserable heap in a corner of the cage. She was snoring, and loudly, but the harrumphing rumble of her lungs was nearly drowned out by the thunder of the roared oaths that was coming from outside. Every so often the entire structure of the giant's lodge would shake with a sound like an enormous drawer of spoons. The whole thing was probably going to come crashing down on their heads any second.

"Yo," Jennifer T. said, whispering at first, though she doubted the giant could hear her, or anything, at that moment. "Yo, Mrs. Sasquatch. Taffy." There was no reply. She raised her voice. "Hey, *Bigfoot*!"

Once again the heap of ragged skins seemed to assemble itself with startling rapidity, and there before her, glowering down with great staring yellow-orange eyes like two glowing chunks of amber, stood the lanky, powerful creature which, only yesterday, Jennifer T. would have been inclined to refer to as *a giant*. Taffy did not look pleased.

"Look at my feet," she said, in a low, steady, angry voice. "Do they look inordinately large to you?"

They were like a human's feet, more or less, big toe, pinky toe, and three in between, but they were covered all over with thick black fur, and the big toe, come to think of it, looked a lot more like the thumb of a *hand*. And they were nearly half again as long as a big man's foot, and half again as wide. If you tried to put shoes on them, Jennifer T. thought, you would need at least a size twenty-nine or thirty. She did not know how to answer. She had no desire to injure the Sasquatch's feelings, but the feet really did look awfully big.

"*Relative to the rest of me*, of course," the Sasquatch said. "I'm nine feet tall. Of course they're bigger than *yours*."

"I guess not," Jennifer T. said. "Actually, when you look at it that way, they're really almost kind of dainty."

The Sasquatch looked more pleased than she had until now, but when Jennifer T. told her that Mooseknuckle John had lost his wager, and explained that she was taking advantage of the giant's being a sore loser to sneak in and spring Taffy, the creature's smile faded.

"I have nowhere to go," she said, with an air of deep bitterness.

"Then come with us," Jennifer T. said. "We're going across the Far Territories."

The Sasquatch's dark face softened in its rich soft mantle of fur.

"The Far Territories," she said, her voice thick. "I haven't seen the Great Woods since the day Suckmarrow John and his trapping party snared me."

"Then come!" The irritating thought crossed Jennifer T.'s mind that there might not be room in a Saab station wagon for a nine-foot Sasquatch, but she dismissed it. "And fast. We may have to make a run for it if that guy settles down."

The Sasquatch had begun to pace eagerly back and forth across her cage but now she stopped and her smile faded once more. She pointed to the immense lock that was bolted to the door of her cage. The keyhole was nearly as high as Jennifer T. herself, and as wide. Even if Jennifer T. had somehow managed to obtain the key, it was plain to see that she would not have been able to wield it. And while a human girl might have been able to slip through, the keyhole was nowhere near large enough to allow a Sasquatch to pass. Jennifer T. glanced at the hinges of the door, at the iron rivets that held the bars to the frame.

"I've been in this thing for two hundred years," the Sasquatch said. "I've studied those hinges and rivets as if they were holy scripture, and raged against and fought with them as if they were robbing me of the dearest thing to me in all the world. Which, of course, they are. It can't be done, little human. Get yourself back to your friends out there, and begone."

And so saying she sank back into a wretched ragged pile on the ground.

Jennifer T. looked around for something she or the Sasquatch might use to break the cage. There were plenty of old tibias and shankbones, but Jennifer T. felt pretty certain that they would just snap in two if you tried them against the thick black bars. There were the burning embers and logs of the cookfire, but she knew that an ordinary fire, even a giant's fire, would never be hot enough to melt iron – otherwise it would melt the big iron stewpot, too. Feeling the hope ebbing from her heart with every inch lower to the ground that Taffy sank, she zipped open her backpack, and saw the *Wa-He-Ta Brave's Official Tribe Handbook* lying there. Maybe there was something in it about fires, something herb or mineral you could add to them to make them burn hotter?

She flipped through the old musty pages, and saw that the point of being a Wa-He-Ta brave seemed to be to collect something called Feathers – maybe they were real feathers – one of which you earned whenever you showed that you had mastered some aspect of True Indian Lore. There were Feathers for Tracking, for Canoe Building, for Fire Making and Spear Fashioning, for Fishing and

Swimming and Climbing Trees and Rocks. There were Feathers to be won in Dancing, Singing, Telling the Truth, and even, somewhat to her astonishment, in Telling Good Lies. And you could – it was right on page 621 – earn a Feather in the Most Ancient Lore of the Knot. It was here, in the chapter on Knots, at the very back, in the final three paragraphs, that she encountered a small essay, almost an afterthought, on the picking of locks. It was illustrated with a series of five drawings that showed what was going on inside of what was called a "warded lock". This appeared to be exactly the type of old-fashioned lock that she was now confronted with. The kind that you opened with one of those clunky old "skeleton keys". Inside the lock there was a kind of metal tube; when you twisted it, it raised the latch. This tube was prevented from twisting, however, by a series of three pins, resting on springs. The pins were set to three different heights. When you stuck in the key, three different bumps on the key's blade pressed the pins down so that they all sat level with one another, out of the way of the tube. That allowed the tube to turn.

Jennifer T. put down the book and pulled herself up to the keyhole. She stuck her head inside, but it was too dark to see. She felt along the narrow passage with one hand. She could feel a pin – it was more like a rod, thick and cold. She pressed down on it and, with an unwilling creak of its iron spring, it gave. She crept along this strange passage until she encountered the second pin, and then the third. A moment later her head poked through into the cage itself, followed by her shoulders. Taffy was staring at her, looking very surprised.

"What are you trying to do?" she said.

"Twist my shoulders," said Jennifer T. She was pressing down, as hard as she could, on the three pins, using her ankles, her knees, and the muscles of her upper arms. The resistance of the springs was stiff and the tips of the rods jabbed her skin.

"What?" Freedom, when at last it comes, rarely resembles the picture the prisoner has longingly painted of it. Taffy's great bearded jaw hung slack, and she blinked.

"I'm being a *key*, Bigfoot! Grab my shoulders and turn me!"

Taffy stood up and shook off two hundred years of servitude. She had watched often enough as Mooseknuckle John operated the lock with the enormous iron key. She knew that Jennifer T. must be twisted – clockwise, from Taffy's point of view – in order to lift the latch of the cage. She took hold of the girl by the shoulders, and twisted.

"Owww!"

Taffy let go of her at once.

"No, it's OK!" Jennifer T. said. "Just do it. Hurry!"

The big furry hands, long-thumbed and steady, grasped the girl's shoulders again and cranked her in a clockwise direction. Jennifer T. pressed with all her might against the pins, until she felt that they were about to pierce her skin. Slowly, almost irritably, the key shaft began to groan and give; the latch lifted and, with a rusty creaking like the wheels of a train, the heavy iron door swung open. Jennifer T., of course, swung with it. Her head was now pointed towards the centre of the great hall – she herself lay on her back, face up, and she missed the moment when the Sasquatch stepped out of her cage a free beast.

A great rumble shook the lodge, and the walls rang like a carillon. Shards and chunks of rock fell and shattered against the hard ground that underlay the furs.

"He's coming!" Jennifer T. said. "Get me out of here."

Taffy swung the door shut again and this time gripped Jennifer T. by the feet. Now that she was on the other side, she needed to turn the girl clockwise once more. The key shaft gave more easily in this direction, and Taffy soon was able to set the latch and tug the girl free. She set the girl on her feet and then surprised her by catching her up into her soft, hard, furry arms and squeezing every atom of oxygen from Jennifer T.'s lungs. Taffy had a smell that was rank but not unpleasant, the way Gran Billy Ann's dogs smelled after they had gone swimming in the Sound.

"Thank you!" Taffy cried. "Oh, thank you, thank you!"

A sparkling dark wave crested and broke at the centre of Jennifer T.'s brain. It was funny, considering that you spent every second of your entire life doing it, that you could forget how important breathing actually was. "Please… put… me…"

SHE WOKE UP in the backseat of the Felds' Saab wagon, jostling and pitching and tossing. There was a sound all around her like pennies being shaken from a bank as the contents of the car rattled and tumbled. Her head struck something hard that turned out to be the head of Thor Wignutt.

"Ensign Rideout has regained consciousness, Captain," Thor Wignutt said.

Ethan turned around to look at her. He was sitting in the driver's seat, with Cinquefoil riding shotgun. The ferisher was sitting very still, with his eyes closed.

"Hey, Jennifer T.," Ethan said. "Hold on tight. John's about to lob us across."

Sure enough, the windows of the car were filled, on the right side, with a view of nothing but the great pale fingers of Mooseknuckle John; on the left side curved his enormous thumb with its long black nail. He was holding Skidbladnir by her underside, pinched between his fingers, like a boy about to launch a paper plane.

"Where's—" She sat up, panicked.

"Shh," Ethan said. He pointed towards the back of the car. Jennifer T. turned around and saw a smudge of black fur at the top of the rear window of the car's hatch. It looked very much like a foot. Now she noticed another bit of fur visible at the top of her window, and one at Thor's that matched. Ethan pointed to Cinquefoil, whose forehead was beaded once more with glinting drops of pale golden sweat. All at once she understood: Taffy was clinging to the roof of the car, probably grasping the stay cables that held the envelope in place. And Cinquefoil – pale, damp, all but unconscious himself – was working desperately to maintain the grammer that was keeping Mooseknuckle John from noticing.

"READY, MORSELS?" The giant's voice rocked the car. It held a note of malicious pleasure, like the voice of a bully just before he "helps" you into the swimming pool – with all of your clothes still on.

They all gripped their thick Swedish safety belts and held on.

"SMELL SOMETHING," the giant said. "SMELL TAFFY!"

He snuffled and sniffed and muttered to himself for a moment. A low moan escaped the ferisher's lips. But the grammer held. As Mooseknuckle John raised his arm they were driven deep into their seats. The cables shivered and sang. Then the wind was in them, and they thrummed like the strings of an enormous guitar, and Jennifer T. was thrown backwards with all the force of a giant's mighty arm. The car squeaked and shuddered, and the wind whistled over the car. Jennifer T. turned, and saw the giant disappearing rapidly behind them, rubbing absently at his belly, very sorry indeed to see his meal go sailing off into the blue.

"WELL, REUBENS," CINQUEFOIL said, after they had been bubbling along over the endless green carpet of the Great Woods for half an hour. Their route, Cinquefoil hoped, would take them clear over the Raucous Mountains, over the Big River to Applelawn, and thence across Diamond Green to the well called Murmury. "That were yer first tangling-up with the greater grammer."

"What's that?" Ethan said.

"It's what's supposed to keep you reubens *out* of the Summerlands," Taffy said, from the roof of the car.

"Not exac'ly," Cinquefoil said. "It won't never keep ya out if yer so hot ta get in as all that. It'll let ya in, you bet. But it won't never let ya get far. Not without making sure that ya gotten yerself all tangled up in grammer."

"What happens to you then?" Ethan said, looking

himself up and down as if for any lingering traces of grammer that might be clinging to his clothing.

"*Stories* happen," the ferisher said. "Misadventures. Exploits. Stumble through at a spot where the greater grammer is laid on all nice and thick, might take ya a hunnert years ta get two miles. Send a reubenish army through – just try! – and they get tangled up in all kinds of sagas and folderol. We're well past it. Fer we'd best get on our way. I fear our time may be very short."

Ethan checked his watch again and found that the numeral 1 at the bottom right corner of the calendar page was now a 2, and that the arrow beside it was pointing *up*.

"I wish I knew what this meant," he said.

"What?" said Jennifer T.

"This little thing here, with the two and the arrow. When we were in the giant's house, I looked at it and it was a one, and the arrow was pointing down."

Jennifer T. pulled his wrist towards her.

"Innings," she said. "Top of the second."

"Top of the second inning?" Ethan said. "The second inning of *what*?"

But even before the question was out of his mouth, he already knew the answer. He could hear Mo Rideout's gravel-bottomed voice echoing in his memory: "*Ragged Rock is a day, the last day. The last day of the last year. The last out in the bottom of the ninth.*"

"Top of the second," he said. "Seven and a half innings left to go."

Just then the guy wires from which they dangled began to thrum, in unison, deep and low. Dark clouds were piling up in the sky all around them, out of the proverbial clear blue sky.

"Mmmmm," said Taffy the Sasquatch, inhaling deeply the free air of the Summerlands for the tenth time since leaving the giant behind. "Storm coming."

"Does this mean that *nothing* is going to happen to us?" Ethan said. "No stories, I mean? Because I kind of think we actually need something to happen, or we'll never find my dad. Finding my dad, and saving the Tree – it's like a story, only it's *true*."

"All stories are true," Cinquefoil said.

"You sound like old Albert," said Jennifer T. "Anyway, Eth, I wouldn't worry too much about nothing happening."

She pointed, and the wind rose to a whuffling gust that made the silvery envelope shudder and hum nervously to itself, and then they were drowned in the shadow of an enormous pair of wings.

10

Mr. Feld in the Winterlands

FINER MINDS THAN my own have forever dulled their edges trying to explain the workings of clocks and calendars among the worlds. A human traveller to the Winterlands may pass a single month – the month of Splike, say, with its forty-three days of stabbing black hail – amid the horrors of the Blue Toeholds, only to find on his return to the Middling that even his great-grandchildren have been dead for fifty years or more. Another may spend her entire life adventuring in the Summerlands and then return, aged and bent, to find, still waiting for her, the supper and husband and children that she left only a few minutes before. So I can't really explain how it happened, but nevertheless it is true that *at the very moment* when Skidbladnir appeared in the skies over the Far Territories of the Summerlands, a motley caravan was approaching the crossroads known as Betty's Bonepit, in the shadowless region of the Winterlands known as the Iceburns.

When Ethan tried, much later, to reconstruct the course of his father's strange and painful journey across the Winterlands in the clutches of Coyote, he came to the conclusion that there were at least six, and possibly thirty-seven, more direct routes the Rade might have taken from

Clam Island to the heart of giantland. There was no reason for Coyote's party even to *be* in the Iceburns – it was totally out of their way. But the Rade rarely travels in a straight line, or takes the most direct route to any destination. In fact, if you consult the old myths and legends, you will see that it has always been extremely rare for Coyote actually to have a destination in mind when he moves among the worlds. Coyote, as the tales tell us – he just sort of goes along. His travelling companions, the vast, shrieking, tumbling, lying, skulking, dancing, shambling crimson-and-black-clad Rade of skrikers, greylings, hobs, goblins, lubbers, fire sprites, and beastmen of every imaginable breed and configuration, including weretrout and wereflies, known as the Rade, almost never knew where they would be sleeping the day after tomorrow.

They did not even always know for sure, as Robin Padfoot tried to explain to Mr. Bruce Feld, if Coyote was even among them as they rambled along. Which was why there was just no way he could take Mr. Feld to see Coyote, or convey Mr. Feld's repeated demand to be released immediately.

"He ain't— heh-heh— he just ain't around right now," said Robin Padfoot. "And even if he – heh-heh – *was* around, no way could I take *you* to *him*. Folks have to wait for Coyote to come to them."

Mr. Feld nodded. He was feeling very low. For the last twenty-three hours and nine minutes he had been lying, blindfolded and with his hands tied behind his back, on a piece of musty foam rubber. For a blanket, he had the skin of something that smelled like a goat and did little to keep off the stunning cold. He knew exactly how long he had been lying there shivering because every ten minutes he checked his watch. For most people, being blindfolded would have made it hard to check the time, but not for Mr. Feld. He had constructed *his* wristwatch, too, and, like Ethan's, if you held down the FUNCTION key and pressed 2*1 it would literally tell you the time. For reasons that Mr. Feld himself could not quite understand, the watch spoke with a crisp little British accent. And while it didn't do him much good to check the time every ten minutes, there was something reassuring to Mr. Feld about the watch's unflappable butlerish tone.

His rude bed was rendered still more uncomfortable by the fact that the room in which he lay did not stay still like a normal room, but pitched, shuddered, and creaked. From time to time it was gripped by a horrific metallic scrape that stood his hair on end and rattled the fillings in his teeth. But the worst of it was that he had absolutely no idea of where he was, or why he had been kidnapped, or what it was that his captors wanted from him. Every time that Padfoot came in with drink (which he said was melted snow) and food (which he claimed was sliced caribou ham) for Mr. Feld, Mr. Feld questioned him. He questioned Padfoot angrily, and he questioned him pleadingly, and he questioned him in a tone of resignation. He reminded Padfoot that he had a son, young and motherless, who could not be left alone to fend for himself. He tried to trick Padfoot into making a slip or revealing some little corner of his true intentions. But Padfoot, snickering his withered little husk of a laugh, just kept on repeating the same set of outrageous lies:

1. Mr. Feld was being held in the cargo hold of a "steam-driven freight sledge."
2. The sledge was part of a large armada of snow vehicles and dogsleds embarked on a mission of conquest.
3. The vehicles and other machines were powered by the electricity of a thousand thunderstorms, "a herd of thunder buffalo", travelling along in the wake of the armada.
4. The object of the mission was to capture a city, called Outlandishton, from some "shaggurts" or "frost giants".
5. In a lonely patch of green at the outskirts of this city of Outlandishton there was a well, called Murmury. Its waters fed "a infinite big fat tree" from which the universe as he knew it dangled like a plum.
6. The leader of this army, a person who called himself Coyote, planned to poison the waters of Murmury and bring down this cosmic tree, for purposes that not even Padfoot himself, as he admitted, quite understood.
7. With 6 accomplished, all existence, life as we know it, would come crashing to an end.

"Please," Mr. Feld said, "I'm begging you. I don't know who you are or why you're doing this to me. If I've done something to hurt or offend you, Mr. Padfoot, then I'm very, truly sorry, and I hope you'll give me the opportunity to make it up to you."

"You're a big fat sceptic, Mr. Feld, heh-heh, it's a sad fact," Padfoot said, sounding exasperated. His voice was rougher, somehow, than it had been back at the ball field that day, his grammar poorer than Mr. Feld remembered it. But there was no mistaking the dusty little laugh, like somebody crumbling a dead leaf in his hand. "What's it gonna take to get you to believe all this, heh-heh, guaranteed one hundred per cent truth I'm handin' you?"

"Well, what you're telling me is pretty far-fetched, Mr. Padfoot," Mr. Feld said, flexing his hands at the wrist. He had long since given up trying to wriggle out of his bonds, but he had learned that if he didn't keep things moving down there his fingers would soon grow too numb to feel. "I guess I would have to see it with my own eyes, for starters. But even then I'm not sure I would believe you."

"Oh, I doubt that," Padfoot said. Mr. Feld could hear him come scraping across the floor of the room. It sounded like a leather sole against something gritty and hard. "I ain't never yet run into the reuben that was able to deny the witness of his own meat body."

"I'm an engineer. I do it all the time. Take centrifugal force—"

There was a sharp jerk at the back of Mr. Feld's head, and then his eyes swam with bands of golden light and blotches of dark shadow. Something loomed over him, gathering itself around what looked very much, as Mr. Feld's eyes adjusted to the dim light, like a great grin filled with crooked, pointed teeth. A grey smile, in the middle of a pug-nosed face, fur-jowled, the red-rimmed eyes weak and blinking but alight with a hungry expression. Mr. Feld cried out, and scrambled up from the mat onto his haunches, hands raised to protect himself. The thing blinking down at him was at once hulking and small, not much bigger than a boy of eleven or twelve, but thick across the chest and with a great sinewy neck like a horse's. Its arms were muscular and long, crooked at the elbows and dangling to its knees, and it was thatched over all of its body with a luxurious growth of pale blond fur. It wore no clothing but a pair of leather boots, high and reddish-brown, and a small purse on a leather belt around its waist. There was no visible trace of the ponytailed investor in alternative and emerging dirigible technologies who had approached him at the ball field on Clam Island.

"Well?" the creature said. "Feast your eyes on the handsome mug of pale Robin Padfoot." He licked the palm of one crooked hand with his broad tongue and smoothed a wayward tuft of fur at the back of his head. "What do you say?"

"I— I—" As unlikely as it seemed that this could possibly be the same Rob Padfoot, the alternatives were so much more unlikely – literally *unthinkable* by Mr. Feld's cautious mind – that he felt a certain pressure to concede the point. "Hmm."

"Am I real, Mr. Feld?" Once more they were joined, in the dim cell, by the grey pointed grin.

"Show me the machines," Mr. Feld said. "These steam sledges you were telling me about. The thunder buffalo. Then I'll know."

This suggestion seemed to make Padfoot uneasy. Aha, thought Mr. Feld. It is all a hoax of some kind. There were no steam sledges, no dangling plum of the universe.

"I dunno," Padfoot said. "Much as I'd like to mop the last nasty spatter of reuben thinkin' from your pointy reuben skull… Nobody said nothin', heh-heh, about lettin' you—*What*—?"

Mr. Feld had sat up, and was leaning in very close to Padfoot, peering at the thick, matted chest hair through the lenses of his eyeglasses. Now he twisted his body to bring his pinioned hands around, grabbed hold of a fistful of fur, and yanked, hard.

"*Yeowch!*" Padfoot slapped with the back of a paw at Mr. Feld's hands. "What are you doin', you hairless son of a bald monkey?"

"Really," Mr. Feld said, unable to conceal his admiration. "The costume is remarkably plausible."

"That does it," snapped Padfoot. He grabbed Mr. Feld by the back of his collar and dragged him to his feet, dangling him by means of one powerful brutish arm, so that Mr. Feld's toes barely grazed the floor. "Mr. Bruce Feld, prepare to lose yourself the remainder of your marbles."

Still holding Mr. Feld at arm's length, like a man carrying a baby who needed very badly to be changed, Padfoot stole out of the room. It was an iron room, Mr. Feld noticed now, floor, ceiling and walls, and the door they passed through was a kind of iron portal, oval in shape. They began to move along a low, narrow passageway formed, like everything else, of sheets of gun-grey iron held together with fat grey rivets. It was like the interior of a Navy submarine in some old World War II movie. Padfoot was not especially careful of Mr. Feld's head and Ethan's father received a number of painful bumps as they went along. The air was close in the corridor, and had a burnt smell of spent matches. But as they climbed a steep spiral of iron stairs – Mr. Feld's poor head smacked the underside of every step as they went up – it seemed to grow at once thinner and fresher, and brutally cold. They emerged at the top of the steps in a low round chamber of iron and rivets. The walls were a bristling mass of gauges, levers, leather-clad handles, and indicators whose functions were not clear to Mr. Feld but which he would very much have liked to examine. Around, among, and in and out of the brass-and-steel tangle, teemed some greyish animals that Mr. Feld at first took for large rodents, some kind of strange nutria or opossum. He just had time to form a disturbing impression that these busy little rodents were talking to each other in a jabbering version of English – that their movements seemed to have a purpose, that they seemed to be going about their business with an unmistakable air of devotion to the work – when Padfoot returned him, with a jolt, to his feet. The next moment Mr. Feld was enveloped in a sudden darkness that was soft and heavy and stank like a goat.

"There, best put that on," Padfoot said. "It's, heh-heh, wicked cold up top."

There was something about that laugh that made it sound like Padfoot was still pulling Mr. Feld's leg. It was a vast robe of rank brown fur, hooded, belted at the waist, trailing to the iron surface of the floor. It had been slashed up the back almost to the waistband, and there were straps to bind the long flaps around each leg, making a pair of furry chaps. Mr. Feld watched as Padfoot tied his own robe.

"Well?" Padfoot said, seeing that Mr. Feld was not getting dressed.

"My hands," said Mr. Feld.

And so Padfoot, fingers nimbly dancing amid the difficult knots, untied Mr. Feld's hands and helped him into his foul-smelling robe. There were thick fur gloves to go with it.

"What is this stuff?" Mr. Feld said, wrinkling his nose as he held one glove up to his face.

"Mastodon, natcherly," said Padfoot, as if this were an idiotic question.

Then, in spite of everything – in spite, above all, of his absolute refusal to believe that any of this was really happening to him – Mr. Feld felt something wriggling inside him, fizzing like a plume of bubbles in a glass of beer. It was a feeling that, as an engineer with a strong background in physics, he knew very well. In another moment, a window that opened onto the ceaseless mechanism of the universe was going to be thrown open, and he, Bruce Feld of Philadelphia, was going to get a chance to peek through it.

"Come on, then, reuben," Padfoot said. "Monkey on up that ladder before you get my fur-lined hiney in trouble with the Boss."

The ladder in question was a column of narrow rungs, clamped at its bottom to the floor and reaching up towards a small hatch at the centre of the circular roof. It was not easy to scale in the cumbersome robes, and Mr. Feld had no idea how it was supposed to open. But when at last he reached the top of the ladder there was a metallic groan, a soft hiss, and the hatch spun open like the aperture of a camera. He cried out, and shrank back as a giant wall of cold and sunlight fell on top of him. But something was pressing him, shoving, really, from behind – it was Padfoot, of course – and in the next moment he was tumbling forwards out of the hatch, into the dazzling cold. From all around him came a deafening iron grumble, under or over which he could just hear what sounded like the yipping and yapping of dogs. And every so often there would be the tooth-shattering iron scrape that had so tormented his hours in the cell.

"Help," he said. "Can't— I can't see—"

"Here," Padfoot growled. "Slap these on. I used to have me some good ones but I lost them back on that mouldy old island of yours."

Mr. Feld felt around until his gloved fingers encountered something at once flexible and hard that turned out to be a pair of heavy goggles. They were constructed of canvas and hide. The lenses, when Mr. Feld got them down over his eyes, cut down considerably on the painful glare, though they gave a pronounced yellowish tinge to everything. He saw that he was sprawled on a kind of crow's nest or observation platform, with Padfoot beside him. Padfoot was standing up, clutching with his gloved paws a low brass rail that enclosed the platform. Mr. Feld grabbed hold of the rail and slowly pulled himself up. It was a good thing there was a railing, as he quickly realised, because they were moving across bumpy ground at high speed, and the footing was unsteady. As they rumbled along the ground, Mr. Feld noticed that it was gleaming, with a light that was yellowy through the lenses of his goggles, but hard and bright as the glint on a china cup.

"It looks like ice," he observed. Even as the remark left his mouth it sounded sort of embarrassingly obvious.

"Of course it's ice. These is the *Ice* burns we're scooting across, down deep into the Winterlands. What else would it be?"

And so the last of Mr. Feld's doubts was ploughed through and swept aside. He could not deny the vehicle in which he was riding – a remarkable machine, part snowmobile, part Sherman tank, painted black. He could not deny the deep piston *chunk-kachunk* of the machine's engines, nor the collective drumming rumble of the dozens and dozens of other steam sledges all around them, sliding and scraping over the hard shiny bones of the ice. There was no getting around the untold numbers of dogsleds lurching and streaking amid the steam sledges, driven by little creatures wrapped in fur and pulled by what had to be – what could only be – straining, yelping teams of *werewolves*. They loped along on their strong hind legs while by means of heavy tow-straps with their great furred paws they dragged the sleds behind them. And there was nothing at all that the cool, sensible part of Mr. Feld's mind could do about the great sparking thunder clouds, roiling and steaming and boiling with red lightning. They trailed in a ten-mile thundering train, a herd of thunderheads blackening the sky.

"Ah," Mr. Feld said. He could not seem to think of anything else to add, and so he just said, "Ah," again.

"When Coyote wants to see you, heh-heh," Padfoot said. "Then Coyote will come to *you*."

Just then, as if Padfoot's words had been the cue, the drumbeat of their steam sledge's engines abated somewhat, and they began to slow. All the sledges around them slowed, as well, and the werewolves dropped their towlines. The sled drivers climbed down from the sleds. They threw back their fur hoods, revealing pinched and leering faces furnished with long black beards.

"Mushgoblins," Padfoot said. "The wolfboys don't listen to nobody else."

The mushgoblins tore open heavy sacks and, grinning, spilled their startling contents onto the ice. Big frozen chunks of blood-red meat went skittering in all directions. A frenzied yipping went up from the werewolves, horribly reminiscent of human laughter, and then they fell on the meat, while the mushgoblins cracked their long black whips and sang a tuneless tune. The meat disappeared in under a minute. The werewolves began to roll around on the ice, shoving, playing leapfrog and biting at each other's throats with savage glee. Somebody broke out an ancient football and they got up a great bruising scrimmage, tearing across the ice.

Overhead, the thundering black buffalo of storm caught up to them, and the shadow of the great herd fell upon a wide stretch of ice. Wherever it fell, the ice began to creep and writhe like something that was alive. After a moment Mr. Feld realised that it was not the ice moving at all, but tiny creatures, a million tiny white mice.

This sight really cracked up Robin Padfoot. "They think it's night-time! Poor little ice mice of the Iceburns! They've never seen a *shadow* before!"

The werewolves broke off their game of football and fell in among the mice, scooping up big pawfuls of them, tossing them back like salted nuts.

A thought – nothing too fancy – that been struggling to make its way out of Mr. Feld's brain finally arrived, somewhat the worse for wear, at his mouth.

"*Where are we?*" he said.

"We're at a crossroads. A big one. It's called Betty's Bonepit. This looks good for you, heh-heh! Mr. C. loves crossroads, you know, rube. And this is one of his, heh, absolute favourites!" Padfoot seemed quite excited at the prospect of seeing his boss again.

Mr. Feld blinked his eyes, squinting through the yellow stain of his lenses. He hadn't realised before that they were actually travelling a road. It was a gigantic road, wide enough for an entire town of humans to march abreast. In the sunshine it sparkled like a road of diamonds. In the shadow of the thunder herd it glowed like a pearl. Just ahead, where the lead sledges had stopped, it ran into six other roads, some as wide, some narrower, forming a crooked, misshapen star of seven rays. Like all crossroads in the Winterlands this was a desolate spot; treeless and unmarked; a place where mortal adventurers came to grief. At the very centre of the ragged star lay a hole, roughly circular, and filled, as Mr. Feld could not help but see from atop the steam sledge, with bones. Bones of every description, wind bitten and grey. Skulls, too – antlers, jagged nasal cavities, wicked curving jawbones studded with sharp teeth. One look at this pit and somehow you sensed that it went very, very deep. Someone or something had been eating an awful lot of animals for a very long time.

"Angry Betty was a hungry lady," Padfoot said. "She, heh-heh, nearly ate my dad, back when he was just a puckling."

As the steam sledges drew to a halt, one by one, they sputtered, groaned, and then, with a sigh of their engines, fell silent. Their hatches were cranked open from inside. Great grey clouds of vapour came pouring out, followed in short order by the little greyling crews. They spattered the ice like handfuls of pebbles tossed into a snowbank. As they ran towards the crossroads they were joined by the mushgoblins, and by a bewildering variety of other smallish, yowling creatures, who leapt from beneath the fur tarps that covered the dogsleds and lurched and tottered across the ice. Some of them brought out bagpipes and tambourines. Others beat on iron shields with little black swords. They set up a terrible racket. In the house in Philadelphia where Mr. Feld had grown up, the old iron radiator grilles rang, banged, pounded, and screeched all night long. The sound disturbed your dreams and then when you woke with your heart pounding in the quiet of the night you could hear the radiators, all nine of them, going at once, all over the house. That was how the Rade sounded to Mr. Feld, iron and ugly and joyful.

"What are they all so happy about?" he said.

But there was no answer from Robin Padfoot. The shaggy demon (there was nothing else he could be) was already halfway over the side of the observation platform. As Mr. Feld watched, Padfoot lowered himself to the ice and loped towards the vast crossroads, tossing greylings and mushgoblins and who-knew-whats out of his way as he went. His animal style of getting along was unnerving to watch.

"Padfoot!" said Mr. Feld. "Where are you going? What's happening?"

"It's a crossroads," said a small, droll voice at his elbow.

Mr. Feld turned. On the brass rail, its feathers stirred and ruffled by the bitter wind, sat a raven. Its eyes were ink, its beak lead, and its scaly legs and talons a rusty red like cedar shavings. It had the deadpan, crafty look common to its species, as if it were trying to conceal its thoughts. "That's where you'll always find Coyote."

"Is he here?" Mr. Feld said, turning back to watch Robin Padfoot go shambling across the mirror-bright surface of the Iceburns, deciding not to care, finally, that he was conversing with a bird. He wiped the frost from his goggles, trying to see through the swarms of greylings and goblins that were flooding the crossroads at Betty's Bonepit. "Can I speak to him?" He turned back to the raven, which had its head tucked under one wing and appeared to be searching its feathers for something to eat. "Do you know where he is?"

"Of course I do," said the raven. "All ravens know where Coyote is, at all times. It's just a little gift we have. Got it from Coyote himself, as a matter of fact, back when he Changed the world."

"Is he here? It's very important that I speak to him."

"Relax," said the raven. "He wants to talk to you, too. He's heard about you."

Screeching greylings, grinning like boys, came sledding down the ramps.

"I've gathered that," Mr. Feld said. "I think he wants my— He sent Padfoot to— He wants my airship envelope design."

The low chuckle of the raven took on a suave quality, less

raspy and harsh. Mr. Feld looked back at the bird. What he saw made him jump so quickly and carelessly that he nearly tumbled over the side of the observation platform. Where the raven had sat, perched on a length of cold brass pipe, there now stood a man. He was a slender person, slight of build, an inch or two shorter than Mr. Feld. He wore a short, hooded tunic, of scarlet shot through with gold, trimmed at the collar, cuffs, hood, and hem with thick black fur. The hood was thrown back to reveal a flaming shock of red hair. The face under the fiery hair is, and has always been, difficult to describe. It was handsome, but the bones of the nose, cheeks, and chin were drawn too sharply; youthful, but the skin was lined and weathered; merry, but the eyes were cold and unkindly; wise, but the thick red lips were drawn into a cruel and stupid smirk. It was the face of someone who could see no difference between looking for trouble and looking for fun and who, though since the beginning of time he had succeeded in stirring up no end of trouble, had seen nothing of fun in a very long, in much too long, a time.

"It's not your precious *envelope* I want, Mr. Feld," said the person. "It's the truly *marvellous* stuff you spin it from."

Mr. Feld was about to guess (correctly) at the identity of his mysterious companion, when his attention was distracted by the sound of a high, thin voice, uttering the worst string of curses that he had ever heard. Mr. Feld looked towards the wild mass jig now taking place in the crossroads, all around the bonepit, to the icy skirling of the pipes. Some of the greylings, he saw, had formed a ragged line, leading back from the edge of the pit to the place where the lead steam sledge had come to a halt. Down this line they were tossing along a small, furry bundle, over their heads, from one pair of wicked hands to the next. The bundle was of a fiery orange colour that stood out boldly against the colourless expanse of the Iceburns, and it was from the centre of this bundle that the truly scabrous cursing seemed to be coming.

The language spoken by the bundle was unknown to Mr. Feld. (In fact it was a dialect of West Reynardine.) But so deeply outraged was the bundle's tone, and so fiery its rhetoric, that the meaning of unknown words was nevertheless as plain to Mr. Feld as if he were speaking them himself. The ancestors of the greylings were first compared to a variety of loathsome animals, fungi, and bacteria, and then were accused of having perpetrated on themselves and one another a number of vile and probably physically impossible acts. All this seemed to amuse the greylings considerably. Next the bundle – it had a tail, Mr. Feld saw now, a great red brush of a tail – began to describe to the greylings, who were sending it, inexorably, towards the giant pit of bones, all the horrible illnesses and afflictions that would befall them, and their offspring, and the offspring of their offspring, if they did not, this minute, set the bundle down. Skin lesions, boils, sores, deformities of limb, failures of crucial organs. None of this appeared to make any impression on the greylings. The thing with the tail arrived at the grasping hands of the last greyling before the pit, and then with a heave, and a group shout of "Ho!" was sent sailing. It arced high out into the frost-blue air, kicking and shaking its tiny black fists. Then it landed, with a nasty crunch, on the pile of bones. Its head struck with a thud against something hard. After that it lay there, unmoving, a poor, tiny little creature, familiar somehow to Mr. Feld – a fox, or a monkey, or—

"A bushbaby!" said Mr. Feld.

"It's a werefox, actually," said the young-old man with a polite cough. "Bushbabies, I believe, are rather smaller."

Mr. Feld turned, filled with a pity for the werefox and also, belatedly, for Ethan, stuck with a father who shunned the unlikely and refused – foolishly, as it turned out – to believe in the impossible. He started to reproach the young-old man, to protest the treatment of the innocent werefox whose life had been spared, on the Clam Island Highway, by the sharp gaze of his lost little son. But as soon as he looked at the man, Mr. Feld found that his thoughts grew fuzzy and confused. It was as if Coyote shone with some kind of invisible light that you could see with the deepest animal layer of your brain.

"What's going to happen to it?" he managed to get out.

"Nothing you'd care to see. He served his purpose, old Cutbelly. I told him, he really ought to feel honoured. Shadowtail for the last great leap between the Worlds." His gaze flickered like a leaping spark in the direction of the madness in the crossroads, then back at Mr. Feld. "Idiots," he said, affectionately, with a grin so large and cheery that it warmed Mr. Feld from the depths of his fur-wrapped belly to the frozen tips of his ears. "Let them have their fun. In the meantime, Mr. Bruce Feld, you and I can get acquainted."

Nothing changed. There was no sound, no hint of motion. And yet from one heartbeat to the next the endless white world around them vanished completely, and with it the sound of the pipes and drums, the growling of the werewolves, the rumble of engines, the strange half-light of the sky. Instead Mr. Feld found himself seated in a large, soft chair. A fire flickered gaily in a stone fireplace. The walls were dark and handsome. The lamps cast a warm, buttery light. Mr. Feld was holding a cup of coffee, black with sugar, exactly as he preferred to drink it. In his other hand there was a chicken sandwich, with mayonnaise and tomato, on egg bread, the chicken warm from the soup-pot and well salted. His favourite kind. He took a bite of the excellent sandwich and then washed it down with a slug of good hot coffee.

The red-haired man sat across from him, in an even larger chair, in a pair of Chinese pyjamas decorated with capering embroidered monkeys. He cupped his slender hands around a steaming mug, looking every bit as snug and comfortable as Mr. Feld was feeling. But Mr. Feld was not fooled. He knew that he was about to be asked to do something that he was not going to want to do.

"You are a man of sense," the man said, with a sigh of impatience. He smiled. "It's always so much harder to bargain with a creature of sense. Fortunately such creatures are blessedly scarce. Another of Old Woodenhead's many oversights. Hello. How are you? Comfortable, I hope? Coffee all right? It's Peruvian Organic, that's what you like, isn't it? And the salt in that sandwich was harvested from French salt marshes. One really can taste the difference, can't one, between sea salt and the ordinary kind? Isn't that what you always say?"

"Are you the boss? Are you the Coyote?"

"Some people call me that. Also the Changer. Monkey. Raven. Weasel. Snake. Loki, Herm, Legba, Glooscap, Eshu, Shaitan. Prometheus."

"Shaitan," Mr. Feld said. "Isn't that another name for—?"

"Yes, yes, but that Satan business is a bunch of bologna," Coyote said, looking bored with the subject. "It gives me a pain. All right, I've pulled a few fast ones over the years on you people. Ha-ha, oh, my goodness, yes, OK, I grant you, there have been times when I've been just awful. But that's only part of the story. Name one thing you enjoy in that woebegone world of yours. Go ahead. I guarantee you, I'm responsible for it. Go ahead. Name it."

"Pizza," said Mr. Feld.

"Fire," Coyote said at once. "Try running a wood-burning oven without *that*."

"You invented fire." Mr. Feld sounded doubtful.

"Middling fare was a nasty, tough, bloody, stringy business before I tricked Old Woodenhead out of his precious flickering stuff." As he recalled the incident of the theft of fire, Coyote's entire body itself seemed to flicker, like a flame, with pleasure. "Name another."

"Physics," said Mr. Feld.

"Let me ask you this," Coyote said. "According to physics, can a box possibly contain a cat that is both dead and alive at the same time?"

"Schrödinger's Cat," Mr. Feld said. "Nothing is ever one way or the other until you observe it. Theoretically, yes. The cat is both a dead cat *and* a live cat until you open the lid of the box and see which it is."

"Well, you can thank me for that, too. So much for physics. Now, one more. Come on. Something that you really, honestly love about life in the Middling."

And, as if to give Mr. Feld a hint, he began to whistle. *Take me out to the ball game. Take me out with the crowd.*

"Baseball?" Mr. Feld obediently guessed.

"They don't tell you *that* about old Shaitan, do they now?"

"You invented baseball?"

"Oh, a while back now. On a fine summer day on Diamond Green."

"What about death?" Mr. Feld said. He set down his coffee on a little table next to his chair. "My son has a book of Indian folk tales. I recall reading to him about Coyote in that book. It said there that Coyote brought death into the world. I remember that we talked about that, Ethan and I."

"Ah, yes, Ethan," Coyote said. "Such a *spunky* little youngster. They all start out so *spunky*, these heroes of the Middling. Always come to such *regrettable* finales. Poisoned by the blood of centaurs. Crushed in the toils of a dragon. Crashing their rescue planes into the Caribbean Sea on the way to Nicaragua."

Mr. Feld stood up. Real or not, he was tired of this business now. He had not slept in over a day, his belly felt bloated and overfull, his head spun from the warmth of the fire.

"I won't keep you against your will, Mr. Feld," Coyote said. "You may go at any time."

Mr. Feld looked around for a door out. The room did not seem to contain any. He went to a large drapery dangling in one corner and brushed it aside. There was nothing there. He peeked into the corners. He even searched the floors and ceiling for a trapdoor.

"Does this room have a way out?"

Coyote sighed.

"No."

"I thought you said I could go."

"I lied."

Mr. Feld started to protest, but then he remembered. "Oh, that's right," he said. "You're a big liar, aren't you? The Prince of Lies."

"Suppose I say no to that?" Coyote said with a grin. "Where are you then? On the other hand, suppose I say yes?"

Sadly Mr. Feld circled back around and sat down in his chair. All the feeling of comfort and warmth had dissipated. He needed to go home. He needed to see Ethan again.

"What do you want from me?" he said.

"I'm going to be requiring your brain," Coyote explained. "Your brain, your hands, your way of seeing things. For this little project I have underway."

"Right. Look, I see the kind of operation you have here. You already have my Zeppelina. I'm sure it would be no problem for some of those smart little grey guys you have working for you to figure out how I array my picofibres."

"Actually, I have them at work on it even as we speak. Oh, one thing." He winced. "I'm afraid my boys have made a *terrible* mess of your lovely little Zeppelina. Cut it to bits, the little monsters."

Mr. Feld let out a groan. He had poured all of his sorrow and passion into the building of *Victoria Jean*.

"I'm truly sorry," Coyote said. "I know how much she

meant to you. But it couldn't be helped." And he really did look very beautifully sorry. "Now, listen. For reasons that are hard to explain to reubens – believe me, I've tried – I would like to put an end to existence as we know it. But the way I've been going about it is so very slow and inefficient. Along about, oh, three or four thousand years ago, I realised that I would never be able to undo everything, take everything back to zero, as long as magic and its by-product, story, were constantly flowing back and forth among the Worlds through the pleached branches of the Tree. So I've been trying ever since to cut apart those irritating galls. But it's a very time-consuming business, and what's more, new galls are popping up all the time. For quite some time, therefore, I've been looking for a *faster* way. Then, one day, I happen to get word of a modest little gall tucked way in a spot corresponding to the place you know as Summerland. I had some of my people look it over, and sure enough, not only is there a mob of highly irritating ferishers living there, but it turns out they've been *warned* of my arrival. They've sent for a champion, to defend against me. Hopeless, of course, but that lot never seem to learn. And then, of all things, this so-called "champion" turns out to be a very small, forgive me, not very impressive *boy*.

"The boy's *father*, though. There's an interesting fellow. Turns out he's somehow managed to stumble onto a substance with some very interesting properties. Inert. Nonreactive. Yet infinitely malleable. Just the sort of thing that might be used to contain and deliver a, let's call it volatile, substance. More poisonous than a death's-head mushroom. Nastier than vomit. More corrosive than acid. Hot stuff. Hard to handle. The sort of substance you might use, say, to *dissolve the entire underlying structure of the universe.*"

"I'm in aviation," Mr. Feld said, doubting Coyote's tale without being able completely to disbelieve it. "Sounds to me like you need a materials engineer."

"You understand picofibres as well as any chemist," Coyote said. "With one difference – you taught yourself. You have a fine, independent, uncluttered mind. All I need to do is touch it. Just once. With my little pinky finger. As I did for, oh, Tesla, Goddard, Tycho Brahe." These were three of the scientific thinkers whom Mr. Feld had always most admired. Coyote might have mentioned Daedalus, Werner von Braun, or Robert Oppenheimer, but he did not. "As I did for the men and women who brought pizza and physics and baseball into the Middling."

"What if I say no?" Mr. Feld said.

"Oh, I'll manage without you, in time. Everything will just take me longer. But I have been waiting for a very long time already. I can wait a bit more." He smiled another of his bright, cheery, cruel smiles. "You will never see your son again, however. I promise you that. The universe as you know it will come to an end before that happens."

"I see," Mr. Feld said. "Well, all right then. I suppose I have no choice."

"Oh, you *always* have a choice," Coyote said. "That's another little fun feature of life you can put down to me, if you like."

"But I can't do it myself," Mr. Feld said. "I'll need an assistant."

"Fine. I'll send over a half dozen of my brightest—"

"No," Mr. Feld said. "Not the greylings."

WHEN THE SUN rose over the crossroads at Betty's Bonepit the next morning, there was a horrible gnashing, an outburst of cracking and snapping like ten thousand nutshells being ground to paste under an enormous boot-heel. It was the creaking of the ice, stirring and rippling like the hide of an enormous frozen beast. In the next moment there arose a terrible tinkling and chiming, as if a gigantic bell were being pelted with thousands upon thousands of wineglasses, each of which shattered on impact with a sharp *ping*! That was the sound of the Rade, thawing out. They had danced through the night, gorging themselves on ice mice until their bellies squirmed, slaking their thirst with sweet, evil liquors, waiting for the Boss to appear in the crossroads. After a while they grew so wild and intoxicated and stupid with mouse that they failed to notice that Coyote never showed. Then as the deep, heavy, eldest cold, the cold of the Winterlands, settled upon them like the effects of a strong drug, their movements slowed, grew less frantic, and their singing and banging faded to a few ragged shouts. Finally, about an hour before daybreak they had all, at the same moment, frozen solid as statues, and toppled over. Those who had congealed while standing on an incline or slope went skittering down and across the endless ice, some of them for miles and miles. When the sun at last defrosted them, those scattered greylings who were not immediately set upon by packs of dire wolves made their way back towards the crossroads as quickly as they could, found their sledges or steam-sledges, and rejoined their companions. The mushgoblins blew their special whistles (hollowed-out shards of moonstone), and, grudgingly, the furry creatures came limping in from the country all around, their chins gory and greased with the fat of seals and caribou. The thunder buffalo were stampeded, and took off at once across the cloudless Iceburns sky. If anyone noticed that the body of the werefox was no longer lying in the bonepit, its absence was marked down to the stealthy ravenings of a dire wolf.

When the demon known as Padfoot finally awoke, his head still pounding with weird drums, his throat parched from the copious horns of fermented haint's milk he had drunk the night before, the Rade had long since rambled on. He had to run across the ice for seventeen miles, without stopping to feed, before he caught and went aboard the steam sledge known as the *Panic*, his flagship as commander-in-chief of the greylings. Hung over, out of breath, and very, very relieved not to have been left behind by his troops, he was only mildly surprised and not at all put out to discover that the large private quarters on the middle deck of the *Panic*, formerly his own, had been reassigned to Mr. Bruce Feld, of Clam Island, Washington, and was now a laboratory for his researches into new applications of picofibres, those curious molecules that when properly arrayed were as flexible as rubber and impermeable as diamond.

"So," he said, sucking greedily on an icicle, "you going to make us a nozzle to spray poison on the roots of that great old Weed?"

"That's right! And then we're going to turn the hose on you, you nag-shouldered, pigment-free mop with no handle!"

"Allow me to present my laboratory assistant," Mr. Feld said with a small smile. "I believe you already know Mr. Cutbelly?"

11

The Herald

A THUNDERSTORM! TAFFY cried from her lookout perch atop the car, amid the humming guy wires. "A great, big, old-fashioned, singe-your-nape-fur, Summerland thunderstorm!"

"It's on a direct heading for this vessel," Thor reported. Jennifer T. had noticed that Thor tended to get especially androidish whenever he was afraid. Actually the storm was well above them, hovering, as if trying to make up its mind what to do about them.

"Nevertheless," Taffy said. "It's so *beautiful*!" They could hear her, snuffling up a deep nostalgic breath of stormy air. "It smells so *wonderful*!"

It was, Jennifer T. had to agree, a beautiful thunderstorm, its black wings beating at the summer air. It had lightning for talons and rain for plumage and its eyes were alight with a static charge of ozone. It was a creature of storm, a big black bird made of thunder.

"Tell me it isn't," she said. But she knew that it was.

"Course it is," Cinquefoil said.

"Thunderbird!" Taffy said. "Hey there, you thunderbird!" Up on the roof of the car there was an awful thumping. Jennifer T. grabbed hold of Thor Wignutt as the car began to shake and rock violently. Taffy the Sasquatch, somewhat ill-advisedly in Jennifer T.'s opinion, was jumping up and down on top of Skidbladnir. She had been in that cage, Jennifer T. supposed, a few hundred years too long. "Hi! You-hoo!"

"Quiet, ya shaggy old she-bigfoot!" snapped Cinquefoil. "Ya think this wired-together heap a junk and grammer could stand up ta a brush with that?"

Taffy quit her leaping about, but it was much too late, of course. The thunderbird had noticed them long before. It was circling over them, about half a mile up, with an easy malevolence.

"Why does it want to hurt us?" Ethan said. "Is it on Coyote's side?"

"Wouldn't think so," Cinquefoil said. "Coyote stoled storm-bringing from Thunderbird, like he stoled fishing from Eagle, and war from Ant, and fire from Old Mr. Wood hisself."

"Wait a minute." Certain features of everything they had experienced since her first crossing, back on Clam Island, had struck Jennifer T. as familiar from the old people's stories, of course, in particular all this talk of Coyote and the Changer. But a thunderbird? "Is the Summerlands, like, is it an *Indian* world?" she said.

"Well, we use ta see a fair number o' Indians in the Summerlands, at one time. Adventurers, shamans, rogues and trickster men, witches and princesses. They used to get all tangled up in the greater grammer and take some terrible fine stories home with them when they found their way out agin. But we don't see too many Indians these days." Cinquefoil levelled his heavy-lidded gaze at Jennifer T. "Something musta happened."

Jennifer T. felt that the ferisher was looking right into her, into everything that had always troubled her about what old Albert called her "Indian side." How she loved all the old stories so much that it made her angry, everlastingly furious, with her Indian ancestors, for having lost everything, land, language, legends, so completely. Even though she knew it was not fair to blame them, not fair at all; there was nothing that those poor old Squamish and Salishan and Nooksacks could have done, not really, in the face of white-man inventions and white-man viruses and white man wanting them dead. She couldn't help it; she blamed them anyway. She even blamed them for not having had antibodies against smallpox and measles. Nevertheless, all the old people's stories were still in there, locked away in her brain or her heart or wherever such things were kept. And now, somehow, they had brought her this far, to a place where they had never been lost.

"Well," she said. "I'm here, now."

"So ya are."

Jennifer T. rolled down her window. A strong fresh breeze, with a bright, coppery tang like burning wire, blew into the car. The storm was nearly upon them. Just the smell of it seemed to fill her with the sudden certainty of all the marvellous things it was in her power, as Jennifer T. Rideout, to do.

"Hey! Thunderbird!" She thrust herself, head and shoulders, out the window of the car. "Shame on you! Doing Coyote's work for him, you big dumb turkey vulture! Don't you know what's coming? Don't you know the day is here? The day of— *ack*." She lost her purchase on the car door, lurched forwards, and fell out of the window. The deep green forest far below her seemed all at once to leap up.

"Ensign Rideout!"

Thor's reflexes were android-sharp and he grabbed at her right ankle with his thick fingers. But the force of her fall yanked her loose of his grip, and she fell. Even in the Summerlands certain laws hold true, and she fell very fast, at a rate of thirty-two feet per second squared. The world of green in which she was going to die rushed towards her with breathtaking eagerness. Light drained from her head like the air running out of a balloon, and she began to lose consciousness. She was just barely aware of a sharp upward jerk of her body, a firm grip on her ankles. At first she thought that it was Thor again. As if in a dream, she saw him reaching down from the car, his robo-arms telescoping out of their sockets, section by titanium section, to snatch her out of the air. Then she opened her eyes, and looked up into the seething black breast of the thunderbird, caught in the grip of its lightning claws. There was a roar of wind all around her that deafened her almost to the sound of her own thoughts. It blew past her ears, growling, then broke and billowed into little whistles and eddies. Her hair hung down in her face, damp from the rain of the bird's black plumage, clinging to her cheeks, flapping in her eyes, and standing out in all directions as the charge of the bird's body flowed through her. Her ankles thrummed and tingled, and burned. But somehow, in the face of all that, she managed to finish the sentence that she had begun in the car.

"—RAGGED ROCK!" she told the thunderbird.

That was when something very strange happened. The arching wings of the storm bird seemed to grab hold of her voice, to catch it up, and roll it around between them, and then to send it forth into the world *enlarged*. It was as if a pair of invisible hands, as huge as those of Mooseknuckle John, had clapped themselves like the bell of a trumpet to her mouth. The two words were shaken out across the sky, in every direction, like a blanket, scattering every other sound before them. Then the spreading blanket of echoes and re-echoes seemed to settle, billowing, down over the world below, in the form of an immense silence. The wind died. The rivers and streams ceased murmuring and ringing on the rocks. The birds of the Summerlands left off singing their endless songs. From the Big Fella Country to Turtle Ocean to the snowcaps of the Raucous Mountains there was only the echoing last traces of her voice. In this way the news of the end of the world was brought to the Far Territories of Faerie.

And then, as if in reply, Jennifer T. heard, from a great distance, a sound that broke her heart. Someone was weeping; a woman, bitterly and freely, runny-nosed and moaning and half-laughing, the heavy grunting laughter of grief, the way you weep only when you are certain that you are absolutely alone, letting out the sadness in all its ugliness and animal strength. It was faint but unmistakable, and hot tears sprang to Jennifer T.'s eyes in response, and sorrow clutched her heart, and she forgot that the world was ending, and that she was hanging upside down with her hair falling into her face and pennies and dimes dropping from her jeans pockets one by one. For an instant longer the world was racked by the sobbing of a poor lost woman in the woods. Then the weeping faded and died. The birds resumed their songs, and the squirrels their chatter, and the beavers their toil, and the butterflies their drunken rustling flight, and the silence, and the weeping, and the echo of Ragged Rock's coming, were all drowned out by the old, stubborn life of the Summerlands.

The thunderbird circled in low over the forest, to a spot where the tree cover thinned as the land rose towards the foothills of the Raucous Mountains. Jennifer T. saw a wide clearing, a vast stretch of grey-brown land that looked – it was hard to tell, in her current position – as if it had been stripped, or paved over, or maybe burnt. In the centre of this ruined meadow rose a high grassy hill, spangled with dandelions. The contrast was stark between the lovely hill and the patch of blighted earth from which it rose like a green island in a sea of ash. As the great raptor circled lower Jennifer T. saw that tennis courts had been drawn in white lines on the grey surface of the wasteland, as well the circles, grids and parallelograms of other games, some of which she thought she recognised – marbles? foursquare? – and others that were strange to her. Ferishers were scattered across the waste, interrupted in their pastimes, clutching rackets and mallets and leather balls and gazing up at the sky, and at her, the girl who was hanging down from it. One of them, taller and larger than the others, raised a hand in a bewildered warning or salute. And that was when the thunderbird dropped her.

She landed at the back of the hill, away from the ball field, and tumbled down all the way to bottom. She sat up, rubbing at her legs where they bore the throbbing purplish-red mark of the thunderbird's electric grip. The ground beneath her backside was at once hard, springy, and cold to the touch, a strange kind of clay or dried mud, and with an acrid smell of charcoal. It was like the skin of some kind of loathsome animal and she tried to roll off it, back up onto the grass and flowers of the hillside. Ferishers came running towards her, jabbering excitedly in the local dialect of Fatidic, helping her to her feet, brushing the dirt and grass from her jeans. She just had time to thank them, in English, for the kindness of their welcome when ropes were fetched, and the ferishers began to tie her arms to her sides, comfortably enough, but with very strong knots.

"Wait!" she said.

Now a group of ferisher women appeared at the top of the hill. They unslung longbows from their back and nocked arrows with black barbs and bright red feathers to their bowstrings. They took aim at the sky. For an instant Jennifer T. thought that they were shooting at the thunderbird, but she could see the great creature soaring off away towards the mountains, already a tiny unhittable speck and growing smaller all the time. No, the ferisher archers were aiming for something much nearer to hand, and much easier to hit.

"No!" she said, but it was too late. With a kind of whispering sizzle the arrows took to the sky. Jennifer T. knocked her captors to one side and whirled around to watch as the arrows arced towards Skidbladnir. Three of them glanced harmlessly off the tough picofibre hide of the gas bag, and then a fourth, and a fifth, and Jennifer T. began to leap up and down. 'Yes! Way to go Mr. *Feld*! Picofibres rock!" The sixth arrow was plucked from the air by the swift black hands of Taffy the Sasquatch, who snapped it in two and tossed the halves back down to the ground. "Nice catch!" Jennifer T. said. "Ha, ha, ha, you stupid little— Oh."

The seventh arrow entered the front window of the Saab station wagon, on the passenger side. There was a cry that sounded unmistakably like the voice of Cinquefoil, and then Skid lurched, and shuddered, as the grammer ran out of the envelope of magic the ferisher had woven around the envelope of picofibres, and the station wagon dropped, slowly and then swiftly, to the ground.

12

The Royal Traitor

THE PRISONERS WERE lodged deep in the roots of the fairy hill, or knoll, in a clean, warm room with whitewashed walls and a floor of beaten dirt covered with rushes. There were two wicker hampers of food. One was filled with little bricks formed from some kind of paste of nuts and dried fruits. They were salty, sweet, a little dusty, and gritty in the teeth. The other hamper held packets of some kind of boiled thing like a potato, with a taste like nutmeg, wrapped in an edible leaf. A large clay jar, with a dipper tied to the handle, held fresh water that somehow stayed cold hour after hour as the ferishers who held them prisoner debated their fate. Though there were five in their party – Ethan, Jennifer T., Thor, Taffy, and Cinquefoil – the cell held six prisoners. The sixth was a ferisher, a little red-haired female in a short green jerkin and baggy buckskin trousers. She called herself Spider-Rose.

She was a member of the Dandelion Hill mob – that was the name of the tribe that had shot them from the sky. Though age seemed to be more or less an unknown thing among the ferishers she seemed somehow younger than Cinquefoil. She had a springy, impatient way of stalking back and forth across the cell. And then there was the matter of her doll. It was a horrid little thing, a knot of chamois leather with a hank of black yarn for hair. Ethan couldn't tell if it had a face or not.

It was Spider-Rose who told them that the dusty nut bricks were called *durpang* and the mushy tamale thing a *guapatoo*. Both, she assured them, were sure to give a reuben "a dire case of the runs."

"Don't take it personally," she said, when they asked her why they had been treated so badly. "They're in a terrible state around here these days. Have been ever since—" Her voice caught and broke, and she squeezed the horrible twist of skin, and nuzzled it with her cheek. "Ever since the ballpark was lost."

"What happened to it?" Ethan said. He and the others had been struck by their brief aerial view of the sad grey waste around the knoll. "How did it get lost?"

But at this Spider-Rose only squeezed her doll more tightly, and looked away.

"What are they going to do to us?" Jennifer T. said. "That's what I want to know. We have to get out of here. We have stuff to do."

"Oh, they're talking it over now. Talking and talking. They'll be talking for days. Course in the end it won't turn out any different for you than it would if they *didn't* waste a week in chatter. The punishment for intruding on a ferisher hill's a, what's the word, a *no-brainer*." She smiled sadly. "You reubens'll be driven mad, then sent back to the Middling to tell wild tales no one will ever believe. The Sasquatch there'll be bound with grammers and put to work in the kitchens for the rest of eternity."

"And Cinquefoil?" Ethan said, looking anxiously at the little chief, who lay on a pallet by the water jar, unconscious.

"*Cinquefoil*? Of the *Boar Tooth mob*? The Home Run King? That's who that is?" She went over to the pallet and looked down at him. "How about that? Oh, well, he's going to wither up something *bad*," said Spider-Rose. "Them arrows were tipped with iron."

"Iron is poisonous to fairies," Ethan remembered. They had bandaged the meat of the little slugger's right hand – the arrow had entered the back and exited through the palm, luckily missing the bones – but the ferisher had shown no sign of stirring, and as Ethan sat beside him he seemed indeed to have dwindled, somehow. His face was hollow, his rib cage sunken. I finally remember something I've read about fairies, he thought, and he's not awake to hear it.

"Please! Poisonous!" Spider-Rose shuddered, and stroked her cheek with the black yarn hair of her dolly. "We don't even like to touch the stuff. Those archers, we done trained them up specially since the time they was girls. Dressed them in little shoes of iron. Hung iron chains from their necks. Twisted the iron-jimjams right out of them. Ironbroke, we call them. But if iron goes *through* a ferisher, that's just, well, it's just sad. Ferisher dries up like a seedpod. Even a ironbroke girl. There's life inside her, still, but she's never waking up ever again. Nah, he's doomed."

"Why tip your arrows with it, then?" Jennifer T. said. "Are you trying to kill other ferishers?"

"Iron works hard on the Cousins. Greylings. Skrikers. Reubens, too. Rough customers come troubling the ferishers of the Far Territories. They like to find a spot in the Middling that brushes up to the Summerlands and push on through the gall that way. We can't be too careful."

Ethan thought of the attack on Hotel Beach, the trucks and earthmovers blazoned TRANSFORM PROPERTIES, the pile of slaughtered birch trees. Coyote's forces had pushed and pushed against the grammers of the Boar Tooth mob until they finally got through, and the ancient ban on summertime rain was broken.

"Is that what happened to your ball field?" Ethan said. "Did Coyote's things destroy it?"

Spider-Rose didn't answer right away. She stopped pacing the cell, and lowered her doll to her side.

"In a sort of a way," she said, looking down at her little feet in their green slippers. "Not quite exactly."

"Taffy, is it true?" Jennifer T. turned to the Sasquatch. "Is he going to shrivel up and die?"

Taffy shook her head. "Not die. Nothing can kill them but the grey crinkles, as far as I have ever heard," she said. "But iron gives them a deep, deep hurt."

"Isn't there anything we can do?"

Spider-Rose shook her head. "Not in these stinking dull times I got myself all ended up with," she said, sounding somehow younger than ever. If there could be such a thing as a ferisher teenager, Ethan thought, Spider-Rose appeared to qualify. "Use to be you could just go out walking into the deep woods, find yourself a piece of the Lodgepole. A nice little slivereen of that Oldest Ash. Wave it around the hole a few times, draw out the bit of iron and the hurt along with it." She stopped, and sighed, shaking her head. "But all the bits of the Lodgepole got finded up a long time ago. Coyote's been searching 'em out."

Ethan leapt to his feet in excitement.

"I have one!" he cried. "I mean, I *had* one. A piece of the Lodgepole itself, that's just what Cinquefoil called it. I found it in the Summerlands, back at the Tooth. Only those guys must have taken it from me, your people. After they crash-landed thc car. It was lying across the foot-well in the backseat and I... I know there's something special about it, I can feel it whenever I pick it up. It knocked the head clean off one of those skriker things." He flexed his hands a few times, choking up on an invisible bat handle and taking a pantomime swing. His palms ached for the cold hard pressure of the wood against them. In all the confusion of the attack, the plunge from the sky, their capture, somehow he had lost track of his piece of the Lodgepole. Now he felt ashamed. He ought never to have let them take it from him. "We have to get it back!"

He ran to the door of their cell and began to pound on it with both fists.

"Hey!" he said. "Hey, you! Out there! Give me back my stick!"

After a moment Jennifer T. came and started banging on the door, too. But the wood – oak, it seemed to Ethan – absorbed the blows like the softest of cushions, sound and all. They might have been pounding on a sheet of empty air. Taffy came over, then, and the children stepped aside. The Sasquatch hunched down in front of the door – her head nearly brushed the ceiling of the cell – and glared at it steadily for a moment with her mild, intelligent eyes. Then she raised her right leg in front of her, bent at the knee. Her enormous right foot quivered with the intensity of the blow she was about to deliver.

"Yah!" she cried. "Bigfoot this!"

The next moment Taffy lay rolling on the soft rushes of the floor, clutching her great, big foot in pain.

"Don't you know anything about grammer?" Spider-Rose said, shaking her head. "And a door grammer is just about the strongest, you know. A slab of good heart-oak can hold an awful lot of grammer. A door grammer is proof against any blow, charm, or picklock you care to employ. You can go on and kick it till Ragged Rock if you like. Not as how that's apt to be a very long time. We're all *doomed*." She sighed, and knelt down on the floor beside the sleeping Cinquefoil. "That's really Cinquefoil, then? Poor little fay. Not bad looking, neither."

"Let me try?" Thor Wignutt said.

Thor had barely moved or said a word in all the time since they were first thrown into this cell. Instead he sat in a corner, with his eyes rolled back in their sockets. From time to time he tapped on his left temple and murmured to himself. When Jennifer T. had gone over to see if he was all right, he had waved her away. Now he approached the oak door of the cell. Gently he stroked it with the fingers of one hand, fluttering them delicately as if they were the most sensitive of instruments.

"OK, Thor, you're strong and all," Ethan said. "But not stronger than Taffy."

"But, OK, here's the thing. You told me that that werefox guy, Cutbelly, could scamper anywhere, as long there was a way through, a branch or a twig of the Tree. Not just *between* Worlds, but *inside* a World. And these twigs and branches are everywhere. I can feel them all over the place." Thor reasoned, slowly, and thoughtfully, but with no trace that Ethan could see of his flat TW03 manner. "I leapt from one world to another, remember? What's to stop me from crossing just one little grammery door?"

And with that, he got right up against the door, until his face, chest, and hips were pressed tightly to it. He closed his eyes and began muttering to himself. The stout door seemed to ripple, for the briefest instant, like a curtain stirred by a breath of wind. Then it fell still, solid and impenetrable as before. But Thor was gone. He had passed right through.

"I knowed there was something haintish about that boy," Spider-Rose said.

"He's a shadowtail," Ethan said, watching to see if Thor was going to reappear. He hoped that his friend wouldn't take it upon himself to set off alone, inside a fairy hill, looking for a piece of wood that might be anywhere. "Cinquefoil said he's the—"

"He's a changeling, is what he is," Taffy said, pulling herself upright and gingerly testing her outraged foot. "Oof. I knew it the first time I laid eyes on him."

"A *changeling*?" Ethan said. "Do you mean— Are you saying— Thor Wignutt is a ferisher?"

"Wow," Jennifer T. said. "That kind of explains a few things."

"But he's so tall," said Ethan, feeling that the explanation begged as many questions as it answered. "And his blood is red, I've seen it."

"No doubt he was fed on human milk," Taffy said. "Nursed by his human mother. If that's the case, then—"

"Then he ain't neither ferisher nor reuben," Spider-Rose said. She had resumed her pacing now. "And that's how come he can walk on through a door all loaded up with grammer. A changeling shadowtail. Huh." She shook her head gloomily. "I predict all kinds of trouble for you with that one."

"With what one?" said Thor. He was standing there, in the cell again, breathing steady and carefully, as if his heart were pounding and he was trying to slow it down.

Everybody stared at him as if he had just returned not from the other side of a door but from the land of the dead itself. Then Ethan looked at Taffy, hoping she would know what to do. The Sasquatch tugged thoughtfully for a moment on her brush of a beard, then went over to Thor and laid one of her big soft paws on his shoulder.

"Can you get me through with you?" she said.

Thor nodded. "Yes, Ms. Sasquatch, I really think I could."

"Then let's go find that stick."

She spun Thor towards the door and stood behind him, ducking her head. Thor reached a hand towards the door.

"*No*," Ethan said.

Taffy turned back, looking a little startled. There was a strange edge, almost but not quite angry, to Ethan's voice, one that took even him by surprise. He had meant only to say "No."

"It's my stick," he said, feeling a little sheepish. "I shouldn't have let them take it from me. Cinquefoil told me to hold on to it. Besides, Taffy, you're too big and, well, Sasquatchy, to go sneaking around inside a ferisher hill."

"We call it a *knoll*," Spider-Rose said. "And I wouldn't try it if I were you. They'll catch you for sure."

"You are not a very optimistic person, are you?" Ethan said.

Taffy gave another tug at the luxuriant silvery tuft at her chin, staring coolly at Ethan. Then she nodded.

"All right," she said. "The girl and I will stay here and look after the chief. We can't leave him, and I don't think we should try to move him, either."

"What?" Jennifer T. sprang to her feet. "No *way*. Eth and Thor and me are a *team*."

"Three of you are much more likely to attract attention than just a pair," Taffy said. "Be sensible, girl. But listen to this. If this boy and this other boy aren't back in what I consider to be a reasonable period of time for such an enterprise, then we are going after them. I'll kick my way through a wall if I have to."

"Oh, the walls are *miles* thick," said Spider-Rose, kissing her doll's ragged head. "You'll never get through."

"You can just be quiet," Jennifer T. said. Ethan could tell that she was mad about being left behind. "For some reason," she told Spider-Rose, "you give me a great big pain. Why don't you just go, too, huh? You and your stupid doll. Now's your big chance to escape."

"Oh, sure," Spider-Rose said. "That's *just* what my mother is looking for me to go and do. As if I'd give her the satisfaction." She stopped her furious pacing and sat down in an angry tangle of tiny legs and arms. "She said I could stay here till Ragged Rock, and that's just what I'm going to do."

Jennifer T. shrugged, and then came over to Ethan.

"Hurry back," she said in a low voice that was not quite as low as it might have been. "Or I can't be responsible for what happens to that fairy."

Spider-Rose stuck out her tongue.

"OK," Ethan said. He turned and put his hand on Thor's shoulder. It felt appealingly steady and firm.

"All right, shadowtail," he said in a low voice. "Let's find that stick."

The door rippled again, and they passed through it, and were gone.

HOURS PASSED. TAFFY and Jennifer T. took turns sitting beside Cinquefoil's pallet, bathing his forehead in cool water from the jar and trying not to think too much about the greenish-black tinge that had begun to spread like spilt ink across the skin of his right hand. Spider-Rose watched them, for a while, and paced for a good while longer. Finally, when Jennifer T. had almost forgotten she was there, she exploded.

"I'm tired of this place! I should have gone with those two little reubens while I had the chance! What was I thinking?"

"It appeared to me as if you were trying to spite your mother," Taffy said reasonably.

"True enough," said Spider-Rose.

"Who *is* your old mother, anyway?" Jennifer T. said. "Why would she want you to be in here until Ragged Rock?"

"My mother? My mother is Filaree, the Queen of the Dandelion Hill mob!" She stood and drew herself up to her full height of just under the top of Jennifer T.'s kneecap. The little feather in her headband quivered. The headband was worked with a beaded pattern of decidedly spidery-looking rose vines. "Don't you know I'm a *princess*?"

Taffy and Jennifer T. exchanged looks. Somehow this information did not surprise Jennifer T. particularly. She nodded. Taffy nodded, too.

"So why'd she put you in here?" Jennifer T. said. "Your highness?"

"Because she's a leathery old garfish with a heart like the spiky case of a buckeye, that's why!" Spider-Rose declared. "And they're all a bunch of hidebound old farts without an ounce of imagination in them."

"Just what was it you were asking them to imagine?" Taffy asked.

"Yeah, what did you do?"

"What did I do? What did I do? I gave them an idea, that's what. A simple, brilliant idea that changed things around here for the better, no doubt about it. Everyone thought so. At least at first. Then I guess everything went wrong."

"An idea about what?" said Jennifer T.

"About baseball, of course."

Spider-Rose stood up, and started pacing again, warming to her subject, waving the little doll around by the tattered rags of its tail. "Actually. Well. The idea wasn't mine. I mean, I *embellished* it. Improved upon it. But I wasn't the one to come up with it at first."

Jennifer T. had a sudden certainty. "Coyote," she said.

"Well, he invented the game, didn't he? Why shouldn't he want to change it? He's called the Changer, after all. And like he said to me, that first day when I met him, out walking in the woods. You could study the question, he said, and think some about it, and research it just a little bit, too. And in the end, if you were going to be honest, you were going to have to admit it to yourself. The game—" Here her brashness seemed to abandon her somewhat, and she stopped pacing, and lowered her voice. "The game was boring."

Jennifer T. scowled. She had known from the first that she didn't like this Spider-Rose. Now she knew why.

"Not over*all*," Spider-Rose put in hastily, catching the murderous look in Jennifer T.'s eye. "Just here and there. Let's take one example. And this is the example that Coyote made to me. Is there anything duller in all the game of baseball than watching the pitcher hit? Pitcher goes up there, if she even gets the bat off her shoulder it's to give it a few weak waves like she's shooing a little moth away. And then, big surprise, three or four pitches later, she's out. Well, Coyote said, and I couldn't argue with him, why *does* the pitcher have to hit? That's all. Just a little thought. Let somebody else hit for the pitcher. One of the old-timers, somebody whose legs, maybe they're not what they were. Or one of your born sluggers who can't catch or run or field a position too well, but can knock the hide off a ball with one swing. Somebody who ain't—"

"The designated-hitter rule," Jennifer T. said, shaking her head. She took a rush from the floor, soaked it in a dipper of water from the jar, and then laid it across Cinquefoil's forehead. "You *deserve* to be in here for that."

Spider-Rose sank to the ground, and laid her little doll in her lap. For a long time she didn't say anything, staring sadly at its blank and wrinkled face.

"For that alone," she said. "But it's so much worse than that."

"What happened?" said Jennifer T., regretting now, a little, her harsh words.

"I wouldn't never have done it," Spider-Rose said. "Even though I seed merit in the idea, I wouldn't never have listened to his talk. Only he offered me something. In return for bringing this idea to the mob. Something I wanted."

"What was that?" Jennifer T. said.

"Her heart's desire," Taffy said.

"That's right," said Spider-Rose. "You don't know— nobody knows— what it's like to be a young ferisher in these worn-down latter days. To be the only baby in the knoll, the only child, the only young person, for hundreds and hundreds of years. Even if you are a princess. Coyote said that he would grant me my dearest wish if I would turn the mob to the new rule, and so I set about persuading them, one by one. Some of them agreed to it right away, and others took years. My mother was the very last to change her mind. But change it she did. And the very next day, she found herself with child. A boy."

"A little brother," said Jennifer T., thinking of Dirk and Darrin and all the times she had made a precisely opposite wish. "You wished for a little brother."

Spider-Rose nodded, unable to speak. Amber tears splashed the ground before her.

"The day he got born was the happiest of my life," she said at last. "But we done saw from the first that there was something... lacking... to him. Something was missing. He didn't never make a sound. Just stared all around him like, eyes big and scared, like everything he saw was more than he cared to contend with."

"And the ball field," Taffy said gently.

"Took us a while to notice," Spider-Rose said. "Somehow the change in the rules unworked the grammers that done kept our grounds green, tamped and raked our infield dirt, fixed and laid our chalk lines, for the tens of thousands of years that we been living in this hill. Which was just what Coyote intended. Later we heard that other mobs all across the Summerlands fell for his idea and went with the new rule, and the same thing happened to them. Of course we gave *up* the new rule. We went back to the Old Style of play. But it was too late. The field kept fading and withering and dwindling, until one fine morning we came trooping out of the hill and saw that it was as you see it now. Grey and lifeless, a kind of scab on the earth. No amount of grammer and praying could heal. And the very next day when I came into the nursery, I found my brother. What I'd thought of, and loved, as my brother. But it was only another one of the tricks of the trickster."

So saying, she raised the twisted rag to her chest again, and kissed it tenderly on the coarse woollen top of its head. Then she lay back, and rolled over with her face to the wall.

Jennifer T. looked at Taffy, who shrugged. *Say something*, her expression seemed to implore.

"That's, uh, that's pretty harsh," said Jennifer T.

She just didn't *want* to feel sorry for this betrayer of her people and of the game. But somehow, staring at the tiny, slender back of the young ferisher, she found that she couldn't help herself. She picked up a ragged square of greasy felt that was lying in a corner, carried it over to Spider-Rose, and draped it across the horrible blank face of the shock-haired doll.

13

The Housebreakers of Dandelion Hill

THE INTERIOR OF a fairy knoll, as Thor Wignutt explained to Ethan, is invariably laid out on the plan of a spiral. In the case of a great ferisher court such as Caer Sidhe, Lyonesse, or the Fields of Even, there may be several hills, and spirals linked to other spirals linked in turn to more spirals, in a grand and intricate labyrinth of tunnels. But the court of Filaree, Queen of the Dandelion Hill, was just an ordinary sort of ferisher knoll, rustic and plain. It plays no role in any tale or record, aside from this one, and until the appearance there of the traitor princess, Spider-Rose, no personage or hero of any particular interest had ever turned up within its confines. Once Ethan and Thor were on the other side of the cell door, therefore, it was immediately apparent that there was only one way to go – up. The cell into which they had been tossed was the lowest room in the hill – the spiral died, so to speak, at its door. Going up it led, in long, gentle but ever-narrowing loops, to the council chamber at the very summit, in the usual and predictable ferisher way. Perhaps the most remarkable thing about the whole situation in which they now found themselves, as they set up the curving tunnel in search of Ethan's lost stick, was that Thor Wignutt was explaining the whole thing. He was whispering, so it was harder to tell, but it seemed to Ethan that his friend's voice really had lost, perhaps for good, the slightly irritating flatness it took on when he was being TW03 and explaining about thermal vents, or how you could plot a human being on a sheet of graph paper, if you really wanted to. He was just talking, in that gravelly voice of his. It made Ethan feel oddly sad. It *had been* annoying, true, to be referred to as "Captain" all the time, and to be kept constantly informed of the coordinates of this, and the ion-emissions of that. But then again there was something kind of nice about the way Thor was always trying so hard to behave like a real human being. That was a lot more than you could expect from some people. The actual significance of what Taffy had told them back in the cell – that Thor was, in fact, not a real human being at all – well, that was just too much for Ethan to think about right now.

As they climbed, they passed dozens and dozens of low ferisher doors, most of them elaborately carved with tangling shapes that might have been vines or flames or the characters that spelled out a grammer. Many of the doors had been left ajar, even wide open. The rooms inside – kitchens and sculleries, bedchambers and salons, card rooms and galleries, had all been abandoned to the urgency of council. They were lit by rows of tiny windows that let in the afternoon sunshine, though Ethan was sure he had seen no windows on the outside of the knoll.

"Grammery windows," Thor said, passing his hand through a slanting beam of illuminated dust.

"Is that what they're really called, or did you just make that up?'"

Thor considered the question, his big serious head cocked to one side.

"I really don't know," he said.

At first Ethan and Thor crept into the rooms cautiously, looking all around, checking under the doll-sized beds and card tables, peering behind the draperies, touching nothing. But before long the complete desertion of the rooms by the ferisher folk was apparent, and the two boys grew bold. They helped themselves to cheeses, handfuls of pumpkin seeds and wild strawberries, and to the dazzling array of candies that they found piled high in dishes in nearly every room. Ferishers love sweets, and the variety of candies was positively baroque. There were candies like snowflakes, and candies like stars and planets, and candies like the striped domes of Russian churches. The boys stuffed their mouths, and dirtied their faces, and loaded their pockets, too. They opened wardrobes and rifled drawers. They got up on tabletops and peered behind dusty rows of books on the shelves of the mouldering library. There was no sign anywhere, though, of Ethan's stick, and meanwhile they climbed ever higher in the knoll, and the circuit of the tunnel narrowed, and now they could hear, faintly, the shouting and blustering of the assembled ferishers, away at the top of the hill.

Then, after they had been climbing and searching for a long time, they came to a door that was nearly as tall as they. Unlike the others, it was shut tight, and its knotty expanse featured neither latch nor handle. For a moment

Ethan thought that they might have stumbled onto the council chamber itself, and he drew back, then crept forwards and put his ear against the door. Silence. The mutterings and shouts of the ferisher debate continued to drift down, as before, from farther up the tunnel. He pushed on the high door, but it was stuck fast. He crouched down, and put his shoulder against it, and pressed with and all his strength.

"The *treasury*," Thor said softly, and his hand went once more to his temple to scratch. "All kinds of grammer on this door."

Ethan looked at his friend. The information, though it came so easily to his lips, seemed at the same time to be causing Thor a certain amount of pain.

"Is there a Branch you can—?" he began, but Thor was already pressing himself against the door. Ethan grabbed hold of him by the waistband of his jeans, and in half a second, with a shivery chiming as of icicles, they had crossed the massively thick door.

Say *treasury* and the thought springs to mind, perhaps, of glinting mounds of doubloons and swag, golden candelabras, ornate caskets choked with emeralds and diamonds. But that is not the sort of loot that interests a ferisher. No, a ferisher's treasure is something else entirely. When Ethan and Thor crossed into the treasury of the Dandelion Hill ferishers, by far the tallest room in the knoll – it was nearly high enough for Taffy to have stood erect – they found AAA batteries, picture hooks, and rubber doorstops; shoelaces, neckties, and the strings of bathing trunks; watchbands, watch works, watch crystals, and the loose hands and faces of watches; loops of wire, baling twine, packing twine, bungee cord, rappelling rope, and electrical wire (coated in plastic, rubber, and fabric); ten thousand shirt buttons of bone and vinyl, wood and shell; tubes, gearboxes, coils, and grilles filched from the backrooms of radio-repair shops, hardware stores, and garages; Christmas ornaments, firecrackers, and the Easter eggs that roll deep under the hydrangea and are never found again; uncountable, but no fewer than two hundred and fifty, ferisher-sized balls of tinfoil, aluminium foil, gold leaf, Mylar, and coloured cellophane; canvas stolen from painters and lace from fine ladies; handkerchiefs, bandannas, headscarves, and ten thousand rags of gingham, flannel, corduroy, denim, and terry; no end of house keys, car keys, motel keys, safe-deposit keys, and the keys to locks from the diaries of girls long since grown old and buried, along with their deep and tedious secrets; hair combs, hair clasps, and barrettes; rhinestone brooches, imitation-pearl earrings, and cheap finger rings given out by a century of dentists; unmatched but otherwise perfectly good argyle socks; catnip balls, sun-bleached Frisbees, lawn darts, rubber pork chops, and the fuselages of a thousand balsawood gliders… In short, everything that you (or someone very much like you) has ever lost track of and stood, in the middle of your bedroom (or one very much like yours), holding on to that other perfectly good argyle sock, saying to yourself, "Where *do* they go?"

"We are never going to find my stick," Ethan said glumly. "Not in all this. Not if we had a hundred years to look for it. I mean, I sort of think it would be right in the front here." He poked with his toe at some brass buttons, of the sort found most often on men's navy blazers, which were piled by the door. "But they could just as easily have heaved it up somewhere in this mess way back there and then we..." He trailed off, and stood for several moments feeling overwhelmed by the sheer variety and size of the pile of junk. Spider-Rose was right: Cinquefoil was doomed. And without the ferisher chief to lead them and guide them, they would never find Ethan's father.

At the thought of his father Ethan took out the dark glasses and put them on. To his surprise the scene that had become so familiar – his father huddled on a patch of dark grey, in a pale grey room – was gone. In its place was a scene so bizarre and unexpected that it took him a moment to realise what he was seeing. At first he thought it was a billowing banner or sheet hung in the wind. Then he decided that it was a carpet of some kind, over which ran a rippling stream of water. Finally he realised that what he was looking at was *mice*, thousands of them, millions of them, tiny white mice running for their lives. And in the lower part of the lenses a pair of clawlike mitts was reaching down into the running river of mice and scooping them up, in the general direction of Ethan's *mouth*. The image jerked and swung as whoever was eating mice tossed his head and worked his jaws with evident pleasure.

Ethan whipped the glasses off his face and stuffed them down into his pocket, shuddering. He was going to have to think twice about putting them on again. He looked around for Thor, and presently found him, perched halfway up a mound of what looked like binders or notebooks, sitting on his haunches, turning over a pleated packet of paper, holding it this way and that, folding it, opening it, folding it again.

"What is it?" Ethan said. Thor said nothing, wholly absorbed in studying the sheet of paper, which looked to be about as big as an open newspaper. If they were still back on Clam Island, and it was a few days before, Ethan would have said that Thor was scanning the paper into his database. "Thor?"

Ethan found a toe-hold in the mound of binders and hoisted himself up. The little binders, he saw now, were actually address books, plastic- and leather-bound, purse-sized and pocket-sized and briefcase-sized, representing the total acquaintanceship of a couple of thousand people, easy. He remembered his mother's having lost her address book, once, the day before she went in for her biopsy— "the worst week of my life," she had called it at the time, though there would of course be worse to come. He wondered idly if his mother's address book could be somewhere in this mountain he was climbing. Whose addresses and phone numbers would have been in that book? What would those people say to him if he called them now? How many address books out there still had his mother's name in them, neatly pencilled, with a phone number that was disconnected and an address that was no longer good?

Even before he reached Thor's perch he could see that what the other boy was studying with such interest was a map, a large one, which had been ruined by repeated and slapdash refolding. There were a number of such maps in the glove compartment of Skidbladnir, puzzle-maps, Rubik's cubes of paper so thoroughly "bollixed up," as Mr. Feld put it, that they couldn't ever really be opened anymore. They had been folded so many times and so incorrectly that they were now forever sealed by some mysterious origami of carelessness. At best you could peel back a pleat and peer inside, looking for a street or highway in a cramped, crazy-quilt terrain where the Pacific Ocean, say, bumped up against downtown Phoenix. Thor was not studying the contents of the map. He was still trying to figure out how to arrange and collapse the coloured rectangular sections back together the right way. There were whitish rectangles, and greenish rectangles, and brownish rectangles, painted, covered in tiny black writing, and shot through with curling lines of grey. And then there were the blue rectangles, serenely blue and blank as the sky with no grey lines, no writing or marks on them at all.

"What's it a map of?" Ethan said, crouching down alongside Thor, accidentally starting a landslide of address books towards the floor. As he leaned in to get a closer look, he saw that the paper on which the map was printed looked old and yellowed, and had chipped considerably along some of its edges. Then he looked closer still and saw how crooked and quirky were the letters in which the names of the various features of the map were written. It was the same alphabet he had seen on the letter-scroll used by Johnny Speakwater to spit out the future as seen by the oracular clam. "Can you tell? Do you see any place names you recognise? Is there a legend? Is there a compass rose?"

But Thor did not answer. He just went on peeling back sections of the map from one another, folding it in half, then in quarters, then opening it into brand-new quarters and halves.

"Come on, Thor," Ethan said. "We don't have time for you to play with that. We have to find that stick." Thor ignored him. He had folded the map down to a single thick rectangle, one of the blue ones without any text or markings. Now he began to open it up again, one tentative fold at a time.

"Thor," Ethan pleaded. "Thor, come on, we have to—hey. Way to go."

He'd done it: opened up the map all the way, smooth and unpleated. He held it out in front of him and Ethan, arms spread wide. From one end to another, from top to bottom and from right hand to left, there hung before them a single, uninterrupted expanse of blue, like a detail of a close-up of a tiny blue section of the wide-open sky. It was six rectangles high and nine wide, like this:

"What kind of map is that? What's it of? Turn it over."

The reverse of the map was made of thousands and thousands of overlapping green splotches, pointed ovals, some large and some small, each one painted carefully and edged and shadowed to give them the appearance of depth. Ethan looked closer and saw that they were not splotches but *leaves*, painted green leaves connected by a bewildering tangle of the curling, twisting, bending grey lines that were meant, he understood, to represent the branches of a tree. Each leaf was marked, in turn, with little picture symbols for rivers and woods, mountains and lakes, hills and cities, and countless other places, all of them named in the crabbed little ferisher alphabet.

"What happened to the mostly brown parts there were a minute ago?" Ethan said. "And the mostly white ones?"

Thor turned his head towards Ethan, and looked at him. Though it lasted only a second, Ethan never forgot that look. He had been so often the recipient of Thor's information, of his facts and his preposterous theories. But he had never until this moment seen in Thor's eyes – in anyone's eyes – such a look of utter knowledge. Whatever else happened to him, whatever became of him, in spite of his being too tall, too red-blooded, too mortal, too *human*, Thor had found his way into a world that he understood. Back in the Middling, Thor had been like one of those meteorites you heard about that fall from space and land at the bottom of the ocean. Though it lies half buried in mud and half encrusted in a skin of plankton and molluscs, though it is warmed by vents in the earth and gives shelter to all manner of fish, at its heart lie the chemicals and elements, the sparkling mysterious stuff of outer space. Without saying a word, Thor quickly folded the map down to a single rectangle, this time a greenish one – Ethan saw a patch of rippling black lines meant to represent a sea. Then Thor opened the map back up again, and turned it over. This time the reverse was made up of a mass of pale brown leaves, neatly painted and linked as before by intertwining branches, thick and thin, painted in grey. Ethan opened his mouth but for a minute nothing would come out. Then at last he finally managed to say, "White?"

Thor nodded, and with the practiced ease of a magician, folded the map down to a single brownish rectangle, then out once again into a map of brown leaves. He turned the map over; the other side of it was covered in clusters and masses of white leaves, traced with ink of pale blue-grey, and all interconnected with the veins and arteries of grey.

"Four sides," Ethan said. "Four worlds! It's a map of the Tree!"

"That's right," Thor said. "The white one is the Winterlands. The green one is the Summerlands. The brown one is the Middling. And the blue one is—"

"The Gleaming. Which is blank. Because no one knows what happens there. Or how you get there. Or even who lives there."

"I know who lives there," Thor said. "Old Mr. Wood. And his brothers and sisters. The— what Mr. Rideout called the Tahmahnawis. The spirits. The gods. They— they're all up there, or over there, or in there. In the Gleaming. They're trapped there. Yeah. Yeah, Coyote did it. There's a— there's a whole story, like, a song, or a poem or I can't quite..." He shook his head. "It's all about how Coyote tricked them. Got them in there and sealed the Gate. And now it's been sealed ever since. And none of them, not even Old Mr. Wood, can get out. It's part of all this... data that seems to have been... uploaded to my head since we got to the Summerlands."

"Thor?" Ethan said. "You know— you know that you aren't an android. Not really."

"I know it," Thor said.

"But you know— you know that you aren't— I guess you aren't really human, exactly, either."

"Tell me about it," Thor said. "Like I haven't known *that* my whole entire life." He shrugged. "I guess being an android was the best explanation I could come up with for how I always *felt*."

"And you're all right— I mean, it's OK? You're OK? With being, well, a changeling?"

"I guess so," Thor said. "I don't really have any, you know, choice. It's just— well, there's this one thing I'm sort of wondering about. A little. Looking around, you know, at all this stuff these ferishers have *taken* from people over the years. They do take it, you know. It's not like they just find it lying around."

"Yeah?" Ethan said. "What? What do you wonder?"

"Well, it's just, the Boar Tooth mob, if they're the ones that, you know, left me. When they left me..."

"Yeah?"

"What did they do with the baby they took?"

This was not a question, Ethan found, that he had any great desire ever to find the answer to.

"Come on," he said. "Fold that thing up and take it with us. I'm sure it'll come in handy. And let's get going after that stick."

At this point, though it's a little late, I should probably mention that while ferisher treasures differ from those of dragons, dwarfs, gnomes, etc., in nearly every respect, they resemble them in this one: they are always, but *always*, carefully, and fearfully, and very often fatally, left in the hands of an ill-tempered and none-too-well-fed guardian.

"Stick, is it?" said a small, hard voice behind them.

14

A Mother's Tears

THE CANDLES IN the sconces that lit the little cell guttered, spitting and smoking, and then, one by one, went out. At last only a single flame flickered weakly in the sconce just over the spot where Jennifer T. sat, her head pillowed against the soft fur of Taffy's lap, in the shadow of one of the Sasquatch's heavy breasts. Jennifer T. and Taffy lay that way for a long time, without speaking. They listened to the shallow breathing of the wounded chief and the rowdy snoring of the ferisher princess. The Sasquatch's breath slowed. After a while it occurred to Jennifer T. that it had been a long time since either of them had moved.

"Taffy?" Jennifer T. said at last. "You awake?"

"Yes, Jennifer T."

Taffy shifted a little, and Jennifer T. tilted back her head to look past the coal-black boobs at the Sasquatch's face. Taffy's little dark eyes glinted in the dim light from the sconce overhead.

"Did you, well, did you hear anything... strange? Today, I mean. Back when that thunderbird had me hanging there like that."

"Hear?" Taffy said, and a low growl of amusement

rumbled in her throat. "I heard plenty. The whole Far Territories heard you, my dear."

"No, I mean, did you hear anything else?"

But Taffy seemed not to have noticed the question.

"When I was just a little squatchling," she said, "I remember the old ladies used to tell us that the Last Day would be signalled by the crowing of a rooster. But I guess they were wrong."

Jennifer T. thought about this for a moment. Then she said, "Well, I am a Rooster, in a way."

And she explained to Taffy all about the Clam Island Mustang League, and Mr. Perry Olafssen, and the Angels, and the Reds, and the Bigfoot Tavern Bigfoots, whose team nickname drew another growl from the Sasquatch, though this time it sounded like a growl of irritation.

"Why must they?" Taffy said, shaking her big head. "It's just so *cruel*."

As Jennifer T. talked on about the Mustang League, she found herself, somewhat to her surprise, missing Clam Island. She had been born and had spent nearly every moment of her eleven years there, except for the summer when she was five, which she had spent at the home of her mother's mother, in Spokane. Clam Island was the only home she had ever known. Now she was very far away from it, separated from that rainy grey-green patch of island not only by miles but also by time and enchantment. So perhaps it is not terribly surprising if, lying cold in the darkness of an underground cell, in the midst of the utmost wilderness of the Summerlands, she was suddenly wracked with homesickness. Nonetheless she was surprised. She missed the dirt and the smell of the grass at Ian "Jock" MacDougal Regional Ball Field. She missed her bicycle, and the scratchy cheeks of her uncle Mo, and even the three ancient and irritable ladies in their enormous recliners. She missed Mr. Perry Olafssen!

After a while she left off talking, but thoughts of home ran on in her mind. Only now they began to meld and entangle themselves in one another, like sections of a map being carelessly folded: she was falling asleep. As she drifted off, she found herself missing, in a kind of dream-stew of homesickness, old Albert Rideout himself, who was standing beside her now, at the controls of *Victoria Jean*, with the fly of his trousers half zipped. He was piloting the airship, with a steady hand, over the Cascade Mountains. When they reached Spokane he flew right over Grandmother Spicer's house, with its pointed turret, and there on the front porch stood Jennifer T.'s mother, whose given name was Theodora. She was more beautiful than Jennifer T. remembered her – in fact she looked much more like *Ethan Feld's* mother, at least as she appeared in a framed photograph on the buffet in the Felds' living room. As Albert and Jennifer T. sailed overhead, the beautiful, Mrs. Feldish Theodora raised her small white hand and slowly, with a sad smile on her face, began to wave. And then the smile faded, and from somewhere deep inside the house with the pointed tower came the sound of someone roughly weeping, dark barking sobs of terrible pain.

Jennifer T. sat up, in the semi-darkness, her heart pounding. Taffy was crying – thundering, rough-edged Sasquatch sobs.

"You *did* hear something, didn't you?" Jennifer T. said,

with the utter certainty of someone who is not yet fully awake. "You *heard* it. After I shouted out 'Ragged Rock'. A woman was crying. A mother was crying." She didn't know why she was so sure that the weeping woman was a mother, but she was. "Taffy, I know that you heard it."

Taffy snuffled, and wiped her snub nose on the back of a shaggy forearm. Slowly she hoisted her huge bulk into a more upright position, and let out a long shuddering breath. She nodded.

"I heard it," her voice thick with grief. "But I thought it was only the sound of my guilty conscience. Because of what I did, a long time ago. To my children."

"What did you do?"

That question started poor Taffy crying all over again. "I left them," she said.

WHAT FOLLOWS, IS, as far as I have been able to reconstruct it, the sad story told by Taffy the Sasquatch. It will turn out later to have some importance for *our* story, or else I would never interrupt things in this way to relate it. Not with Cinquefoil shrivelling into a seedpod on his pallet in the corner, and Ethan and Thor in the clutches of the guardian of the ferisher treasure, and Mr. Feld and Cutbelly somewhere off in the Winterlands, prisoners and slaves of that smiling, rust-red rogue who means to bring the universe to an end. Fortunately Taffy's story has the virtue, shared by most really sad stories, of being fairly short.

Sasquatches have acquired a reputation, in the Middling, for being solitary creatures. But as a rule it is only the males who spend their lives wandering alone. They range widely in the vast forests of the Far Territories, and from time to time one of them will stumble onto a gall where the Branches of two Worlds are pleached together. These are the unlucky specimens who wind up crashing into the camp of some terrorised party of trappers or fishermen up in Alberta, or, once, directly into the path of a man named Roger Patterson and his 16mm movie camera. The male Sasquatch is a shy and unsociable creature, who prefers his own company to any other, and when he gets around those of his kind it is usually only long enough to exchange some news of the woods and to get some female or other pregnant. Then he is on his way again.

With the females, however, it is an entirely different story. They spend their whole lives, generally, in the woods where they were born, among their mothers and grandmothers, sisters and aunts, helping to look after the squatchlings, gathering food – they are strict vegetarians – and listening to the endless stories of the very old ladies. These stories, few of which are notably sad, tend therefore to be very long indeed, often two weeks, or more, in the telling. Since the old ladies, like their grandmothers and great-grandmothers before them, have never ventured beyond the local neighbourhood of hills and trees, their stories are not especially rich with the wonders and marvels of the world. Instead, they tend to be what might be called wisdom tales, cautionary stories, which for all their length and elaborate language boil down, in the end, to pretty simple ideas like Short-Cuts Usually Turn Out to Be Very Long Indeed or Never Throw Anything Away, Because You Never Know.

But then, every once in a very great while, when there are two full moons in a single month, or when one of the less antisocial males has come to pay a visit, a great-grandmother Sasquatch will break out a story from the Beginning of the World. In the Beginning of the World, before Coyote changed everything, when the Sasquatches were still fresh from the making hand of Old Mr. Wood, things were not as they are now. All the Sasquatches wandered, unprotected and lost, a gang of stragglers, through the deep, deep shadows of the First Forest. They had adventures, all right – and terrible misadventures. Because they had no families, no clear lines of motherhood, no organisation, no wisdom tales, they could not defend themselves very well against the various nonvegetarian creatures with whom they shared the earliest world. They were stalked and caught and, because Coyote had brought hunger and death into the world, devoured. It was not long before only two Sasquatches remained, a male and a female. They called out to Coyote to help them. As usual, his help took the form of a choice: wander the woods in an unruly way, heedless of each other's safety, but knowing the marvels and wonders of the world; or settle down, make order, find wisdom – stay home. In the end, as you may have guessed, the male chose the first, the female the second, and they have stuck stubbornly by their choices ever since.

These ancient tales of adventuring females and devouring beasts unsettled their listeners, and ended up feeling pretty cautionary, too, in the end. But on the mind of Taffy the Sasquatch – that was not, of course, her real name; her real name was very long and deeply secret – they had a peculiar effect. They filled her with *longing*. And when the visiting male, having eaten his fill, and told a tale or two of his own, and fathered another squatchling, had gone off again to resume his wanderings, Taffy would feel as if a small part of herself, of her contentment, had gone off with him. It was not many years, as Sasquatches reckon such things, before all the remaining bits of her happiness had been carried away.

By this time she was a mother, herself, twice over, and the aunt of seven squatchlings more. Her oldest nephew, whom she loved dearly, had reached the age when his homewood had begun to feel more like a prison than a shelter. He began, tentatively at first, then for longer and longer periods, to go beyond the streams and fields that were the recognised bounds of their territory. When he returned, his face would be alight with the memory of the things he had seen. One day he was gone for a very long time, and when he returned he told a story of a marvellous bridge of stone that stretched, in a single continuous arch, across a great river gorge, across which there passed a steady traffic of creatures – ferishers and werebears, talking squirrels and blue jays and minks, and strange adventurers, like hairless Sasquatches, from the land known as the Middling. This bridge, he said, was no more than a good day's walk to the west.

Now, Taffy had heard many outlandish tales in her life – she had even heard, once or twice, about this marvellous bridge, which some said had been raised by Coyote, so that he could leap across the worlds more easily, and which others said was a remnant of the time when Old Mr. Wood and his spirit kin still walked the First Forest. But she had never realised that it was so near to home, and she had never heard it spoken of by one who was, himself, so near to her.

"I would like to see that bridge," she blurted out, and then covered her mouth, because it was not a very polite remark for a female Sasquatch to make. And her young nephew, because he was young, and loved her, said, "Go, Auntie! Leave now! Yes! Oh, you must! You can be there by midnight and back again by dawn and none but we two will be the wiser."

"And who," she asked him, "will stay with the squatchlings while I am gone, and lay a cool cloth on their foreheads if they get feverish, and lie beside down them to stroke their forearm fur if they have bad dreams?"

"I will!" said the nephew, laughing. "Go! Go now!"

And so she had gone, taking nothing with her but the memory of his face alight with the wonders he had seen, and of the murmuring of her children sleeping by the fire.

"I NEVER DID see that marvellous bridge," she told Jennifer T. now, in the darkness of their cell at the bottom of the knoll. "Before I arrived, I was set upon, in the dead of night, by a raiding party of giants – those rotten John brothers. The Sasquatch-mania among the giants was at its peak. They were regularly prowling the woods for—" She shivered. "Pets. Later Mooseknuckle John told me he had heard that the bridge collapsed, or was destroyed. Long ago. So I never will see it. And I never will see my dear, sweet squatchlings again, either."

"Why not?" Jennifer T. said. "You're free. You're home, or close enough. Listen, oh, Taffy, once we get out of here, you don't need to stay with us. You can go off and find your way back to your homewood. You can find your kids. I'm sure they're dying to—"

But Taffy shook her great shaggy head.

"They're gone," she said. "Long gone. I wasn't sure at first. It took a while for my nose to readjust."

"Gone?" Jennifer T. was confused. "Your *nose*?"

"We Sasquatches have very sensitive noses. We can smell things that you can't possibly imagine, my dear. We can smell an idea forming in the brain of a fish. We can smell the first heartbeat of an infant in its mother's womb. And we can smell the passing of time itself. At first, as I say, I wasn't sure. But once that thunderbird storm blew through my nostrils, I had the full smell of the Summerlands again after all those years in the cage in that stinking hall of stone. And I knew. There just isn't any way that any of my children, or even my grandchildren, could still be alive. I was stuck in that cage for much too long."

"But you said it was only a few hundred years," Jennifer T. said. "And if *you* could live that long..."

"Ah," Taffy sighed. "But the cage I was in – it was not made of true iron. It was weird-iron, mined in the Winterlands. And as long as I was kept within it..."

"Time moves different in the Winterlands, so they say." It was Spider-Rose. She rolled over now, and sat up, her face as she looked at Taffy creased with a faint wrinkle of sympathy. "It was a couple of hundred years for you, maybe, but all the while, out here in the wide world—"

"Nine hundred years have passed, here, since the day I left," Taffy said, hanging her head. "I can smell each and every one of them gone by."

Jennifer T. reached over to stroke the smooth dark cheek of the Sasquatch, and Taffy drew her against her side, and then they lay there, in the cell under the ferisher hill, listening to the hollow echo of all those vanished years.

15

Grim

"CLIMB DOWN FROM there. Come on, now. Be quick."

Ethan and Thor turned, awkwardly, sending fresh avalanches of address books to the treasury floor. At first, when he saw their captor, Ethan wanted to laugh. It was a boy, roughly the age and height of Ethan himself, perhaps a little smaller. An extremely ugly boy, true, with a nose like an empty spool of thread, ears like two shrivelled apples, and a pair of pink, staring, bloodshot eyes much too small for the rest of his face. He was brandishing Ethan's stick of ashwood, swinging it carelessly back and forth, like a policeman in the cartoons with a nightstick. There was something familiar about him, to Ethan, and at the same time something very wrong. His expression was far too hard even for the unluckiest child; it banished Ethan's laughter, and encouraged him and Thor to scramble down from atop the pile as quickly as they could.

"What's your problem, rube?" said the not-boy, with a sneer of irritation. He was looking at Thor Wignutt. Ethan turned to his friend and saw that Thor had gone white as a sheet.

"Are you…?" Thor began. He swallowed, with such difficulty that Ethan could hear the muscles of his throat. "Did they— take you?"

"What's that? Did who take me?"

"The ferishers. From the Middling. Are you— a changeling?"

For a moment, Ethan was puzzled by the question, but then he understood. The not-boy gave off such a powerful air of *wrongness*. Maybe that was what seemed so familiar about him. It had reminded Thor of *Thor*.

Now, however, it was the not-boy's turn to laugh. He threw back his knobby head with its thatching of stiff yellow hair, and emitted a series of harsh guffaws, like a trash can banging down a flight of concrete steps.

"Me? You think I'm *human*? Feh!" He wiped his eyes with the sleeve of the loose buckskin tunic he wore. "A *changeling*?" He had to kneel for a moment, he was laughing so hard. "By the Starboard Arm, how did a pair of idiot reubens like you manage to come so far?"

"Well," said Ethan, in his mildest Invisible Boy tones. He was unpleasantly reminded, for some reason, of Kyle Olafssen. And it was just as well, because he was used, by now, to dealing with the Kyle Olafssens of the world. "What are you then?"

"What am I? What *am* I?" cried the not-boy, springing to his feet with startling speed. He rushed Ethan, crowding him up against a teetering heap of stolen mailboxes, most of them still on their posts, some still with dirt and tufts of grass clinging to them where they had been yanked from the ground. He raised the ashwood stick with both hands and rammed it up against Ethan's throat, choking him. The mailboxes clanged and rattled. "I'm a *giant*. I should think that would be obvious."

It was hard to tell – especially when the oxygen supply to your brain was being cut off – whether the not-boy could possibly be serious. When he had said he was a giant, he had sounded as if he meant it. But when he said that it ought to be obvious, his voice had taken on a edge of bitterness or sarcasm. And, after all, he could not possibly have been taller than four feet nine.

Such questions had, for the moment, to be set aside. Thor Wignutt was never one to stand idly by when his captain was under attack.

First he grabbed hold of the not-boy's thick shock of yellow thatch. Then he got around the not-boy from behind, and jerked his head back by the hair with one hand. With the other hand he grabbed hold of the stick, twisting it sharply down and away from Ethan's throat. At the same time he poked his right knee into the back of the not-boy's right knee. The not-boy went down with a grunt of surprise, and Ethan fell back against the tangle of mailboxes, gasping. When next he looked, Thor and the not-boy were whiplashing each other around, rolling on the ground, always with the stick gripped between them. First the not-boy was on top, then Thor, and all the while they kicked and slapped and spat at one another. The not-boy tried to chew off Thor's left ear. It was the ugliest fight that Ethan had ever seen.

Thor won. He ended up on top of the not-boy, with the stick pressed heavily down against the not-boy's throat, and the not-boy going red, then blue, and finally a sickly yellowish-green in the face.

"Say 'uncle'," Thor said.

"You mean 'nuncle', " grunted the not-boy, through his teeth.

" 'Nuncle'? "

"That's what we say here."

"Say 'nuncle', then."

"Nuncle!"

Thor let him up, taking the stick with him, and the not-boy rose to his feet, making a disgusting array of gagging and choking sounds and hawking up great yellow oysters of spit which he deposited all around himself with evident pleasure. Finally he drew himself up to his full (and, as has been mentioned, not considerable) height and looked Thor carefully up and down.

"Not bad," he said. "For a jambled-up mishmash of a changeling."

"Not bad," said Thor, "for a shrunken-down little pinky-toe of a giant."

"What?" Ethan said. "He really *is* a giant?"

"Of *course* I am, scat-for-brains," said the not-boy, and, scowling, he bowed very low. "And a wicked mother cursed me with the sorry name of Grimalkin John. If you prize your life, though, you'll just leave it at Grim. Grim the Giant."

"But— but what happened to you?" Ethan said, recalling a poem he had once read about a little grey kitty cat whose name was Grimalkin.

"I was born this way," Grim the Giant said. "What happened to *you*?"

"Are you a boy giant? Or—?"

Grim the Giant sneered his toothy sneer, and looked ready to fight all over again.

"I'm a full-grown, tried-and-true man of a giant, boy! And don't you forget it!"

"Here," Thor said to Ethan, handing him back the stick. Thor was badly torn up. Bloody scratches on his cheeks as if he had been fighting with some kind of irascible animal like a wolverine or a stoat. Shirt collar ripped. A bead of blood on his lower lip. Actually he looked sort of angry with Ethan about the whole incident. "Don't ever let go of it again."

"I won't," Ethan said, feeling decidedly scolded. "OK, so, come on. Let's go. Take the little giant."

Grim the Giant took a dangerous step towards Ethan, pushing back a sleeve. "'*Take the little giant?*' Where do you think *you're* going?"

At this point they faced the uncomfortable question of who was now the captive of whom. Ethan, who doubted if he would ever be able to win in a fight against the little giant, even with his bat in hand, decided to take a psychological approach. That was what he was best at. It usually worked on everyone, except for Jennifer T.

"OK, just tell me this," he tried. "Just say that we are your prisoners. Just say."

"Right," said Grim.

"Which means, in other words, that you are working for them. Those stupid Dandelion Hill ferishers who can't stop talking long enough to realise that, OK, one of their very own species, and the Home Run King of three Worlds, is dying right now, in their dungeon, which is because he's got iron in his body from one of their arrows, and two, that *the entire universe may be about to come to an end.*"

"They sure does like to hear themselves talk," Grim the Giant agreed, spitting again.

"So that's what I'm asking, then, is just why would you want to work for them? You're a giant. They're ferishers."

"Well," said the giant, "the fact of the matter is, since you ask, I wouldn't work for that mob by choice or for money. Alas for poor Grim that he doesn't have no choice in the matter."

"You're grammerbound," Thor said. "A slave."

The little giant pressed his thin lips together as if biting back an angry rejoinder. Then he just nodded, once, shortly.

"Ferishers use slaves?" Ethan said, dismayed.

The giant spat. "Some do. This mob does. One. That's me. Grimalkin John. Chief Mechanical, and Senior Equipment Manager for the Dandelion Hill mob. And"— he flushed— "Head Mouser. But that don't—"

He broke off, and stood still, listening, and then Ethan heard it too, a musical cry, a cracked note of song from the other side of the treasury door. When Ethan and Thor had passed through the door, the uproar of the ferishers' council died away. Now, in addition to the exuberant voice of a singing ferisher, there were other raised voices from out in the winding hall. The next moment there came a loud rapping; the sealing grammer had been taken off the door. Grim the Giant turned bright red, and looked wildly around the treasury.

"Damn them!" he said. "They'll have my hide if they see you've beaten me."

He looked quite upset, in a way that did not at all fit with his brash features and hard little twist of a smile. Ethan had no desire to be taken prisoner again, but at the same time he felt sorry for the scrappy little giant. He turned to Thor, whose knowledge of the ways of the Summerlands – Ethan supposed it was really a kind of deep memory, returning to his friend after years of amnesia in the Middling – seemed to be growing by the minute.

Thor was studying Grim the Giant now with expression that showed traces of the pity that Ethan had been feeling. The wiry creature who only moments before had seemed to believe that his shoulders brushed the treetops and his shadow blotted out the very sun now listened to the increasingly irritable knocking at the door to the treasury with an air of misery and even dread.

"He means it," Thor said at last. "They really could take his hide."

"Don't I know it," said Grim, glumly. "Didn't the old bat craft her very mitt from the thigh skin of my great-grandpap?"

Ethan thought of the pile of great bleached bones out of which the Boar Tooth mob's ballpark had been built, and found that he could not doubt the little giant's grisly claim. Just like that, all the sympathy that he had built up towards ferishers, especially after witnessing the brutal treatment they had received from Coyote's minions, seemed to drain away. Ferishers had shot him and his friends from the sky, unprovoked, and without asking any questions, thrown them into the deepest dungeon in the knoll. They had enslaved – grammerbound – Grim the Giant. They had stolen all the human possessions piled in this dank and echoing chamber. And they had, once upon a time, *stolen Mrs. Wignutt's baby,* leaving a strange changeling boy behind. Dizzyingly, all the dark stories that he had read about fairies came flooding into his memory: stories of their heartlessness, their cruelty and indifference to human life and desires, the bewitchments and tricks and the harsh curses that they laid on hapless mortals.

"If we let you capture us again," he said finally, as the knocking grew ever more imperious and sharp, "you have to help us get back to our friends."

Grim's breath came out of him in a single gust as if he had been holding it tight. "Yes!" he cried.

"And then you help us get *out* of here."

Grim pressed his palms together. "I swear it."

Ethan looked at Thor. "What should we make him swear by? That 'by the Starboard Arm' thing they're always saying?"

"Not serious enough." Thor hand lingered on his temple. "Say 'by the Lone Eye'."

"It's Eye*ball*," the giant corrected. "All right then. I swear it, by the Lone Eyeball. A swear can't be more serious than that. Now you got my apologies, rubes, but hope you'll understand I'm going to have to tie you fast."

He grabbed one of the coils of rappelling cable and quickly wound it around and around Ethan and Thor.

"I'll not cinch it overtight," he said. "It's only for show anyhow, and they don't never look too close at nothing, 'less they have some money riding on it."

He went to the door, took hold of the latch, gave them a solemn wink, and threw open the big door. There was a burst of angry jeering and several dozen ferishers trooped in, jabbering and shouting at Grim the Giant in what sounded like Old Fatidic, slapping him on the bottom and kicking at his shins, then dissolving into raspy little gusts of mean laughter. They were dressed in leggings like Cinquefoil's mob, and they had the same strange golden eyes and ruddy skin, but their tunics were cut from some silvery stuff that glowed softly in the firelight. Ethan supposed that it must be some kind of ceremonial garb they wore especially for their Councils. Leading them all was a grand personage, a full head taller than the rest of the mob, and more than twice as wide. She was dressed in leggings and a silvery tunic, like the others, but she wore a silver circlet around her head, and she was unmistakably a queen. Her skin was powdered white. She was the only one who neither laughed nor taunted the little giant. She swept past him without a look, and began to say something, in a quavering, operatic voice, when she saw the boys tied up by the pile of mailboxes. Her mouth snapped shut, and her eyes with their strange rectangular pupils grew wide, then narrowed. She turned to Grim, and gazed up at him with an eyebrow arched, her arms folded tightly under her magnificent bosom.

At the sight of the ferishers Ethan felt a hot shiver run up his spine, and his toes curled and uncurled inside his shoes.

"Might I ask, then, what in the name a yer highest-pocketed and lowest-browed forefather these reubens is doing in my treasury, Mr. Grimalkin John?" Though she had Cinquefoil's broken grammar and accent, her voice had none of his raspy warmth. It was cold and barren of feeling. In her size, her pallid skin, her silvery gown, she made Ethan think of a tiny, cold moon.

There was a silence that grew very long and stretched very thin, and then Grimalkin John, somewhat to Ethan's surprise, laid a hand on his belly and cast a rather evil stare in Ethan's direction, and said,

"Don't hold it against me none, ma'am, but I been living somewhat overmuch on mouse and rat and whatnot for quite some time, as what I'm sure you'll acknowledge. It's an awful long time since I done sucked the good sweet marrow of a nice, meaty little reubenish bone." He lowered his head and managed to work a convincing flush of shame into his cheeks. "I just couldn't, you know. Resist."

At this the ferishers burst out laughing, Queen Filaree the loudest of all. Several little clinking sacks of gold-pieces changed hands, and Ethan marvelled that the ferishers had found enough time to wager on what Grim the Giant's excuse was going to be in the brief seconds between the asking of the queen's question and its answer. It was a little worrisome to think that some of them could have been so certain that he planned to devour the boys. Then the queen stopped laughing, and came over to stand beside Thor and Ethan. She gazed up at them, her expression blank but not unpleasant, the way you might stare at the rainbow in a greasy thumbprint on a windowpane, the instant before you wiped it away. Then she turned back to the little giant.

"Well, Mouser, yer in luck," she said. "Fer here we are, spent all the day in a considerable palaver, and in the end come ta no decision whatever but ta go out and play in the sunshine o' the afternoon. Would that it might be nine innings of baseball. But alas."

There was a general sad murmuring among the ferishers at the prospect, and Ethan wondered how much of the meanness of these ferishers was due simply to the loss of their ball field.

"So look here, Ratcatcher," the queen went on. "Just ya be fetching us our *racquets*" – she uttered the word distastefully – "and balls, and the mallets, and so on, and we'll leave ya ta yer meal."

The giant nodded, and wandered back into the shadows, where Ethan now saw another, smaller door, standing ajar. This must be where Grim the Giant had been concealed when he and Thor first crossed into the room. As the little giant pushed the door open, Ethan caught sight of two long racks filled with dozens and dozens of baseball bats. The little giant banged and clattered around in the equipment room – Ethan supposed that this might form, in a ferisher's opinion, the heart of the treasure – and then came back out carrying several small canvas sacks and pushing a wheeled croquet set.

The queen looked at them with revulsion, and Ethan saw her eye stray wistfully to the baseball bats ranged on the walls of the equipment room.

"Alas, Spider-Rose, what ya done to yer mother," she said, with a sigh. And a great golden tear rolled down her cheek. She wiped it away, and turned to Grim. "Carry that rubbish out," she said curtly, nodding towards the croquet and tennis gear. With a backwards look of warning, Grim followed the ferishers out of the treasury.

Ethan and Thor set about trying to get out of the ropes that tied them together, but giants have the knack of knots, and in the end they were forced to wait until Grim returned. Rapidly he untied them, and then he disappeared into the equipment room again, and began rattling around. Ethan and Thor followed him. The little giant was crouching down beside a straw pallet no different from those that had furnished their cell, stuffing some clothes into another of the canvas equipment sacks.

"What are you doing?" Ethan said.

"Leaving," the little giant said. He tied up the sack and rose to his feet. "Been thinking about it often enough lately. Might as well do it now."

"But *can* you leave?" said Thor. "Aren't you a bound giant?"

Grim nodded, looking quite grim.

"What will happen to you if you run away?" Ethan said. "What kind of a grammer is it?"

"I told you, scat-for-brains," said the little giant. "They'll have my hide. I'll start walking away from this hill in any direction and little by little, I guess, though tell the truth I ain't never seen it done, my skin'll start getting, well, *skinnier*. Less and less of it, until I'm a day's walk from her that binds me, Queen Full-a-rot, I calls her, and then it's all gone, and the bones and such are showing plain as anything, and there's nothing at all to hold the inside of me in, nor keep out everything what's meant to be outside."

"Ick," Ethan said.

"Don't matter, though, because once they found out I helped you and your friends, they'd have it anyway, wouldn't they?" He shouldered the bag and took a last look around at the room, the neat ranks of ferisher-scale bats, the ornate baskets overflowing with bright little white balls, the spare bases and extra gloves and sets of catcher's masks and old leather shin-guards. At the very back of the room was a long workbench, well stocked with tools, and beside this a great hulking old wooden machine, busy with flywheels and belts. This must be where the Chief Mechanical crafted the various fanciful machines in which the ferishers so delighted. A look of disgust, but not unmingled with regret, filled his eyes. "Maybe if I'm strong, and *this* much lucky, myself will hold together until I can get back to home and wrap the blood and bones of my fingers around the throats of them what bound me into the service of this mob in the first place. The pack of great snakes and weasels that my mother gave me in the stead of brothers."

"Mooseknuckle John?"

"Aye, he's one of 'em. And like as not the first I'll seek to liberate from his breath should I get the chance."

He smiled a thin, mean smile, and then his gaze fell on the stick in Ethan's hands.

"We're in some'at of a hurry," he said. "But before we skedaddle, I wonder if you doesn't want me to try and work that splinter of yours into a usefuller shape than it has at present?"

"Useful?" Ethan said. "You mean you know how to—can you make a *bat*?"

"It's not five minutes' work for me, on that gin of mine," the little giant said, pointing to the big machine. "But I'll do it only on a condition, and that's this: you got to let me keep all the shavings that get shedded off in the turning. If I can stuff my pocket with woundwood, who knows but that the binding grammer might not fit me just a little more loose."

Ethan looked at Thor, who nodded.

"I have a feeling we're going to be needing to hit some things, and not just balls," Thor said. "If a bat wasn't better for hitting stuff than a plain branch, why would people bother to make them?"

So Ethan handed the stick to the little giant, who took it with a certain rough tenderness and carried it back to the big machine at the back of the room. It was kept so far from the outer room and the halls of the knoll, he explained, because of the iron in it, and in the sharp-edged tools he needed for carving. He screwed the ends of the stick between the two spindles of the lathe, and gave it a slap with his hand.

"It's an awful fine piece of wood," he said, almost as if he regretted having to alter it. "*Awful* fine."

He began, with deep, regular strokes of his left foot, to work a great black treadle that lay in the dusty shadows beneath the hulk of the machine. Slowly at first, and then faster and faster the wood began to turn. The little giant reached for a large metal tool, and held its edge very close to the dark blur of the whirling wood. He paused. Ethan and Thor crowded in behind him.

"This here shank's conformulated out of weird-iron," Grim the Giant said. "Wouldn't nothing else do."

He touched the tip of the weird-iron shank to the wood.

Ethan was never sure afterwards exactly what happened next. Something long and thin seemed to reach towards him from the whirling blur at the heart of the lathe, a jagged streak, dark at one end, blazing gold at the other. It lanced out from under the blade in the little giant's hands and struck Ethan, with a bright, stinging sizzle, full in the chest. It could only have been – and afterwards both Thor and Grim insisted that it *was* – an especially long shaving of ashwood, peeled off by the first flashing strike of the shank. But to Ethan it looked and felt like nothing so much as long, jumping spark of electricity. It burned the air in his nostrils, and left a strange pulsing ache in his breastbone. A strange haze filled Ethan's eyes, tears and smoke and the sparkle that fills your head when you have been crouching, and then too quickly rise to your feet. He was filled with a powerful longing to handle the ashwood branch. The palms of his hands ached and tingled – they *bothered* him – as if something that he had lost, whose absence was as much a part of him as his name or the taste of his own tongue in his mouth, were about to be placed, at long last, in his grasp.

The air around the little giant was filled with a shower of glittering sparks that hit his crooked features with a weird light. For an instant the three of them stood, human, giant, and ferisher changeling, at the heart of the earth, lit by some ancient fire of making. Then, hours or minutes later, the sparks died, and the haze lifted from Ethan's eyes, and Grim the Giant turned to Ethan. His face was rimed with sawdust; sawdust had settled like snow on his hair and eyebrows.

"There's but one stroke remaining," he said. "A heart-knot, deep in the wood. If I cut it, you will have yourself a right fine piece of lumber, the best that I can work; and no more. If *you* cut it, you might craft yourself, if I'm not terrible mistaken, a bat for all the ages. Or else, lacking practice, you might turn that there chunk of fine woundwood to nothing more than a great flimsy toothpick fit for my old pappy's gums. It all depends."

"On what?" Ethan said. He leaned in to peer at what the giant had done. As promised he had, in a few minutes, turned the knobby hunk of wood that Ethan had found into a smooth, handsome baseball bat, delicately tapered at the handle. The unfinished lumber looked as soft as suede and shone pale and inviting. It was still attached to its former tree-branch self by a narrow pin at either end, where rough blocks of greyish branch remained clamped to the spindles. At first Ethan thought that what Grim wanted him to do was cut the bat loose, but then he saw, about halfway down the slender handle of the bat, a raised ridge of wood, of a darker hue than the rest, that had not yet been cut away. It was like a ring or collar, circling the grip. He could see that if you didn't cut it away, it would dig right into your hand. "What does it depend on?"

"Why, on *you*, natcherly," the little giant said, just as Ethan had known that he would. "On what you got inside you. On what's in those hands of yours, and in the heart that feeds them."

"Why?" Ethan said, filled with sudden dread of failure, of striking out, exactly like that which seized him when it was his turn to step up to the plate. "Why does it have to depend on *that*?"

But, of course, he already knew the answer to that question, too.

"Why?" said the little giant. He was busily scooping up handfuls of sawdust from the floor around the lathe and filling his pockets with them. "Because that's the nature of these things!"

"Come on, Feld," Thor said. It was the first time in a long time – maybe the first time ever – that Thor had not referred to him directly as *Captain*. "We have to get it back to Cinquefoil."

"Right," Ethan said. He took the lathe tool from Grim the Giant. It had a wood handle, and its metal shank was long and curved strangely in on itself lengthwise, as if it had been stopped just short of turning itself into a tube. The tip of it was curved like the moon of your thumbnail and glinted softly. Grim put a foot on the treadle and began to work it up and down. As the bat began to spin again, the ridge became a dark blur and then finally seemed to disappear altogether except as a fleeting shadow Ethan was not even sure he really could see. Slowly he lowered the tip of the shank towards the general area where he felt the dark ridge might lie. He knew that if he pressed too hard, he might very well cut clear through the handle of the bat. What was left might be useful for healing Cinquefoil, but no good whatever for hitting baseballs, and not much good for smacking at the heads of skrikers, either.

"Not so tight," said Grim. "You ain't trying to choke the life out of it!"

Ethan loosened his grip on the shank a little, afraid that if the blade made too glancing contact with the wood it would go skittering off along the length of the bat, digging out little gouges as it went. He felt the pressure of the little giant's hand on his shoulder, and of Thor's intent gaze. He lowered the tool again, going as quickly as he dared, absolutely certain that he had absolutely no idea where or how firmly he ought to touch the bat. The thumping and screeching of the lathe belts was painfully loud. All at once, just before he brought the shank down once and for all to the wood, he heard, or thought he heard, the voice of Jennifer T. Ridcout in his car, calling out "And keep your eyes open!" That was when he realised that he had, in fact, closed his eyes. He was just blindly poking around his beautiful bat with something that could ruin it forever.

"I can't do it!" he shouted.

He handed the tool to Grim the Giant, who took his foot from the treadle. The bat came whuffling to a stop. The dark lump was still there, of course, right in the middle of the handle.

"I'm sorry," Ethan said. "I— I'm not ready yet. You do it."

Grim raised the tool, and put his foot on the treadle. Then he stepped back, and turned to Ethan, and looked him up and down in a curious way, rubbing a little doubtfully at his bony chin. He took a long, narrow saw, wicked as the jaw of some carnivorous fish, from his workbench, and quickly ripped through the unturned ends of the stick, cutting loose the bat. He gripped it by its handle and took a couple of practice swings. He nodded.

"Going to drive you mad, that knot," he said. "But let's leave it there for now."

Ethan took the bat from him, and ran his hands along its surface. The touch was at once hard and satiny, like the coat of a horse's forehead.

"It wants sanding, of course," Grim said. "And oiling. But I reckon there's no time for that."

Ethan nodded, though he had only half heard the little giant's words; the shame of his failure throbbed in his chest as wildly as after any one of his countless strikeouts. For the first time since leaving Clam Island, he was glad that his father was not around to witness another display of Ethan's ineptitude. He gripped the handle, and the knot bit softly into the meat of his hand.

"Later," he mumbled, his cheeks burning. "I'll take care of it later."

He followed Thor and Grim out of the workshop, across the echoing treasury, and through the door to the spiral corridor – this time, of course, they just opened it and walked on through. They glanced up and down the arcing hall, but there was neither sound nor sign of ferisher – the whole mob, the giant said, had trooped out into the fields for their games. Quickly they ran down and around, and around, and around, past all the doors they had passed on their way up, until at last the corridor ran out, and they were face-to-face with the great oak door of the cell. Thor laid his hands against the wood, and closed his eyes – and the door swung open. Grim grinned as Thor jumped back with a cry.

"No need to wear yourself out with scamperings," he said. "I know the door grammers, took it right— oh."

Ethan and Thor crowded in behind him, and stood there, gaping at the jumble of empty straw pallets that were all that it contained.

"Come on," said Thor. "Let's get scampering."

16

A Rat in the Walls

"I'M SICK OF this!" said Jennifer T. "What happened to those guys? Where are they?"

The lone candle had nearly burned down; there was no way to know how long they had been waiting in the semi-darkness, but it felt like hours.

"They were probably captured," Spider-Rose said gloomily.

"Then why didn't they bring them back here?"

"Maybe they gave them to Grimalkin John. They sometimes do that with the ill-behaved ones."

"Grimalkin *John*?" Jennifer T. said. "A giant?"

"The tiniest giant in the Summerlands," Spider-Rose said. "He's no bigger than your friends are themselves. Mostly we has him around to keep down the mice and rats, better than a cat. Powerful hungry for rats, he is. Clever with his hands, too."

There was a low moan from the ferisher in the corner. Taffy was kneeling alongside him, mopping his brow with a damp rush, but it was clear that Cinquefoil was past any relief that cool water could provide. He had shrunk visibly, inward rather than in length, his chest collapsing and chin sinking down. His skin had turned the yellowy grey of a very old bruise, and felt leathery and dry to the touch. His feet had curled like the corners of a burning page. Meanwhile his wounded hand had swollen to four or five times its normal size, the tiny fingers protruding from it like teats from an udder; the sight of it turned her stomach.

"Well, then we just got to get ourselves out of this," Jennifer T. said. "We have a better chance of finding a piece of ashwood out there in the world than we do in here."

"How do you propose we do that?" Taffy said. The long hours of captivity seemed to have stirred glum memories of her years as the house pet of Mooseknuckle John. She sat, idly dribbling water across the ferisher's brow and staring off into shadows as if seeing in the faces of her long-dead children.

"You." Jennifer T. looked at Spider-Rose, who jumped. "Ferishers can scamper. I know they can, because Cinquefoil did it."

"Maybe that one can," Spider-Rose said, shaking her head. "He's at least a thousand years old, and a chief, and a very great athlete besides. I'm just a kid. I can't even work a proper grammer yet, not really. I'm not good at anything."

Jennifer T. sat down on her pallet and then lay back. But she could not get comfortable – the crazy book her uncle Mo had given her was poking her in the behind. *That crazy book*. Half-idly, with a snort of disgust with herself for even entertaining the idea, she sat up again and took out *The Wa-He-Ta Brave's Official Tribe Handbook*. Maybe there was something in the lockpicking section again, or a recipe for explosives using only dried rushes and Sasquatch spit. She smiled grimly to herself, paging through the old handbook, wondering what in the hell had become of Ethan Feld. She found the chapter on lockbreaking, and held the book towards the guttering light of the last candle, but there was nothing of any use that she could see. She flipped through the next few chapters, devoted in turn to earning Feathers in Boat-Craft, Knife-Throwing, and Building Igloos and Snow Houses, which might come in handy, she thought, if they ever did find themselves in the Winterlands. She had to hand it to those lame old Wa-He-Ta guys – even with all the fake Indian stuff, those kids must have had some fun. There was even a whole chapter for those who hoped to earn a Feather in De-Ghosting a Haunted House. This chapter featured sections on poltergeists, knockers, spectres and revenants, with a number of ghoulish illustrations, and, towards the end, detailed discussions of such common haunted-house features as Shifting Staircases, False Panels, and…

"Secret Passages," she whispered.

"Eh?" Taffy said. "What's that?"

Jennifer T. got up and, carrying the handbook, began searching the walls of the cell for what the book described as Telltale Signs of a Secret Passage. "Look for a section of the wall," the anonymous author had written, "or, as it may be, of the ceiling, which is of a different shade or hue, however slightly, than the rest." The walls of their cell were whitewashed, but quite poorly, and not recently, and so they were fairly awash in patches of different hues – in fact you might almost have said that no two stretches of sloping wall were quite the same shade of white. The next recommended technique was, of course, tapping. Jennifer T.

knelt down at the bottom of the wall by the door and began to tap, working her way up and down, using the spine of the handbook itself, listening for that Telltale Hollowness. Taffy, catching on to what Jennifer T. had in mind, started on the other side of the door and began to rap with her hairy knuckles, working herself around the room in the other direction.

"I get what you're looking for OK," Spider-Rose said. "But it isn't going to work. I been poking around this old hump a dirt these last hundred and seven years and I would— hey."

"*Shh!*" hissed Jennifer T., though Spider-Rose, having heard the same extraordinary sound, had already fallen silent. At the bottom of the wall, where it met the floor, just a little to the right of Cinquefoil's poor curled-up feet, Jennifer T. held the book tightly between her fingers and tapped, once, twice, three times. And there it was again: *tap-tap-tap*, as if somebody on the other side of the wall were tapping back.

"Is there another cell on the other side of that wall?" Taffy wondered.

Spider-Rose shook her head, her eyes wide, her mouth a tiny dot.

"Could it be rats?" Jennifer T. was kicking now at the spot at the bottom of the wall whence the tapping had come. It seemed to her that the spot on the wall distinctly kicked back. "You said there are rats in this place?"

"Precious few," said Spider-Rose. "That Grim the Giant is *crazy* about rat. Rat kebab. Rat goulash."

"Rat goulash," said Jennifer T. Though she had never tasted goulash of any kind, its name, encountered in books or on television, had always struck her as highly suspicious. She was not at all surprised to learn that it could be made from rat meat. "Yuck."

"In any case," Taffy remarked, "rats are certainly intelligent creatures, but they are not, so far as I am aware, capable of counting to three."

With a crunch of plaster, and a pebbly scrabbling of dirt, Jennifer's T. foot disappeared into the wall. A small, scratchy voice said, "Oh, *hell*," and then a moment later a little black snout appeared, tipped with a moist black droplet of a nose, whiskers aquiver.

"What *you* know about *rats*, Bigfoot," said the creature, stepping into the room, slapping the dust from his breeches, "wouldn't fill the jockstrap of a weevil, I'm sure."

It was, Jennifer T. would have said, a very small man, perhaps one-half as tall as a ferisher – but a man with the tail, narrow snout, whiskers, and tufted, softly curling ears of a rat. He walked upright, though with a stoop, and had an impressive pot belly.

"Dick Pettipaw!" Spider-Rose said. "You stinking thief! I should have known!"

"And I should have strangled you in your cradle when I had the chance, but there you have it, life is nothing but a string of missed opportunities."

"A wererat," said Jennifer T.

"A *thieving* wererat. Been raiding our larders for years."

"True enough," said Pettipaw. "And here today for the very same purpose. Though one look at you lot and I can see the day's fun is spoilt. What's wrong with this ferisher, then? Ironshot, is he? Alas, alas. What a pity." He didn't sound sorry in the least. He crept forward, and peered curiously, snout aquiver, at Cinquefoil. "Not one of you rustic lot, by the look of him, neither, though it's hard enough to tell with him all shrivelled up that way." He turned his attention now to Taffy and Jennifer T., tugging thoughtfully on a whisker. One of his eyes, Jennifer T. noticed now, was covered in a dashing silk patch, purple trimmed with black. "A ferisher princess, a Sasquatch, and a reuben girl. Interesting assortment. Not the usual fare, to be sure. I don't doubt but what you all have some connection to that rattling bucket of reuben enginery I passed on my way into the hillside."

"Our *car*," Jennifer T. said. "Listen, Mr. Pittypat or whatever your name is. How wide is that tunnel of yours?"

"Wide enough to fit you, I'd wager, and these ferishers. But your hirsute companion would have herself a difficult time."

"It doesn't matter," Taffy said, sinking into a corner. "Leave me."

"No," Jennifer T. said. "No way." She grabbed hold of the sides of the hole she had kicked in the wall and began to pull at the edges. The plastering was thin here, and in a rush of small stones and root-choked earth she succeeded in widening the hole enough to get her head and shoulders through. It was surprisingly dark in the tunnel behind the wall – no light entered from the cell – but she felt around, and confirmed what the wererat had told them. There was just enough room for someone as large as herself. She crawled backwards into the cell and discovered the reason for the darkness in the tunnel – the last candle in the cell had finally gone out.

"Well, that's it then," Spider-Rose said. "Stuck in the dark till they come to change the tapers. Who knows when that will be."

"*You* may be stuck," the wererat said. "But I can see perfectly well, thank you. Some of us are more fortunately gifted than others, perhaps. And now, if you ladies will excuse me, I'll just be—"

Jennifer T. sat down, hard, in front of the hole in the wall. Her back just managed to block it, with perhaps an inch to spare on either side.

"Wait a minute," she said. The wererat's mention of his *gifts* had triggered something in her memory. "You're a wererat. Part rat, part human."

"That's a distasteful way of putting it," Dick Pettipaw said, sounding offended. "Now get out of my way."

"Are wererats like were*foxes*?"

"Are reubens like baboons? No, don't answer that, you'll only hurt your own feelings. But, yes, we're part of the greater kinship of the werebeasts. Shaped by the playful hand of the Changer, a very, very long time ago."

"Then you know how to scamper! Don't you?"

"No."

Jennifer T. had been feeling quite excited by the idea of getting Pettipaw to scamper them right out of the cell. Now her heart sank.

"But I thought that all creatures who— who are..." She didn't want to offend the creature again, not if they were going to need his help.

"Not me," came the brusque reply. "Never bothered to learn."

"He's lying," Taffy growled out of the darkness. "He does it all the time. His heartbeat, the timbre of his voice—believe me, I know. I can hear lies." The Sasquatch's voice turned acid. " 'Some of us are more fortunately gifted than others, perhaps.' "

There followed, in the darkness of the ferisher cell, a prolonged silence.

"When I was passing that rangabang heap of yours," the wererat said at last, "it seemed to me that my mighty organ of olfaction detected a distinct odour of Braunschweiger sausage."

"It's yours," Jennifer T. said at once. "Just help us find our friends, and then when we get to the car, you can have everything we've got."

"Nope," the wererat said. "It's straight to the 'car' and the liverwurst, or nothing. Your friends will have to find their own way out."

Jennifer T. was about to say no – she couldn't imagine leaving her friends lost or recaptured, somewhere in the knoll – when Taffy spoke up again.

"Don't forget, girl," Taffy said. "That boy, Thor, he can scamper right out of this hill anytime he wants. Maybe he already has."

"True," Jennifer T. said. "All right, then."

It took a few minutes to arrange themselves in the dark. Jennifer T. had to feel her way carefully, keeping her body between herself and Pettipaw in case he decided to make a break for the tunnel. The wererat pressed himself against the far wall of the cell, where his shadowtail sense detected a thin shoot of the Tree leading out.

Jennifer T. reached towards him and her hand settled, with a start, on a patch of long, coarse fur, under which she could feel the delicate bones of his shoulder. A moment later Jennifer T. felt Taffy's great hand feel its way onto her own shoulder. The Sasquatch was cradling Cinquefoil in her other arm. The ferisher's breathing sounded low and rattling and frighteningly slow in Jennifer T.'s ears.

"Ready then?" the wererat said. He sighed. "All this bother for a Braunschweiger sandwich."

Jennifer T. could feel him shaking his head at his own greed. Then all at once the dark around them turned very cold. She followed him forward, and there was a tinkling of ice. In the corner of her eye, something flickered. She stopped.

"Keep moving!" Pettipaw snapped. "You must never stop when you're scampering! Keep moving!"

The darkness through which they moved had begun to shiver. Great dazzling cracks of colour, green and blue and gold, broke through the darkness like veins in a leaf or forks of lightning. The colours starred the darkness. They broke the darkness into bright little squares and patches. They were patches, she thought, of the outside world, but they were scattered, like pieces of a puzzle. And somehow the patches had a different look or feel, as if they were the pieces perhaps of two *different* puzzles jumbled together. And through the jumble of world and darkness three figures moved, shadowy silhouettes walking in single file.

"Keep moving!" the wererat cried. "We're losing our way!"

"There's— there's someone there!" said Jennifer T. "They're coming this way!"

One of the figures, she saw, was carrying something in its hand, a kind of wand of light. As the figures drew nearer, the wand of light burned brighter and brighter, throwing out light in all directions. The patches of tree green and sky blue began to whirl around each other, mingling with purple and yellow and orange and red. The darkness dissolved in the swirl of colour and light until it was spinning all around, a great rushing swirl of colour in bands like the glowing stripes of Jupiter, and the light from the wand flowered and burst over everything. Jennifer T.'s ears hummed, and a burnt smell like tar filled her nostrils. The ground began to rumble and shift under feet, and she lost her balance and fell with a cry, throwing out her hands to break her fall. In the instant before the light of the wand filled every last corner of her vision she had the strange sensation of clutching two thick tufts of grass in her fingers.

17

The Research of Mr. Feld

CUTBELLY THE WEREFOX had spent a good portion of his very long life observing the habits and behaviour of the interesting creatures known in the Far Territories of the Summerlands as *reubens*. As a shadowtail he had done a fair amount of travelling to the Middling. He had seen more of it than any reuben ever had, that much was certain. He had seen war and torment. He had seen illness and destruction. He had seen a lot of sad sights. But he had never seen anything quite like the case of Bruce Feld, Ph. D.

"Here," the werefox said, backing into the laboratory, carrying a tray laid with caribou-butter tea and a plate of those rude Winterlands biscuits known as cracknuckles. The makeshift laboratory in the bowels of the steam-sledge *Panic* rattled and lurched. The beakers and glass pipes chimed steadily, a carillon that never ceased. Cutbelly had often wondered if it were not the endless ringing of all those damned tubes and pipes that had finally driven Bruce Feld mad. "I brought you something to eat."

"No time," Mr. Feld said. He did not take his eyes from the flask whose contents he was heating with an autoclave. The autoclave (a kind of super–pressure cooker used by chemists), and all of the other fancy equipment in the laboratory, had been manufactured by Coyote's greyling smiths, to Mr. Feld's exact specifications. Coyote's plan was founded on Middling science. So his toxin-delivery system had to be created by Middling means. Except, of course, for the fact that all the electricity was provided by Coyote's herd of thunder buffalo. And except for the fact that the flasks and beakers had been blown by fire gnomes, and the tools wrought from walrus bone and Winterlands weird-iron.

"You have to eat something, reuben," Cutbelly said. "What good will it do your son to see you again if you've starved yourself to death first?"

"Later," Mr. Feld said. His conversation, never plentiful, had long since dried up completely. An elaborate skyline of glassware separated him from his assistant. "I'm in the middle of a trial."

"Which trial?"

"Number five hundred and twenty-seven," Mr. Feld said. "Get ready."

Dutifully Cutbelly set down the tray and scurried over to a wooden table in a corner of the lab. As Mr. Feld's assistant, his only real duties consisted of taking down Mr. Feld's laboratory notes and trying without success to get him to eat. Mr. Feld had been working nonstop for ages, without taking more than a nibble of a cracknuckle now and then, and a sip of caribou-butter tea here or there. He slept less than Cutbelly, and werefoxes need very little sleep.

Exhaustion had made deep bruises under Mr. Feld's eyes. His beard grew at Winterlands speed, half an inch per day, and it was a wild tangle. Someone had found him a real lab coat, and he wore it all the time. Because all he ever did was work.

"I observe picofibreisation and it appears to be quite evenly distributed," he said in the dry, high, nasal voice he used when he was dictating his notes to Cutbelly. *P-fib distrib,* Cutbelly wrote. *Even*. Mr. Feld held the beaker up to eyelevel and tipped it back and forth. The clear liquid it had once contained had turned a pale white colour and thickened like a pudding on the cool. Mr. Feld poked at it with the tip of a long, thin probe. Inset into the bone handle of the probe was a spring-loaded gauge with a red wire needle. The probe slid in with ease but then when Mr. Feld tried to remove it, the thick white stuff refused to let go. Mr. Feld had to set the beaker down, clamp it to a brace, and jerk the probe out with both hands. "Auto-adhesion index off the chart," he said.

"Is this it, then?" Cutbelly said. His heart sank. "Did you do it?"

"It looks good," said Mr. Feld. There was little emotion in his voice. You would never have known that he had come to the moment he had gone for weeks without food and sleep to reach. The liquid in the flask condensed, turning thicker and shinier until at last it lay glinting in the flask like a pool of mercury. Mr. Feld tipped it from the flask into the palm of his hand. The shining stuff spilled outward in all directions and lay draped over his hand. But it did not drip or run out of his palm. It held together. He grasped it with the other hand and balled it up. Then he kneaded it a few times and smacked it against the workbench. It flattened into a disk. He lifted the silvery pancake and began to stretch it like pizza dough. He tossed it spinning into the air and it stretched and stretched until it hung silky as a parachute, then drifted, billowing, to the floor.

"Bring me a skriker," Mr. Feld said.

"I don't like to touch those things," Cutbelly said. "You know that, Bruce."

"Fine," said Mr. Feld. He went to a small metal door at the back of the lab. It looked like the door of a locker, narrow and slitted at the top. He opened it with a twist of a bone handle and then turned to one side to squeeze himself halfway in. There was a nasty yipping snarl from inside the dark closet. As Cutbelly watched Mr. Feld reach around inside the locker, he noticed something very odd about the back of Mr. Feld's head. It looked— well, it looked *flat*. As if his head were made of putty, you would have said, and he had been lying on his back too long. Mr. Feld jumped, and flinched. Then he smiled. It was a smile that made Cutbelly shiver.

Mr. Feld held out a large black wire cage, carrying it by a ring at the top. The skriker in the cage thrashed and snarled at Mr. Feld. It snarled at Cutbelly. Skrikers were reputed to feel no emotion but spite and no pain but hunger. But this skriker looked to Cutbelly very much as if it were afraid.

"Bruce," Cutbelly said. "Mr. Feld. Don't. Please."

"I have no choice," Mr. Feld said. It seemed to Cutbelly that his voice still had the nasal tone it took on when he was dictating notes. "If I don't do what he asks, I'll never see Ethan again."

"You may never see him again even if you do," Cutbelly said.

"Be that as it may," Mr. Feld said. The dry dictation voice was still there; it seemed to have become a permanent condition. He put on a pair of thick elk-hide gloves. He raised the restraining device, a pair of long handles with an adjustable noose at one end, which he would use to grab the skriker, and prepared to reach into the cage. Even though the skriker was injured – it had lost its wings in a skirmish with a tribe of wild shaggurts outside Grunterburg a few weeks back – it was still dangerous. "I have no choice."

He unlocked the cage with a weird-iron key and eased open the door, reaching in with the long-handled noose. The skriker cursed at Mr. Feld with the simple grammar and rich vocabulary of the skriker's palindromic tongue, which was called Azmamza.

"*Katnantak!*" the skriker cursed. "*Tav vatve gala gevtav vatkat nantak!*"

Then the noose snared the skriker by its neck. Mr. Feld jerked the creature out of the cage and in a single smooth movement tucked the skriker's body under his arm like a bagpipe, and gave its head a sharp twist. The skriker's head came off with a moist pop. From the joint of its neck a single black drop swelled into a shining bead.

"*Tavvat!*" growled the skriker's head. "*Vizgon og zivtav vat!*"

Mr. Feld set the head down on the table beside him and then covered it with a towel. It continued to chatter for a moment longer, then fell silent. Mr. Feld turned his attention to the bead of black liquid at the tip of the skriker's dead neck. Lowering the body towards the surface of the table, he dabbed at the stretched crêpe of picofibre he had just rolled out. The black stuff smeared across in a long streak. Almost immediately it began to steam and smoke. There was an awful smell of sizzling tooth.

"That's just the residue of my hands," said Mr. Feld. "The oils and dirt."

Indeed as he said the words the steaming stopped, and the smoke curled to the ceiling and then began to disperse. Mr. Feld watched the black streak of skriker blood, the second most vitriolic stuff in the universe, as it lay on his shining silver stuff, cooling. The picofibrous material refused to react with it. That, as Mr. Feld had explained to the werefox, was what picofibres did: they refused to react. To Mr. Feld's picofibre pancake the skriker blood was as inert and uninteresting as a splatter of spilt coffee. It was not particularly interesting to Cutbelly, either. But Mr. Feld gazed at the streak of ichor as if it were the most beautiful thing he had ever seen. Tunelessly he sang to himself:

Na na na na
Na na na na
Hey hey hey
Goodbye

"Biosolvent test," he said after a moment, his voice higher and dryer than ever. "Negative. No indications of molecular interaction on any level." He glanced over at Cutbelly, who sat, not moving, the notebook neglected. "Take that down."

"No," Cutbelly said. "I'm not going to help you anymore, reuben."

Cutbelly liked Mr. Feld. He liked most reubens, as a rule, preferring their company to that of ferishers, among whom he had been born. Ferishers were spirited but shallow and incapable of pity. They were immortal. Only things whose lives were too short, like reubens, were able to feel pity. And he was grateful to Mr. Feld for having intervened to save his life at Betty's Bonepit. But he was increasingly uneasy around Mr. Feld. Something had to be done.

"Take it down!" Mr. Feld said, through clenched teeth. "I'm extremely close now! Take it down! Don't you want me to see Ethan again?"

"What are you going to do, pop my head off? Take it down yourself!" Cutbelly said.

Mr. Feld set down the beaker, then snatched up the notebook and began furiously to jot.

"This has nothing to do with you seeing Ethan again," Cutbelly said. "You're doing this, sir, because you like what you're doing. You enjoy the work. Admit it. If Coyote walked in here right now and told you could stop, you'd keep on working, wouldn't you?"

"No," Mr. Feld said. "Of course not."

He looked away, and Cutbelly saw that the back of his head was flatter than ever. In fact, now that he considered it, the entire back of Mr. Feld's *body* looked flatter than it ought to. His buttocks looked as if they were pressed up against a clear sheet of glass.

The iron portal of the laboratory rolled open, squealing, and Coyote walked in. He was dressed in his snowgear, a tunic and trousers of white fur. His white fur hood was thrown back and his bright coppery hair blazed with droplets.

"So!" he cried. "Hard at work, I see! Excellent! Fine! Splendid! And how goes it? Excellent? Fine? Spendid, even?

That's good. Mr. Feld, that is just so good. I am *this* close to obtaining an adequate supply of the vitriol. A friend of mine is working on the problem right now. I think she's found someone – someone close to your son, intriguingly – who can be persuaded to get me the stuff." He balled his hands into fists and pounded on his own forehead. He yanked on his own hair. "Oh, I'm *pleased*. I'm *very* pleased. In fact, I am *so* pleased that I would like to reward you. As of now, as of this very moment, you are free of my service. I cannot release you from my *custody*, of course, not, at least, until we have overthrown Outlandishtown and captured Murmury Well. But you need no longer work on the delivery system. My smiths can take over from here."

He said this all with perfect sincerity and a kindly tone. Mr. Feld glanced at Cutbelly.

"Uh," he said. "Well."

Cutbelly spat on the floor. "What did I tell you?" he said.

"It's just, I'm so close," Mr. Feld said at last. "I really hate to stop now."

Coyote nodded.

"Knock yourself out," he said. Then he nodded to Cutbelly, and the werefox saw a mean little Coyote smirk on his face. He started back out of the laboratory. "Or should I say, knock yourself *flat*?"

18

On Three Reubens Field

ETHAN STOOD IN the middle of a large, green field, with one perfectly square corner, that opened like a grassy fan. Near the perfect corner, inside of a square traced in rich, brown dirt and filled with green grass, stood a tumulus or little round hill of more rich, brown dirt.

"Hey," Ethan said, as he stared across the bright green diamond at Jennifer T. He found himself standing squarely at the back of the circle of dirt where home plate belonged. Jennifer T. was standing on the pitcher's mound.

"Hey," she said, looking around with an expression on her face of perfect wonder. "Did you do this?"

"I… I didn't *mean* to," Ethan said.

The last thing he remembered was letting go of the burning bat in his hands – burning not like a fire, or even an electric light, but with a cold kind of flame like starlight. It had begun to flicker almost from the moment he followed Thor into the side of the knoll. They had gone no more than a few steps when the light blazed up, blindingly bright, and then it was as if someone had put the worlds in a blender. After that he remembered nothing. And now here they were, standing in the middle of a baseball diamond, in the shade of Dandelion Hill.

When they saw the miraculous ball field that had swirled into existence at their doorstep, the ferishers of Dandelion Hill threw down their tennis rackets and croquet mallets, and left behind the scarred grey patch in the grass where their old field had lain. They dived into the thick, new grass, and swam in it like water, and rolled over onto their backs, and floated on it, and sighed.

"Ethan Feld," Taffy called from the angle of third base. "We need that wood, and quickly."

It was on top of the pitcher's mound that they laid the featherweight husk of Cinquefoil the ferisher. Ethan was shocked by his appearance. He looked less like a living creature than the imitation of one, a bundle of rags, like the doll carried by the ferisher girl, Spider-Rose. Ethan wanted to believe that his newly forged bat could somehow reverse the process, but it didn't seem likely. And even if the bat turned out to be up to the challenge, he had no reason to believe that *he* was.

"Here," he said to Jennifer T., offering her the bat that Grim had made for him. Jennifer T. took it, gripped it in both hands, studied it with her fingertips. She had been eyeing it with interest from the moment she and Ethan had first faced each other across the infield, with the swirling winds and green chaos of a disturbance in the Worlds settling all around them.

"It's got to be you, rube," Grim said to Ethan. "It's your wood. You found it."

"But I've used Jennifer *T.'s* bat before," Ethan protested. "People share bats all the time. She can use mine if she wants to."

"I don't know," Jennifer T. said, giving it a few practice swings. "There's this little bump on the handle. This knot, or whatever. It sort of hurts my hand."

She passed the bat back to Ethan and he took it. Jennifer T. was right; the knot – he came to think of it as the Knot – on the handle spoilt the feel of the bat in the hands. That was his fault, of course; he hadn't owned the nerve, at the last, to carvc it away. He put the shame of his failure out of his mind and turned his attention to the crumpled form of the ferisher lying on the pitcher's mound before him. The Dandelion Hill mob crept closer now, hoping to get a better look at the proceedings. Some of them called out advice and hints to Ethan; others began to lay odds on whether it was going to work at all.

Like all advice, most of the ferisher's suggestions were contradictory – it had been a long time, after all, since anyone around here had seen ash used to draw out the withering sting of iron. Some of them shouted to Ethan to kneel down, and lay the head of the bat right on the wound. Others seemed to feel that he was supposed to remain standing, but wave the bat around over the wound. In the end Ethan settled for some of each. He knelt, and began to draw little circles in the air over Cinquefoil's ruined hand. He closed his eyes, because he couldn't stand the sight of the poor, shrunken chief.

When he opened them again, he saw to his surprise that things were looking much better. The hard little kernel into which Cinquefoil's life had curled itself sprang forth again and sent shoots to uncoil in his face, hands, and feet. His hands opened like buds. His eyelids opened like petals. He was looking right at Ethan.

"Shaved yer splinter, I see," he observed.

A cheer broke out; it was the first time the sound of cheering had been heard at the Hill since the loss of the old ball field to Coyote the Changer's deceit. Then Queen Filaree approached the mound. Her face, alone of everyone's on the field, was severe and unsmiling. Her walk was haughty. She stopped at the edge of the grass and scowled at each of them in turn – Ethan, Jennifer T., Thor, Cinquefoil, Taffy, Grim the Giant, and at the strange little pot-bellied rat-creature – a wererat, Ethan decided, who was standing beside Jennifer T. The wererat stared right back, with his one bright eye. Longest of all, though, the Queen glared at the ferisher girl, Spider-Rose. Spider-Rose admired the line of beech trees beyond right field, as if unaware of all the scowling and glaring that was going on.

"We've been bittered, and ruint, and soured, and mean," said the queen at last. "And worst, we done dishonoured the Laws o' Hospitality most disgraceful." She looked at Ethan and Jennifer T. "And ta repay us fer this ill-doing, ya have healt up our long-broken hearts."

"It was kind of an accident," Ethan said, looking down at the bat. "I'm not really sure what I *did*."

"I ain't sure, neither," Grim the Giant said. "But here's the way I figures it. That lot" – he gestured towards Jennifer T. and Taffy – "and us, now, we was all scamperin' through the hillside at the same instant. I done heard of such things happenin' from time to time, an' the way I heard it, people cross each other in a scamper, why then, you always ends up with somethin' very interestin'. Now, let's just say, with this little reuben carryin' that old hunk of woundwood there – what with all that glowin' it did – I think... I think he done pleached two worlds together. This one and the Middling, I'll warrant. Just for a minute, like."

The wererat crept forwards and gingerly ran a dainty forepaw along the shaft of Ethan's bat.

"Woundwood, is it?" He frowned. "Then much as it pains me to havc to do so, I fear I must agree with that midgety pudding-head over there. Put a piece of woundwood at the spot where two branches cross, it's like you created a tiny, little temporary gall – you know what a gall is? But it wasn't a real gall. It didn't last. And it only stayed open just long enough for a little bit of the two worlds to involve themselves with each other. Just long enough to make a little tiny patch of a magical place."

"A ball field," said Jennifer T.

"It's got all the magic and size we require," Queen Filaree said. "An' we're deep, deep in yer debt."

"Oh," said Ethan, a little put off by her solemnity, and still trying to take hold of the idea that he had, even if only for a moment, brought two worlds together, and made something so beautiful where there had been only mud and grey ashes. "Well, that's OK."

"It is not," the queen said. "Name a price fer yer gift, and it'll be paid."

"Well—" Ethan began. They had already wasted so much time. "I'm really worried about my dad. He's been taken prisoner by Coyote."

"Plus we're trying to keep Ragged Rock from coming," Thor reminded him.

"Oh, yeah," Ethan said. "Also we're trying to stop the end of the world. And we have a really long way to go. So—well, OK. Could we please have our airship back?"

The queen's cheeks flushed until they were the colour of blood oranges. She glanced down at herself, then away. A certain amount of dark laughter bubbled up from the assembled ferishers. A certain amount of money changed hands. Ethan took a closer look at the queen's shiny tunic and at those worn by nearly all of the other members of the mob. Now that they were out in the sunlight he could see that they had been sewn – hundreds of tiny garments, glowing soft and silvery as the moon – from the picofibre envelope of Skidbladnir.

"Oh," he said. "Oh."

"I'll have yer wagon fetched out o' the stables," said the queen. "But I regret ta say that it may not fly so well as it did afore now."

A few moments later, the old Feld Saab appeared from around the other side of the hill, pushed by two dozen huffing ferishers wearing thick gloves to keep the touch of metal from their hands. She was dented and dirty and looked, in this enchanted spot, more incongruous than ever. But there was plenty of gas in her tank, and when they tried the ignition, she turned over at once.

"Good thing I couldn't grammer the engine away," Cinquefoil said. "But we got a long ways ta go on a tank o' gas." He looked worried, and he trembled, still pale and drawn, peering in at the gauge labelled BENSIN.

"I'll work a feasting grammer on her for ya, Chief Cinquefoil," the queen said. "What can turn a heel o' bread inta a banquet fit fer a mob. That should stretch things a bit fer ya. And a course we'll outfit ya as we can with foodstuffs and such gear as ya may need."

"Pardon me," said a small, crisp voice at Ethan's feet. "But as long as we find ourselves on the subject of foodstuffs, there was a small matter, I believe, of some Braunschweiger sausage."

It was the wererat. He was staring up at the rear hatch of the car, his tiny black nose aquiver.

"Oh, hey," Jennifer T. said. "Right."

She went to the back of the car and opened the hatch, and rummaged around in the cooler her great-aunts had packed. She re-emerged with a stack of sandwiches, wrapped in wax paper, and handed them down to the wererat.

"Pettipaw," said Grim the Giant, shaking his head. "You'd sell your own mother for a hunk of liverwurst, wouldn't you, now, you one-eyed lesser half of a rodent?"

"And yours into the bargain, Shorty," said Pettipaw, with a grin, gazing lovingly down at the sandwiches. Then, with a rapid bow, he scurried off across the grass and disappeared into the trees.

"Cinquefoil," Ethan said. "We don't have a ship anymore."

"True enough," the ferisher said.

"So then how will we ever cross the Raucous Mountains and the Big River and all?"

Another murmuring started up among the ferishers, and the queen looked shocked.

"Ya don't mean ta say— ya aren't seriously bound for *Applelawn*?"

"Farther than that," Cinquefoil said. "We hope to cross Diamond Green itself, and come at the Winterlands through the backdoor. We mean to raise Outlandishton itself, on its high Tor."

"We think Coyote's trying to do something to that Well and kill that Tree thing," said Jennifer T. "My freaky old auntie had a dream."

"Only we don't know what," Thor said.

"Well, then I'm sorry we cut up yer skybag," the queen said. "Applelawn." She shook her stately head. "Damn. I wanted ta see it my whole life long."

"Can ya tell us how ta find it, then, sister?"

But here the queen could only shake her head.

"There ain't been news from Applelawn in a age," she said.

"I can find it," Thor said. Everyone turned to look at him. He was standing in front of the car, with the map he had found in the Treasury spread out across the hood. "Applelawn. Uh-huh. OK." He traced a route with the tip of his finger. "So. We just need to go through those mountains there. The Raucous Mountains. Right." Ethan looked off, beyond the trees, to the hazy purplish-grey mountains they had seen, far off, worn and ancient-looking, when they first crossed over from Clam Island. "Then, yeah, OK, then we come down the other side of the mountains, through the Lost Camps, and cross the Big River, here." He jabbed with a finger. "After that we're right there. Applelawn."

The Queen of Dandelion Hill exchanged a look with the Chief of the Boar Tooth mob.

"Crossing the Big River," the Queen said. "That could be tougher ta arrange than any leap o' the Worlds, if them stories I heard are true."

"What stories?" Ethan said.

"It says here, I think it says... '*Old Bottom-Cat*'," Thor read, tracing the snaking course of the Big River. "Is that it?

"Who is Old Bottom-Cat?" Ethan said. "Is it a who or a what?"

"I heard too many outlandish tales ta repeat," Queen Filaree said. "He might be a sort of a giant; he may be a fish; he could be a snake or a dragon." As she mentioned each of these possibilities, a different bunch of ferishers nodded their heads. Several arguments broke out, amid cries of "Fish!" and "Snake!" She chopped at the air with the back of a pale hand; they fell silent at once. "At any rate I reckon you'll find out soon enough."

Ethan looked at Thor, who nodded. They really had no other choice. Then Ethan looked over at Jennifer T., standing staring off into the trees where Pettipaw had vanished.

"Food, and a grammer," she said finally. "That's all I've heard said about paying us back." She looked around now at the new green expanse of grass that surrounded them. "Doesn't seem like quite enough, somehow."

"Well, I'll grant ya that map," the queen said. "Which otherwise I would have ta consider stoled from my treasury."

"And which you could never get to lie *flat*, much less make head nor tails of," Spider-Rose spoke up sharply. She had been hanging back, until now, clutching her doll, as if afraid, somehow, of stepping onto the ball field. As if the merest touch of her foot might blight it. But now Ethan saw her creep up behind Thor Wignutt, and clamber up onto his shoulder to get a better look at the Four-Sided Map.

"Applelawn," she said with a dreamy look on her face. "And to think that it's really just a little ways on the other side of those mountains."

"A *long* way," Thor corrected her. "Especially if we have to *drive*."

"We definitely want the map," Ethan said.

Jennifer T. nodded.

"And, OK," Ethan went on, seeing how much he could get just by asking. It was the Jennifer T. style of doing things, and new to him. "We want you to release Grim here from the binding you put on his hide."

This produced a silence that was deep and long-lasting, filled almost to the brim with birdsong and the sound of the wind in the trees. For once no bets were settled or laid.

"And we want to take the princess with us, too," said Jennifer T. Then she covered her mouth as if she herself felt she had gone too far. The only person present who looked more surprised than Jennifer T. Rideout at that moment was Spider-Rose. "I mean, like, if she, you know, *wants* to come." She glanced at the ferisher girl, whom Ethan understood for the first time to be the daughter of the queen. "But probably she doesn't."

The queen looked at Spider-Rose, who looked down at the map again, then at Jennifer T., studying her afresh, doubt replacing surprise in her expression – and maybe the littlest beginning of interest.

"It isn't going to work," she said finally, gazing down sadly at her doll. "But even if all you fools end up doing is *bother* old Coyote a little bit, I guess that's something I wouldn't mind seeing."

"Ya ask a good deal, reubens," the queen said. "An awful great lot. My daughter's behaviour is her own bizness, since I'm prepared ta say now that her debt ta me and ta her people has been paid – though not by her. But as fer this giant, that's another matter."

"It's awful kind of you," Grim said to Ethan, and there were tears in his eyes. "But a bound giant is bound for ever."

"Then we'll bind you to *us*," Thor said. He looked at Cinquefoil. "We can do that, can't we? Isn't there a way?"

"Yeah," Cinquefoil said. "There's a way."

The queen shook her head. "No," she said. "It's too much. The map itself is priceless. Consider yerself paid."

Ethan looked at Spider-Rose. He wondered how it would feel to have your mom be more willing to give you up than anything else she possessed.

"This is an awfully nice field, isn't it?" Taffy said, sitting in the grass. "Maybe you ferishers would care to try it out? Test your ballplaying skills against those of myself and my colleagues?"

There was a sharp buzz of excitement from the Dandelion Hill mob, and the chiming of coins began again.

"Are ya offering us a *wager*?" the queen said.

"Nine innings," Taffy said. "To settle the fate of this little giant's hide." Ethan was startled by the proposal, but only for a moment. Taffy knew intimately, of course, the pain of being bound. But he had his doubts.

"I don't know," he said. He checked the watch, scrolling quickly to the calendar screen. The arrow beside the two was now pointing down. "Bottom of the second!" He was suddenly panicked. "Jeez! It's going so fast! I don't think we have time for baseball, Taff."

All the ferishers burst out laughing, including Cinquefoil. After a moment Taffy and Grim joined in.

"Ya don't think yer going ta cross the Summerlands a thousand miles or more without playing baseball?" Cinquefoil said. "That would be like trying ta cross a thunderstorm without stepping on a raindrop. Can't be done. What's more, it *shouldn't* be done. Baseball is good for ya, little reuben. Yer going ta need ta be a fair sight smarter and tougher than ya are now, Ethan Feld, before this here adventure of ours comes down ta the final at-bat. Catching a couple thousand o' yer girlfriend's fastballs and sliders will make ya that, an more." Ethan's cheeks buzzed from Cinquefoil's description of Jennifer T. as his 'girlfriend'. The chief made a rapid calculation on his fingers. "But we're still be two players short of a team."

At that moment Ethan detected a distinct smell in the air of liverwurst, slightly rancid.

"Just a minute," came the thin, strong voice from behind Grim the Giant. The wererat stepped out from behind his old antagonist. "You don't think I'd be content knowing that you were off living a life of adventure and stimulation, without me hanging around to drive you off your nut?"

"Make that *one* player short," Cinquefoil said.

I HAVE BEFORE me Volume 117 of Alkabetz's Universal *Encyclopaedia of Baseball* (Ninth Edition). The line score, according to the infallible Professor Alkabetz, for the game played that day between the rough and contentious team fielded by the Dandelion Hill mob and a ragtag, ad-hoc nine captained by Cinquefoil, Chief of the Boar Tooth mob, reads as follows:

	1	2	3	4	5	6	7	8	9	R	H	E
Visitors	0	0	0	0	0	0	0	0	1	1	1	3
Home	0	0	0	0	0	0	0	0	0	0	1	5

As is often the case with unscheduled and interworld games, details are sketchy – there is no box score, and the ninth man on the Visitors team is referred to only as Chickweed (3b).

He was one of the Dandelion Hill mob, a wiry, taciturn fellow who said nothing at all, to anyone, for the entire length of the game. The other Dandelion Hill ferishers teased him mercilessly for being a turncoat, and warned his new teammates that they ought not to trust him. But he made every pick that came his way, snagged a tricky short-hop grounder in the bottom of the sixth, and started two double plays. Cinquefoil was still quite weak, and four of the other Visitors – Taffy, Ethan, Jennifer T., Grim the Giant – had of course to be grammered down, limbs burning, bones crackling, to ferisher scale. Whether it was the disorienting effects of the shapeshifting, or a deliberate spike in the grammer worked by

Queen Filaree and two of her most powerful grammerwrights, they hit poorly – Ethan in particular. He struck out swinging three times, with the Knot on his bat handle chafing viciously against his palm. On his third at-bat he reverted to his old Dog Boy ways, just leaving the cursed stick on his shoulder and hoping, forlornly as it turned out, to coax four balls across the plate before three strikes.

On the other hand, it had been over a century since the Dandelion Hill mob had played a game of baseball, and they were sorely out of practice. One look at the Errors column will show you that. The lone run – the winning run, as it turned out – by the Visitors, in the top of the ninth, was scored by Jennifer T., who reached on a fielding error, moved to third on throwing error, and scored on a passed ball. The home team's hitting was, if anything, even worse than their game in the field. They could not seem to find their timing; the bats, after years of tennis and croquet, felt at once cumbersome and ineffectual in their hands.

In any game where the hitting is weak, of course, it will all come down to pitching, and this, according to Professor Alkabetz in his brief summary, was the story of the game. Jennifer T. pitched for the Visitors, and here the change in size seemed to work to her advantage. Though she was now only about eighteen inches high, somehow her sense of the distance to be travelled by the ball "retained a certain 'grandeur' " as Professor Alkabetz puts it, and with the help of a sympathetic umpire, a local werebear★ named

★Werebears, methodical and sharp-eared, able to *hear* the difference between a strike and a ball, being the race that has traditionally produced the finest umpires in the Summerlands.

Smacklip, she was able to mow the home nine down, giving up only a cheap single in the bottom of the fourth. Ethan, who read feverishly from *How to Catch Lightning and Smoke* whenever he was on the bench, tried to mix his calls as much as he could, but since Jennifer T. only had two pitches, the fastball and the slider, he couldn't get too fancy. Mostly he just called for the heater. It was enough; and the run that she finally scored, on three errors, stood up.

Queen Filaree herself made the last out, popping up weakly to her daughter (2b) in shallow right. She threw down her bat, cursed, spat, and then uttered a strange series of coughing barks in Old Fatidic. Grimalkin John took off his glove, turned and knelt on the ground before Ethan.

"I'm bound over to you, little reuben," he said.

"Cool," Ethan said. "Only stand up, OK?"

Chickweed walked past Jennifer T. on his way towards his fellows, head down, watching his feet. As he went past her he looked up briefly, and gave a tug on his long mustache.

"Nice game," he said.

After the larger beings had been restored to their normal sizes, the queen issued a proclamation – henceforward this ball field, in honour and commemoration of its generous donors, would be known as Three Reubens Field. This went some way, in Ethan's mind, to making up for his terrible afternoon at the plate. After that the promised provisions were brought and packed into the rear of the car; and then the Visitors piled themselves, as well as they could into the car – except, of course, for Taffy, who resumed her familiar station on the roof. Apart from Jennifer T., of the eight of them, only

Grim the Giant had *really* driven a car – once, years before, in Trondheim, Sweden. ("Long story," he said, licking his lips in a nasty way that did not encourage questions.) Oddly enough, that other car had also been a Saab. This coincidence more than qualified him, in Ethan's opinion, to serve as driver for the group that now and hereafter styled itself, at Jennifer T.'s suggestion, the Shadowtails.

"Because it sounds to me," she explained, climbing into the backseat with Thor, Ethan, and Spider-Rose, "like we got a lot more scampering to do before we scamper across Home Plate."

"Farewell, daughter," Queen Filaree said to Spider-Rose through the rear window of the car. It took two of her subjects to hold her up. They staggered and strained under the weight of her. "Perhaps ya'll return one of these days."

"Not likely," said Spider-Rose, without looking at her mother.

"If ya do, I can't help hopin' it's not before ya done found some *sense* in that head o' yers."

Spider-Rose turned now and glared at the Queen of Dandelion Hill.

"Not likely," she said again, more carefully.

Then Grim started the engine, and glanced over at his old nemesis, Pettipaw, who shared the front passenger seat with Cinquefoil. "The better to criticise," the wererat said, "what promises to be a display of some truly horrendous driving."

"Ready, rat?" Grim the Giant said, with a grin.

"That all depends," said Pettipaw, "on whether you plan to drown us or drive us off a cliff."

Then Grim put the rattling old car in gear, and they set off into the woods, following the wide, ancient giant-built track that ran up into the Raucous Mountains. Some of the Dandelion Hill ferishers ran after them for a while, and then they fell away, whistling and calling farewell. The noise of the engine, the crunch of the sandy road under the tyres, and the squeaking of Skid's old springs, combined to ensure that as the car plunged into the dark green shadows of the Great Woods, only Taffy the Sasquatch, sitting on the roof, heard the distant sound, faint but unmistakable, of a woman, disconsolate, weeping for the children she had lost.

THIRD BASE

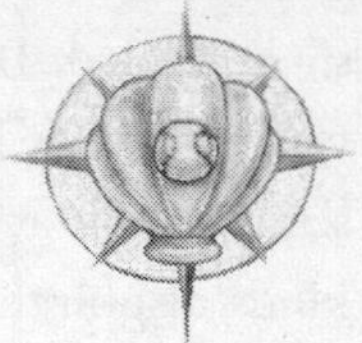

19

The Lost Camps

BIG CHIEF CINQUEFOIL'S Travelling Shadowtails All-Star Baseball Club made its way up into the Raucous Mountains, through Sidewinder Pass, and down into the Lost Camps of the Big River Valley. Every day brought new signs of the coming of Ragged Rock: vast rustling coverlets of crows that blotted out the sun; weresquirrels and werechipmunks carrying reports of earthquakes, of great tracts of forest turned to empires of fire, of mighty rivers that reversed their courses or dried up overnight. The moon turned first the colour of apple cider, and then the next night – full now – to a deep rusty gold, like ferisher blood. And one morning they woke in their bedrolls to see the glint, on the tip of Kobold Mountain's peaked cap, of snow – snow, in the Summerlands!

Their record, when they came down from Sidewinder Pass and into the Lost Camps, was two and seven. One of those victories was a forfeit (9–0) by some hill ferishers On Account of Excessive Shyness, and the other was a blowout, 15–3, against a team of wizened old Bowling Men who were drunk on honey beer and had not played a game of baseball, by their own admission, in 216 years.

They were, at best, an uneven ball club, and chronically

shorthanded. Because of her annoying habit of regarding every game as lost before it even began, Spider-Rose did a slapdash job at second, hotdogging it on one play with all kinds of pointless but pretty tumbling and diving, and then drag-assing it on the very next play so that she just barely got the ball to Cinquefoil over at first. The ferisher chief had yet to get his hitting game back, but he was steady as usual at his corner. In the outfield, there was Pettipaw in left – he was, if anything, even more of a hotdog than Spider-Rose, all one-handed catches and over-the-shoulder catches and crazy grass-churning dives towards the fence, but he did everything with such style, from hunting squirrels to rolling ragweed cigarettes one-handed, that it was impossible to imagine him playing any other way. Centre field was Taffy, and even grammered down to the scale of a ferisher field she remained too lumbering and slow for the position, so that every routine fly became something of an adventure. The truth was that Sasquatches have never been passionate about baseball. In right, there was the outsider, a blinking pale ferisher or a Bowling Man drinking steadily from his flask. And playing shortstop was Grimalkin John. ("What else?" as he had said on first taking the position.) The novelty of a miniature giant never quite wore off and just having him there, glowering and gnashing his teeth gigantically, whenever one of the opposing ferishers came to the plate, messed with their minds a little bit.

As for Jennifer T., every day she could feel her arm getting stronger. Each time she threw, her fastball had more of a shimmy in it, like the wobble of a bit of metal caught between opposing magnets, so that it might veer at the last instant just a hair from its apparent trajectory as it left her hand. And she was learning, with coaching from Cinquefoil, to "take something off it", so that when Ethan put down three fingers, she could begin to experiment with throwing the change. But it was her slider that gave the other side fits. It was a hard slider that Jennifer T. threw, one that she had learned from watching big-league players throw them on TV. It broke not only downward but also a little to one side, away from the right-handed hitters. "A slurve", the announcers sometimes called it, a shadowtail kind of pitch, part slider, part curve. The Raucous Mountain ferishers had never seen anything like it.

But the most uneven feature of the Shadowtails, by far, was Ethan Feld. On the one hand, his hitting was the scandal of the team. It was funny the way such a small bump could give you such fits, but Jennifer T. had tried swinging the magical bat herself and the Knot really did throw you off, somehow. It was like how you heard sometimes about a pitcher, Dizzy Dean or somebody, whose whole career was ruined because a broken toenail grew back in a different way, or a callus on his thumb changed from round to oval. For the first five days he swung, and swung, and swung, and struck out swinging in twenty straight at bats; after that he reverted to his sad old Dog Boy ways, waiting for a walk. Then the crafty ferisher pitchers ate him up. Yet though his hitting game languished, Ethan's mastery of the craft taught by Peavine improved daily. Every game brought him face-to-face with situations – the pitchout, the swinging bunt, the slide into home – that Peavine described in *How to Catch Lightning and Smoke.* He grew accustomed to the sticky pressure of the mask against his forehead, the endless crouching and rising, the brutal treatment he got from foul-tipped balls and careless swings that smacked his mask and made his head clatter like an iron lid.

One afternoon, amid the long shadows and bright grass of a ferisher ballfield at the summit of Sidewinder Path, with the score knotted at four apiece, Ethan caught his first glimpse of Applelawn. It was just as he was rising to his feet to start the happy little around-the-horn ceremony (catcher to first base to second to shortstop to third and then home again) that his infield performed after every strikeout. The sun had been caught behind a towering stand of alders for the last few innings, but now as it moved clear of the trees something sparkled, far in the distance. It was just that – a faint metallic glint, as of a coin, a lost hubcap, a pool of water, a heat mirage. But as Ethan stood there, watching that far-off sparkle of the Farthest Territory beyond the wide green river valley, and the next batter came swaggering up to the plate, smelling of tobacco, and Jennifer T. rearranged the dirt of the pitcher's mound with a thoughtful toe for the nine hundredth time, and the shadows lengthened, and the hummingbirds made their sounds of kissing the air as they thrummed among the rhododendrons, and Cinquefoil and Pettipaw kept up their steady low chatter "*Easy-out-easy-batter-two-down-come-on-kid-you-can-get-him-guy-couldn't-hit-a-bull-in-the-butt-with-a-shovel,*" and the ferisher baseball lay warm and almost animate, a living thing, in his fingers, he recalled Peavine's words: "A baseball game is nothing but a great slow contraption for getting you to pay attention to the cadence of a summer day."

And then, nine days after leaving Dandelion Hill, in a patch of green scrub and blackberries near a ghost town called Dutch Courage, they ran out of gas. It happened all at once, without warning. One minute they were puttering along, with the wind flowing in through the open windows of the car, and the next they were rolling to an ignoble stop in a cloud of their own dust. The air was tinged with smoke that turned the sunlight, even in the afternoon, a wistful golden colour, the very colour of homesickness. The river was always before them, now, a reddish-bronze band twisting like a copperhead through the lush green bottomlands. It was so wide that as they came down to its level they could no longer see its other side – it might have been an ocean, muddy and dull. It was Thor Wignutt's opinion, based on careful study of the Four-Sided Map, that at Skid's top speed of fifteen miles per hour (running on enchanted fuel, magically stretched to last longer), they were at least three days drive from Old Cat Landing, from which they hoped to cross that wide bronze river to Applelawn. On foot – a bunch of children and various foot-high beings – it would take them much, much longer to get there.

"This is not good," said Jennifer T.

According to the tiny doomsday scoreboard in the corner of Ethan's wristwatch, it was now the Top of the Seventh Inning. What was more, the pace of the Game of Worlds, or whatever you wanted to call it, seemed to be accelerating. Ragged Rock was coming faster now. Just yesterday the little indicator had read Bottom of the Fifth.

Baseball games were like that. Get a pitcher into a jam, send a bunch of guys to the plate, and half an inning could take an hour to play. And then the next two full innings might fly past in under thirty minutes. Baseball moved at a Coyote pace, now wandering, now moving at a steady lope, now bearing down hard and quick.

"Top of the Seventh," Cinquefoil said, shaking his head. "Coyote must be nearly ta Outlandishton by now. And here we are with miles and miles left ta go and the greatest river in the Summerlands ta cross."

They had all taken to consulting Ethan's watch, frequently, like a team in the hunt for a pennant watching the out-of-town scoreboard. They had the same sense of disconnected connection to the unimaginable events in the Winterlands that the Red Sox feel when the Yankees play the Orioles: there was nothing they could do to influence the outcome of that other crucial game. They just had to keep moving forward, to keep on playing their best.

"We needs to find some fuel for this heap, and quick," Grim the Giant said. "Or we ain't never gonna make it across the river in time."

"I wish that map of yours showed gas stations," Jennifer T. said to Thor, climbing out of the car, grateful to have stopped – even if it meant they went no further—for one reason: in the last nine days they had played *three* hard-fought, losing games of baseball, and bathed only *once*. It had never smelled wonderful inside of Skidbladnir to begin with. Fill the car up with unwashed children and eldritch creatures, put a Sasquatch on her roof, and after a while the word *stench* became unavoidable.

Everyone piled out of the car, leaving the doors open to air things out. Everyone except for Ethan. He remained in the backseat, just sitting there, staring at the face of his watch. He was working on an 0-for-36 streak since they had left Dandelion Hill, and it was making him a little moody.

"It does show gas stations," Thor said. "But only Sinclair stations." He demonstrated to Jennifer T. how the Green Side of the map was dotted, here and there, with little Sinclair Oil brontosauruses. "Those all went out of business a long time ago."

"There's a gas can in back," Jennifer T. suggested. "Maybe we could scamper through to the Middling on foot, get gas, bring it back, put a gallon in, then go back and fill her up."

Thor unfolded the map, whistling through his teeth, then folded and refolded it, so that it showed the green leaves of the Summerlands and on the reverse showed the leaves of Middling brown. Then he held it up to the light of the sun that had just started its long slow way down towards the crooked cap of the mountain. As he did so, the map turned pale and dappled as the waters of a stream, starred with tiny spots of light. These spots, Thor had discovered, represented places where the branches of the different worlds lay near enough for a shadowtail to leap across the gap. If you looked *through* one of these spots you could clearly read, reversed of course, the name of the place on the Other Side to which a place on This Side corresponded. Thor peered through the map in this way for a while, then shook his head.

"There's no good spot to leap to the Middling until we get farther down into the valley," he said.

"Cinquefoil?" Ethan said. "What about you? Isn't there something you could do?"

"Once upon a time," said the ferisher. He was still trying to recover from being ironstruck, from the strain of the mighty grammers he had worked to get them airborne, from the lingering ill effects of his solitary scamper, back on Clam Island, and, at the bottom of it all, from the loss of his home and his mob to Coyote. "I mighta filled old Skid here with the everlasting gas o' grammer. But alas." He had been unable to work even the simplest firelighting grammer since Ethan had drawn out the iron from him, on the mound of Three Reubens Field.

"We'll go on foot, then," Taffy said. "I'll carry everyone, if I have to." With this bold speech she went around to the back of the car and started to unpack their gear.

Jennifer T. stretched, and yawned, and felt that she had to pee. A little ways up the slope she found a ferisher trail concealed among the blackberries. The bramble was thinner across the trailhead, as if it had been travelled not so long ago. The Raucous Mountains were shot through with these trails, steep punishing paths that led everywhere and nowhere, deep into fabulous mines aglow with treasure, from which you would never be permitted to escape alive, or up to high and dry ledges where you lay down amid the bones of your unlucky predecessors and died.

Jennifer T. squatted down behind a scrub pine. Everybody else – even Spider-Rose and Taffy – did their peeing right in front of the rest of the party. But Jennifer T. liked her privacy. They spent all the rest of their time together – eating, sleeping, passing the endless hours in the car. It was nice to have even a minute to yourself at the end of the day, crouched under some huge Summerlands oak or redwood, with the smell of the campfire, the bats in the dark blue air, and Taffy in the distance singing some sad, slow, endless Sasquatch tune.

It was as she stood up again that she heard it: the weeping woman – La Llorona. Pettipaw the wererat had told them the story of this ghostmother who had, in life, been led by a trick or a promise of the rascal Coyote into killing or abandoning her own children, and then was ever after doomed to roam the Far Territories, and those portions of the Middling that brushed up to them, until the day of Ragged Rock. They had heard her terrible weeping, the racking, horrid, laughter of her sobs, at least once, on each of the preceding nine nights. Sometimes it came from very far away, sometimes from alarmingly near at hand. It was hard not to get the idea that La Llorona was following them, though for what reason none of them, not even Pettipaw, who was the richest in lore and understanding of anyone, could say or imagine. Jennifer T. shivered, now, at the sound, and ribbons of ice rippled through her belly and down her back. If you saw La Llorona, according to Pettipaw, standing at the edge of the fields where the woods began, or by the banks of a river, in her tattered white dress, it meant that you were about to die.

When she returned to the car, Pettipaw was getting dinner together, his fire snapping and smoking merrily in the lee of some standing stones. It was a known fact, he claimed, that wererats had the most refined palates in all the Worlds, and he refused to eat anyone's cooking but his own. Grim the Giant was lying sprawled in the grass, among the stones, amiably criticizing the rat-man's technique.

"Don't put no more of that wild garlic in there, baldtail," he said. "You know it gasses me up."

"Burgoo needs a bite," Pettipaw declared unanswerably.

Grim answered him by cutting a thunderous fart.

"Ahh," he said contentedly, settling deeper into the grass.

"Why is it," Pettipaw wondered aloud, not for the first time, "that the sole one of your features to turn out properly giant-sized should be your *flatulence*?"

But he scraped away, into the dirt, some of the wild garlic he had been chopping, before sliding the rest of it into his bubbling stew.

Thor and Cinquefoil were practising fielding one-hops. Thor was learning to play right field, which was the position they regularly had to fill, being only eight in number, with a player from the opposite team. Though ferishers took the game so seriously that you could usually rely on them, even against teams from their own mobs, giants were far less reliable. And now that the Shadowtails had reached the Lost Camps they would, according to Pettipaw, soon face teams made up of a different sort of untrustworthy creature: human beings. Or at least some version of human beings; Jennifer T. didn't quite understand exactly who, or what, were the denizens of the Lost Camps. At any rate, Cinquefoil was hitting sharp little bouncers to Thor and having him go down on one knee, to his left, to his right, now charging the ball, now waiting on it, over and over again. Jennifer T. stood for a while, enjoying the mechanical *crack-spluff-thwop* as the ball left the bat, dusted the grass, and then settled comfortably into Thor's mitt. Then she heard Spider-Rose huffing and whooping, down at the bottom of the clearing. The ferisher girl had found a creek, and was having herself what looked to be a fine, freezing-cold bath. As for Ethan, he was still, she saw, sitting in the back seat of Skidbladnir. Jennifer T. ached to strip off her clothes and join Spider-Rose down in the creek for her first real bath in longer than she cared to remember. But instead she went over to see what it was that was so bothering Ethan Feld.

He hadn't moved, but she saw that he had on the dark glasses, and her heart sank. While she didn't blame him for wearing them, she supposed, she couldn't understand why wearing them didn't give him the creeps. To Jennifer T., wearing them felt like wearing another person's *hair*. Touching them was like touching your hand after it had fallen asleep – it was your hand, but it felt like somebody else's. She had tried them, once or twice, looking for clues as to Mr. Feld's whereabouts, or just hoping to catch a glimpse of the man. Everyone had. But with Ethan, wearing the dark glasses had become almost an obsession. He would sit for hours, perfectly still, breathing through his mouth, looking as stunned as Darrin and Dirk sitting in front of pro wrestling or *Power Rangers*. This in spite of the fact that the image transmitted by the inky lenses of the glasses had grown increasingly dim and fragmentary over time, harder to see. The glasses themselves had darkened to a colour like stained teeth, and now, she saw, they had even started to shrivel like the skin of a very old pear. It was as if

Padfoot's glasses, which had always felt weirdly alive somehow, were, like cut flowers, slowly withering.

"Hey," she said.

"Hey."

"What's up?"

Ethan didn't answer. He just sat there, staring into the dark lenses, picking with a fingernail at a sticky patch on the vinyl of the driver's seat.

"Yo, *Feld*," she said, punching him on the arm. "What are you doing, Holmes? Is he there?"

That was the other sort of disturbing thing about Ethan's increasing use of the dark glasses. As the quality of the images deteriorated, Mr. Feld also appeared in the lenses less and less often. When he did appear, his face was often averted, or tilted down. You could see that he was concentrating on some work of his hands. The work itself, and his face as he performed it, could not be seen. And as the weeks passed, Padfoot seemed to have less and less to do with Mr. Feld. It had been days since Ethan had caught a glimpse of him.

"Nope," he said softly. "He's not there."

"Then what are you looking at?"

Ethan didn't answer at first. Then he said,

"Nothing."

"Nothing?" said Jennifer T. "*Nothing* nothing?"

She snatched the glasses from his face and, holding her breath, slid them on. They had gone cold as a mushroom. Her skin crawled, and she ripped them off her face again. But before she did, she saw that the images of the Winterlands, which had been flickering and dimming for days, were gone. The glasses had truly gone dark.

"Get rid of these things," she said. She was tempted just to toss them into the trees, but that would have been mean. So she handed them back. "Jeez."

Ethan sat, turning them over and over in hands.

"We aren't going to make it," he said. "It's already the Top of the Seventh."

"Stay positive," she said. "We'll make it. We'll find him."

"That's what I'm sort of, like, starting to worry about," he said.

"What do you mean?"

"I don't know. It's just— the last time I saw him. The last time the glasses really worked. I saw something… He looked…"

"What?"

"I don't know." But he shuddered, and she saw that he *did* know. He just didn't want to say. "It was like something from a bad dream. It was my father, but I knew it wasn't my father."

"They were malfunctioning," she assured him. "Now they're dead."

"Yeah," Ethan said. His smile looked a little brave. "That was probably the thing."

He put a hand on the door handle, then left it there without opening the door.

"Did you hear her?" he said.

Jennifer T. nodded. She knew that Ethan's mother had broken his heart, too, by leaving him. She could imagine how it felt to him to listen to the sobbing of that wild old La Llorona, night after night.

"Whatever," he said.

He tossed the glasses onto the floor of the car. He got out of the car, and they went over to see what they could do to help with dinner.

"You can keep out of the way until it's time to wash the dishes," Pettipaw said, shooing them away with a flick of his tail. He was a deadly hunter – he hunted with his bare hands and the twin daggers of his foreteeth – with a special fondness for ground squirrel. Tonight he was boiling up a fine ground-squirrel burgoo. "Maybe you can figure out what became of the megaloped."

This was his nickname for Taffy. Jennifer T. looked around, and realised she had not seen the Sasquatch since her announcement that if need be she would carry them all down to the river. Now, Jennifer T. saw, their gear stood stacked in orderly piles, or laid to dry or air out on the rocks, all with the Sasquatch's telltale neatness. But there was no sign of Taffy herself. They hiked back up to the trail Jennifer T. had found, then down to the stream to ask Spider-Rose if she had seen Taffy.

"Nope," the ferisher said. She had her little doll-brother – its name was Nubakaduba (Old Fatidic for "little rocket") – in the stream with her, and just now she was beating its woolly hair clean with a small, flat stone. Since leaving her native knoll, her temperament, if not her outlook on life, had improved somewhat, but she was if anything more attached to the tattered remnant of her lost brother than ever. She sang to it endlessly at night, lulling herself to sleep. She drove Pettipaw wild with her demand that he provide her brother with a bowl of supper every night, suitably mashed. And woe to the one who inadvertently sat on or squashed Nubakaduba in the backseat of the car. "But I think she said she was going for a walk."

"Was that before or after La Llorona started up?" Jennifer T. wanted to know.

"Couldn't say. After, I guess. Why?"

"No reason," Jennifer T. said.

Shaking off her misgivings, she chased Ethan away, and had a brief, frigid, glorious bath in the stream, washing out her socks and underwear and laying them to dry on a stone. Then she changed into her other clean set of clothes and went to find Ethan. He was sitting by the fire, working over the handle of his bat, which someone – Jennifer T. wasn't sure anymore just who – had dubbed "Splinter." She had to admire Ethan for his persistence, or maybe it was *loyalty*. He had decided that, though it caused him to swing late, to swing early, to swing too soft and too hard, to swing himself right out his shoes, he was meant for Splinter, and Splinter for him. In spite of its failure to perform on the field, it had, after all, slain a skriker and healed Cinquefoil. But something must be done about the Knot. And so night after night, he sat glumly working it over with the wicked blade of Grimalkin John's hunting knife. But though the knife blade was finger-severing sharp, all his hours of dutiful scraping failed to do more than peel away a few scant fingernail-parings of ash. It was as though the Knot were not wood at all, but iron or stone.

"I need a sharper knife," Ethan said, stabbing the little giant's knife into a rotting log beside him. As if to belie his words, it sank into the wood all the way up to its haft.

"It ain't a question of the blade," Grim said. "It's the one that's doing the wielding. And that Knot ain't going away till you're ready, like what I told you a hunnert times already. And I guess you ain't ready."

"But I'll wager he's ready for supper." Pettipaw beat on a pot with a metal spoon, and the thin sound of it carried far up into the hills above them. One by one the scattered Shadowtails gathered around the fire and took their steaming bowls of chow. All except for Taffy.

"I'm worried," Jennifer T. said. "She's never wandered off before."

"And I made her a fine poke salad," Pettipaw sulked. "Don't know why I bother."

From far off there was low rumble, and they all looked up. It might have been thunder, or the sound of the little mountain men playing at ninepins, or the bellowing of some distant moose or bull elk. It was nearly night. The sky was a deep, rich colour like the heart of a gas flame. Bats swooped and wheeled and stitched their crooked way across the blue, embroidering the night. The moon rose, gibbous and huge, far bigger and brighter than the moon of the Middling. Somewhere off in the woods an owl hooted. And, away down beyond the road, the stream in which she and Spider-Rose had bathed that afternoon bubbled and muttered and spilled down the mountainside. It was beautiful – the Summerlands were beautiful – but at night sometimes it got a little strange. There were things in the woods, all kinds of night-things, both familiar – owls, bats, wolves, foxes – and creepy.

"Ah, now," Cinquefoil said, returning his attention to the burgoo. "Sasquatches love ta wander. 'S just their way."

"Not the girls," Jennifer T. insisted. "They like to stay close to home."

The stew was rich and brothy, spiced heavily with bay laurel, and since eating little chickeny chunks of cut-up ground squirrel was no stranger than anything else that had happened to her since the day she threw her first fastball on the little field at Clam Island Middle School and a werefox had appeared, she ate it. Then she, Ethan, and Thor went down to the stream with the clay ferisher bowls and drinking gourds. They did not say much as they passed the dirty bowls and drinking gourds through the chattering cold water of the creek.

"I want to get a hit," Ethan said.

"You will," said Jennifer T. "Tell him, Thor."

"Absolutely," Thor said. "I think you should try a different bat."

"Maybe one that doesn't, oh, make your hand bleed, for example," suggested Jennifer T.

"No," Ethan said. "You heard what Grim said. It isn't the bat. It's me." He blew on his hands. The water of the stream was so cold it made your fingers hum. "Maybe I'm just supposed to learn to hit *around* the Knot. You know, like that ancient Greek guy who taught himself to talk with stones in his mouth."

"Demosthenes," said a lugubrious voice behind them.

"Taffy!" Jennifer T. stood up and ran to the Sasquatch, and put her arms around her. "I was so worried about you! Where were you?"

Taffy didn't answer right away. Jennifer T. looked up. The daylight was failing and the firelight dim, but nonetheless

Jennifer T. could see that the Sasquatch's tiny bright eyes were red from crying.

"I went for a walk," she said at last. "That's all. I'm fine."

Even though she knew that they had been dead for hundreds of years, Jennifer T. could not shake the thought that Taffy, like La Llorona, had been out looking for her lost children.

"Were you—" she began.

"In a way, dear," the Sasquatch said softly. "In a way, I suppose."

They heard the deep rumbling again, nearer this time. It was a rumbling, Jennifer T. decided, in the ground. It caused the soles of her sneakers to buzz. Something big was coming their way. They heard a cry from up towards the camp. It was the sharp little voice of Dick Pettipaw. He sounded as if he might be excited, or afraid.

"What did he say?" said Jennifer T.

"He said, 'Big Liar coming!' " said Thor.

"Big Liar coming," Taffy said. "How about that? They're still around. One of them is, at any rate." She smoothed down the spray of black fur at the top of her head. "Come on. I want to see this."

She gathered up all the dishes and gourds in a single armful and started up the hill, picking her way on her experienced feet. There was another rumbling in the earth. The children followed the Sasquatch up to camp. They kept behind her, not sure what to expect. They knew that the Lost Camps were Big Liar country, because it said so on Thor's map. And their team-mates had told them some of the old lies. Lies about shooting contests in which hairs were shot from the hind legs of houseflies. Lies about grinning contests between men and raccoons. Lies about knife fights, poker games, fishing trips, and mosquitoes. Lies about women who rode alligators and carried razors in their boots, and about working men who outworked the Devil and the Machine. Some of them were lies that Jennifer T. had heard before.

"Which one is it?" Ethan said, struggling up the hill behind her. "Can you see?"

She reached the camp. All of the other Shadowtails were standing with their backs to the campfire, watching as a tall man came out of the woods. Jennifer T. had, naturally, been expecting someone *big*. She was somewhat disappointed to see an ordinarily large man come striding from the trees. He was not quite as tall as Taffy, broad chested, thick necked, with a full, black beard. He wore a plaid flannel shirt, red as a flag, black dungarees, and black boots. The boots were so large and so thick-soled that for a moment Jennifer T. thought that they must have been causing all the rumbling. But he was walking now, the Tall Man, coming towards them, and there was no rumbling. Then she saw the great red-headed Axe. It was as long as an oar and the edge of its blade glowed like halogen.

"Wal," said the Tall Man with the Axe. "Lookit this. Visitors."

He grinned, and even though he was not a giant anymore, there was something about the smile that made you feel very small.

"Howdy, cuz," said Grim the Giant. "Nice to see you."

"Visitors!" said the Man. "Heard there was Visitors, and so there are. Ain't had no Visitors in a terrible long time!"

"We're the Travelling Shadowtails," said Cinquefoil. "We're on a little tour o' these parts. Only, as it turns out, the team bus done run out o' gas."

"We need to get to Applelawn," Ethan said. He went over to the Man, sticking out his left arm. "Ragged Rock is coming."

The Man squinted down at Ethan's watch.

"Do you?" he said. "Is it?"

All at once the joy of Visitors seemed to drain from his face.

"You really purpose to get to Applelawn, then. It warn't just some rot the crows and weresquirrels was handing us."

"Is there a problem with that?" Cinquefoil said.

"Not a bit," the Tall Man said. "Not a bit. Only that I cain't let ya pass."

"You don't own this road," Cinquefoil said. Jennifer T. admired him for standing up to the Tall Man. Like his grin, his manner had something giant about it.

"Oh, but I do." Then went over to the nearest tree, a stout fir, and raised his axe to one side. He turned the handle until the blade lay horizontal and then took a sweeping hack at the trunk of the tree. That was when Jennifer T. figured out what the rumbling was. The tree shuddered, and its leaves all seemed to sigh. It hung for a moment, motionless, teetering on the point of the huge notch the Man had gouged into its trunk. Then, silently, it fell. When it hit, the earth shook so hard that Jennifer T. lost her balance, and fell down. Her ears were still ringing when the Man spoke again. "Ya don't wanna mess with me."

There was silence. Cinquefoil looked at the tumbled ruin of the fir tree, then up at the Man's giant grin.

"Fine," he said. "We'll turn and find another road across the river." He gestured towards the children. "Come on, rubes."

He went over to Taffy and took a gourd from her. He stuffed it into the canvas sack they carried their mess stuff in. It really looked like he was planning to leave. Jennifer T. couldn't tell if he was bluffing.

"Wait just a minute, there. Hold on."

The Tall Man reached down and snatched the sack from Cinquefoil.

"I think ya might have misunderstood me, there. No need ta be hotheaded, eh?"

"You said you won't let us pass!" Pettipaw said.

"Did I?" He looked genuinely shocked. "Well, I meant, not without a proper *hello*. Down by the Landing. Me and all the old Liars, we're all staying down by there these days. I know they're all gonna want ta meet ya."

"How far is it, by foot, then?"

"Three days fer the likes of you, I reckon, more or less."

Jennifer T. heard the breath go hissing out of Ethan. In three days it might already be the Ninth Inning.

"We need to get there sooner!" Jennifer T. said. "Have you got anything we could use for fuel?"

The Man grinned, and reached into the hip pocket of his dungarees. He pulled out a silver flask.

"What is that stuff, cuz?" Grim said.

"Put it this way, little giant," the Man said. "Friend of mine makes this stuff. Takes the shining edge of my axe, the crash of timber ya just heard, and puts them in a bottle. Calls it prunejack."

"Prunejack!" Grim said. "You can't run a engine on prunejack!"

"With grammer, ya could," Cinquefoil said.

"Prunejack!" said Pettipaw, taking a deep appreciative whiff of the Man's flask. "You can't waste a fine flask of good jackass liquor on a *car*!"

IT TOOK THE better part of the day to make their burbling way down to Old Cat Landing. The character of the land changed, as they descended into the grassy foothills of the Lost Camps beyond the Raucous Mountains. There were fewer ferisher knolls, and the caves of Bowling Men were left far behind. The road widened out again to a kind of highway. It ran, mostly straight, occasionally dodging around a piney hill or barren knob of black oak, through a country of Indian camps and hunters' lodges, of miners' flats, of farms and ranches, of lean-tos and lonely cottages with a pale watching face from the kitchen window. To Ethan's surprise, the dwellers in these habitations were, for the most part, of women and men. There were gold-panners, wolf-trackers and bear-hunters, farmhands and cowboys, freed slaves and Buffalo soldiers, pig-tailed Chinese labourers whose bats and gloves were stamped with the words PROPERTY OF BIG JIM HILL. But though the form of these creatures was human, they were not reubens, not at all. They were solid, living creatures, and yet they were not human beings so much as the compounded memories, preserved in the Summerlands like mayflies in amber, of human beings. They were ghosts, shades and reflections. They were lies and legends made flesh. And the greatest of these ghost people were the Big Liars. At one time they had ranged all across this part of the Summerlands, striding a quarter mile in a single step. Now they hung around Old Cat Landing, haunting its bars and brothels. When the Shadowtails showed up on the main street, right by the Jersey Lily saloon, the Liars all came out to laugh.

The street was paved in a mixture of chalk, oystershells, and broken whiskey bottles. You had to watch where you walked.

"So, here they are, then. The saviours of the Summerlands."

It was a large man who said this, bearded, in a vast blue pea coat, with a stocking cap on his head and the stub of a pipe jammed into the corner of his mouth. He carried, slung over his shoulder, a long harpoon, tipped with a glinting barb. The Tall Man with the Harpoon threw back his head and laughed, very carefully, somehow, as if the laughter would not be as humiliating, nor the laugher himself quite so big and imposing, if he did not stop first to throw back his bearded head. They were all large, the men and women who crowded around Skid and the Shadowtails, and one of them was wearing a cowboy hat, with an enormous live rattlesnake twined around his throat like a living necktie. Together with the Man with the Axe, they numbered nine, the seven men as tall as Taffy, the two women nearly so, broad-shouldered and thick-legged and strong. Two of the men and both of the women were dark-skinned, with hands as big as the family bible that Jennifer

T.'s gran Billy Ann kept on the television. One of the black men carried an immense black iron hammer, and his smile though more kindly was no less mocking than that of the man with the pipe.

"Old Ringfinger done said you was a motley crew," said the Tall Man with the Hammer, peering down at the Shadowtails, "but didn't nobody said you was this motley."

With that all nine of the giant people burst into laughter, slapping each other on the back, and spitting foul juices into the street, and exchanging high fives with the man holding the great big Hammer.

"You might be laughing now," Jennifer T. said, and Ethan loved her for it before she even got the rest of the sentence out of her mouth, "but you're going to be *crying* when we get through whupping your fat butts!"

That brought out an even greater explosion of laughter. One of the big white men, a little smaller and fatter than the others, with close-cropped red hair, laughed so hard that he dropped his long pole, fell over, and had to be righted by one of his fellows, a huge ox of a man with a snub nose, beady red eyes, and skin that glinted like polished bronze who carried a huge hammerlike tool, spiked on one side, that they afterwards learned was a steelworker's maul.

"Chiron Brown?" Ethan said. "Is he here? Has he been around?"

The Tall Man with the Axe pointed – his index finger as thick and long as one of Cinquefoil's legs – and they turned back to see the old white Cadillac coming down the main street. It was Ringfinger Brown behind the wheel. He was dressed in a green-and-gold suit – green overlaid with a kind of diagonal yellow grid. He eased his old body out of the car and walked right up to Ethan and Jennifer T.

"Well, now," he said. "Well, well, well. Look like old Ringfinger wasn't en*tire*ly wrong about you two." He chuckled, clearly delighted with himself, as though his failure in scouting Ethan and Jennifer T. had been rankling for a long time. "You done come *far*, come a *long* way. Been playin' halfway good baseball, too, what I hear."

"Been playin all-the-way *losin'* baseball, what we hears," said another of the Tall Men. He was a very dark, very handsome man dressed in a grey-and-white pinstripe suit, with a purple brocade vest, that made Ringfinger's look dull and conservative. From the top of his tooled-leather, Cuban-heeled boot, protruded the horn handle of a very big knife. "Come a *long* way to get they hineys tanned."

"We aren't here to play any stupid baseball," said Spider-Rose. "We're on our way to Applelawn, so that we can get through to find the Coyote" – she thrust forwards the scrunched little ragdoll husk of Nubakaduba – "and get him to turn my brother back into a *baby*!"

The Shadowtails all turned to her, mouths open, eyebrows knit. It sounded like a preposterous idea to Ethan, who had seen Nubakaduba only as a gross little hank of chamois and yarn, and never as a cute, plump, burbling little ferisher whose face lit up every time his sister walked into the room. But more surprising still was the wildly powerful blast of hopefulness that seemed to be behind this strange idea.. Spider-Rose had long since won for herself the Shadowtails title of Most Negative Player.

"And stuff," she finished, blushing a deep peach-flesh gold.

Jennifer T. put her arm around Spider-Rose's shoulder. "You bet we will," she said.

"I'm acutely sorry to disappoint you travellers," said one of the Tall Women, "because you done come so powerful far." She was a wide-built lady with beautiful green eyes and freckled skin, dressed in a pair of vast denim overalls, with a long-barrelled rifle slung over her shoulder. "But we are not here to engage in no diamond antics with you, neither. We are here, in fact, to see that you *never get across that there river*."

"And who, I'd like to know," Grim the Giant said, "is fixing to stop us?"

"Annie Christmas," said the woman in the overalls. "And her friends."

They all stepped forward now, the Tall Man with the Axe, the Tall Man with the Hammer, the Tall Man with the Big Maul, the Tall Man with the Harpoon, the Tall Man with the Rattlesnake Necktie, the Tall Man with the Knife in His Boot, The Tall Man with the Pole, and the other Tall Woman – who wore a tight red dress so shiny that it put to shame the slick grey suit of the Man with the Knife in His Boot – and a pair of red shoes whose heels were nearly as high as Spider-Rose herself. Around her neck hung a straight razor on a silver chain.

"These here are my friends," Annie Christmas said. "The Big Liars of Old Cat Landing."

"Yeah? Well, if you're so big and all, why are you so short?" said Jennifer T. She went right up to the Tall Man with the Axe and looked him up and down as critically as she examined opposing pitchers before the start of a game. "I've been wanting to ask you all day. I thought you were supposed to be, like, a *giant lumberjack? Supposed* to, I don't know, supposed to use a whole redwood tree for a toothpick? And Lake Superior for an ice rink? And stuff like that. So, where's the *blue ox*?"

The Tall Man with the Axe rubbed at his grey-blond beard, peering down at Jennifer T. Ethan was astonished to see tears in his eyes. The other Big Liars gathered around him, and the Tall Man with the Hammer put an arm across the Man with the Axe's shoulders. And then the Man with the Axe buried his face in his hands, and sobbed.

"I'm sorry," he said, after a moment, wiping his nose on his sleeve. He tried to gain control of himself, but every time the tears abated somewhat he would let out a heartrending cry of "Babe!" and then start crying all over again. Finally the Man with the Hammer had to lead him away, into the Jersey Lily saloon, with a backwards look of reproach over his shoulder at Jennifer T.

"I'm sorry," she said. "I didn't mean to— I didn't know. Did something happen to the ox?"

"What happen to Babe is what happen to all of us," said the Man with the Big Maul. He had a little bit of an accent, it seemed to Ethan, Russian or Polish or something like that. "Look at me. One time, I am big as slagheap. Legs like rolling mills. Heart like Bessemer converter. Now look. Tiny guy. Only six foot six, and shrinking. Use to take bath in blast furnace, melt myself down and pour myself a fresh new body from the ladle. Not no more. Steel mills gone. Everything gone."

"Whaling ships."

"Railroad crews."

"Keel boats."

"Sternwheelers jes' bursting out with pigeons for the pluckin'," said the Man with the Knife in His Boot.

"Not to mention the good old Indian fights," said the Man with the Rattlesnake Tie.

"Yeah, well, we're better off without *that* crap," Jennifer T. said. "Whaling ships, too. Whales are sentient beings, or didn't you know that? They are, like, smarter than people, and they have language, and myths, and histories." She turned on the Tall Man with the Pole, and for all his six-plus feet and considerable bulk, Ethan saw him take a little step backwards. "And I don't know what a keel boat is exactly, but I'll bet we're better off without keelboat *men* too. I mean, jeez, it looks like somebody bit your ear off."

The Man with the Pole rubbed at the nub of his left ear tenderly. "Yeah," he said, with a dreamy expression. "Gouged out mah eyeball, too, but Ah stuck hit back in ag'in."

"Er, be all that as it may, Miss Rideout," said Pettipaw, stepping forward now to stand between Jennifer T. and the Man with the Pole, and tugging delicately on one of his whiskers. "While I never had the pleasure of making the acquaintance of the late ox, I do not believe that there is anyone now living in the Summerlands who has not, at one time or another, lamented the passing of the Old Days."

"Yer right, there, Pettipaw," Cinquefoil said. "These is shrunken times, indeed."

"But I confess," the wererat continued, "I do not understand why it is that you fine people believe that allowing Coyote to carry out his intentions will *improve* the lot of us Summerlanders."

There was a silence, and the Big Liars shuffled a little, and shifted back and forth, as if the answer were so obvious that they were embarrassed, for Pettipaw's sake, to have to answer it. Finally the Tall Man with the Harpoon struck a match, and got his pipe lit, and then looked up.

"We don't hope to improve our situation, sir," he said. "We hope to *end* it. We *want* that old Kye-oat to bring the Lodgepole down."

A gull cried, and the air went crackling through the clay pipe, and the cooling engine of Ringfinger Brown's Cadillac ticked like a clock in the sun.

"These-here folks," Ringfinger said. "They been feelin' for a while now like there wasn't much point to it all."

"But they don't get to decide," Jennifer T. said.

"They have no *right* to stop us from crossing that river," Thor said.

"We don't need no right, changeling boy," Annie Christmas said. She pushed back her sleeves, revealing a set of powerfully muscled brown arms. "Not to stop the likes a you."

"There *is* a point," Ethan said, surprising himself a little. The others all turned to look at him. "I mean, OK, I want to find my father. My dad. I need my father, and he needs me." He looked at his watch. It still read Top of the Seventh; then, as he glanced at it, the little triangular arrow flipped over and pointed down. Two innings left before the end. "So, ha, that's a point."

"There's one other point," Cinquefoil said, "and I'm shamed a ya fer fergetting it."

The Big Liars all looked blank.

"*Baseball*," Cinquefoil said. "Long as someplace they play baseball the old style, the Summerlands style, with patience and abandon, then there will always be a point ta it all."

This sounded nice to Ethan, and true, though he wasn't quite sure he knew what Cinquefoil meant by "abandon".

Annie Christmas turned to the Man with the Knife in His Boot.

"Honeybunch," she said. "Go on into that saloon and escort those two gennulmens back out here. We needs to indulge in some elongated palaver. No, better yet, let's go in there and get 'em. I could use a drink."

The seven Big Liars trooped off into the Jersey Lily, leaving the Shadowtails with Ringfinger Brown. They wandered down to the landing, and out a little way along the dock. The sluggish water of the Big River churned and slapped against the pilings.

"Well," Taffy said. She had been silent throughout the deliberations. Now she went to sit down at the edge of the dock, and trail her celebrated feet in the water. Her back was to the rest of them. "Looks like we've come to the end." She sounds *relieved*, thought Ethan.

"Even if they said we *could* go, well, I mean, look," said Jennifer T., pointing out across the water. "Applelawn is all the ways across *that*. How are we supposed to get across?"

"Yeah, and what about this Old Bottom-Cat thing? Who or what is it?"

"Ain't nobody really knows for certain," Ringfinger Brown said. "Them that have seen him nice and close up, well, they ain't come back to *describe* him. But he big. He *very* big. I knows that."

"How?"

"Because, children, he what *hold up* the Lodgepole. All clutched up in his tail. Just like that great big muscled-up arm you done seen back there, holdin' tight to that nine-pound Hammer. And that why some people just call him 'Slug'."

"The Slugger," said Pettipaw, nodding. "I've heard that. The Slugger of the Bottom of the Last. And there are some that just call him 'Old Cat'."

"Some way or another, to reach Applelawn, you have to get past him."

"Yeah," Jennifer T. said. "But before that, we got to get past *them*."

The nine Big Liars came down from the Jersey Lily and stood on the pier, gazing out across the river that had once carried an endless cargo of stories and brags, tales and whoppers piled so high on the docks of the Big River that they had to be hinged to let the moon get past them.

"All right," said Annie Christmas. "We will play you nine innings of old-style ball, with all the abandon we capable of. And if you all win, you get to get past us, and try your luck with the Ole Cat. Because if you can beat us, then you *meant* to beat us, and if you *meant* to do somethin', well then, ipso facto you got some kind of *meanin'* enterin' into the situation." She turned to her strapping comrades, and Ethan could see pretty clearly who was the Boss of Old Cat Landing. "That just simple *logic*. Q.E.D."

Pettipaw scrambled straight up the trouser leg of Grim the Giant, hoisted himself to the little giant's shoulder, clambered onto the top of his head, and then leapt into the air, turning a back flip on his way back down. Ethan and Jennifer T. high-fived and then punched each other's fists, one two.

"Yes!" said Spider-Rose, hugging Nubakaduba tight.

But Thor stood rubbing softly at his temple.

"There's only one problem," he said. "We're eight. You're nine. We need another player."

"That *your* problem," said the Tall Woman with the Dice and Razor. She had changed out of her flaming red dress and into her old white flannels and baseball spikes. Across her chest, in flowing blue script, it said LIARS. "You got but eight, you gonna have to beat us with eight."

"I count nine," said the Tall Man with the Axe, looking at old Chiron Brown.

"Not me," said Ringfinger with a soft chuckle. "I'm a scout. I got to maintain my impartiality. What's more—" He bent down and pulled up his right trouser leg, revealing a prosthetic limb of tan plastic. It was wearing a white athletic sock. "I ain't got but one leg."

ANNIE CHRISTMAS PUT them up at her place – the grandest house on the Landing – and after they had bathed and rested, they met down in the dining room, where Annie laid out a vast spread of hog jaws, chitterlings, pork chops, turnip greens, cornbread, whippoorwill peas, macaroni salad, and sweet potato pie. She joined them for supper, of course, and ate more than anyone except for Pettipaw, who consumed several times his own weight in pork, downed frightening amounts of macaroni salad, seven and a half pies, and two gallons of hand-cranked vanilla ice cream. He declared that he had met his match in the kitchen. After they had eaten, Annie sat back in her rocking chair, lit a delicate little porcelain pipe, and blew out a long trail of smoke, and said, "What you people need, if you doesn't object to accepting advice from the opposition, is to locate yourselves a *ringer*."

"I was thinking the same thing," said Jennifer T.

"So was I," Cinquefoil said. "There was some fine players up ta the Lost Camps. That man Oakdale, fer example. Soft hands. A natural hitter. I think we ought ta—"

"No," Grim the Giant said. "Not no local piddly-bit Sunday afternoon slugger. I mean, look at us. We're OK. We're getting better. Now and again, somebody lookin' at us, and feelin' just a tiny bit generous, might even be tempted to say we was a downright fair-to-not-so-bad ball club. But if we goin' to take all the trouble to find ourselves a ninth man, then I say that ninth man ought to be, well—"

"A *champion*," said Ringfinger Brown. "A hero."

Grim smacked the table, and set all the plates dancing. "That's just what I'm tryin' to say!"

"Well, ain't that droll," Ringfinger said, mopping up the last of the gravy with a crumbling scrap of cornbread. "You needin' a hero, and heroes bein' my sole and proper line of business, and me turnin' up here at near onto more or less the end of the world, where you leas' expect to find me."

There was an unmistakable glint in his eye.

"Who is it, Mr. Brown?" Ethan said. "Who did you get us to play right field?"

"Well, now, I don't know as I exactly have a partic'lar person in mind, but, uh, look here. Mr. Wignutt. Why don't you get out that crazy map of yours, and fluster it all around like you do, and tell us what we might find if we was to go looking right around heres for a nice spot to leap over to the Middling."

Thor dutifully pulled out the Four-Sided Map, and pleated and scored it and turned it around until it showed green leaves and grey branches on one side and brown leaves and grey branches on the other. Then he went out into the dooryard of Annie's house, and held it up to the rays of the setting sun.

"Well, huh, I— I'm not sure. But it looks like—" He brought the map very close to his face, and held it a little higher. "Yeah, there is a spot right by here. On a very, very small little branch. On this side it says Old Cat Landing. And on the other side… it says…" He lowered the map, and looked at Ethan. "Ethan, it says 'Anaheim'."

"Anaheim," Jennifer T. said. "*Anaheim*".

"Oh, my God," Ethan said.

"Mr. Brown," Jennifer T. said, turning to Ringfinger. "Did you scout us up Rodrigo Buendía?"

"Rodrigo Buendía," Ethan said. "Oh, my God."

IT WAS EVENING when they left the Summerlands. They were standing on the ball field at Old Cat Landing, on some bluffs overlooking the river. Tall, delicate trees stood like spectators beyond the right field fence. That was the direction that Thor started walking, towards the cottonwood trees. It was just the three of them, once again: Jennifer T., Ethan, and Thor.

"I know your map shows where the spots are," Ethan said. "But how do you really find them, in the world, I mean. How do you know which way to go?"

"I... don't know," Thor said. "I just start walking along a branch until I feel it."

"Are we walking along a branch right now?" Jennifer T. said, gazing down at her feet. There was just grass there, as far as she could tell. And she couldn't feel anything apart from nervousness about the mission they were about to undertake. She tried to imagine what it would be like to be able to feel your way into another world.

"Could you find a way to Rodrigo Buendía even *without* the map?" she said.

Thor kept walking. The summer night, that had been soft and lit by lightning-bugs, darkened, and turned cold. Thor closed his eyes.

"I think I could probably find anyone," he said.

"Could you take us to my dad?" Ethan said.

"Uh, yeah. Maybe. It would be hard. I would need a really long time. A lot of leaping. I would probably make a lot of mistakes. We might leap into some bad places."

All at once it turned very much colder. The trees were gone. The stars were gone.

"Thor?" Jennifer T. said. "Can I ask you a question?"

"Yes," Thor said at once. He opened his eyes. "I could take you to your mother. I'll do it whenever you want."

"OK," Jennifer T. "I'll think about it."

"Could you take me to mine?" Ethan said, with a laugh.

Then Jennifer T. took his hand, and Ethan took Thor's cold and callused one. And then Thor started walking again, and they followed him, holding hands, into the blazing mouth of day.

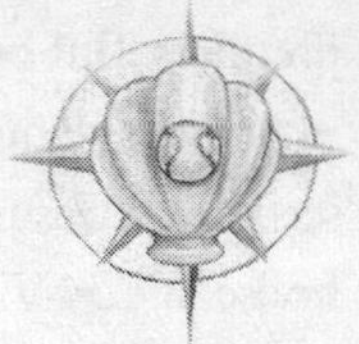

20

Rancho Encantado

THE CRIME RATE in Rancho Encantado, California, pop. 27,000, is very low – "unmeasurably low," as the Director of Municipal Security likes to boast. No doubt this is due, in part, to the fine work done by the men and women of the Department of Municipal Security. Another reason may be that the entire perimeter of Rancho Encantado is surrounded by twenty-four miles of electrified fence.

Within these formidable city limits there is one lovely tract of very large houses, Italian-style rather than the usual Spanish, called Villa Borghese. This fashionable subdivision is surrounded by another wall, a more prosaic one of wood and stucco, taller than a man and topped by an array of decorative pale green iron spikes. Inside these dagger-tipped walls, the streets of Villa Borghese are patrolled not only by the Municipal Security Officers (MSOs) but also by representatives of private security firms. The houses of Villa Borghese, in which some twenty-seven hundred people live, are themselves surrounded by walls and fences, some of them also electrified. Of those eight-hundred-odd houses, all have built-in alarm systems; some have systems of closed-circuit security cameras; others are protected by mean dogs; and a few even have permanent personal bodyguards living on the premises. But only one house, in all of Villa Borghese – in all of greater Rancho Encantado – employs *every one* of the security measures I have described, all at once. This is the house at 234 Via Vespasiana, the home of the Cuban defector and three-time batting champion, Rodrigo Buendía.

It would have been very nice, in other words, if Thor could have found a way to leap right into the guy's living room. Maybe someday he would develop that kind of control over his talent. For now, however, they would have to settle for a spot down at the very bottom of Rodrigo Buendía's street. It was a long street that wound its way up to the very top of the hill out of which, a few years earlier, all of Villa Borghese had been carved. Buendía lived, Thor declared, in the house at the top of the hill. This time Ethan didn't ask him how he knew. They started walking up Via Vespasiana. The day was very warm. The succulent plants in the landscaping strip along the sidewalk shimmered in the heat, as did the sidewalk itself. There was absolutely no one in sight. Not even in the loneliest hollow of the Raucous Mountains had they encountered such silence, such emptiness. Only a distant lawnmower whine, and the nearby *chiff-chiff-chiff* of a lawn sprinkler.

When they came to the corner of Via Vespasiana and Via Aureliana, they were spotted by an MSO, sitting in his patrol car in front of 441 Via Aureliana. The MSO radioed to Central Unit to report what he had seen. Central Unit duly logged the report: three children had been observed walking up the street, at 14:13 hours, on Via Vespasiana.

"This place is strange," Jennifer T. said.

Considering where they had just spent most of the last month, Ethan thought, this was saying quite a lot. But he agreed.

"It's so quiet," Ethan said. "I can hear it when I swallow."

They passed a great big beautiful white house with a red tile roof and a green, green lawn. After so long amid the shifting hues of earth and leaf and sky in the Summerlands, the big white house looked so clean and bright to Ethan, its colours so bold, that it might have been built of Lego bricks.

"Now you got *me* hearing it when I swallow," said Thor.

"Yeah," Jennifer T. said. "Thanks a lot."

"Look," Ethan said. He pointed to the house with the Lego-red, clay-tile roof. One of its upstairs rooms had a little Juliet balcony, with a pretty wrought-iron rail. On this balcony there stood a child, a girl, of about their age. She was watching them walk up the street, just standing there, holding on to the wrought-iron rail. There was no expression on her face that Ethan could see. "There's a kid."

They stopped. They had not seen another child, a little reuben, in weeks. Children were as scarce in the Lost Camps as they had been among the ferishers, and those few they *had* seen were like the children in old photographs, silent and rustic and ghostly, dressed in tan britches and dust-coloured frocks. This girl had on a sweatshirt as pink as a spoonful of antacid.

"Hi," Jennifer T. said, with an uncertain little wave.

"Hi," said the girl on the balcony.

The MSO, who had been trailing them silently in his patrol car from an average distance of three driveways away, informed Central Unit that the children he had reported at 14:13 now seemed to have become engaged in conversation. This was duly noted in the record at Central Unit.

"Where are you going?" said the girl on the balcony.

Ethan started to tell her, but Jennifer T. stepped on his foot.

"For a walk," said Jennifer T.

The girl wrinkled her nose. "Huh," she said.

Ethan could not tell if the idea of going for a walk struck her as interesting, tiresome, or merely bizarre. After a moment she turned and went back into the house. They kept walking, and the MSO kept tailing them. When the MSO realised that they were walking up to Rodrigo Buendía's house, he informed Central Unit, who agreed that the MSO was now confronted with a CT or Credible Threat. Central Unit authorised interdiction. The MSO got out of his silvery-grey patrol vehicle. He approached the children, a hand reaching for a fearsome-looking electrical-shock pistol that he carried on his hip.

"Hey," he said. "Hey, you kids."

They turned around. Then the girl and the smaller of the two boys looked at the bigger one, and they joined hands, and ran up the driveway of Rodrigo Buendía's house. They ran – the word that came to the MSO's mind was *scampered* – straight through the garage door, which must, after all, have been open, even though the MSO felt certain, and indicated in his subsequent report, that at the time the children approached it, it had definitely seemed to be closed.

THERE WERE TWO cars in the garage – a large BMW sedan and a Land Rover, with space for two more – but it looked as if the house was abandoned. They ran through a series of large, high white rooms with bare wood floors and no furniture. Ethan could hear the crackle of the policeman's radio from outside the house, harsh and angry-sounding. His vague idea of their throwing themselves on the mercy of the great Buendía faded with the emptiness of the house; they were simple trespassers, now. They would be arrested, and imprisoned. But then they fell into the kitchen, a great expanse of white cabinetry and steel appliances, in the midst of which there lay a heap of empty yellow cans of black beans. The cans tumbled over the side of a steel counter and down onto the floor. They were crusted with black ooze and there was something almost vandalistic about the mess they made. The labels were in Spanish: FRIJOLES NEGROS. On the stove there was a huge black pot, like a cauldron in a witch's kitchen, and when Ethan looked inside it he saw clinging to its side a brownish skin, with here and there a pristine grain of rice.

"*He's here*," he whispered.

"I know he's here," Thor replied, in his ordinary voice. Was it Ethan's imagination, or was there a trace of TW03 flatness to his tone? "Otherwise I wouldn't have—"

The doorbell rang, a long time, playing a series of churchy tones like a carillon. They froze, looking at each other. Then Jennifer T. crept over to a tall, narrow door by the refrigerator, and opened it. It was a broom closet, equipped with mops and dustpans. There was just enough room for one of them. Jennifer T. motioned for Ethan to climb in. He shook his head.

"*You*," he whispered. "*If they get us, at least you—*"

"They are not going to get us," said Thor. "We can just scamper out."

The doorbell rang again. Then the policeman began to knock, firmly and loud, and for a long time, as if somehow he knew that his persistence would be rewarded. At last they heard, somewhere off in the far reaches of the house, the sound of a man's voice, deep and grumbling. Buendía. The floors resounded with a thunderous tread, a big man pounding down a flight of steps to the front door. He was talking, either to the policeman or to himself, in Spanish. Whatever he was saying, it did not sound particularly kind.

"I'm sorry to bother you, Mr. Buendía," the policeman began, but after that his voice fell, and they couldn't catch what he was saying, nor any of Rodrigo Buendía's muttered replies. It did not sound, however, as if he was particularly interested in what the policeman had to tell him. Ethan crept towards the kitchen door, so that he could hear better – they were in the house of Rodrigo Buendía! That voice, muttering and thick, was the voice of the great Buendía! – and as he did so, his foot kicked one of the cans of beans. He winced, and whipped around to find his friends scowling at him for the idiot he was. The voices by the door fell silent, and then there they were, the strange police officer in his tight black coverall, and Buendía, *El Gran Oso*, the Big Bear, tall, dark and shambling, with the tiniest white terry-cloth bathrobe yanked carelessly around him. His hair was all mashed on one side, and under the robe he wore only a pair of tight blue underpants and one sock. But he was glaring right at Ethan, over the top of the policeman's head, and he looked, almost in spite of himself, very much awake.

Ethan knew that he had to say something, that instant, and that what he said had to be a kind of grammer, a series of words that were the right words, the only words, to dissolve the bonds of the ordinary world that were about to be tied tightly around them.

"Chiron Brown sent us," he said, ignoring the policeman entirely, aiming his desperate little grammer directly at the ears, at the big, strong, heroical heart of Rodrigo Buendía.

Buendía, however, seemed not to have heard the magic words. He blinked once, slowly, and then pursed his lips, and looked down at the policeman.

"Get them out of here," he said.

THE POLICEMAN, OR MSO, as they heard him refer to himself in his communications with Central Unit, put them into the back of his patrol car and drove them downtown. Ethan looked over at Thor, every so often, but Thor just shook his head. At the Municipal Security building, a kind of Lego fortress in a sunsplashed plaza with a fountain, they gave their names to a pleasant woman wearing a headset telephone. Then their MSO led them into a small room, silent, carpeted, furnished with toys that were much too young for them. There were mirrors on the walls that Ethan suspected must be one-way. No doubt the whole place was bugged. They sat down in three chairs of moulded black plastic, side by side. They kicked their feet. A clock on the wall hummed, and occasionally clicked as its minute hand lurched forward. Ethan looked at his watch. It was the Top of the Eighth Inning. Ordinarily he would have informed his friends of this terrible fact, but they were already upset enough.

"'Chiron Brown sent us'," Jennifer T. said, shaking her head. "Way to go, Feld."

"Well, he did," Ethan said. "I thought he knew Buendía. It sounded like he did."

"He's from *Cuba*," Jennifer T. said. "How could Mr. Brown have scouted him there?"

"Chiron Brown's territory is very big," Thor said flatly. "And I think he's known them all."

Ethan looked over at him, on the other side of Jennifer T., staring down at a red plastic fire truck on the ground.

"Can I ask you a question?" Ethan said. "Who are you, right now, Thor?"

Thor looked thoughtful. He seemed to know just what Ethan had meant by his question: Was he still Thor, the ferisher changeling with the blood and body of a reuben, or had he somehow reverted, now, to TW03, the boy who believed himself to be an android who was trying desperately to be a boy?

"I may never know the answer to that question," he said at last. He looked pretty sad as he said it, and for a second – just for a second – Ethan thought he might be about to cry.

"Let me ask you another question," Jennifer T. said gently. "Can you get us out of here?"

"Sure," Thor said. "I couldn't do it the car because – well, it's hard to explain. I could scamper *with* a moving car, but not *out* of one. It has to do with momentum, I think." He knelt down beside the fire truck and pushed it with one hand. "See, we'd be moving this way, but I would be trying to scamper us *away* from the car." He grabbed one of the plastic fire fighters and pulled it to one side. "But our bodies would still be going *forwards*, because of the car." He tossed the little firefighter over his shoulder and it smacked against a wall. "I wouldn't be able to control our momentum. And I really didn't think we wanted that police guy scampering *with* us."

He stood up, and walked over to one corner of the room. He took a deep breath. Ethan went over and turned out the lights, in case anyone was watching from the other side of the mirrored glass.

"OK, then," he said. "Back to Old Cat Landing. We'll have to tell them—"

"No," Jennifer T. said. "Not to Old Cat Landing. Back to Burger Village or whatever it was called."

"But he—"

"I don't care what he said, Feld," said Jennifer T. "I'm not going back without him."

And that, as was always the case when Jennifer T. had made up her mind, put an end to the discussion.

THEY FOUND HIM in bed, still wearing only blue skivvies and a sock, snoring with all the ferocity that his nickname would have led you to expect. He was on his back, one arm cradled under his head, the other fallen over the side of the mattress and clutching the extinct remains of a fat cigar. The room stank of cigar, and cold beans, and unwashed large ballplayer. They knew from their search of the house that this was the only one of its seventeen rooms, aside from the kitchen, that showed signs of human habitation. In addition to the bed there was a nightstand, a dresser topped with scattered coins and unwrapped cigars, and an enormous television with a flat screen. The television was tuned to the Fauna Channel, with the sound off. On the screen a big-eyed little furry creature with dexterous paws helped himself to a nice sticky pawful of tree gum.

"A bushbaby," Ethan said, and suddenly the memory of his lost father, steering their car along the Clam Island Highway, was like a cold, heavy stone in the pit of his stomach. What was going on, there in the world that Padfoot's dark glasses could no longer show him? What if something terrible had happened? What if his father was dead?

Buendía snuffled, and coughed, and then sprang up to a sitting position. He stared at them, eyes wide and uncomprehending, then at the digital clock on his nightstand – it was 3:12 in the afternoon – then back at the children. Recollection flooded his expression, and he fell backwards on the bed, and groaned.

"I should know this will be happen," he said. And then he let off a string of Spanish curses, which I could transcribe but had better simply characterise as foul and imaginative. They ended, unmistakably, with the words "Chiron Brown," which Buendía pronounced "*kee*ROAN BRON."

"You *do* know him," Jennifer T. said.

"Yes, I know that man. Since I was smaller than you." He sounded disgusted, Ethan thought, as if he wanted them to know that he was fed up, for some reason, with Ringfinger Brown. But looking around at the smelly, empty house, at the squalor in which he lived, it was hard for Ethan not to think that maybe Buendía was just disgusted with himself. He was having, Ethan knew, a terrible year. This was his second season with the Angels. He had played almost all of his career since his defection to the United States in the National League, first for the Phillies, and then for the Mets. He had played centre field, and then as his legs gave out and the surgeries mounted he switched to right; but since coming to the American League he had played nothing but designated hitter, never taking the field, spending the whole game on the bench until his turn to bat came around. Sometimes an aging player can flourish as the DH, smacking home runs at a decent clip and stretching his career by a couple of years. But hitting, though he did it magnificently, had always been only one part of Rodrigo Buendía's game. As a younger player he had been one of the top outfielders in the game, covering vast distances, making legendary catches, throwing out runners at home plate from deep in the outfield grass. He had not been moved to the DH position, so much as *reduced* to it.

Ethan knew a lot about Rodrigo Buendía, who was one of Mr. Feld's favourite players. He knew that Buendía had escaped from Cuba on a small boat, and that during the journey to Florida he had supposedly saved the lives of three people. He knew that Buendía was the first player to win the Triple Crown in batting – highest average, most home runs, and most runs batted in – since Mr. Feld himself had been a boy. He knew, from having watched a Barbara Walters TV special about Buendía, that Rodrigo Buendía had a pretty blonde wife, and a daughter, a girl whose name, he suddenly recalled, was Jennifer. And he knew that at some point in the past couple of years it had been in the newspapers and on TV that Buendía had, as it turned out, not saved anybody during the crossing from Cuba. Not that he'd let them drown. Just that there weren't any such people at all.

"Where is everyone?" Ethan said. "Where's Jennifer?"

Buendía had thrown an arm over his face.

"Gone. Gone, gone, they all gone. Lawyers. Psychologists. Judges." One of his big hands strayed down to his knee. It was notched and seamed with an impressively hideous array of scars. "Now that damn scout Bron. I told him already two time. Buendía's already enough a hero. So I din't save no two womens and a baby from the Gulf of the Mexico. I got the Triple Crown. I got lifetime three hundred ninety-six home runs. Career average three-fifteen. That pretty good, I think. Ought to get that damn BRON off my ass. Because, I tell you what, Buendía goes out someplace, the peoples coming up to him, everybody say, Rodrigo, you my *hero*."

He sat up now, and with a glance at Jennifer T. tugged the bedclothes up over himself. He looked at the cigar butt in his hand and brought it to his lips, drawing on it as if some spark remained. Then he set it down on the corner of his night table.

"Now, Buendía, he *done* being a hero. Buendía came to this country with something *big* inside him, something Mr. Keeroan BRON maybe was the only person to notice it, back in the day, give him credit for that. But now, look at Buendía. *Look at him, dude.* In this all-white house. With all these white people all around him. In this white country." He pointed towards the long blue ribbon of bedroom windows. From atop the pile of white houses that had once been a desert hill, alive with lizards, there was a view of all Rancho Encantado, and below it, separated by electric fence and by powerful grammers of wealth and privilege invisible to the human eye, the endless greyish-white grid of Greater Anaheim. You could see the false mountains of Disneyland, and beyond them another mountain of glass, and beyond all that still, the shining white band of the sea. And you could see the stadium where the Angels played, with its scaffolding of lights. "Buendía is *tired*, dude. That something big inside is all little now. My wife, my daughter, they knew it. They saw it. They saw it because—" Here his voice cracked, and his big, sweet-natured face crumpled. "Because, I showed them."

And he covered his face with his big brown hands.

"Mr. Buendía," Ethan said. "If you come with us, I promise you, you won't be so tired anymore. I think it would be really good for you, don't you guys?"

"Definitely," Jennifer T. said. "Rejuvenating."

Buendía peered out from behind his hands. "Where is it?" he said, and his voice sounded pitifully small.

"I think you may have been there before," Thor said. "A long, long time ago."

Buendía stared at him. His expression was pretty close to the usual expression that Thor Wignutt's behaviour elicited from adults.

"I been there," he said. "A long—" He closed his mouth, and afterwards they agreed they had all seen the memory seep into his face. "Huh," he said, and for another moment his thoughts wandered again into the light and shade of the Summerlands. Then he picked up his cigar butt again. He studied it for a moment, then looked up, sharply, at Jennifer T. "What's your name, girl?"

Jennifer T. hesitated a moment, glancing at Ethan. Then she answered. Ethan could see how much it cost her to say the word.

"Jennifer," she said, snipping it off before the T. with a visible wince. Then, to make sure the point was not lost, she added, "Just like your daughter."

"Yeah? That true?" He nodded, and rubbed at the back of his head. "OK, Jennifer, *hija*, run get me one of those cigars from the dresser there."

"No way," she said. "First of all, they give you oral cancer. Second of all, they give you lung cancer. Third of all, they *stink*. Maybe if you didn't smoke so many cigars, you wouldn't be all old and sad and broken down."

Ethan thought she had pushed it a little bit too far with that last remark, but to his surprise, Buendía smiled.

"Maybe not," he said. "But I can tell you right now, no way is Buendía going into that crazy place with you without no damn *cigar*."

RINGFINGER BROWN WAS waiting for them, on the ball field on the bluffs above Old Cat Landing, when Rodrigo Buendía returned to the Summerlands for the first time since he was seven years old. As so many children who carry a deep grief into a lonely place seem to stray into the galls and magic places of the Worlds, on that day thirty years before he had left the little house in the Zapata Marshes outside the town of Trinidad, running from the news that his *abuela*, who had raised him, was dead. That was the day, perhaps, that he had first come to the attention of Chiron Brown, who haunted the places where the branches of the Tree were pleached together, looking for hot prospects in the joyous and heartbreaking Game of Worlds. On this day of his return, at the age of thirty-seven, divorced, alone, broke-kneed and stuck playing DH in the bottom of the American League West, only Rodrigo Buendía knew all the things that he was running from. Or perhaps it was only one big thing: the burden and pain of being Buendía, the Great Bear, El Gran Oso. He stepped into the green field on the bluff, carrying a bag with a change of clothes, two bats, a mitt, and a box of El Rey del Mundo cigars. When he saw Chiron Brown, in a plain white suit, with a white Panama hat, standing on the edge of the grass along the third-base line, he stopped, and dropped his duffel. He walked, half stumbling, over to the ancient man. They shook hands. Then Buendía sank to his broken old knees in the grass.

"*Lo siento*," he said.

"What you sorry for, bear cub?"

"I'm sorry I didn't turn out the way you wanted. I know you had more in mind for me than just being a ballplayer. I'm sorry I didn't save nobody's life."

"Shoot, Rodrigo," Ringfinger said, and with one hand, without seeming to strain at all, he dragged the big man to his feet. "It don't matter. Some peoples, they just gets off to a late start."

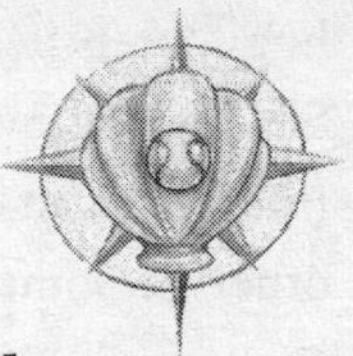

21

Jennifer T. and the Wormhole

SO FAR ALL the games played by the Shadowtails had been more or less private affairs. Though accounts and box scores were duly filed, in time, with Professor Alkabetz and his crack team of baseball gnomes at the Society for Universal Baseball Research, they were played under no official auspices or sponsorship. They were wildcat games, unscheduled and largely unwitnessed.

But the night before the game between the Big Liars of Old Cat Landing and Big Chief Cinquefoil's Travelling Shadowtails All-Star Baseball Club, they came down from the hills. They came from all over the Far Territories of the Summerlands, inuquillits from the snow country, ferishers from the riverbottom mud hills. There were waterknockers, whole families of them, poling into town on their waterlily rafts. Wereotters lolled about the riverdocks, drinking shocking quantities of beer and then getting into quarrels with the stolid werebeavers. The beavermen were teetotalers, for the most part, and between the two families of riverine werebeasts there was certainly no love lost.

Miss Annie Christmas repainted her tin-roofed house, sewed herself a new uniform, and then, as she later reported it, went up into the hills and shot seventeen giant razorback hogs. After she came home, she made breakfast for all of the Shadowtails, went up to the ball field and shot a mosquito (the size of an eagle, according to Annie) as a warning to the other mosquitos to clear out of town. Then she returned home again and started barbecuing hogs. The Tall Man with the Harpoon broke out his last five-dozen casks of good Jamaican rum. The Tall Man with a Knife in His Boot began to drink it. It was a great big party, up and down the main street. There were fireworks, and then firecrackers, and then, when they ran out of firecrackers, the men from the Lost Camps got out sticks of dynamite and blasting caps. People in the Summerlands have old-fashioned ideas of fun. They tied firecrackers to the tails of cats and sent them shrieking and yowling down the streets. All the Summerlands folk found this extremely amusing, even Spider-Rose and Grim the Giant. There were appalling fights fought with shivs and straight razors. Gouged eyeballs were squirting and bouncing all over the place, rolling under beds and into the corners of Jersey Lily. Late that night there were whispered rumors of hoodoos and bone-faced baykoks straying in nearer to the campfires than they ordinarily cared to do, news of the contest have reached even to their lonely and forsaken haunts.

"I hate to see the party if they *win*," Jennifer T. said. They were watching the antics from the sleeping porch of Annie Christmas's house. They had gone to bed hours ago – right around the time that people started setting cats on fire – but with all the noise and the excitement of the game tomorrow, there was no way to sleep.

"Do you think they will?" said Ethan. "Win?"

"They might."

"We aren't that great, are we?"

"Actually, I think we are kind of great," she said, after a moment. "Just that we aren't very good."

"If we were back on Clam, playing in a game, you know, a Mustang League game, do you think you would be as good of a pitcher as you are here in the Summerlands?"

"No," she said. She was definite. Tough on herself, was little Jennifer T. "No way. I think it's all that size-changing, all those grammers for this and that. I just don't think they have quite the same – would it be *physics*? – here as there."

"Do you think it's the kind of thing where if you *believe* you could throw as hard as Randy Johnson, then you could throw as hard as him?"

"I've tried it," she said. "No good. But you know what?"

"What?"

"I think that you would be as good of a catcher. Back home, I mean."

"Really?"

"All pitchers have a favourite catcher," she said. "I would tell Mr. Olafssen I wanted you."

"Thank you," Ethan said, or tried to say, but found that his voice was gone. The memory of home, of Mr. Olafssen and Arch Brody, of the strawberry shed behind the house, of his room, his pillow, of the smell of flannel cakes burning in the kitchen, flooded over him.

"At least you're finally keeping your eyes open," said Jennifer T.

"Where's Taffy?" Thor said. He had remained silent so far, just sitting on the railing of the sleeping porch, in his underpants, watching the people and creatures having a good time down at the Landing. "She said she was going to bed."

"I saw her walking along the river," Ethan said. "All by herself."

"La Llorona goes by the river," Jennifer T. "I think Taffy was going to see La Llorona."

The weeping woman had continued to dog them with her lamentations and howling, but so far, nobody had seen her.

Unless, of course, Taffy had seen her.

"Can you do that?" Ethan said. "Can you just walk outside and go see her?"

"I think she's been talking to her," Jennifer T. said.

"Why would she do that? What could she possibly have to say to La Llorona? 'I'm sorry you killed your children and have been cursed for eternity?' "

Jennifer stood up and started rummaging around in the dark corner of the sleeping porch for her clothes.

"I'm going to look for her," she said, frantically pulling on her jeans. "I'm afraid she's going to drown herself. Like La Llorona. She's been acting so *weird*."

"We'll go with you," Ethan said. "Somebody might try to tie a firecracker to your tail."

"Here I am," said Taffy. They turned. The Sasquatch was crouched in the door of the sleeping porch. She was stroking at the fur on her head with one hand, and Ethan saw that she was more mudstreaked and twig-matted than usual. In her other hand she held a large object, oblong and bumpy, with a stopper at its skinnier end.

"You know what?" Jennifer T. said. "If you keep going away like that, and making me worry about you?"

"I'm sorry," Taffy said.

"I'm going to just stop worrying about you."

"I know. I'm sorry, dear."

"What is that thing, Taf?" Ethan said. "It looks like an egg."

"This? This is an egg. A hodag's egg. Here."

She handed it to Ethan. It was cold as stone and twice as hard, and crusted with rocky little warts and carbuncles.

"Is it a bottle?" He gave it a shake but heard nothing. He tried to pull out the stopper. Taffy yanked it out of his hands.

"Whoa, there! Don't do *that*, by the Starboard Arm!" She clapped a hand over the stopper. "No, it's a not a bottle, it's a hodag's egg, I told you! A hodag is a kind of armoured cow, it has spikes on its back… you used to see them all the time, great stinking herds of them, but they're mostly all gone now. Like all hodag's eggs, it's precisely nine times larger on the inside than it is on the outside, absolutely indestructible to all known substances save one, and hence extremely useful as a universal storage device, in particular for corrosives or bad medicine. And though I believe it now to be empty, I have no idea what was in it *before*. There may be fumes, boy! By the *Arm*!"

"I'm sorry!" Ethan said.

"Where did you get it?" said Thor. "Can I see it?"

"No!" Taffy said. "I don't know what I was thinking. I— I won it." Her voice changed – just a little, but noticeably. A moment ago, she had sounded almost like her old pedantic and irritable self. Now she turned hesitant, and her eyes drifted away to the street. "In a dice game."

"From who?"

"A friend of the Tall Man with the Knife in His Boot. Called himself Billy. Billy Lyons."

"And what are you going to keep in it? Perfume?"

"Perfume! I am not the one who requires perfume in this group," Taffy said, standing up. "Now, you three, go to sleep. We have a game."

"Taffy?"

"What, girl?"

"Would you sing us one of those long, really boring Sasquatch songs of yours?"

"Yeah," Ethan said. "Sing us that one you mentioned, about 'A Snake in Need Is Still a Snake'."

"That would take eleven days, my dear."

"Well, then *sing* the really dull parts," Jennifer T. said.

Then they climbed back into their bedrolls, and Taffy squeezed out onto the porch with them, causing it to creak and wobble. She stroked their heads, and crooned to them, and little by little the sound of revelry died away, and Ethan heard only the slow, Sasquatch rumble of his dreams.

BREAKFAST WAS, OF all things, flannel cakes. They were prepared by the Tall Man with the Axe, right in the middle of the street, on a griddle the size of a pool table, with a spatula as big as a catcher's mitt. They were quite delicious, fluffy and springy at the same time, with a hint of vanilla—nearly as good as Dr. Feld's had once been. But they were enormous, and most of them went to waste because there was hardly anybody up until well after eleven, and those who were up were either still too drunk or too hungover to eat. Ethan and Jennifer T. shared one, and Thor ate two, which was quite a feat because they really were each of them big enough to sew a pair of pyjamas from. Then Cinquefoil showed up, having spent the night carousing with and obtaining scouting reports on the Liars from various of the local ferishers, and he and Jennifer T. started talking about strategy for the day's game. Rodrigo rolled out of bed, looking ten years younger, and dressed in a Hawaiian shirt. The baseball talk was interesting to Ethan at first, but after a while it became more philosophical than practical – his father would have loved all this talk about "timelessness" and "infinite innings" – and at last he drifted out of the conversation.

He left the table, and went off looking for the Tall Man with the Knife in His Boot.

Ethan had heard some things about this Knife. It was said that the Man could slice a flea's whisker into thirds with this Knife, and carve his initials in the door of a bank vault, and cut the insides from a man without his even knowing they were gone.

"What you want it for?" said the Man. He was sleeping it off in a hammock under a persimmon tree, out back of Annie Christmas's house. His big Stetson was lowered over his eyes and nose and he did not bother to lift it as he spoke to Ethan. "You purposin' some form of mischief?"

"No," Ethan said. "It's just there's this Knot on the handle of my bat. I can't get it off, and it's really annoying. I thought maybe your Knife."

"You need Antoinette to cut a *bump*?" Now he lifted the hat. "On a little-bitty boy-size piece of wood?"

"It's kind of a hard bump," Ethan said.

The Man swung out of the hammock, and reached into his Boot. The Knife was neither especially long, or pointed. But she came singing from the Boot in a low voice, cutting the air, and she had a tigerish look about her. She seemed to be happy to be freed from the Boot. You could tell that she was looking forward to cutting something.

"Lay it on me," the Man said. Ethan handed him the bat. The Man held it up to the sky, sighted along it as if it were a rifle, and swung it back and forth a couple of times. "Rube, this a pretty nice bat you gots here. Where you get this?"

"I found it," Ethan said. "Its name is Splinter."

"Yeah, this a Splinter all right," he said. "Splinter of the *Old* Tree." He gripped the bat by its barrel and aimed the handle away from his body. Then he knocked Antoinette against the little ridge. "Say goodbye to your old bump, huh." The blade dug a little ways into the meat of handle, and then stopped, having cut a hairline nick in the wood. The Man set his jaw, and glared at the bump, and gripped Antoinette's handle. He pressed against it, harder and harder, until his eyes were popping out and his Stetson had begun to rattle and shimmy on top of his head like the lid of a teakettle. At last the skin of his hand, where it gripped Antoinette's handle, began to sizzle and steam, and then, with a sound like the snapping of a giant piano string, the Knife snapped off at the handle. The blade went flying off into the woods, and struck a hickory tree. Afterwards the Man went around saying that when the knife hit the hickory, it up and split it into fence rails, firewood, and chips for Miss Annie's smoke oven. This may, however, have been a slight exaggeration.

"Sorry, boy," he said, handing Ethan back his bat. "Look like you jes' gonna haveta git *use* to it."

JENNIFER T. RIDEOUT stood four feet eight inches tall, and weighed ninety-one pounds. She featured three pitches, a fastball, a slider or nickel curve, and a change-up that was sometimes unreliable. In the Middling, where she was born and raised, her control over the locations of her pitches would have been judged better than average for a determined and talented eleven-year-old. I am sure that she could have struck me out, and she probably could have struck you out, too. But she would have struggled even against, say, a gifted young high-school player; and against a player like Buendía, in the Middling, she would not have stood a chance. In the Summerlands, as she and Ethan were both well aware, things were different. It may have been, as Jennifer T. had wondered aloud to Ethan, the strange physics of that world. Or it may have been the unexplored kinship between what some people call magic and a deep, true talent for *concentrating really hard on something*. Or perhaps it was simply the workings of all those wild grammers, layer upon layer and millennium upon millennium, that have always made the Summerlands such a congenial place for young adventurers. I can't say for sure. But the fact remained: in the Summerlands, Jennifer T.'s fastball hurtled, her slider dipped and dived like a swallow, and her change-up was as deceptively slow as old Coyote himself.

And yet that day the Big Liars of Old Cat Landing jumped all over her. They wore her out. They ate her lunch, and her supper, too. From the very first pitch the Liars appeared, as the announcers on television like to say, to have "solved" her. The Man with the Knife in His Boot led off with a slap double, stole second, took off running on a solid single by the Man with the Pole, and scored on the very next pitch, which Annie Christmas sent screaming up the first base line. It rolled into a corner of right field so deep that Buendía had to dig it out from under a rhododendron bush, where it lay next to a lost eyeball. By the top of the third, the score was Liars 7, Shadowtails 2. By the middle of the fifth, it was 12–6.

As a whole – in spite of the uneven score – Cinquefoil's team, all of them grammered up, for the first time, to the size of their shaggy centre fielder, played good baseball. They fielded their positions well, and even managed to turn a smash grounder by the Man with the Big Maul, which probably should have been a hit, into a double play. And if by the fifth inning things were not even more of a disaster for the Shadowtails, there was one good reason: Rodrigo Buendía. He resumed the outfield, as a fish that has been caught and released resumes its native stream. He ranged its broad expanse with a grin on his face, flipping down his shades with a cavalier snap, chasing down flies as if each one promised to carry good news from the farthest blue reaches of sky. He saved a run in the third with a deadly strike to home, and then another in the fourth in the very same way, getting the ball back in to Ethan at the plate before the runner at third, the Woman with the Razor and Dice, had even made up her mind to slide.

Through all this, it was not as if Jennifer T. pitched poorly. Her slider was heavy, and she kept her fastball moving. She could feel the ball leaving her fingers charged up with verve and liveliness; in fact if she hadn't seen the Liars running free on the bases, she would have said she was pitching better today, with the possible continued existence of All Worlds at stake, than she ever had before. In the top of the sixth, Spider-Rose turned a swinging bunt into a gift triple on a bobble at short by Annie Christmas, and when Grim walked, Rodrigo Buendía brought the Shadowtails to within three with a mighty home run, to the deepest part of the outfield. It really looked as if their ringer, imported from another world for this very purpose, really was going to save the day.

In the bottom of the seventh, the Liars scored four more, on seven hits, to make the score 16–9.

That was when the Shadowtails' Player-Manager called for time. He walked very slowly from first base to the mound. Jennifer T. dreaded what she felt must be coming – Cinquefoil was going to pull her. They had no bench, of course; he would have to switch her with someone, probably Pettipaw, who had done some pitching in his distant youth as a rat-boy on the shores of the Kraken Sea. Ethan trotted out from behind home plate, thumbing through that stupid Peavine book of his, probably looking, Jennifer T. thought, under the chapter entitled "What to Say to Your Pitcher When She's Getting

Her Butt Kicked by a Bunch of Liars." Grim clomped in from shortstop, and then Taffy came in from the outfield. Yep, they were going to have themselves a little wake, out there on the mound, for the death of Jennifer T.'s career as a pitcher.

"Tell me what ya think is happening," Cinquefoil said to her, in a low, calm voice. She had expected him to be angry, or at least exasperated, but he sounded so reasonable and even hopeful that she was immediately forced to battle an overwhelming desire to cry. To prevent this from happening she pulled the wool collar of her jersey up to her mouth and began to chew it. She said nothing.

"Here's the thing I been reflectin' at," Grim the Giant said. "That weren't no ordinary hoop-de-do they had themselves last night. That was sort of a kind of a Last Party Ever, seems to me. I sincerely do believe they mean to *win* this game. And then just let the whole Sad Story of Everything come to an end."

"Don't talk nonsense," Cinquefoil said. "Every good team means ta win. Don't mean they *can*. I mean ta win, too. But I guess ya don't, is that it?"

Grim looked away, embarrassed, scratching at his single long bushy eyebrow with a fingernail.

"Listen," Taffy said. It was strange to be looking her in the eye. "You've pitched a good came so far, girl. You truly have. But they just have your number. Maybe they have all of our numbers. Maybe Grim's right. Maybe it would be better if you don't win."

Grim squinted at the Sasquatch. "Did I say that?"

Taffy said, "Better if Coyote does bring the Pole down,

maybe. The story of these Worlds is so tangled and tired and played out."

And at that moment she herself looked ready to give it all up, forever and ever.

Jennifer T. didn't know how she felt about the world coming to an end, exactly. She supposed that on the whole she was against it. But Cinquefoil was her manager. If he wanted her off the mound, then she had no choice but to do as he said. She reached out to hand him the ball. To her surprise, the little ferisher knocked her hand away.

"What is wrong with ya people?" Cinquefoil shouted. "We got somebody trying with all her heart ta win a baseball game here! Giant! Bigfoot!" He yanked the cap from his head and, taking advantage of the shapeshifting grammer, began to beat them about the head and shoulders with it. "Get back to your positions, and field them with every ounce o' whatever it is ya got. And if I hear any more o' that kind a talk, I'll pluck every hair from the one o' ya and stick it ta the other with a great wad o' tar!"

Chastened, Taffy and the giant trudged back to their positions. The crowd, which had turned restless as the time-out dragged on, now began actively to jeer the Shadowtails. Cinquefoil seemed not to hear.

"You!" Cinquefoil said to Ethan, who jumped. He had been lost in a page of *How to Catch Lightning and Smoke*, and now he looked up, blushing, embarrassed to have been caught reading in the middle of a game. "This is yer pitcher! What have ya got ta say ta her?"

"Oh," Ethan said. "Just a minute." He flipped through the book, moistening his thumb with the tip of his tongue.

"Right. OK." He scanned the page, nodded, then looked at Jennifer. "Hang in there, Jennifer T.," he said. "Just bear down, and keep it close, and we'll get right back in this, OK?"

Though she knew he had just read them in a book, Ethan said the words with just the right amount of meaninglessness, and they made her feel better. She was about to say that she would hang in there, when the Hangin' Judge, proprietor of the Jersey Lily saloon, started to make his rolling, stoop-shouldered way to the mound.

"Awright," he said. "How about let's break up this little confabulation and play some baseball? Or is that too much to ask?"

At the same time, there was a scatter of footsteps behind her, and Jennifer T. turned to see Pettipaw come scurrying in from left field. He was out of breath and clearly excited.

"I just heard something from one of the riverboat boys in the stands," he said. "With these fine, fine instruments of mine." Lovingly he caressed one of his nicked little earflaps. He looked at Ethan. "Little reuben, is it possible that a bit of your bat might have come into the possession of the Man with the Knife in His Boot?"

"I said *break it up*!" said the Hangin' Judge, shambling up to the mound, reeking atrociously of whisky, with a strange undercurrent of vanilla from having consumed seventeen of the Man with the Axe's flannel cakes.

Jennifer T. saw that Ethan did not like to have to answer Pettipaw's question.

"Yes," he said softly. "It's possible. I asked him to try to cut the Knot for me. But the Knot broke his Knife. Maybe he got a little shaving. I didn't see."

"The Man has a conjure eye," Pettipaw hissed, keeping his voice low. "Didn't you notice his blue gums? Give him a sliver of baseball power like that, even the tiniest chip, and there's no telling what he could do with it."

"Most likely he'll put a quickeye on them Liars," Cinquefoil said. "Ya can throw as hard and as smart as ya want, kid, if they can quickeye the ball, they'll hit it a ton."

Jennifer T. stared at Ethan. He was her friend, and she loved him, but at that moment she could have whittled him to a pile of very tiny shavings indeed. Him and that freaking Knot of his! It was bad enough he let it mess with his hitting game – now it was messing up *her* game, too.

"No sweat," she said. She took a fresh ball from Ethan, not looking him in the eye. "Let's get 'em."

Cinquefoil and Ethan returned to their positions, and Jennifer began to work over the mound with a toe. She had no idea whatever of how to pitch to a team under the force of a quickeye conjure, but she certainly wasn't going to let anybody else see that.

"Court is now in session," cried the Hangin' Judge, raising his sallow hands, with their manicured nails, over his hairless head. The spectators cheered, whistled, paid off their various bets and side bets, and then settled down to watch play resume. The Man with the Harpoon stepped in, a wicked grin peeking out from his sandy beard, his great bat tipped, in Jennifer T.'s imagination, with a jagged whale-piercing barb, ready to strike. Then, to Jennifer T.'s surprise, Ethan threw up his hands.

"Time!" he said. There was a curious look on his face, as if he had something to say to her that he wasn't sure she was going to like. She had seen him look at her this way many times; usually he was right.

With an exasperated growl, the Hangin' Judge informed the players that Time was, once again, officially Out. The crowd groaned and mocked the time-wasting Shadowtails. Ethan paid no attention. He trotted out to her, and started to talk.

"Cover your mouth," Jennifer T. said. "We don't want them reading lips."

"Oh, right," Ethan said, glancing over at the Liars' bench. He raised his mitt to his mouth, and spoke softly into it.

"I had an idea," he said. "Something I was just reading about in Peavine."

"What is it?" Jennifer T. said. She didn't like holding up the game, but she was more than willing to listen to anything on the subject of what the heck she was going to throw next.

"See, Peavine talks about a pitcher he caught, once, in a game way, way far away, near the Kraken Sea."

"Yeah?"

"The pitcher was a *selkie*. Like a seal, but he could sort of undo his seal skin, I guess, and turn into a man, or—"

"I know what a selkie is. I saw that movie with the seal lady."

"Well, this guy, because a selkie's a kind of a werebeast, see, he was a shadowtail. The only shadowtail pitcher Peavine ever caught. And this guy? The selkie? He could *scamper* a baseball."

Jennifer T. felt that she understood the idea immediately,

on some deep level. At the same time she had absolutely no idca what Ethan was talking about.

"He could pitch the ball along a tiny little branch of the Tree, you know, make it disappear, and then at the last second, just before it crossed the plate, he could pop it back. Just like when Cutbelly got me from my house to the Tooth in like five minutes."

"A wormhole," she said. "They call it. I read about it *Eli Drinkwater: A Life in Baseball* by Happy Blackmore." Eli Drinkwater, as you know, was a great catcher for the Pittsburgh Pirates, and a noted theorist of pitching, who had been killed in a car crash before Jennifer T. was born. "You throw the ball into a wormhole, he said, and it comes out someplace totally different."

"Right!"

"But a wormhole isn't real, E. It's just, you know, a way of saying there's a lot of *movement* on your fastball."

"Maybe in the Middling," Ethan said. "Not here."

"Huh," said Jennifer T. "But, OK, what are you saying? Pettipaw should take over the pitching because he's a shadowtail? Or Thor?"

"Well, that's my part of the idea. But it's sort of trippy. But here it is." He leaned in very close, speaking through the webbing of his old stained pieplate. She could smell flannel cake on his breath, too. "*Maybe you're a shadowtail.*"

"That's enough, now," the umpire shouted. "Now, play ball or I'm callin' this game a forfeit."

"What!" she said. "Get out of here!"

Ethan's face fell, and he looked very shocked. He started to say something.

"Go on!" Jennifer T. said. "Get back behind the plate where you belong!"

He nodded, then turned and walked slowly back towards home plate.

Jennifer stood there, turning the ball over and over in her fingers. A shadowtail? To be a shadowtail meant – what had her uncle Mo said? "You have to be something neither fish nor fowl, a little bit of this, a little of that. Always half in this world and half in the other to begin with." She was a little bit of a lot of different things, she supposed. Her mother was half Scots-Irish and half German, with some Cherokee in there, too. Her father was half Suquamish and half Salishan and half junkyard dog. Everyone said she was a tomboy; that was a kind of a half and half, too. According to her Aunt Shambleau – it had not seemed to be intended as a compliment – she was half a girl and half a woman. She had grown up on Clam Island, and yet because she was a Rideout she was never fully a *part* of Clam Island, and had passed most of the days of her childhood living in a world of her own, out in the wintry grey at Hotel Beach. She had, over the years, thought of herself at one time or another as a half-breed, a mongrel, a mutt, a misfit, and an oddball. It had never occurred to her think of herself as a shadowtail, or to consider that you could find power in being caught between two worlds.

"Huh," said Jennifer T. to the baseball, turning it over and over. "How about that?"

When the Man with the Harpoon stepped in again, the grin even brighter and harder, there in his beard, than before, he had not a thought in his head. Ordinarily a batter tries to guess what the next pitch is going to be, and tries to adjust not only his swing but also his way of looking at the pitch. Since there was a quickeye on him, however, as on all his team-mates, thanks to the wily conjure-man ways of the Man with the Knife in His Boot, there was no need for him to guess, or to adjust anything at all. He just stood there, waggling the bat up behind his head, knowing that when the pitch left the reuben girl's hands, he would see it as plainly as if it were a yarn ball rolled across a thick rug by a weak little kitten.

The girl looked in to the reuben boy, shook her head, shook it again – and then nodded. She had her pitch; well, so did the Man with the Harpoon. He had her pitch all nice and wrapped up in a neat little conjure-man package.

The girl settled the glove against her belt, the hand with the ball tucked deep inside it. Then she raised glove, ball and bare hand up over her head, and held them there. For an instant some wild idea seemed to flit across her face, and the Man with the Harpoon felt a momentary doubt about the conjure man's work. Then she brought her glove down again. The hand with the ball whipped free, coiled back behind her head, and then uncoiled with a smooth, corkscrew motion, and the ball sprang from her fingers. The conjure held; he saw it all. The ball rolled across the air towards him, fat and floating as a bumblebee. The stitches advanced, one slow tick at a time, steady as the second hand on his old brass pocket watch.

And then it disappeared, vanished completely, in a curl of steam that looked to the Man with the Harpoon like a puff of breath on a frosty morning. Baffled – spooked – he lashed out with the bat at the empty air. Then, to the utter and undying astonishment of the Man with the Harpoon, there was a thick smack as the ball hit the webbing of the catcher's mitt.

"Strike ONE!" howled the umpire.

Ethan looked down at the ball in his mitt, then grinned, and held it up. Even from the mound Jennifer T. could see that it was still covered in the frost of its crossing.

The crowd hooted and whistled in delight.

"I think you better have a look at that ball, ump," said the Man with the Harpoon.

"Quit your whinin'," the Hangin' Judge said. "And git back in that box."

She struck him out, looking, on two more pitches, and then struck out the side, and struck them out again in the eighth and ninth – nine strikeouts in a row. And she needed only twenty-eight pitches to do it – one more than the minimum. Her only mistake came in the bottom of the ninth when, pitching to the Man with the Knife in His Boot, she caught sight of his weird bluish-grey conjure-man gums, and it unnerved her a little. The next pitch that she sent spinning out through a tiny hole in the worlds vanished with a puff of steam, never to reappear in the Summerlands again.

The Hangin' Judge only hesitated a moment before making the call.

"Ball one!" he said.

As for the Shadowtails – they were as good as Ethan's word. She held the Liars close, and her team came back for five runs in the eighth (one of them batted in by Jennifer T.

herself), and then three more in their half of the ninth, defeating the Big Liars of Old Cat Landing, and winning, in the process, the right to pass across the Big River. It's all there in Alkabetz's *Universal Baseball Encyclopaedia*.

You can look it up.

22

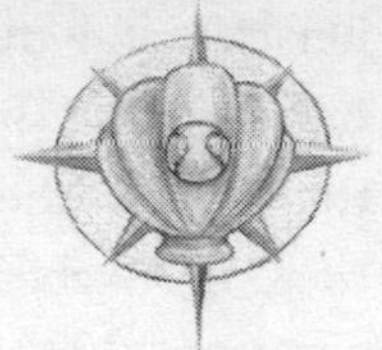

The Bottom-Cat

EXCEPT FOR THE Tall Man with the Knife in his Boot, who took the overturning of his conjure rather hard and slunk off downriver, to raise hell and console himself at dice and cards, the Liars, to their credit, quickly put the defeat behind them. In fact, at Annie Christmas's insistence, they set about doing what they could to help the Shadowtails complete the final leg of their long pilgrimage. The Tall Man with the Harpoon and the Tall Man with the Pole set about framing a vessel that would hold all nine of the Shadowtails and Skidbladnir, too, though she had long since run through her supply of lawalawa joy juice. They sent the Tall Man with the Axe up into hills to fell the trees for the great raft, and then reduce the logs to rails and planking. The Tall Man with the Big Maul and the Tall Man with the Hammer drove the nails, and the Tall Man with the Harpoon lashed the timbers with complicated knots into which he wove old nautical grammers for fine weather and smooth seas. Annie Christmas forged the oarlocks in her smithy, swinging a six-pound hammer, sewed the sail from stout canvas, and baked eighteen of her signature funeral pies (raisins and molasses). The Tall Woman with the Razor and Dice went out hunting hogs, armed only with her great Razor, and returned from the hills with ham, bacon, and fatback; she claimed that when the hogs saw her coming they were so afraid that they had slaughtered and smoked themselves. As for the Tall Man with the Rattlesnake Necktie, they did not see very much of him until the morning, two days after the game, when the raft was loaded, the winds favourable, and the Shadowtails ready to shove off.

He appeared just as Ethan was carrying his equipment bag towards the gangway. The rest of the team were all aboard, and the Man with the Pole was giving Rodrigo and Taffy, the two broadest backs, some last-minute instructions about poling. Ethan was late because he had stopped by to see if he could obtain one last flannel cake from the Man with the Axe; it was rolled up now in a sheet of waxed paper, like a scrap of carpet, and tucked between the handles of his bag.

"Hey, kid," said the Man with the Rattlesnake Necktie. He was leaning against a piling of the dock, picking his teeth with tip of his Bowie knife, one boot crossed over the other at the ankle.

"Oh, hey," Ethan said.

Of all the Big Liars, the Man with the Rattlesnake Necktie was the only one that made Ethan feel nervous. It was partly that dead-eyed Rattler, of course, endlessly coiling and knotting itself around the Man's throat. Even though he didn't have a conjure eye, or anything, there was just something about him that unsettled Ethan. It might have been that of all the Liars, his was the lie – of fire-snorting broncos and thousand-mile cattle drives and duels in the dusty streets of Tombstone and Abilene –

that had lingered the longest in the Middling. The sparkling residue of it seemed to flash, at certain moments, from his eyes, and to wink from the golden bicuspid in his jaw.

Ethan stopped, and looked at the Man, because it appeared that he had something he wanted to say. But the Man just went on picking big horseteeth and looking down at Ethan the way you might watch a sparrow peck at a bit of tasty cookie that you dropped, sort of disgusted and resentful at the same time. His face was long and bony, his eyes pale, his cheeks raw.

"Ever ride a cat?" he said at last in his bowstring twang.

Ethan didn't know how to answer this. That is, he knew, of course, that in fact he had never ridden a cat. But he felt there must be some part of it he wasn't understanding.

"Mah bride rode a cat once," the Man said.

"Uh-huh," Ethan said, wondering if perhaps the old Cowboy weren't a little bit *tetched*. "That's nice."

"Rode it all the way down the Rio Grande."

"Rio Grande," Ethan said. "Right. In Texas."

"Said yuh have tuh grapple 'em. Jes' reach right in and noodle the suckers."

"I have to be going now," Ethan said.

"Jes' thought yuh should know," the Man said.

"What did he say?" said Jennifer T. when Ethan had come aboard the raft.

"Nothing," Ethan said. "Something about his bride sticking noodles into a cat."

"He shot his bride, you know," Pettipaw said, tugging on a whisker. "So they say."

"That doesn't surprise me at all," Ethan said.

Then they called out their last farewells to the people of Old Cat Landing and the surrounding Territories who had come down to the docks to see them off. Among them, sitting on the hood of his Cadillac and waving a white handkerchief, was Ringfinger Brown.

"Not me," he had said, when Ethan and Jennifer T. begged him to come with him. "Until the world ends, if it do end, I'm proceedin' on the old assumptions. I gots scoutin' to do. 'Sides, a scout suppose' to be there in the *beginnin'* of things. He like Moses – one of mine, by the way. He out there in the bushes, pokin' around for seeds of greatness. Ain't get to be there when the promise land get found or the championship get won."

Now Ethan and Jennifer T. stood leaning on the split-log railing of the raft, waving goodbye to the old scout as he and all the others receded, and Buendía and Taffy reached their long poles into the deep mud of the river, and the thick brown soupy water splashed up against the fresh-cut planks of the raft. They could see that he was calling something to them, but they were already too far away to catch the words.

"What's he saying, Pettipaw?" Jennifer T. said.

The rat-man leapt up onto the rail and thrust his head towards the shore, cupping a hand to his ear. His tail quivered with the strain of listening.

"He's saying, 'Sometimes you just got to take time to bring them *along* a little bit'," Pettipaw said.

It was the last time either Ethan or Jennifer T. ever saw the old scout, in any world.

AFTER AN HOUR, the river was too deep for the poles. they hoisted the sail that Annie Christmas had sewed them, and at once, as if summoned by the eldritch knots of the Tall Man with the Harpoon, a breeze sprang up behind them and pushed them towards the opposite shore. They were sailing towards the heart, the axil point, the very centre of the Tree of Worlds. No one could say for sure just how wide the river was. Some claimed that it grew narrower the closer you were to death when you crossed it, and some that it narrowed with the nobility of your intentions, but after they had been on it for most of a day they began to see a ribbon of green on the horizon.

"Land ho!" Thor called. Ethan and Jennifer T. were sitting on the edge of the raft, with their feet in the water, ruining one of Annie Christmas's funeral pies with their hands, and licking their fingers, but Thor was perched on Skid's hood. Taffy lay sprawled atop the roof of the car, moaning softly, worn out from poling the raft all morning, racked with seasickness, and arguing with Grim the Giant about whether or not you could actually *be* seasick on a *river*. He kept after her until finally she reached out and took a swipe at him with one of her hairy paws, almost knocking him into the water. Rodrigo Buendía lay on the planks, on his back, smoking a fat Rey del Mundo. As for Spider-Rose, unlike Taffy, her long years of imprisonment had left her feeling uncomfortable in wide-open spaces. She sat in the car, with her doll, staring fixedly out the windshield at the land of all her unhopeable hopes.

"It ain't going to work," she kept murmuring to Nubakaduba. "No way is it going to work."

An hour later they could make out clouds of white lying thick on the green land; Cinquefoil said they were apple blossoms.

"This breeze picks up a little," he said. "We ought to make Applelawn by nightfall."

At the moment he said it – as if at last his ability to work grammers, so long depleted, had returned to him – the sail began to rumble, and the athletic sock which Buendía had tied to his pole, which he then planted in the planking for a flag, danced in the breeze. Then abruptly it spun around to the hither shore and strained at the knot, snapping and fluttering until at last it wriggled loose, and sailed off towards Old Cat Landing.

"Storm coming in," Pettipaw said, sniffing the air.

"Storm?" Cinquefoil said, looking up, his gaze travelling towards the west. "But the sky was as clear—"

They all looked up at the sky that only a minute before had been cloudless and blue. The next moment a flock of what Ethan took at first to be butterflies, frantic white butterflies, blew in from the west. The fluttering mass engulfed the raft, blowing into their hair and eyes, clinging to their clothes, blotting out Skid's windshield and clotting her radiator. Ethan, his skin creeping at the insect touch of them, scraped away a silken handful and found they were not butterflies at all but blossoms, thousands and thousand of apple blossoms blown from the trees of the land in the west. Now when they looked that way they saw the green ribbon overtopped with a thick dark band that billowed and heaved and flickered, now and then, with lightning.

"Storm buffalo," Cinquefoil said, in a low, grim voice. "Coyote's done come ta the Land o' Apples."

The storm spilled out from Applelawn towards them, sending great black tendrils to coil and flower over their heads. The river was scaled with waves, like the skin of a great bronze fish, and the raft began to pitch and reel. Buendía seized his pole and plunged it down, hand over hand over hand, until the river seemed to catch hold of it, and snatched it from his grasp. The next moment there was a terrific hissing as the water began to churn and fizz around them, and then Ethan heard a deep, disturbing *thump* as of something knocking up against the underside of the raft.

The next moment he felt himself being lifted up into the air. He had just enough time to reach out behind him and grab hold of Splinter before the entire raft stood on one edge and slid them all into the water, like onions on a cutting board being scraped into a bubbling pot.

Cold metal filled his mouth, and his nostrils. Cold fingers of water were poked into his ears, and pressed at the sockets of his eyes. He struggled and kicked and tumbled in the water, and then all at once something, some calm voice inside him, told him to lie still. As soon as he stopped moving, Splinter seemed to take hold of him and to rise, with him in tow, towards the surface of the water. At last in a shivering burst of light his head broke through to the air, and he spat and coughed and gasped for breath, clinging to Splinter. He thought he heard voices – Buendía's, Taffy's, Jennifer T.'s – and he looked around to see. The water was filled with Shadowtails, strewn everywhere along with the shattered bits of the raft, and in the middle of them all he saw Skidbladnir, the Wonder Ship, wheels to the sky, bobbing on the surface of the water. Then he heard, for the first time, a sound like rain, like water running ringing down a culvert after a rainstorm, and he turned, and what he saw nearly caused him to let go of Splinter.

There, filling all the sky between him and the place on the horizon where Applelawn had been, rose a vast shining column of water. It was strangely tinted a rosy orange, and it streamed down towards the surface of the river from a dizzying height. A waterspout, Ethan thought, until, tilting his head so far back that his ears filled with cold water, he saw that at the top of the column there sat, thick-lipped, goggle-eyed, ugly and wise, an enormous whiskered head. The whiskers were as long and twisting as anacondas, the lips fleshy and black, the eyes sly-lidded and unimpressed with the struggling flotsam that lay far below. What Ethan had taken for a column of moving water was only the runoff, the skin of water shed by the coils of an immense body, snaky and pink, as it rose from the river high into the air. A pair of green fins like sails, veined with bone like the wings of a bat, projected from its sides a quarter mile or so up, and another long fin began just above the waterline and ran down to whatever unimaginable depth represented the creature's terminus.

The Bottom-Cat, Ethan thought to himself.

"The Bottom-Cat!" Jennifer T. said. She swam up behind Ethan, kicking her legs, and he scooted down to the handle end of the bat and let her grab the barrel.

"Thanks."

"No problem."

The Bottom-Cat narrowed its bulging eyes, pursing its lips into a great blue-black plum.

"What you got there, midge?"

Ethan felt something bump up against his legs, something big that caught him, and lifted him and Jennifer T. out of the water. He reached down, and felt, beneath him, a surface – the skin of the thing – that was at once slick and rough, like half-cured cement, and gave to the touch of his finger. The Old Cat had caught them up, like ladybugs on a kid's forearm, on a bend in its long snaky tail. Now it began to hoist this humped loop of itself into the air, raising Ethan and Jennifer T. towards its head.

There was a grunt beside them, and Ethan saw Taffy scrambling up onto this living hill with them, as it climbed into the sky. In her arms she carried the hodag's egg, saved from the wreck of the raft.

"Taffy!" Jennifer T. said. "What is it doing? Is it going to eat us?"

But Taffy didn't answer. She just stood, legs apart, on the coil in the body of the Bottom-Cat, riding this strange elevator into the sky.

The stench from its gills was like mud and mould and rot, and it wafted towards them in thick rolling waves. The lips shone like wet rubber; the eyes, set wide in the face in a way that was disturbingly human, gazed at them with bright interest. Its voice was surprisingly small and soft, almost tentative, as if it were unused to speaking.

"So. You bring the slugger a piece of his great stick. His weary, weary burden. That it, midge? Well, you too late! The slugger

thanks you kindly, but it looks to him like it's nigh on time to lay his weary burden down. A storm in Applelawn where no storm ever was. Strange rumblings up and down the Tree all day long. Something inside Slug telling him it time to wake up."

"E, look." Jennifer T. was not really listening to the Bottom-Cat – she had never had a whole lot of patience for speeches.

"*Been asleep a long time, little midges,*" the Old Cat said. "*Pretty hungry.*"

Jennifer T. was pointing down to the river, where they could see their friends, tossed and scattered by the coils of the Cat and by the storm-choppy waters of the river. In another minute they were all going to be eaten or drowned.

Ethan lowered his voice, and put his mouth to Jennifer T.'s ear. "You know that thing the Man with the Rattlesnake Tie said to me about noodling a cat? I thought he meant a cat cat, but do you think he was trying to tell me about—"

"Noodling," Jennifer T. whispered. "We saw that on TV, one time, on this fishing show, remember? Those guys down in Alabama or wherever. Shoving their hands down inside catfishes to catch them." She made a face. "But we could never...."

"We can," Taffy said. "We have to."

The Sasquatch ran towards the edge of the coil to which they clung, the hodag's egg tucked under her arm like a football.

"Eat me first!" she cried. "These two are nothing but strings and bones."

"*Powerful hungry,*" the Cat agreed. It stretched its lips back in a grin and, slowly, opened its great mouth, a few slow inches at a time, as if its jaw were almost too large for its muscles to bear. Taffy danced right up onto its lip, and the mouth strove to open wide enough to fit her.

"Splinter, Ethan! Splinter, now!"

"She means jam it in there!" Jennifer T. said. "We have to grab hold of the inside of its mouth!"

Ethan slipped and scrambled up the coil towards the thing's mouth, and then shoved Splinter as far into its jaw as he could reach. The roof of its mouth, he saw, was lined with hundreds and hundreds of teeth, long and sandy grey. At the same time he heard Jennifer T. run up behind him. Without stopping, without even hesitating, she dived right into the mouth of the Cat and stood up. She looked wildly around, as the voice of the thing came rumbling up from its distant throat in a roar of outrage.

"I don't know where to grab it," she yelled. She dithered for a moment more, than reached up and took hold of one of the grey teeth embedded in the raspy roof of its mouth. Ethan held on to Splinter, feeling it throb with the force of the Cat's desperate struggle to close its jaws. Then, all at once, the struggle ceased, and the Cat's voice rose again from its innards, pleading this time. Jennifer T. rode the rippling and flappings of its mighty tongue as if she were surfing on its words.

"*Please let go of my tooth,*" it said, quite piteous and tame as a kitten. Though it came out more like *Hease let go a I too.*

"When we get to Applelawn," Jennifer T. said. "And all our friends, too. Pick them up. Now."

Ethan looked down over the lower lip towards the water below. Slowly great slick coils of the enormous fish began to writhe and twist, reaching here and there to lift the

Shadowtails. It hunched and shifted and stretched until it had tumbled them all together onto the top of one coil. Then it lifted them, en masse, into the air.

"Well done, reubens," Cinquefoil said as he and the others rose, waving, past the Cat's mouth, towards the crown of its head. "Ya got her by the mouthparts. Only what's become a Bigfoot?"

Ethan looked around. Taffy had been there a moment ago, perched on the lip of the Bottom-Cat. Now she was gone.

"Taffy!" He looked down at the river. There was no sign of her. There was also no sign, he saw now, with a sharp pang, of Skidbladnir. "Taffy!"

"Here."

Ethan was surprised to see Taffy emerge from the back of the Cat's mouth, from behind Jennifer T., who stood desperately clutching the big tooth, her gaze fixed on her hands. She was carrying the egg more carefully now, and Ethan saw a thin rime of black ooze spilling down one side of it from the stopper. Taffy knelt, and wiped the ooze away against the rough, greyish stuff of the Bottom-Cat's tongue. The great beast shuddered, down its whole length, and at that moment the whole of the Summerlands gave a great heave, and in the Middling a chain of earthquakes rippled outward from the Pacific Rim and rocked the tembler-prone countries of the world in a manner that was very surprising to seismologists.

"Let's go!" Jennifer T. "The sooner you get us there, the sooner I let go of your tooth."

And so they escaped the wreck of their vessel, and were

borne the rest of the way across the Big River in and on top of the bewhiskered, outraged head of the Bottom-Cat. It was a journey of less than five minutes for the enormous beast whose coils reach down, down, down to the very roots of the Tree. Delicately, like a child cupping a chick, the great head lowered itself to the green grass of Applelawn. The grass was starred with blown blossoms, and the skies overhead were corrugated with vast steel bands of storm. One by one the Shadowtails climbed or slid down from the top of the Cat's head, and then Taffy leapt from the mouth.

"*Too, hlease,*" said the Bottom-Cat. "*Let go.*"

Ethan looked at Jennifer T.

"If I pull Splinter out, it might eat you," he said.

"But if I let go, we don't control it anymore," she said. "It could just take off and knock you out against a mountain or something."

"Huh," Ethan said.

"*Ket hromise,*" the Cat said, reminding them that it had kept its promise. "*Let go.*"

"On the count of three. One— two— three!"

She let go of the Cat's long tooth, and at the same time Ethan jerked Splinter free. They tumbled out of the mouth and went sprawling in the soft grass of Applelawn.

The Cat glowered down at them, hissing, and seemed briefly to be considering inhaling them all, like the nozzle of an immense Hoover. At the last it changed its mind.

"*I should have stayed in bed,*" it said, with a great sad shake of its head. Then it turned and, with a long, cascading ripple of its ninety-nine uppermost coils, slipped back down into its gloomy haunt at the bottom of the world.

It took them a while to catch their breath, and regain their land legs, and generally recover from the crossing. Then they took stock of their losses.

"Everything," Cinquefoil. "We lost everything. Everything but Splinter."

"And the egg," Ethan said. "And whatever that gross black stuff was Taffy had inside it."

"Yeah," Jennifer T. said. "What is that stuff, Taff? Taff?"

But though they searched the orchards for two hours, until it turned dark, they could not find Taffy the Sasquatch.

23

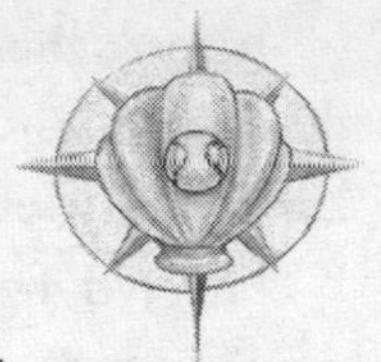

The Conquest of Outlandishton

AT THE EDGE of the Winterlands, near the centre of the Tree, there is a pool of water. Though no wider than a country pond – you could throw a stone halfway across it – this pool is deeper than any lake on earth. It is deeper than sleep, and blue-black as the winter night sky. Some say it has no bottom; others that it flows into the Summerlands as the Big River and the Witch River and the River of Dreams, and down into the Middling to feed the Nile, the Amazon, the Volga, the Mekong, the Mississippi, the Congo, the Yangtze, the Colorado, the Rhine. It was on the banks of the pool of Murmury, some say, that She-otter caught Salmon. Instead of devouring him, she admired his steady eye and shining brow and fell in love. Salmon spat a cool jet of the water of Murmury Well at She-otter's hindquarters. Nine months later, She-otter gave birth to a child, a boy of silver, a fireballing phenomenon who eons later grew into Old Mr. Wood, the Maker of the Worlds. The waters of Murmury sustain the Tree; they also bring wisdom to all who drink of them (about six people ever, so far).

All around the still banks of Murmury Well the perpetual ice of the Winterlands begins to melt away. It fades and thins and streaks until green shows through the greyish white. This in-between land, the Greenmelt, marks the end, and the start, of the Winterlands. On the far side of the pool, the ice gives out altogether in the sweet lush grass of Diamond Green. On the near side of Murmury rises a high frozen crag called Shadewater Tor. Atop this icy hill stands Outlandishton, citadel of the shaggurts.

Cutbelly had never cared for shaggurts, and nothing he had seen in their journey across the Winterlands so far had inclined him to change his mind. They had all the poor qualities of greylings – noisy, cruel, ill-tempered, quarrelsome – but they were twenty feet tall. So they had *more* of all the greylings' faults. They claimed descent from Owlmirror John, the very first giant, and like their distant cousins, their appetites were vast and bloody. They were also addicted to fighting, courageous in battle, and horribly strong. At their hands the Rade had suffered tremendous losses in the course of the journey over the ice. Only its great numbers, and the relative scarcity of shaggurts, had enabled the Rade to make it to the jagged walls of Outlandishton.

The citadel rose into the sky, massive, black and spiky, like a pile of hammerheads. It had been raised in the dawn of time to mark the border of the Winterlands at the centre of the four worlds, and to keep out wanderers and invaders. It stood high on frozen Shadewater Tor, glowering down now on the surviving steam-sledges and werewolf teams, daring them to try to take its walls.

Cutbelly clung to the iron rail atop the *Panic*, craning his neck to look up. All the mushgoblins and greylings were craning their necks, too. Now that they had reached their goal, they wanted Coyote to instruct them about just what he wanted them to do. But they had not seen Coyote in some time.

"He's, heh-heh, already in there," Padfoot said. He alone was not gawping up at the iron ramparts of Outlandishton. He sat on the roof of the *Panic* with his legs crossed, filing his teeth with a chunk of grey stone. "That's the scam, see? He's working some kind of bamboozle on the brains of them shaggy-bags this minute. Messin' with their minds, such as have them. Any minute those gates is going to swing open from the inside and we can just stroll on in."

"If he could just waltz into Outlandishton so easy as that," Cutbelly said, "he wouldn't have needed this Rade at all, nor taken so long a journey."

"Maybe," Padfoot said. "You might be right. Heh-heh. But you might be wrong. You might not be takin' into considerable-ization that the Boss didn't want to get here too soon. That he might've been waitin' for certain other things to occur, like."

"What other things?" Cutbelly said, but the conversation was cut short by the rumble of shaggurts, far up on the top of Shadewater Tor. The next moment there was a howling, lonely and sad, and then a series of sharp yips, and then something whistled through the air. It was coming right towards them. It hit the ice alongside the Panic and went skidding along for several hundred yards, kicking up a powdery roostertail, before it slammed into a steam sledge that was bringing up the rear of the Rade. The steam sledge crumpled in on itself with a deafening clang, and its greyling crew flew like ninepins in all directions. The thing that had dropped from Outlandishton kept on sliding along for another ten yards or so beyond the shattered sledge, where at last it came to a halt.

For a moment it seemed to Cutbelly as if nothing was moving in a thousand-mile radius. The wind whistled sadly to itself. The ice tinkled and sighed. Then the thing that had fallen stirred. Slowly, shakily, it rose to its feet. It shook itself off. It was Coyote. He had been tossed out of Outlandishton like an empty beer can from a passing car. He staggered back across the ice towards the Panic, lurching and reeling.

"I guess the shaggurts weren't very bamboozled," Cutbelly said. "Looks like this scam needs more work."

"Shut up," Padfoot said. "The Boss has everything under control."

"Since when?" Cutbelly said. "He's never had everything under control once in his entire long, wild career. Not once. Why should it be any different now?"

"It is different this time. The Boss has been really tryin' to pay attention. Stay focused. Keep his eye on the ball."

"I think," Coyote said, "that I just made a terrible mistake."

He was just there, somehow, standing beside Padfoot. He sank to the roof of the sledge and buried his face in his hands.

"Boss," Padfoot said. "What happened?"

But Coyote just shook his head.

"Tell us," Padfoot said. "We've come all this way. We deserve to know."

"I took my eye off the ball," Coyote said. "There was somebody I neglected to reckon with."

"Who was that boss? Boss, who?"

"WITH HIS WIFE!"

Even from high atop the citadel, the voice came down, so loud and so irritable that even at a distance it deserves to be written in capital letters.

"Oh, brother," Padfoot said. "Not again."

"I thought she was dead!" Coyote said. "I thought that champion from the Middling – what was his name? Beowulf – he was supposed to take care of the old bag." He grabbed two handfuls of hair and began shaking his head back and forth. "Oh, Betty. Angry, Angry Betty. What did I ever—?"

But he broke off before he could finish his question, which no doubt, Cutbelly thought, would have been, *What did I ever see in a great stinking shaggurt like you?* Coyote let go of his hair, and smoothed it back, and gazed up at the citadel. A startling look of affection – even adoration – entered his bright mocking face.

"Betty!" he cried. "Oh, Betty! Please don't be angry with me! I came all this way to see you!"

At this point there arose from the assembled remnant of the Rade a sound that Cutbelly had learned to recognise. It sounded like three hundred saws tearing all at once through three hundred planks. It sounded like fire snapping through a dry meadow. It was the sound of the werewolves trying to suppress their own laughter. The Boss was up to one of his tricks.

A head appeared over the gates of Outlandishton. It was thatched with unkempt white hair, and though at this distance its features were hard to make out, the tone of voice was unmistakable.

"COYOTE ALWAYS DID THINK BETTY WAS STUPID," Angry Betty said.

Coyote looked shocked. "What?" he said. He turned to Padfoot, the fingers of one hand pressed to his chest. Padfoot shrugged, as if to suggest that he had no idea what Betty could possibly have meant by this strange and mistaken remark. "*Stupid?* On the contrary, dear, you know I—"

"CLEAR OUT!" Angry Betty said. "BEFORE BETTY COMES DOWN THERE AND EATS EVERY WRETCHED ONE OF YOUR WRETCHED LITTLE FRIENDS."

The werewolves stopped snickering. Angry Betty had a taste for wolf that was legendary.

"Darling," Coyote said. "Come on down! Help yourself. They're a bit stringy by this point, I imagine, living on nothing but ice mouse for these last weeks and months. But you're more than welcome to a snack."

The werewolves had stopped capering and rolling in the ice. They huddled together amid the sledges, looking up at Coyote with an expression of reproach.

"BETTY CARES ONLY FOR THE NEXT MEAL, THAT'S WHAT COYOTE THINKS! THINKS BETTY CARES NOTHING FOR THE LIFE OF THE MIND!"

"Nonsense, Betty. Come down, dear. Bring your family. Come on. Eat my werewolves. Come, you can have them all." An audible whimpering started up in the werewolf pack, threaded with a few angry growls. "I only got a glimpse of those brothers of yours, of course, before you… showed me the door. But my goodness they have grown, haven't they? How is little Geryon?"

The rumbling from the citadel grew louder. Individual voices could be made out among them, clamouring for wolf. Cutbelly saw some of the werewolves began to slink away, back into the Winterlands. The werefox didn't blame them. It was hard not to imagine that someone with a taste for wolfmen might look on a foxman as a nice little appetizer.

"SHUT UP!" bellowed Angry Betty, and the rumbling of her wild relations ceased. "ANGRY BETTY IS THE SHAGGURT QUEEN, NOW. SHE LAYS DOWN THE LAW. AND THIS THE LAW IS: NOBODY NEVER FALLS FOR THE TRICKS OF THE CHANGER AGAIN."

"How very wise," Coyote said. He was pacing back and forth now, limping a little from his fall to earth. "And may I say, I'm not at all surprised to learn that a woman of your intelligence has risen to such lofty heights. You always were a clever girl, Betty dear."

There was a silence in the wake of this remark, and then a low sound, a trembling in Cutbelly's eardrums. It sounded, or felt, like nothing so much as the purring of an enormous cat. Angry Betty was pleased – in spite of herself, no doubt – by Coyote's flattering words. A moment later a squeal tore the frigid air, and then a deep iron groan. The great gates of Outlandishton were swinging open.

"Were you listening? Did you catch it?" Coyote hissed in an undertone to Padfoot. "Did you hear the keygrammer that opens the gates?"

Padfoot nodded eagerly two or three times, then stopped. He shook his head.

"Sorry, Boss," he said.

"Werefox?"

"Even if I did, I wouldn't tell you. Much as I bear no great love towards shaggurts, if they stand in your way then I consider them to be—"

"Yes, yes," Coyote said. "Thank you."

He turned back to the citadel, from which a great stack of greyish-white hay seemed to be tumbling down the tor towards them. It was, of course, Angry Betty herself. The gates closed behind her and she came skiing down the hillside on the flats of her great shaggurt feet. She was covered all over in the sparse pale fur of the shaggurts, and she carried over her shoulder a heavy wooden club spiked with wicked tusks. Her face as she schussed nearer appeared steadily more human, and Cutbelly had to admit that in spite of everything she might have been an attractive enough lady were it not for the long white beard, braided into nine thick plaits that swung from her chin.

Coyote leapt down from the top of the *Panic* and strode limping across the ice towards her. As he went he signalled brusquely to his greylings, and they went after the werewolves who had been edging away. They rounded them up with lashes and prods and drove them towards the shaggurt.

"Eat! Eat!" Coyote cried, with a broad chef's gesture towards the fine table he had laid for her.

What followed was horrible and I see no reason to describe it. Betty Ann had not feasted on wolf meat in a very long time. The snow steamed with the blood of werewolves. When she had finished eating, Coyote clapped his hands and a large tarp was produced and handed up to the shaggurt queen for use as a napkin. Daintily she wiped her chin, then belched and sat down in the snow. She beamed at Coyote. He grinned at her.

"WELL, WELL, WELL," she said. "OLD COYOTE HISSELF. IT'S NOT HALF BAD TO SEE HIM. BETTY IS SORRY SHE PITCHED HIM OVER THE WALL LIKE THAT. BUT HE STARTLED HER. HE SHOULD KNOW BETTER THAN TO SHOW UP AS A NASTY OLD RAVEN IN THE MIDST OF BETTY'S COURT. BETTY HAS A HORROR OF BIRDS. NASTY CREATURES. COYOTE KNOWS THAT."

"It's been too long, Betty. I've forgotten all your charming ways."

Again Cutbelly heard the low purring of her flattered heart.

"OLD RED LIAR."

"Great big thing."

"OLD SNAKE."

"Fuzzy-wuzzy-wuzz."

Coyote clambered across the ice to her, and then he startled Cutbelly by climbing right up into the shaggurt's immense lap. He reached up and touched the lowest-dangling of her nine beard-plaits. It was smeared with werewolf blood.

"Look what the great silly cow's gone and done, she's gotten her beard all bloody. Remember how I used to sit for hours and groom it?"

Betty nodded, closing her eyes. She remembered. Coyote signalled again to his greylings, and one of them went scuttling across the ice and disappeared into the belly of a steam sledge.

"I wonder that she's so trusting of him," Cutbelly remarked.

"She ain't," Padfoot said. "It's just that she can hear a ambush the day before it's laid for her, smell a sneak attack, feel the footstep of a cat a mile away. Her hide is tough as steel. And her fists could splinter a mountain. She don't trust him. She just ain't afraid of nothin'."

A moment later the greyling reappeared, carrying a large brush with stiff wire bristles. Coyote took the brush and began, one by one, to untwist the braids of Betty's beard until it hung down in a bloody pink fringe from her chin. Then he got down from her lap, gathered up an armful of snow, and carried it back up to her beard. Slowly and lovingly he washed the gore from her whiskers with armfuls of clean snow. The rumble of her purring shook the very roof panels under Cutbelly's feet.

It was as he was working the comb through her beard that Betty opened her eyes. She sniffed the air, working the immense nostrils of her long pale nose.

"BETTY SMELLS A REUBEN," she said. "HAS HE GOT ONE? A REUBEN IN THE WINTERLANDS?"

Cutbelly's heart seized. Mr. Feld, of course, was the only reuben component in all of Coyote's Rade. He was lying on his pallet down in the *Panic*, still and staring. Cutbelly knew this without looking because Mr. Feld had been lying thus for a long time now. His work for Coyote was accomplished; and Coyote's wicked work on him, as well.

"Oh, I might," said Coyote. "What would it be worth to you?"

"BEEN A LONG TIME SINCE BETTY TASTED THE FLESH OF A REUBEN. A LONG, LONG HUNGRY TIME."

"Would you be willing to trade it for the keygrammer to your fine stout gates?"

Betty sat up straight, and glowered at Coyote, and jabbed an immense thick finger in his direction. He ducked.

"Just kidding," he said, pinching at a strand of her beard. He looked across the ice towards the *Panic.* Cutbelly felt all the deep chill of the Winterlands in that look. "Padfoot, my lad, fetch our poor old friend, Mr. Feld."

"No!" Cutbelly ran to the rail and shouted with all his might. "You can't do that!"

"Of course I can," Coyote said mildly. "I've gotten all the use from him I need. And he's not much good for anything anymore."

Padfoot rolled open the hatch and dropped down into the sledge. Cutbelly could hear him clambering down the rungs to the main deck. If he didn't do something now, Coyote would feed Bruce Feld to the insatiable innards of Angry Betty and to his own voracious plan. But what could he do? Her skin was as hard as steel. She would hear him before he was halfway across the ice.

The greylings inside the *Panic* began to curse and chatter as they dragged Mr. Feld towards the hatch. Cutbelly could hear the reuben's feeble moans of protest. Betty stood up and began to rub her great hanging belly in anticipation.

A moment later, there was a muffled thump from somewhere deep inside Angry Betty. Her eyes got very wide, and her mouth opened, and a great pale pink bubble of blood formed on her lips. It grew and wavered and then blew from her mouth on the last gust of breath the queen of the shaggurts ever breathed. She pitched forwards and fell with a deafening crash and shattering of the ice. Coyote leapt down from her lap just in time to avoid being crushed by the immense bulk of her. The bubble hovered a moment longer in the air over her body and then popped, starring the snow with blood.

A moment later there arose from the top of Shadewater Hill a horrific growling and wailing and banging of drums. The greylings and mushgoblins and the few surviving werewolves all turned to look at each other in wonder.

"What was it?" said Padfoot, emerging alone from the hatch of the *Panic*. There would be no need, he saw, for the Flat Man.

"It was as if her heart burst," Coyote said, shaking the ice from his sleeves. "I heard it."

A moment later the air over her great back shimmered, and then there emerged from the very fur and meat of the dead shaggurt the sharp snout and foxy ears of Cutbelly. He climbed up out of her body, leaving no trace of his shadowtail passage through her. A moment later a great cheer went up from the remnant of the Rade.

"I didn't do it for you!" he cried.

"Nice enough," Padfoot said. "And they'll be mourning her all night in Outlandishton, wandering around confused and queenless. But now we'll never get hold of that keygrammer."

"Don't be so sure," Coyote said, holding up his right hand. The index finger and thumb were still pinched together from when he had plucked at her beard. He made a series of low clicking sounds with his tongue, and after a moment Cutbelly's sharp ears caught the sound of a tiny, faint reply uttered in the same clicking tongue. Coyote's face broke into a smile, and with a tender expression he gazed at his fingertips and then tucked the tiny freight they carried deep into the hair on his own head.

"You will never go wrong," he declared, "teaching yourself a few choice phrases of Flea."

24

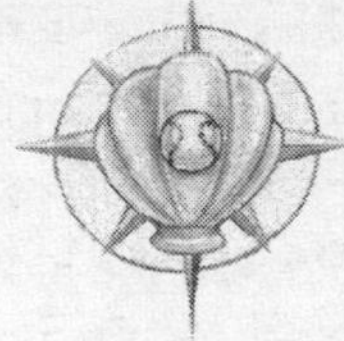

Applelawn

IN OUR WORLD, alas – here in the broken and beautiful Middling – the ways into the peace, the cool air and fragrant grass of Diamond Green have long been lost to us. For a while, as you may know, you could step into Diamond Green through a gall called the Elysian Fields, along the shores of a broad, shining river. It was here, in 1846, that the first game of baseball in the history of the Middling was played. But Coyote unpleached, or cut, that gall long ago. Today an abandoned Maxwell House coffee factory stands on the vanished spot. All that remains of the opening to that fortunate land is one last leafy scrap, a small, modest playground with a swing set and a slide. I once tried to reach Diamond Green from this spot, a big ungainly adult making a fool of himself on the swings; but am sorry to report that I failed completely. Perhaps you will have more success, if you visit one day. Or maybe you will grow up to be the one who finally restores to their former splendour the Elysian Fields of Hoboken, New Jersey.

On the day that the Rade conquered the frost giant's city of Outlandishton, and took possession of Diamond Green, a string of unusually severe thunderstorms lit up the skies of northern New Jersey. Other than that, there was no sign of the impending disaster.

In Applelawn, the peace was utterly spoilt. The storm blew all the blossoms from the trees, and the leaves, and the nests of birds, and strewed them on the ground. Bitter red rain fell on the Lodges of the Blessed, burning through the roofs and ruining the banquet tables and the perfumed baths. The Cattle of the Sun stampeded, and the Sheep of the Moon ran bleating for the distant Hills of Sleep. The three old beaver women who built the Lodges of the Blessed were forced out of their own grand home on the banks of the Big River by a gang of rampaging werewolves who scattered their immense library of romances to the four winds. Everywhere that the Shadowtails went, as they hiked in towards Diamond Green itself, Ethan saw uprooted apple trees, upended carts, and trampled fields. Greylings and goblins had run rampant in the orchards, lighting great bonfires of slaughtered apple trees; and as the vast quantities of fat, sweet apples they had greedily consumed failed to agree with their stomachs, they left foul, steaming piles of grey dung that sullied the apple-sweet air.

At last, after a sad and weary day of walking, the Shadowtails – still minus their shaggy megaloped centre fielder – came down a tree-lined hillside that was fouled with goblin dung, and found themselves in the midst of a broad expanse of grass, ringed with trees. At first Ethan thought that the field was square in shape, but when he looked more carefully he decided that it was shaped like an enormous spread fan. A diamond. Directly across from them, beyond the right side of the outfield, stretched only a cloudless sky, a blank blue mass as tall and featureless as a wall of glass. On their right, all along the first-base side, rose a great dark bramble of enormous vines, thick as the trunks of trees, studded all over with long jagged thorns that glinted in the sun. Along the left side of the outfield lay a long pool of clear blue water, and beyond this a high hill that seemed to be on fire. Beyond the burning hill lay a barren white expanse. Far back onto the expanse of ice, strange armoured vehicles were arranged, scattered carelessly, and all around the pool the army of Coyote had pitched its crimson tents. And everywhere at the edge of the Winterlands lay great piles of what Ethan took at first to be snow. Then he realised that they must be the fallen bodies of shaggurts.

"Well, we failed," Cinquefoil said, stepping out onto the grass. He looked up. The sky was heavy with the herd of storm buffalo. "Coyote got here first. He laid waste ta Outlandishton, what no one has ever been able ta do afore. And he beat us ta the Well."

"No!" Ethan said. Tears stung to his eyes. "He didn't. He didn't!"

He looked at his watch. The little grey screen was blank. He pushed the tiny buttons of the keyboard, delicately at first, then squeezing down hard. Nothing happened. He ripped the watch from his wrist and threw it into the grass.

Jennifer T. sat down heavily. She hung her head, and covered her face in her hands.

"I hate this place," she said.

"So we're too late," Spider-Rose said. Her arm fell, and Nubakaduba dangled beside her. "I knew it. We may just as well sit down and wait for it all to come crashing down or whatever it's going to do."

"Mebbe," said Grim the Giant, "we ought to get back under cover of the trees. Otherwise it's not going to be very long before they notice us."

There was a high, maniacal yipping sound, then, like the coyotes that Ethan used to hear sometimes in the hills around Colorado Springs.

"I think they already notice us, dude," Buendía said. "Here they come."

A low, ragged line of brown figures came bobbing and clambering towards them across the grass. Ethan turned, and grabbed hold of Jennifer T., and tried to pull her towards the trees on the hill in Applelawn behind them, but he could not move his feet. It was as if the soles of his shoes had been staked to the ground. He looked around and saw that Thor and Buendía and Cinquefoil and the others were all doing the same absurd dance, working their hips and flexing their knees, like people sunk to the ankles in mud. And getting nowhere at all. The yipping grew louder, and more joyous, and Ethan saw that the creatures had the shapes of men, and the heads of wolves, and the next moment he could smell their coats, rancid and sweet, a smell like the inside of your lunch box at the end of a warm afternoon. He raised Splinter over his head, and as he did so felt something that he could not see grab hold of its barrel and give a sharp yank. He yanked back, and gripped the handle tightly in both hands. Just before some kind of immense soft hammer came down and engulfed his head in endless silky yards of iron blackness, he caught a glimpse of a man, walking along behind the gang of werewolves, a man in a long black coat, his red hair crackling around his head like fire.

AMID THE CRIMSON tents, between the blue pool and the stumps of fallen trees, there was a patch of trampled earth. It was here, hours or minutes later, that Ethan awoke from the grammer that had been worked on him and his companions. In a panic, he reached for Splinter, and found to his relief that he was still clutching the bat in his left hand, so tightly, in fact, that his fingers had stiffened into a kind of claw around the handle of the bat, paralysed and aching. And that same invisible something was still tugging, firm and steady, at the other end. The Knot was wearing a raw spot into the palm of his hand.

He sat up. The man with the red hair was standing at the edge of Murmury Well, arms folded across his chest, a gentle smile on his lips and a sharp expression in his bright eye. Ethan felt, very much to his surprise, that he liked Coyote from the first moment he saw him.

"Come on, little guy," Coyote said to Ethan. "It's time to let go."

The bat gave a sudden leap in Ethan's fingers, and he redoubled his grip on it, crying out at the sharp pain that racked his hand.

"Don't let him get it," Cinquefoil said. "He can't take it from ya if ya don't let go."

Ethan thought about the other time that he had been separated from Splinter, at Dandelion Hill. While that separation had not been voluntary, it was more in the nature of a burglary – he hadn't been holding the bat at the time it was taken from him. The ferisher had simply plucked it from the backseat of the car.

"What do you want it for?" he asked Coyote.

"What *for*? Well, because I have already *have* everything else," Coyote said, stepping across the trampled grass towards Ethan. "Thanks to the admirable efforts of a very good friend of yours, I've acquired a small but highly concentrated jar of *very* powerful weed killer."

In the instant before the hodag's egg appeared in Coyote's hands, the thought flapped, black and blind, into Ethan's head: *Taffy*.

"Yes," Coyote said. "Taffy. Noble creature, really. Sad story. When I sent that old pill La Llorona to her with my offer, part of me was almost hoping that she would refuse. You know, I really do think that, in her poor Sasquatch mind, you reuben children had very nearly come to fill the hole in her. Very nearly."

At that moment the wind picked up, and with a bulky rustle of canvas one of the crimson tents came unmoored from the ground and took off into the sky, flapping like a big red bird. In its place, like a white dove revealed by a conjuror's hand, Ethan saw a tall, iron cage that strongly resembled the one from the stone lodge of Mooseknuckle John. For all he knew it was the same weird-iron cage. And there, in a soft black heap, just as they had first seen her, lay Taffy the Sasquatch. Her arms were thrown over her face, as if in shame. Standing beside the cage was a hideously bent figure, covered in colourless fur, with a thick neck and bandy legs. He was poking at Taffy, jabbing her with a long stick.

"But in the end she couldn't resist, could you, Taffy, dear?"

Coyote turned towards the cage, and it surprised Ethan to hear that there was tenderness in his tone, and that the tenderness sounded real. "I offered, you see, to return her children to her. I brought death into the Worlds, after all, as you know, little Feld. I suppose it did not sound all that far-fetched that I might be able to send it away again, at least in the case of two Sasquatches. Even if they have been dead for over nine hundred years."

There was low, whimpering moan from inside the cage. The horrible white creature poked her again.

"But— heh-heh— he lied," said the matted white thing, in a voice that was oddly familiar to Ethan.

"Don't I always?" Coyote held up the hodag's egg, balancing it on the palm of one hand, his long elegant fingers splayed. "And thanks, little Feld, to your old dad, who's really quite a *brilliant* person, isn't he, I am now the proud owner of an *extremely* clever toxin-pump system, constructed entirely of a truly revolutionary semirigid picofibre composite. To deliver this fabulous weed killer where it's really needed. Deep, deep down at the very roots of it all."

He raised a hand, and there was an iron clang. Ethan looked towards the ice of the Winterlands, and saw the door of one of the armoured snow-truck things bang open. A crew of greylings tumbled out. There was a mechanical whine from inside the truck, and as the greylings found their footing Ethan saw them begin to tug a long shining string into the light, tipped in a darker silver. The hose played out in silken ripples from the some great spool, and snaked along behind them as they ran. When they reached the edge of the pool the greylings hooked clusters of round black weights to the nozzle of the hose, and then tossed it into the water. It fell with an eerie, soft splash. At once the hose began to slither, hissing, down into the pool.

"If your father's calculations are correct, that ought to reach right down to the very bottom of the Well, where it feeds the roots of the Tree."

"Mr. Feld would never help you," Jennifer T. said. "You're a big liar."

"Oh, the biggest," the Coyote said pleasantly. "But not, hard as it may be for you to believe, in this case. Mr. Feld?"

Somehow, then, Ethan's father was there. Ethan couldn't think how he had missed him before. But there he was, standing beside Coyote, in his old jeans and a clean white T-shirt, his beard tangled and his hair unkempt, his eyes behind their glasses calm and intent. Ethan leapt to his feet, to run to his father, but then he hesitated. Mr. Feld did not quite seem to be looking at Ethan, or rather did not appear to be *seeing* him. It was hard to explain. Ethan took an experimental step towards Mr. Feld. The grammer that had prevented him from walking before seemed to have been unworked. So then he ran, his arms outspread, and waited for his father to bend down, laughing, and catch him up, and lift him into the air, and swing him around and around. But Mr. Feld just stood there, looking at him without seeing him, his hands in his pockets, a grave little smile on his lips. Ethan stopped. It was as if a cold wind blew in from that smile, finding all the chinks in Ethan's heart.

"That will be all, Bruce," Coyote said. "Thank you."

Mr. Feld turned to walk away, and as he did so Ethan saw that – there was no other way to put it – his father had been emptied out. His head, his torso, and his legs had no back. There were no organs, no muscles or bones. Instead there was just a hideous greyish-white *lining*, glossy as fresh paint. It was like looking at the reverse side of a mask, a full-body mask, with indentations for the nose and mouth, for the nipples and penis, for the shoulder sockets and knee caps and the toes of the feet. The worst thing of all was the eyes – they were just openings, through which you could plainly see the white expanse of snow and the blue sky beyond. Ethan watched in horror as the husk of his father climbed up into the armoured truck and disappeared.

"He didn't *want* to help me, you can be sure of that," Coyote said. "Though the problem interested him *extremely*. You can see what it did to him. He's become a Flat Man. Same thing happened to a lot of those A-bomb fellows, you know, back when I was putting that little fiesta together."

Ethan was standing only a few feet from him now, and the pull on the bat was suddenly enormously strong. Ethan fought it with everything he had, and the ache in his hand grew sharper.

"Come on, now, Ethan," Coyote said. "Help me out, here. I've got everything else I need. The venom of Nazuma – that's the right name for the Bottom-Cat, did you know that? It's not ordinary poison, you see. In fact, it's not really *venom* at all."

"What is it?" Thor said.

"Such a *curious* boy. In every sense of the word. Well, Thor the Changeling, I'll tell you. Back when Old Woodenhead was making the Worlds, separating out all the Something from the Nothing, he found himself with quite bit of Nothing left over. Some of it, as you know, he used to fill in the spaces between the leaves and branches of the poor old Tree. But the rest of it, well, you know how these things are done. Corporations in the Middling do it all the time. He just sort of buried it, all that Nothing, where he thought no one would look. Way, way down at the Bottom of it all, lower even than the roots of the Lodgepole. And he set Nazuma to dwell at the Bottom, and hold the Lodgepole up, keep an eye on the Nothing. And then, I suppose, Nazuma found a bit of Nothing that had leaked out, through a hole in the Bottom of it all. And being a gluttonous fellow, he tasted it. And he liked the taste of Nothing quite a bit. Been snacking on the stuff ever since. Holding it in these little pockets at the back of his throat, which, were we to dissect the Bottom-Cat and take a look at them, would likely turn out to be made of the very same kind of organic picofibrous tissue as this hodag's egg, here. It will not merely kill the Tree, this Nothing." He gave the egg a shake. "It will *dissolve* it. Everything will return to the admittedly rather drab grey fog from which it all began. A trackless grey sea in which I will bob, as you did not so long ago in the waters of the Big River, clinging to my little Splinter of the Tree. And then, when you and they and all of it have fizzed and foamed and subsided, I will take my little Splinter, and have something to which I can stake my fabulous *new* creation. And then, as the case really ought to have been all along, the Changer will be the Maker. And you can be absolutely certain I won't make the same mistakes Old Woodenhead made when he was starting out. So come on. Let go."

"No," Ethan said. The pain of the Knot was searing. "It's mine. I hate you. You're crazy."

"Yeah, yeah, yeah," the Changer said. He waved his right hand, waggling the fingers, and the pressure on the end of the bat abruptly dwindled and passed. "All right, look, I can wait. You're bound to let your guard down at some point, and if you don't, despair will change your mind."

WEREWOLVES CARRIED ETHAN and Jennifer T. over to one of the red tents and shoved them in. They were fed some kind of thin but tasty broth, with crusts of flat, sour bread. Then they were left alone to their thoughts, and to the creeping onset of despair.

"What do you think is going to happen?" Ethan said.

"Some more bad things, I guess," said Jennifer T. "Ethan, it's so awful. Your *dad*."

"I don't know what that Flat Man thing was," Ethan said. He shuddered at the memory. "But it wasn't my dad."

"And poor Taffy."

"I can't believe she fell for his stupid lie," Ethan said, uncharitably.

"That's what people do, Ethan," Jennifer T. said. "They fall for his lies."

There was not much more to say. After a while they fell asleep, and in his dreams Ethan saw his father and mother, and they had no backs, and the sky shone through their eye sockets, and they were smiling down at him, and telling him that they loved him, and tugging mercilessly at his hands.

He woke up. Something was pulling on his hands – not on the bat, which he still gripped tightly – but on his hands themselves, at the wrists. Something cool and flexible, and tipped with tiny barbs. A pair of cool little claws.

"Come on, now, piglet," said a voice out of some long-ago, distant dream. "We got to get our ownselves out of here."

CUTBELLY LED THEM through the shadows towards the vast dark bramble of enormous thorns that Ethan had seen along the first-base side of Diamond Green, when they came down the hill from the Summerlands. This place, he explained, was called the Briarpatch. It was a hostile waste that had grown up to fill the borders between the Middling and Diamond Green, as the old ways and roads of adventure were neglected, and travellers and heroes from the Middling ceased to seek the refuge of the Lodges of the Blessed. The thick briarwood had grown so huge and high that it was not difficult for them to find a path through it, ducking under the shaggy vines when they could, and scrambling over them when they could not duck under. The thorns themselves, six and seven feet long and as thick at their base as the trunk of a tree, were almost too large to be really dangerous, as the thorn of a rose poses no great hazard to the aphid.

Our three aphids kept silence for a long time, until they arrived at a place where the Briarpatch thinned somewhat. A slender, horned moon cast a faint light on the clearing in the bramble. Far in the distance there was a steady, low pulse of air, a kind of inanimate breathing, which sounded to Ethan very much like the whiz of traffic along a freeway.

Cutbelly had led them to the very edge of the Middling.

They sank to the ground with their backs against a tree, and for the first time Ethan realised that he was exhausted. They had been walking all day, since the Old Cat had deposited them on the far shore of the river. He had no idea how long it had been since his last sleep. Days? Weeks? He felt as if he could close his eyes and fall instantly asleep; his head seemed to fill rapidly with a fine sand, cool and dark. But then he saw again the emptied shell, the glistening hollow, the Flat Man that had taken the place of his father, and his eyes snapped open, and he cried out, and tried to brush the vision away, slapping at his face.

"It's OK," said Jennifer T., taking his hand. "Take it easy."

"Sleep, piglet," Cutbelly said. "And in the morning we'll see things more clearly, and sniff a way out of our troubles if we can."

"I don't think we can," Ethan said.

"Nor do I, not really," said the werefox. "But nonetheless we have to try. We have the Splinter, and that's something. You were strong to hold on to it as you did, piglet. In particular in the face of… of what you saw. We must do what we can to keep that strength up."

"Cutbelly," Ethan said. "That Flat Man. Is that really him? Is that really my father?"

The werefox sank to the ground, now, too. He took his bone pipe from its pouch, and struck a match, and exhaled a foul cloud of smoke.

"I'm afraid so," he said. "I did what I could to stop it, for he was – he is a good man, your father. He took pity on me when I was in a pickle, and did what he could to make things easier for me. But when a mind like your father's falls into the grip of one of Coyote's deep puzzles, there's not much a rude creature such as my ownself can do. He stopped eating. He stopped talking. Then one day he just turned around and I saw." He lowered the pipe, and shook his head. "What you saw."

"I don't want to wait until morning," Jennifer T. said, standing up again. "I want to do something *now*."

"I know you do," Cutbelly said. "I can feel it coming off you like the heat of a fever."

"There's no point in just waiting here. He knows where we are. He can just come get us."

"He may not try. Coyote wants everything, but he wants it very carelessly, and in no particular order. It's not inconceivable that he could forget about us for hours while he's occupied with the lowering of that hose of his."

"I know about Coyote," Jennifer T. said, sounding almost angry in her knowledge. "And I'll tell you what I know. The things he does, sometimes they come around and bite him on the butt."

"True enough," Cutbelly said. "But in the dark, and as few and weary as we are..."

"Sometimes the way to beat Coyote," Jennifer T. said slowly, and Ethan could almost hear the idea as it came together in her mind. "Is at his own game. Huh. OK."

"What?" Ethan said. "Jennifer T.?"

"Piglet!"

There was a snap of branches and an urgent whispering as the thighs of her jeans rubbed together, and then only the distant rumble of some highway in the Middling. In the dim light of the slender moon she was soon lost amid the shadows of the Briarpatch.

"Why is she going back?" Ethan said. "What's she doing?

"I'll go after her. You stay here. Lie low, stay quiet. And remember, piglet. Two thirds of all the shadows you see are not real shadows at all."

And with that he scampered off after Jennifer T., to the place where the armies of Coyote were encamped.

ETHAN FOUGHT SLEEP for as long as he could, aided in this battle by the occasional suspicious rustle of a shadow in the trees overhead, and by the recurring image, in his memory, of the thing his father had become. But at last he could fight it no more. His head sank to his chest, and he thought to himself, No, no, little E, don't fall asleep. Yet once again his head began to fill with fine black sand. And then he heard it – the low sound that at first you took for the call of some lonely bird, far out on the waters, or flapping stark against the moon. The wild call, so husky and harsh it almost sounded like laughter, of La Llorona.

She was very near. His arms prickled with some strange emotion between longing and fear, and he rose to his feet, so naturally and inevitably that a part of him wondered – and was never afterwards certain – if he were not asleep and dreaming.

He started to walk, neither towards the Middling, nor back to Diamond Green, but keeping instead to the jagged land that lay between them, ducking and weaving among the blades and needles of the Briarpatch. And then a surprising thing happened. As he drew nearer, and the weeping grew ever more sorrowful and wild, all his fatigue and fear and hunger left him. Instead, he felt his heart aflood with pity for this lost and wandering woman, doomed to stalk the ragged borders of the world.

He came into another clearing in the giant bramble, a muddy place, cut in two by a stream that lay glinting in the moonlight. She was standing there, by the mocking laughter of the water, in her tattered white dress. He recognised her at once, and ran to her, and she folded him in her cool soft embrace.

"My boy," said La Llorona. "My own and only boy."

"Mom," Ethan said. "Oh, Mom."

Her sobbing ceased, then, though its ghost or echo shook her frail body from time to time. He could feel the bones through her skin, just as he had when she lay dying in the hospital in Colorado Springs, those hollow angel bones of hers. The sweetness of that bitter memory, of her embrace, of holding her again and hearing her voice, filled his heart so full that all the old healed places in it were broken all over again. And in that moment he felt – for the first time that optimistic and cheerful boy allowed himself to feel – how badly made life was, how flawed. No matter how richly furnished you made it, with all the noise and variety of Something, Nothing always found a way in, seeped through the cracks and patches. Mr. Feld was right; life was like baseball, filled with loss and error, with bad hops and wild pitches, a game in which even champions lost almost as often as they won, and even the best hitters were put out seventy per cent of the time. Coyote was right to want to wipe it out, to call the whole sad thing on account of darkness.

"I'm only a little kid," he said, to himself, or to his mother, or to the world that had snatched her from him.

"Let go, my boy," said the Weeping Woman. "My only boy. Let go."

As she stroked his hair, gently she took hold of the bat with her other hand. The ache subsided, and the rigid claw in which he had grasped it for so long finally relaxed. He felt the bat slip through his fingers at last with a rush of gratitude.

"OK," Ethan said. "I'll let go."

That was when the strangest thing of all happened: La Llorona, the screaming Banshee of the Far Territories, the ragged Queen of Sorrows, smiled.

At that moment, Ethan felt a sharp pain in the palm of his hand. It was the Knot, that little stubborn morsel of something impossible to remove or forget or work around. As he surrendered the bat to La Llorona, the Knot chanced to rub against the swollen blister that it had long since raised on the skin of Ethan's hand. The blister was unbelievably tender and raw, and Ethan yelled. As he yelled, it was just as if – as they say in old stories – *the scales fell from his eyes*. He blinked, once, and found himself in the cold embrace of a ghost, in a smell of dust and rotten cloth. La Llorona's face was a pinched pale mask, a translucent white veil with the bones of her skull showing through. Ethan grabbed at the bat, and just managed to wrench it, at the last possible instant, away from her. As he did so La Llorona shrieked, and snatched at his hair with a ravenous skeleton hand.

"No!" Ethan cried. "No, you aren't her!"

The grief of his mother's death was returned to him, then; it resumed its right and familiar place: a part of life, a part of the story of Ethan Feld, a part of the world that was, after all, a world of stories, tragic and delightful, and, on the whole, very much the better for it. The memory of Dr. Victoria Jean Kummerman Feld was Something, unalterably Something, a hodag's egg that no amount of Nothing could ever hope to touch or dissolve.

"Get off me!" he cried, brandishing the bat. "Or I'll bust you open like an old piñata."

La Llorona's face was blank with sorrow, and she made no sound at all, as though all her tears were finally shed. She stood, floating a few inches above the ground, gazing down at him. For one last second, Ethan thought he saw the face of his mother, projected like a flickering image on the blank screen of La Llorona's face. Her expression was one of infinite reproach, and Ethan was crushed by the knowledge that he had lost her, forever, all over again. Then she backed away from him, into the trees, and was gone.

JENNIFER T. RAN a long way, but as she drew nearer to Diamond Green she had to slow down. The night was filled with iron airs, a music of hammers and shovels, bike chains and manhole covers. There were campfires burning in the Briarpatch, and she carefully picked her away among them. The laughter of the Rade at its campfires was like the barking of dogs straining against choke collars, like the yapping of seagulls. She walked, toe to heel, keeping her breathing low and steady, and managed to slip past the campfires, and out onto Diamond Green. In the moonlight, she could see the great machines that littered the Winterlands side of the Green, trampling the thick grass around Murmury Well. There was the steady *ronf-ronf-ronf* of the spool that was sending Mr. Feld's marvellous hose and nozzle down to the bottom of the universe itself. Up on the hillsides of the Summerlands, more fires burned, and she could hear the angular chiming of their music. The looming puppet-shadows of dancing greylings and other creatures flickered against the leaves of the trees. She wondered briefly why even that nasty bunch of skanky little creatures would want to help Coyote bring about their own destruction. If Coyote did get ahold of Splinter, and the world dissolved in a great sea of Nothing, there would only be room on that skinny little raft for *one*. Then she remembered that the greylings were, or had once been, ferishers, and the skrikers were some kind of strange hybrid of goblin and machine – contrivances of the Changer. Maybe they were dancing, now, not out of the general happiness of evil at all, but rather from joy at the impending end of their miserable little lives.

On the fourth side of the Green, beyond right field, there was a profound darkness, broken here and there by the smudged light of fires that were, she realised, only the reflections of the fires burning in the Summerlands across the way. The Gleaming, sealed forever by some kind of trick of Coyote's that he was unable, or afraid, to undo. Or maybe, since everything was about to come to an end anyway, he just didn't see any point to bothering.

It was hard to imagine someone as powerful and tricky as Coyote being afraid of anything, but standing there in the middle of Diamond Green she got the unmistakable feeling that he was. He had laid waste to the orchards of Applelawn, trampled the Greenmelt around Murmury, and violated the waters of the Well itself. And he had allowed his followers to pitch their red tents in the dark thorny bramble of the Middling. But Diamond Green itself, where she now stood, lay untouched, stretching smooth and unsullied in every direction, the grass dark in the moonlight and glinting with dew. Even with the Gleaming sealed up, it was as if there was a power in the world, on this great grassy diamond, that Coyote still feared.

There was a rustle, just behind her, like a flag in a stiff breeze. She whirled, remembering the shadows that had pursued them into the Middling, back on Clam Island. A black shape, with a smell like the smell of smoke in your hair the day after a barbecue, churned the air beside her. It was a huge black bird – a raven. Jennifer's heart lurched in her chest, but she stood her ground as it dived towards her. Covering her face with one arm, she swatted at it with the other, knocking it away, wary of its sharp beak and claws.

"Take it easy!" croaked the raven. "I'm just looking for a place to sit down."

Once she had heard it talk, she could no longer seem to move her hands to shoo it away. She stood stock still, her heart pounding so hard now that she could hear it as a soft iron clanging in her ears, and allowed the raven to light on her shoulder.

"Now who's afraid?" the raven said, and the voice, though raucous, was familiar to her. "Coyote doesn't *fear* the power of this field. Coyote *is* the power here. This is his ground, the Great Crossroads of the Four Worlds. It was here, oh, ages ago, that he fell asleep, and dreamed a Coyote game of paths and chances. The game you love so much, little girl. So don't go thinking such nasty thoughts about Coyote."

"You don't fool me," Jennifer T. said. "You're *him*."

He was standing beside her then, in the moonlight, regarding her, his head cocked curiously to one side in a way that really did remind her of a cunning and curious old coyote.

"You are a spark plug, all right," he said. "If I weren't about to disband my team, I'd be tempted to sign you to a contract."

"Where's *my* team?" Jennifer T. "Cinquefoil and Rodrigo and Spider-Rose. Where are they?"

"I have them," he said. "As I now have you."

"You don't have me yet," she said. "So shut up."

He smiled. She could see that he really seemed to like her. For some reason that made her even angrier than before.

"You know why I'm here, right?" she said. "You can read my thoughts."

"I can, in fact. And I do." He reached into the pocket of his long coat and withdrew a long tobacco pipe. It was pale grey in the moonlight, but she guessed that, like Cutbelly's, it was carved from bone. He wiggled two fingers and a little gold fish of fire flopped in the air above the pipe and then plunged, with a hiss, into the bowl. "You want to play ball."

"That's right. My guys against your guys. Nine on nine. Right here, on Diamond Green. If we win, you get that hose out of there and pack everything up and, you know. Basically, lose. If you win, then..." She hesitated before saying it. It was not as if she had asked Ethan for his permission; he might not agree. "Then we give you Splinter. The bat. The piece of wood you need."

"Interesting proposition. You know Coyote pretty well, for a gum-chewing half-breed child of television. And I just love the idea of the fate of the entire universe coming down to the bottom of the ninth. *Love* it. But you're neglecting one thing. *I* have all the power here, and *you* have none. I hold all the cards, except one, the bat, but as to that, look around you. I have ten thousand of my freakish little buddies scattered in their tents and trailers all around this field. That's versus nine of you, of whom at the moment all but two are in my immediate control. I have positioned my fellas in a ring in this immediate vicinity, all around Applelawn, the Greenmelt, and the Briarpatch, armed not just with weapons but with powerful grammers to dampen the talents of Shadowtails. You can't get away, and you can't send for help. All I need to do is be patient, and keep your friend Ethan away from food for a week or two. And that stick of his will be mine."

Jennifer T. had used up her entire store of boldness in stealing through the Briarpatch, coming here, and standing up to Coyote as she had. Now she fell silent, and allowed the weight of defeat to hang her head.

"What do *you* have to fight me with?" Coyote said. "What do you *know*? Your father's father's people knew me, once; and got the better of me many times. But that lore is not yours, little girl. What lore do you have?"

When Coyote said *lore* – that was when Jennifer T. thought of the book her uncle Mo had given her. *The Threefold Lore, they called it. All that's nonsense.* She took it from her back pocket and held it up to him.

"I have this," she said. "The Lore of the Wa-He-Ta Tribe."

"What is *that*?" He peered through the darkness at the book's cover, with its three costumed little white boys sitting by a fire while a big Indian in a corny headdress taught them how to tie trout lures or do lanyard. "*That?*" He grinned. "That book was written by a little old man named Irving Posner, in a hotel room in Pittsburgh, Pennsylvania, in 1921. There's no *lore* in that book. There's nothing in there that can save you."

"The Threefold Lore," she said, without much faith in what she was saying – *Irving Posner?* – but taking refuge, as so often in her life, in her own deep stubbornness. "Wonder. And Hopefulness. And Trust."

Coyote laughed so hard that he blew his pipe out; a little comet of burning tobacco shot into the air. He bent over, laughing. He stood up, and smoothed his hair, and dabbed at an eye. And then the pipe fell out of his mouth, and he looked surprised as only Coyote – whose talent has always been that of ridiculous failure as much as of wild success – can look surprised. Jennifer T. turned. At first she thought that it was a mist, rising from the grass, but then she saw that it was clearly stealing in through the Briarpatch itself, from the Middling. It was some kind of silk, milkweed spores or the floats of balloonist spiders, thousands of them, drifting in the moonlight, blowing in from the Briarpatch on a breeze she could not feel.

"They're ghosts, you idiot," Coyote said, with a twisted grin of dismay.

The wisps of silky fog settled on the field like smoke curling inside a bottle. Then each wisp seemed to bloom, instantly, into a small shape, oddly spiky up on top. As she stood there with Coyote, holding the *The Wa-He-Ta Brave's Official Tribe Handbook*, the field of Green Diamond filled with an army of ghostly boys. The ghost-boys were gotten up like little "Indians," in buckskins and warpaint, each of them wearing a dopey-looking feathered headdress on his head. The boys filled in – developed like photographs – as they settled and spread across the field. Their features grew more distinct. They even took on a certain amount of pale colouring. They reminded her of old photographs of her grandmother and great-aunts on the breakfront in the house on Clam Island: black and white, or brown and white, but tinted with delicate pale Eastery colours. Some of the boys were bigger than she, and others smaller, but none of them seemed to be older, as far as she could tell, or as far as you could ascribe an age to a ghost.

"Who are you guys?" she asked the nearest ghost, a snub-nosed kid with wide-set dark eyes and pale cheeks, tinted candy pink.

"We are the braves of Wa-He-Ta," he said. "And we are true-blue to the end."

"That's right," said a second boy, thin and spotty. "Even if you is a girl."

Jennifer T. opened the *Handbook* to its title page and held it out to Coyote. Under the crossed-tomahawk-and-peace-pipe symbol of the Wa-He-Ta braves there was a motto in big slanty letters. She guessed that Coyote's eyes would be sharp enough to read the motto, even by the light of a three-quarter moon.

"Says so right here," said Jennifer T. " '*True-Blue to the End.*' "

"Your uncle Mo wishes he could be here with us," said the pink-cheeked boy. She could see clear through his body to the name tag sewed into the collar of his uniform shirt. It said COOTER SIMMS. "But he isn't dead yet, so he can't."

"He's the last of the Wa-He-Tas," said another ghost boy.

"We doesn't need him," said a third. "We is skitterish as squirrels and toothy as garfish and scrappy as a mess of rat terriers." There was a general excited murmur of agreement among the ghost boys at this declaration, a number of them piping up with feisty similes of their own. "An' they's one of us for every one of them little critters and greylings and whatnots you got doing your dirty work 'round here. An' mister," the boy finished, pushing up his sleeves, "we aim to see that they doesn't do you one lick of good."

"So now it's a fair fight," said Cooter Simms. "Ten thousand against ten thousand."

Coyote spun around where he stood, watching as the billowing ghost-boys fogged up his view of the fires of his troops. Their soft rustling presence seemed even to dampen the sound of the Rade's iron music. The infernal pounding of the unwinding picofibre hose on its clattering spool faded and died. Coyote opened his mouth, and as he did so his lip curled in an ugly way, and Jennifer T. thought she caught a glimpse of a row of snaggled, ugly canine teeth. Then he closed his mouth, and smiled his beautiful smile. He reloaded his pipe, and sent another firefish diving into its bowl. He puffed merrily for a moment, looking around at the ghostly army of boys. Then he looked at Jennifer T., and his eyes blazed with a fire so old and deep that the cockiness she had been feeling over the past few minutes vanished like a drop of water on a hot skillet.

"All right, then," Coyote said. "I'll release your teammates, and return your gear. And we'll meet on this green at noon tomorrow. But don't count on winning. My Hobbledehoys are *tough*, Jennifer T. Rideout. They're spikes-out, swill-spitting dirt players who'll steal your signs and brush back your hitters and load up the ball with Vaseline. They're the original Gashouse Gang, and they play by Coyote rules. And their pitcher, let me tell you..." He sucked on his pipe and it flared up and lit his face from underneath, the way you do with a flashlight when you are telling a ghost story and want to spook your friends. "He has the *nastiest* stuff you've ever seen." He chuckled. "A real *fire*baller."

Then he turned, and walked off the field.

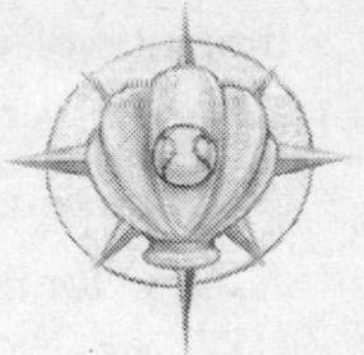

25

A Game of Worlds

THE GHOST BOYS conveyed Jennifer T. through the briars to the place where Ethan lay, huddled by a stream, cheeks silvered with tears.

"E?" she knelt beside him. "You all right?"

He shook his head.

"What happened?"

"I don't want to talk about it," Ethan said. "Is that all right?"

"Sure," said Jennifer T. She held out her hand to him and he took it, and she dragged him to his feet. He looked around at the flickering army of dead boys she had brought along with her into the Briarpatch.

"Who are all these...guys?"

"We're the braves of Wa-He-Ta," said the ghost of Cooter Smith. "And we don't much hold with a boy what cries."

"Oh, like you never cried in your whole life," Jennifer T. said. "I'm *sure*. I'll bet you could have earned yourself a Feather in Straight-up Old-fashioned Indian-style Bawling if they gave one out."

Cooter Smith's ghost glared at her, and the delicate pink tinge of his ghostly grey cheek seemed to deepen. There was a murmur of delighted appreciation among the other Wa-He-Tas.

"Come on," Jennifer T. said. "Let's go find Cutbelly."

They found the werefox scrambling madly amid the hooks and tangles of the Briarpatch, calling out their names. When he saw the boyish ghosts of all the men who had never forgotten their years of service in the ranks of the true-blue Wa-He-Tas, he was alarmed, but when Jennifer T. told him how they had intimidated Coyote, he broke into a foxy little grin.

"So, it's to be a game of baseball, then," he said. "And what did you promise him, should we lose?"

Jennifer T. looked at Ethan, then down at the bat in his hand. It shone softly in the pale light of the horned moon.

"*Splinter?*" Ethan said. "You promised him my bat?"

"It's the only thing he wants, Ethan. What else could I offer him?"

Ethan raised the bat, and hefted it, and then winced. He opened his left hand and she saw the fiery welt on his palm, raw and glistening.

"I guess it doesn't matter if I lose it," he said. "I can't even swing the darn thing."

"Ya want ta spit on that there blister," offered one of the Wa-He-Tas.

"Spit on it, then rub it with some sourgrass," suggested another.

"Spit and lemonade," suggested another. "And then lay a nice hairy cobweb acrost it."

Jennifer T. winked at Ethan. "I guess we know how they died," she said.

They spent the remainder of the night sleeping in a 1977 Ford Citation that had been abandoned in an impromptu junkyard, down a steep embankment from Route 179, outside of Sedona, Arizona. The air was cool and flavoured with the dusty smell of sage. The sky in the distance glowed like the dial of a luminescent clock. They were not sure what had become of the ghost boys – they were not sure, in the tender pink glow of a desert morning in the Middling, if there really had been any ghost boys at all – until Cutbelly crossed them back to Diamond Green, and they saw the ruination of the Rade.

The red tents were struck; the great armoured vehicles had rolled out of sight; even the fleet of storm birds had passed away, leaving behind only the endless blue heaven of Diamond Green. Jennifer T. thought that the braves of the Wa-He-Ta must have driven the Rade away, but Cutbelly said that it was Coyote himself who had sent them packing, now that he could no longer avail himself of them.

"They drive him mad, you know, the Rade," he said. "All that yelling and banging and yammering. Every thousand years or so he just goes off and *eats* them all."

All that remained now of the great rambling Rade was the armoured truck, a great black-and-red katydid crouched on the edge of Murmury Well, from whose belly there played the endlessly unspooling bobbin of Mr. Feld's hose. There was also a painted sledge, like a gypsy caravan on steel runners, drawn by a team of werewolves. As they stepped out onto Diamond Green, Ethan saw the back door of this wagon swing open, and the shaggy white creature with the irritating laugh stepped out. He raised his hand, and then one by one the Shadowtails emerged and stepped blinking into the sun. They ran towards each other and met at the very centre of Green Diamond, where mysteriously in the night a pitcher's mound had been raised, or had sprouted of its own accord from the grass. They embraced, or shook hands. They took stock of their hurts and weaknesses, and confirmed, to their universal regret, that Taffy was not among them. Then they moved into the ruined orchards of Applelawn to rustle up some breakfast.

Aside from the loss of their centre fielder – Cutbelly would have to take the Sasquatch's place – their single greatest liability was Ethan's hand. Overnight the blister on the palm had ballooned to the size of an olive. The skin all around it was fiery and swollen. Furthermore, his repeated struggles to cling to the bat, in the face of attempts by Coyote and La Llorona to take it, had left the muscles of his hand stiff and aching. He could barely fit it into the glove.

"We'll need a salve," said Pettipaw. "A blister like that calls for comfrey."

"Comfrey, my eye," Grim the Giant said. "Comfrey is for boils. What's wanted is yarrow."

A hot dispute might have broken out then, but Cutbelly cut in sharply.

"Clearly the herbal lore you two possess couldn't squidge a blackhead," he said. "What's truly wanted in this case is marshmallow."

The three of them tramped off into the Summerlands, arguing, while the rest of them set about gathering the wood the greylings had left unburnt. Amid the heaps of foul garbage and dubious bones they managed to find a sack filled with loaves of the greyling's sour bread, and a miraculous two dozen eggs that Spider-Rose taught them to roast in the ashes of the fire. They had a strong, rich flavour – Cinquefoil said they were goose eggs – and after he had eaten three of them Ethan felt strong enough to contend with the pain in his hand. It was decided among the three quarrelling herbalists to craft a compound of the leaves they each favoured. Grim the Giant upended an iron hat abandoned by some fleeing skriker and filled it with water. Then he tossed in the leaves and steeped them until the water had all boiled away, leaving a noxious charred paste that stank like tar. Like tar, the smell of it, though awful, somehow reached down into you and reminded you that you were alive. Cutbelly slathered it onto palm of Ethan's hand with a quick paw. They were just going to have to hope for the best.

"You know there's no way we can beat them," Spider-Rose said. "I say we don't even try. Everybody knows the Hobbledehoys are the best. They been playing on Coyote's team since the day he invented the game. That's what I heard, anyway."

"It's true," Pettipaw said. "They were the First Nine. Demons, is what they were, until Coyote put gloves on their off-hands and set them loose right there on the green. They traded in their hell-hammers for bats and their iron slippers for lace-up leather spikes. That's how all the demon virtues – patience, deception, quick hands, craftiness, an eye for the mistakes of others – they all got dragged deep into the game."

"I've played 'em before," Cinquefoil said, and everyone turned to look at him. They were sitting around the embers of the fire as the last chill of the morning burned away. "Tough team. I don't misdoubt the demon tale, though they looked ta me like more or less ordinary reubens, but even uglier. They was making a tour of the Outer Islands, oh, it was long, long ago. Took a best-a-nine series from us in five straight games. Tough, tough team."

"How do we play them?" Jennifer T. said.

"What do they got?" said Grim. "Tell us all about it. Did you hit off 'em? Tell the truth."

"Yeah, Chief," Ethan said. "Can you give us a scouting report?"

"No." It was Rodrigo Buendía. He had been quiet all morning, puffing away at a succession of cigars, walking back and forth across Diamond Green as if taking the measure of it. The confinement he and the others had undergone, in a lightless cell in the wagon sledge, had been hardest on him; Cinquefoil had told Ethan that the great slugger even wept in his sleep. "Waste of time, dude. We should to be out there warming up. Sprints. Bunt work – fielding *and* laying them down. And then a couple hours of BP. You, little fox dude, you going to be in centre today. When the last time you played ball?"

"Fifteen sixty-nine," Cutbelly said at once. "I hit into three double plays."

"That's what I'm saying," Buendía said.

THEY SPENT THE next two hours working out on Diamond Green, and then, when the sun had climbed nearly to the centre of the sky, a crew of greylings emerged from the wagon sledge, carrying chalk-spreaders and bases, and chased them from the field. They went to work laying down the lines, painting the batter's boxes and basepaths. Half an hour later the field was ready. Jennifer T. climbed the mound and began to throw softly to Ethan at home plate, warming up her arm. Little by little she increased the velocity of her pitches until they were snapping pretty well into Ethan's mitt. She was not going to be able to avail herself of the wormhole today. Diamond Green was the hinge of Worlds, the axil point. All branches were born from it, but none crossed it. There was no way to scamper across it.

Each time the ball slammed into the heel of Ethan's mitt, it hurt so badly that he clenched his jaw, and his breath came hissing through this teeth. It was while he was waiting for a curveball from Jennifer T. that he heard Cinquefoil say,

"That's them."

They were just there, the Hobbledehoys, crossing the outfield grass with the great blue sky of the lost Gleaming behind them, as if they had stepped somehow out of that sealed-up land. As Cinquefoil had said, they were like men, lean, rangy men, and one broad, beefy fellow – with sallow, pinched faces. They reminded Ethan of the faces you saw on really old baseball cards, country faces, squinting eyes set close together, noses sharp, mouths lipless and grimly smiling. They wore white flannel uniforms with red pinstripes and black caps with red bills. Across the front in black script it just said HOBS. Their spikes were long and black, with pointed rat-snouts and quivering black laces. They walked right up to the mound and stood in a loose group around it, looking at Jennifer T. She pretended to ignore them – actually Ethan supposed she actually *was* ignoring them – reared back, and let fly with her slider. It dived, and bent at the end like a buttonhook, and smacked like a brick against Ethan's glove. One of the Hobbledehoys grunted, but none of them spoke. Then they went over to their bench and sat down. Aside from grunts and mutterings, they hardly spoke. When it was necessary, they communicated mostly by means of a series of signs, like those used by managers and third-base coaches.

"There are only eight of them," Thor said. "Where's the ninth?"

"Here," Coyote said. "He's here."

He was looking splendid in a dazzling Hobs uniform, standing behind the visitors' bench. Beside him, on its black wheels, stood the great iron cage that held Taffy the Sasquatch.

"I hope you don't mind," he said, "but I really thought it would be a shame if there were no spectators at all for the last game of baseball ever played."

"Taffy!"

Ethan, Jennifer T., and Thor ran to the cage and pressed their faces against the bars. The Sasquatch lay in her old boneless heap on the floor of the cage, an arm thrown over her face.

"Taffy!" Jennifer T. said. "Taffy, are you all right?"

There was no reply. Jennifer T. knelt down beside the cage and reached in between the thick iron bars. The tips of her fingers just reached the ends of the fur on the Sasquatch's head, and she stroked it, gently.

"We're not mad at you, Taff," she said. "We understand."

"Yeah—" Ethan began. He was about to tell her that La Llorona had come to him, too, with an offer of release from sorrow. But then he remembered that, thanks to the Knot, he had managed to resist the temptation of La Llorona, where Taffy, dooming the Lodgepole, had failed. So he just said, "Yeah."

But Taffy didn't stir.

"Hey," Ethan said to Coyote. "I need somebody to hold my bat when I'm catching. To make sure you don't get it."

"As if I would ever resort to such trickery."

"Yeah, well, and I want it to be Taffy."

Taffy lowered an arm from her face and gazed at Ethan with her little round eyes. They shone with tears.

"Will you, Taff? Will you watch my bat?"

Taffy blinked, and puckered her dark forehead. Then, slowly, she nodded.

"All right, then," Coyote said. "Let's begin."

"Wait a second," Thor said. "Who's going to be umpire?"

"Heh-heh," said a raspy voice. "That'd be me."

Ethan turned, expecting to see the foul shaggy creature, pale as a worm, who had been dancing in attendance on Coyote since their arrival at Diamond Green, and saw instead a young man, his longish hair swept back behind his ears, dressed in the pale blue shirt and dark blue trousers of an umpire.

"Padfoot!" Ethan said.

"What's up, dude-let?"

"No *way*!" Ethan yelled, turning on Coyote. "That guy works for *you*. He can't be an *umpire*."

"You have no choice in the matter, first of all," Coyote said. "And second of all, I have discovered, to my surprise, that my old friend Robin Padfoot seems to have arrived, much to my hurt and consternation, on your side of the question of his own continued existence."

"All due respect, boss, heh-heh," Padfoot said. "But I *like* the universe OK. I know, heh-heh, that makes me weak."

"I think that, torn as he is between his sworn oath to serve me, and his inexplicable fondness for his own miserable life, he can manage to be fairly impartial. So come. Let's do it."

"Play ball!" Padfoot cried.

HERE ARE THE lineups, according to Alkabetz, for the game played at Diamond Green, on the ninth day of the ninth moon of the year 1335th Woodpecker (Universal Reckoning):

SHADOWTAILS	HOBBLEDEHOYS
Rideout, J.T., P	Breakneck, J., SS
Pettipaw, D., LF	O'Scratch, J., 2B
Boartooth, C., 1B/Mgr	Bones, J., 3B
Buendía, R., RF	Gobbet, J., CF
Reynard, C., CF	Van Slang, J., RF
Wignutt, T., 3B	Lupomanaro, J., 1B
Dandelion, S-R., 2B	Strzyga, J., LF
John, G., SS	Slaughter, J., C
Feld, E., C	Coyote, P/Mgr

For the first few innings it was a pitchers' duel. Coyote threw heat and smoke and lightning and thunder, pitches so wild yet true that you were certain they were coming at your head and yet when you looked down you saw them there, curled neat and tidy in the heel of the catcher's mitt. Some of his pitches may well have been invisible; others turned the air blue as they ripped on through. Then there were his junk pitches, screwballs and offspeed curves, sinkers and sliders and back-door curves. They were imbued with all the craft and treachery that have made Coyote's activities so interesting over the last fifty thousand years.

Jennifer T., whenever she took the mound, proceeded more deliberately, stopping frequently to confer with Ethan on pitch selection, relying mostly on her fastball, but with her change-up working well and her slider a quick shimmering silvery hook of unhittable air. One or two of Padfoot's calls were questionable, in the opinion of the Shadowtails, but there were as well a pair of Rideout pitches that he called as strikes, when Ethan was sure they had been outside and low.

Yet the Hobbledehoys, as Cinquefoil had said, were a tough team. They chipped away at Jennifer T., a hit here, a walk there, now bunting the runner over to second, now stealing third, until in the bottom of the fifth they lined everything up right – a walk, a stolen base, a fielder's choice, and a sacrifice fly – and managed to get a run across the plate. They went scoreless in the sixth and seventh, then added another run in the bottom of the eighth when Cutbelly lost a fly ball in the sun. By the top of the ninth, the score was 2–0 in favour of the Hobs. And within that zero were contained entire alphabets and inventories of zeroness; the Shadowtails were runless, hitless, and without a walk; Coyote was throwing a perfect game. Of all of the Shadowtail hitters, only Buendía had connected solidly, sending two of Coyote's pitches deep before they were run down by Jack Gobbet, the Hobs' centre fielder.

Spider-Rose led off the top half of the ninth by coaxing a walk out of Coyote, who seemed to be generally unnerved by the sight of the tattered doll that he had once foisted off on Filaree. Grim followed this with a first-pitch single, simple and clean. In spite of this apparent turn for the better in the Shadowtails' fortunes, Ethan came to the plate with almost no hope in his heart of succeeding. He had struck out once – swinging. Though he tried with each swing to ignore the pain in his hand and the chafing of the Knot, it was impossible. In his second at-bat he had hit a towering foul ball to left that was chased and caught by Jack Strzyga, and that was the best he had to show for his afternoon.

Now as he came to the plate for what would likely be his last time at-bat – ever – he stopped. He looked at Spider-Rose, with a lead off second base, Nubakaduba tucked under her left arm, and at Grim lurking behind the Hob first baseman. Ethan turned and looked back at his bench, at Jennifer T. in the on-deck circle, at Pettipaw, Thor and Cutbelly, Cinquefoil, at Taffy in her cage, and at Rodrigo Buendía. Taffy was on her feet, gripping the bars in her great fists and looking right at Ethan. He wondered how she felt, now, about the universe's coming to an end. At this point she probably wanted just to get it all over with. She was probably pulling for him to strike out.

Buendía pointed at Ethan. He put his hands on an imaginary bat handle and swung. Then he pointed at the sky. Ethan nodded.

"Yeah, right," he said.

"Batter up," Padfoot said.

Coyote tugged on the bill of his cap, then went into his stretch. He centred his body around the ball, in his glove, over his belly. Then he rocked back and let fly. Ethan caught a flash of the ball's seams as it came screwballing in at him. He swung, but at the last minute the pitch broke sharply away.

"Strike one!" Padfoot said.

The next pitch was another breaking ball, a curve that started away from Ethan and then dove in. He swung at it, pain lancing through his hand.

"Strike two!" Padfoot said.

Ethan stepped out, and took his left hand off the bat, and shook it. He tried once more to put the pain from his mind, but it was impossible. So he decided to try something new, something that struck him as very much in the vein of an idea Mr. Olafssen would have had. Instead of shirking the pain, he would allow himself to *feel* it. He would *use* the hurt, if he could. Maybe it would make him angry, or help to focus his thoughts. He stepped back in, and gripped the bat. He gripped it as tightly with his left hand as he could, allowing the Knot to press deeply against the tender spot on his hand. The pain shimmered through him like a ripple in a thin sheet of metal. He raised the bat over his shoulder.

"Get a hit, Ethan!" called a voice, reedy and strange, from beyond third base. Ethan looked up and saw his father, the remnant of his father, standing on the steps of the pump truck, watching the game. The Flat Man didn't raise his hand – didn't even move – but Ethan was sure it had been he who spoke. Nobody on the visitors' bench seemed to have heard or noticed, however. Nobody turned around. Ethan wondered if somehow the sound of his father's encouragement could have been simply wishing. He gazed out at Coyote. The pitch came. It was a fastball, straight down the middle. Ethan dug the handle of the bat into his outraged palm and swung. The impact of the ball on the shaft was so hard that Ethan felt the bones of his body shatter. His arms broke at the elbow, and his shoulders snapped off, and then as his momentum carried him around, his upper torso twisted entirely around on his hips, around and around like a stick of taffy, his waist corkscrewing thinner and thinner until it sheared in two and his upper body fell with a thud to the ground.

"Little dude!" cried the voice of Buendía, from somewhere back in a place where time and joy and the acrid tang of a burning cigar still existed. "Dude! Dude! Dude!"

Ethan staggered to his feet and looked up, and caught sight of the ball he had hit. It was rising into the air, over deep left-centre, a seed, a liner, a frozen rope streaking skyward over Diamond Green.

The speed of a home-run shot is determined not only by the velocity of the bat at the moment of impact, but by the speed the ball is travelling towards the hitter. So it must have been the combination of Ethan's pain-driven, father-haunted, wild, desperate swing, and a truly scorching hummer thrown by the Changer of the Worlds, that produced the magnificent shot that rocketed off the bat of Ethan Feld. It rose, and rose, and rose into the sky. It kept on rising, travelling farther and farther, out towards the limitless blue beyond the outfield of Diamond Green. Then, as everyone agreed, it seemed to hang a moment, a tiny grey period, pale against the blue – and disappeared. Ethan stood there, watching the fuzzy little hole it left in the sky, trembling and faint, like one of those optic floaters (actually they are called *phosphenes*) that you catch sight of from time to time, gliding across the empty air at the corner of your eye.

"Run!" came the cry from the Shadowtail bench. "Run, Ethan, run!"

He started running then, and when he crossed home plate, to be caught up in the collective dancing embrace of his team-mates, was amazed to the discover that the Shadowtails, thanks to him, now held the lead, 3–2. The celebration was cut short, however, by a sound, distant and clear as a bell. It was a familiar sound, crystalline and bright and yet at the same time alarming. It was the sound of mischief, of reckless play and impending disaster, of a backyard game of baseball carried just a couple of inches too far. It was the sound, at once unmistakable and infinitely far away, of a breaking window. Everyone, Shadowtails and Hobbledehoys, turned and stared up at the high featureless wall of sky beyond the outfield fence. The silence that fell upon the field was haunted by a tinkling that lingered in the ears.

It was Coyote, in the end, who put an end to the silence.

"Uh-oh," he said. "We're in trouble now." He stood a

moment longer, gazing up at the sky, then turned, and jammed his index and pinky fingers between his lips, and whistled. Across the field, by Murmury Well, Ethan saw his father's shape raise its hand. Then it retreated into the belly of the truck.

"Game over!" called the Coyote, starting to run to Murmury Well. "Forfeit! You win!"

The Hobbledehoys began to gesticulate wildly, chasing after their manager as he ran towards the truck. They were outraged with him for forfeiting; they had played very hard and were only a run down with three more outs to their name. The Shadowtails stood uneasily at the edge of the ball field, some of them watching Coyote as he ran, others staring up at the wavering little hole that Ethan's shot had poked into the glassy seal on the Gleaming. Ethan's gaze, however, was fixed on the armoured truck. The crew of greylings came tumbling out of its belly, rolling a wheeled machine that Ethan recognised as a variation on the kind of pump his father used to inflate his envelopes. Then came the Flat Man, carrying the dragon's egg. Coyote took the egg from the Flat Man and unstoppered it. There was a soft *piff* and then a curl of black vapour snaked like a vine from the opening. Coyote raised it, and took hold of a hose on the pump.

"Hey!" shouted Jennifer T. "You didn't *win*! We had a deal!"

"So I lied!" Coyote shouted back.

Then something large and dark and moving very quickly seemed to shudder up out of nowhere onto Coyote, and he stumbled backwards.

"Taffy!" Ethan cried. "It's Taffy! She got out!"

Snarling, the Sasquatch wrapped her long arms around Coyote's throat. Then she snatched at his upraised hand, on whose palm there balanced the wobbling hodag egg. A black, starless hole splashed across the sky behind them. They fell over backwards, but the Slipperiest One managed to slip the knot of Taffy's great furry arms, and catch the knobbly egg before it could tumble to the grass. He held it up, standing over her with a wild grin on his face. Then he tipped the egg, once, twice, and two long drizzling drops of Nothing splashed against the big leathery soles of her feet, and she bellowed in pain.

Coyote slapped the egg to the intake valve of the picofibre pump, and the Flat Man threw a switch, and instantly the pump started up, *onk-squitch-onk-squitch-onk-squitch*. The silvery hose leapt once, and then again, and then it settled back shuddering to the ground.

For a moment, for an hour, for a year, nothing happened. Then they heard another faint, familiar call, more chilling than the sound of breaking glass. It was the far-off crowing of a rooster. They felt the ground beneath their feet shudder, spasmodically, as if it were the hide of an immense animal trying to shed them like irritating flies. The air was rent with a creaking sound, like the rusted hinges of a giant door, and all about them, echoing against the hills of Applelawn and the craggy burnt brow of Shadewater Tor, came cracklings and rustlings and the groaning of ancient timbers.

"Ragged Rock," Cinquefoil said softly, sitting down in the grass. "Two out in the Bottom of the Ninth. The count is 0 and 2."

The werebeasts, Cutbelly and Pettipaw, whose eyes were sharper than anyone's, were the first to notice what they afterwards described as a window opening in the sky. They cried out, and pointed at a spot high in the blue expanse beyond the outfield. Ethan strained his eyes, but saw nothing – and then all at once it was there, a small patch of darker blue, roughly rectangular, in the midst of which lay the jagged hole that his home run shot had made. Though darker than the sky around it the rectangle was rimmed at its edges with a paler light, and as they watched faint shadows became apparent within in it, flickering and grey.

The shuddering of the ground grew more intense, and Ethan was knocked off his feet. When he looked up at the sky again the blue window had grown larger, and the pale blue light was pouring freely from it now, in all directions, reaching long solid shafts of blue to touch every corner of the world. Then a huge shadow passed in front of the source of the blue light from the sky, and it seemed to Ethan that this shadow had the form of a man. No, it was not a shadow at all. It was dark, but somehow it shone.

"No! *No!*"

It was the voice of Coyote. Ethan tried to look that way, but the force of gravity seemed to have grown abruptly stronger. He could not turn his head, or raise his body. He could only look at the great brilliant gap his home run had broken open in the sky-blue seal on the Gleaming.

"No!" Coyote yelled. He was dipping down to snatch baseballs from a canvas bag at his feet, and hurling blazing fastballs at the sky. "Get back in there! Go away, you big one-eyed bully! I'm not done! I'm not *done*!"

Just before the weight of Ragged Rock drew a curtain down over him, Ethan thought he saw the light around the face in the window shift and gather itself. It seemed to have formed itself into the shape of an immense arm, long, rippled with veins of lightning and a musculature of clouds. The arm reached down out of the sky, fingers spreading like the rays of a star, to grab at something that was flickering on the shore of Murmury Well, to snuff a dancing red flame.

HOME

Epilogue

Life, the World, and Baseball, in the Days After the Flood

NOT SO LONG ago, here in the Middling, there was an hour – it may have been a period as long as sixty-three minutes – during which a number of unusual phenomena occurred. A battered old Mercedes van pulled into the courtyard of a small orphanage outside of Cuzco, Peru, and when the nine children who lived in the orphanage ran out to greet it, they found that it contained their parents, all of whom had been lost in a catastrophic mudslide three years before. In the Jura Mountains of France, a modest hydro-electric dam project, whose completion would submerge an ancient, peaceful, and attractive village, and uproot its residents, vanished overnight. Off the southern tip of Thailand, the next morning, a magnificent coral reef that had been dying for ten years was found by divers to be mad and dazzling with life. Nine thousand terminal cases around the world were informed that their cancers had gone into remission. Tens of thousands of quarreling lovers reconciled, and hundreds of runaway children found themselves with money enough to return to a home that suddenly welcomed them.

Not all of the incidents were so dramatic. As you went farther along the branches of the Middling from Diamond Green, the effects of the unsealing of the Gleaming were less pronounced. People found beloved neckties, photographs, and lucky charms they had long given up for gone. Lifelong losers hit modest jackpots, the leaves of neglected houseplants uncurled and turned green again, and Chihuahuas whose yapping ability had been surgically removed found themselves suddenly able to bark again, and loudly repaid their owners for their cruelty. Much of the world was asleep during this enchanted hour, and on awaking the next morning many reported light and refreshing dreams in which the beloved dead returned to them, or in which, though hitherto they had never displayed any musical aptitude, they composed symphonies of genius.

It really is a shame that through our sad neglect of wonder, hopefulness, and trust we allowed so much clutter and debris to build up in the space that once connected us to Diamond Green. Nearly all the force of the Unsealing, of the great healing flood of pent-up Spirit that flowed out of the hole broken open by Ethan's home run, was dissipated in the effort of clearing through the vast thorny tangle of the Briarpatch. In the end, most of us here received only a trickle, a gleaming droplet, of that mighty flood. In the playground that is all that remains of the Elysian Fields of Hoboken, New Jersey, for example, the sole evidence of what happened at Diamond Green was the appearance, under the swings, of a yellowed Spalding baseball mysteriously signed *Van Lingle Mungo*. Later that day some boys and girls came out and tossed it around.

The good news, however, is that most of the Briarpatch was cleared away, and that the road into the land of perpetual summer, of apple blossoms and green grass, lies open to you, for the time being, at least – if you know where to look for it.

For those who were standing directly in the path of the flood, the effects were dramatic indeed. When Ethan came to himself again, he felt a dry, cool palm on his forehead that he recognised at once as belonging to his father. He sat up, and found himself under the worried scrutiny of a pair of moist brown eyes.

"Hi, Dad," he said. It was almost a question.

"Hi, son."

The Feld men stared at each other, and long weeks of separation and strangeness and horror filled the silence.

"Anything, uh, missing?" Ethan said at last, still a little uncertain.

"Yeah, actually," said Mr. Feld. "My glasses. But, oddly, I don't seem to need them anymore. I can see your beautiful face just fine without."

That was when Ethan finally found himself back in his father's arms, and all the strangeness and horror was washed away.

"I found you," Ethan said. "Dad, I said I would find you, and I found you."

"I heard all about it," said Mr. Feld. "And I'm very proud of you."

Ethan looked around and saw his knapsack lying in the grass, not far away. He went over to it and took out his father's wallet.

"Here," he said. "You left home without this."

His father took the wallet with a puzzled expression.

"That isn't like me," he said.

"You had a little bit of a hard time, Dad," Ethan told him. "I'll explain it later."

"OK," Mr. Feld said.

"It wasn't easy, Dad," Ethan said. "Finding you. I don't want you to ever go away again."

"I won't," his father said.

It was the kind of promise a father makes easily and sincerely, knowing at the same time that it will be impossible to keep. The truth of some promises is not as important as whether or not you can believe in them, with all your heart. A game of baseball can't really make a summer day last forever. A home run can't really heal all the broken places in our world, or in a single human heart. And there was no way that Mr. Feld could keep his promise never to leave Ethan again. All parents leave their children one day. Ethan knew that better now than he had ever known it before. But he was glad to have the promise nevertheless.

They stopped talking for a long time, and just lay there, shoulder to shoulder, in the sunshine on the grass.

"What's that sound?" Ethan said, at last, sitting up. "It sounds like a *baby* crying."

"It's a baby crying," Mr. Feld said. "One of your, uh, little friends, seems to have come across a very small baby."

He helped Ethan to his feet, and they walked across towards Murmury Well. There, by the cool deep wintry waters, they found Spider-Rose, holding her squalling brother in her arms, and kissing his little feet, each no bigger than a butter bean. Like all ferisher babies he was sort of rubbery and scrawny, with an elderly expression on his face, and his hair was still a hank of coarse black yarn, but there was certainly nothing unkissable about his little kicking feet.

"It *worked*!" Spider-Rose exulted. "I *knew* it would work. Didn't I always say?"

There were a dozen ferishers hanging around the edge of the well, lounging in the grass, laughing and mugging at the baby, and it took Ethan a moment, looking at the silly grin on Cinquefoil's face, to realise who they must be: members of the Boar Tooth mob who had been taken during the attack on the Birchwood. It was they who had formed the greyling ground crew that tended to the Diamond Green chalk lines. The pump, hose, and iron black truck had vanished; the sledge wagon had been smashed, as if by a giant fist, to splinters.

"Hey," said Jennifer T. She and Thor came over. They stood for a moment, three points of a triangle, then fell together and hugged. As he was holding Thor, Ethan realised that something was off, something that he thought, at first, might be his friend's smell. It was a *greener* smell, somehow, like that of pine needles or eucalyptus. He took a step back at looked at Thor.

"You're smaller," he said.

Thor nodded. "Shrinking," he said. "And look." He held up his forearm, to show Ethan some scratches below his elbow. The bloody streaks were paler than they ought to be, tinged with reddish gold.

"What is it?" Ethan said. "What's happening? Where's Coyote?"

"Gone," Mr. Feld said. He shook his head. "They came and took him."

He pointed towards right field, and Ethan saw that the expanse of sky over the Gleaming, formerly a vast blue blank, was now rich with clouds, mountainous and tinged purple with thunder. All along right field there now ran a giant wall, a hundred feet high, of high golden posts woven through with slats of silver. It would take a mighty swing indeed to clear those fences. At the end of the wall, right in straightaway centre, there was an immense wooden gate, closed, and barred. Over the gate hung a silver banner engraved simply:

216

"Two-sixteen?" Ethan said. "What's that?"

"The number of stitches in a baseball," Jennifer T. said.

"The number of barleycorns in a fathom," said Cinquefoil. "Which is the distance from home plate to the gates of the Gleaming."

"It's also the number of possible outcomes when you roll three dice," said Mr. Feld. It was exactly the kind of deeply irrelevant remark that Mr. Feld could always be counted on to proffer at a dramatic moment. Ethan could not resist hugging him again.

"I once heard it said," Pettipaw intoned, "that there are two hundred and sixteen letters in Old Mr. Wood's true Name."

"Hey," Thor said. "The *four* sides of my map are divided into *fifty-four* sections. Nine by six. And four times fifty-four is two hundred and sixteen."

"Two hundred and sixteen?" said Rodrigo Buendía. "That the area code for Cleveland, Ohio. I got a sister in Cleveland. Great baseball town."

Then he rolled up the legs of his trousers, and delighted in showing everyone how all of the terrible bright scars were gone.

EVERY FLOOD HAS its eddies, its pockets of resistance, its islands left inexplicably high and dry. They found Taffy lying on a barren patch of ice at the edge of the Winterlands. She was unconscious, motionless, and half-dead. Her fur was singed with frost, her lips were caked with blood. And her feet, those glorious, ridiculous appendages, were gone, dissolved by a fatal splash of fermented Nothing.

"That's not *fair*," said Jennifer T.

She rose from Taffy's side, and took off running.

"Jennifer T.!" called Mr. Feld. "Come back!"

She flew, as swiftly as her strong legs could carry her, out of the Winterlands, across the third base line of Diamond Green, and straight up to the great oak gate that marked the distance to straightaway centre. She threw herself against the gate. She pounded on it with her fists. When that had no visible result, she kicked it, fiercely but without producing a sound louder than the tapping of a fly at a windowpane. She turned around and kicked it again, like a mule this time, with the bottom of her foot. By the time Ethan reached her, she had given up her assault on the gate of heaven, and lay crumpled on the grass at its foot.

"I guess they're kind of busy in there right now," Ethan said. "Dealing with Coyote and all."

"It's not *fair*," she said. "What about Taffy? What about *me*?"

For her scars were intact; her finger, where she had once broken it, was still a little bit crooked. And inside of her she was still just Jennifer T. Rideout, of the ne'er-do-well Rideouts of Clam Island, a shadowtail, a mongrel, a mutt.

Ethan sank down into the grass beside her.

"I like you how you are," he told her, squeezing her rough hand. "I'm glad you aren't any different."

"Yeah, yeah, Feld," she said, tugging her hand away and scrambling to her feet. She jerked her ponytail more firmly through the opening at the back of her cap. But she smiled, and he saw there was a flush of colour in her cheeks. "Blah blah blah."

THEY MADE A rude stretcher out of the debris of the sledge-wagon, and dragged Taffy across Diamond Green into the warmth of Applelawn, the resting place of so many wounded heroes. Here, as all over the Far Territories of the Summerlands, a cool blue rain of light had fallen, extinguishing the raging fires, and repairing the tens of thousand of acres that had already burned. The apple trees were bursting with new blossoms, and the Beaver Women were hard at work rebuilding the Lodges of the Blessed. They spent two days enjoying the legendary hospitality of those Lodges, and caring for Taffy's wounds. And they prepared for their long trip back. Following the detailed instructions set forth in the chapter of *The Wa-He-Ta Brave's Official Tribe Handbook* devoted to earning the Watercraft Feather, they fashioned a sturdy and capacious raft, and Grim the Giant cut and peeled some long sturdy poles. Then they set off across the Big River. This time they passed unmolested, without so much the ripple of a whisker-tip to disturb the smooth flow of the waters.

When they arrived at Old Cat Landing, they received a warm reception from a crew of Big Liars who were now, in the wake of the flood, considerably bigger than before, though still not anywhere near their former grandeur. Nevertheless the Liars had outgrown their former haunts and homes. They had been obliged to level the entire settlement, and to rebuild it ten times as big. The Tall Man with the Axe had grown so tall – taller even than Mooseknuckle John – that it was no trouble at all for him to wade out into the river and dredge up poor old Skidbladnir, slimed over and drizzling brown sludge, from the bottom of the river. In spite of her sorry condition, the Felds were delighted to see her again. Mr. Feld and Grim the Giant took her apart, piece by piece, carefully cleaning and drying each valve, coupling and hose, and then put her back together again (albeit with the functions of clutch and brake pedals reversed). A store of prunejack was fetched down from certain persons in a particular range of mountains, and after a week of Miss Annie Christmas's enormous hospitality they set out once again for Big Kobold, aiming to take it this time from the other side.

Grim had built a kind of open trailer out of an old piano crate and a couple of wagon wheels, and it was in this homemade ambulance that they stashed the twelve Boar Tooth ferishers, and laid Taffy the Sasquatch. She had not regained consciousness since the day they found her lying maimed in the icefields of the Winterlands, and as they journeyed up into the Raucous Mountains and down the other side she emitted only the occasional moan and, from time to time, a dour sorrowing snatch of some ancient Sasquatch lament. Spider-Rose, who with the help of the ferisher women brewed a nourishing formula for her little brother out of leaves and bee-nectars they found in the woods, took to nursing the Sasquatch with the same rich decoction, forcing the clear green liquid into Taffy's mouth through a bit of hose left over from Grim's reconstruction of the car.

The welcome they received at Dandelion Hill was much warmer than the first; and they spent a few days here, resting and watching the tiny cheeks and serious gaze of Nubakaduba, whom everyone called Newboy, melt the frozen heart of Queen Filaree – the healing effects of the flood being, in some cases, a little delayed.

When it was time to leave Dandelion Hill they lost Dick Pettipaw, as well. He was happy to return to the warrens and tunnels and secret ways of the great hill, but sad, too, for no longer would he contest the ratting ingenuity of Grimalkin John. The little giant had decided to carry on with the remnants of Big Chief Cinquefoil's Travelling Shadowtails All-Star Baseball Club as far as his homelands. Though the flood had burned away the thirst for revenge against the brothers who had bound him into slavery, there was still a score to settle.

"I'll be wantin' them to look me in the eye and beg me to forgive them," he said. "Even if they has to scramble down on their bellies to do it." He grinned. "*Especially* then."

"I'll miss your great ham-heeled lumbering footsteps," the wererat said, blowing his nose in a lace handkerchief. "Warning me from a mile off that you were coming."

"And I'll miss your blowhard prattle," Grim the Giant said. "And your mule-headedness, to boot."

So, in the shadow of Dandelion Hill, they parted, the best of enemies.

Skid drove on, taking it slow to conserve juice, headed for a point on a branch several days to the east of Dandelion Hill that Thor had decided, after making a complicated study of his map, lay within leap of a spot in the Winterlands called Gnashville, which in turn lay a leap away from Bellingham, Washington, where they could catch a ferry home. When they were two days out from Dandelion Hill, Grimalkin John began to smell something familiar in the air – "the good old rotten stink of giant." After another half a day, he asked Mr. Feld to stop the car and let him out. This was a calculated risk on his part, as they all knew. Cinquefoil felt that it was likely the Unsealing had washed away the binding grammer on the little giant's hide, but there was no way to know for sure until Grim had put a day's march between himself and Ethan Feld. So, having stuffed his pockets with what remained of the shavings he'd taken from Ethan's bat, he shook hands with his friends and with each of the ferishers in turn. Then Grim the Giant climbed out of the car, slung his knapsack over his shoulder, and, with a backwards look and a wave of his hand, walked off into the Summerlands and out of this story.

Three days and two crossings later, they found themselves at the Bellingham ferry dock.

"Well," said Rodrigo Buendía. "This it, little dudes."

"Yeah," Ethan said.

Rodrigo sighed. He was at sixes and sevens. He had decided to rent a car in downtown Bellingham, but that was the extent of his plans. The Angels had been set to leave for a twelve-day road trip the day Ethan and Jennifer had snatched him away, and he was certain that his unexplained, unexcused absence meant that his contract with the team had been terminated. He walked over to the newspaper vending machines and bought a Seattle *Times*, to see if it said anything about the mysterious absence of the Angels' faded slugger. But there was nothing, aside from the information that the Angels were off today, travelling to Seattle. Then his mouth opened, and his eyes got almost comically wide.

"Whoa!" he said. He pointed to the date on the newspaper, and then all their eyes widened. Though they had spent nearly two months in the Summerlands, in the Middling it was, according to the *Times*, only *two days* after they had left Clam Island; and, at the same time, a week *before* they had spirited Rodrigo Buendía out of Rancho Encantado. Don't try to figure it all out; just take my word for it.

"Do you know what that mean?" he asked them. "I remember this day. It was an off day. Yes! We had a game in

Seattle… yes… and I— I— forgot my wife's *birthday*. And she was so… that was the start of the… Oh! Oh my gosh, dudes."

"Go," said Jennifer T.

"I have to go! Goodbye, now! Come to see me in Anaheim, I will put you in the best seats."

Another delayed effect of Ethan's home run, then, was the healing of the marriage of Rodrigo Buendía, who called his wife from a Dairy Queen and asked her to meet him at the Four Seasons Hotel in Seattle, in the honeymoon suite. As you know, he subsequently went on to a .299 season, with 32 home runs and 98 RBIs, and was voted Comeback Player of the Year by the Sportswriters Union.

They waited for the last ferry of the night, which was likely to be the least crowded. Mr. Feld had bought a tarp at a hardware store, and they threw this over the trailer to cover their hairy, moaning cargo. The ferishers, of course, would be invisible to anyone who did not believe in ferishers. Now, Bellingham, Washington, is a freethinking town, and it was not a completely safe bet that there was *nobody* who held such beliefs. This was why they waited for the 1:14 A.M. to Clam Island.

As it turned out, old Albert Rideout was returning to Clam Island that night, as well, from one of his aimless Coyote rambles along the borders of Canada and the United States. He spent the passage from the mainland in the ferry's snack bar, drinking whisky from a can of 7-Up. He was in a uniquely sour mood. He was never exactly satisfied or happy when he came crawling home, trailing arrests and accidents. But this time it was worse than usual. About ten days earlier, ten days into his latest bender, he had happened to cross paths with a full-length mirror. This was, unbeknownst to him of course, at the very moment when the ebbing tide of the Unsealing came foaming over the particular town in the Idaho panhandle where he found himself. It was a clear, cold, truthful look at himself that he got at that moment – at the ruin he had made of his life and, in particular, of his failure as a father. Though the moment had passed, the memory of it had been bothering him ever since.

When he felt the series of iron shudders, deep in the belly of the boat, that meant they were slowing for the approach to Southend Dock, he belched, tossed the can into the trash, and then stumbled downstairs to the car deck. The wind was from the west, carrying with it all the familiar smells of the island of his birth and early promise: Douglas fir, tidal flats, and a faint ghost of the old strawberry patches. He saw the lights of the rapidly approaching ferry dock. He had better get into his old junkheap, then.

He turned, looking for the 1976 AMC Matador that had recently come into his possession. It was not where he had left it. He did not, in fact, remember where he had left it. Suddenly he was not sure if he had even boarded in his car, or if a lady named Shermanette had not dropped him off at the Bellingham dock. He set out among the few late cars, imagining that the island people in them were staring at him with the usual disapproval, imagining that he did not care. It was then that he heard what sounded to him like someone hawking up a really big loogey. He turned around. There, chained to an old orange Saab that he vaguely recognised, was a funky-looking wooden trailer, covered in a brand-new tarp. As he stared, wondering if the sound could possibly have come from the trailer, he saw the tarp twitch. Something *was* there, thrashing and moaning. Albert's heart began to beat faster – he had a feeling that something very wrong was about to appear from beneath the tarp. And then a moment later he found himself staring into the bleary, baffled face of what he took at first for a man in a gorilla suit, until he saw the long pink tongue emerge from the thing's mouth, hawking and smacking its lips as if to rid itself of a nasty taste in its mouth. Then the tarp shifted abruptly, and Albert saw how huge the thing was, and just as his clouded mind began to assemble all the necessary components of the idea *Bigfoot* – that was when he saw that the huge, hideous thing *had no feet at all*!

When the last car drove off the ferry, a ferry worker named Big Dave Cardoon, who had graduated from high school with Albert, found him lying there, passed out drunk in the middle of the empty deck. He dragged his old classmate to his feet, and then when it developed that Albert had no ride home, stuffed Albert into his truck, and drove him back to the Rideout place. It struck him as amusing at first that Albert kept muttering "Bigfoot spat on me," over and over again, but it quickly grew annoying, and he was glad to get the poor fellow out of his car and up the sagging steps of the house.

THEY HAD JUST rolled off the ferry when one of the ferishers climbed from the trailer onto the roof of the car, and peeked in through the window to say that Taffy had revived, and seemed to be in pain. Ethan heard her heavy moaning, then, and saw from the way one of the dockworkers was staring at the car that other people could hear it, too.

"We better get her to a doctor," Mr. Feld said. "I'll turn the car around. We'll take her to St. Joseph's in Bellingham. God knows how we'll explain—"

"Dad," Ethan said. "Would Mom have known how to take care of her?"

"Your *mother*? Treat a *Sasquatch*?" He had slowed the car, preparing to turn it around for the long ride back to the hospital on the mainland. Now he stopped. He frowned. "You know something, Ethan? I sort of think she would have. Is there a vet on the island? There must be."

"There is," Jennifer T. said. "Her name is Margaret something. Down by the tree nursery. We took one of the dogs there when one of the other dogs bit its ear off."

"Sounds perfect," said Mr. Feld. And he turned the car around.

DR. MARGARET PEDERSEN lived in a small, neat house of brick and siding, behind the sign that bore her name. The house was dark, at this hour, except for the porch light. As they pulled into her gravel drive, what sounded like a hundred dogs all began yapping and howling at once. Lights came on inside. The aluminium screen door banged open. A large woman in a long housecoat stepped onto the porch and peered into the shadows.

"Yes?" she called, sounding sympathetic and annoyed at the same time, and maybe a little bit afraid. "Who is it?"

"Dr. Pedersen?" Mr. Feld said, as he climbed out of the car. "It's Bruce Feld. I live out at the old Okawa place."

"*Yes?*" This time it sounded a little more purely annoyed.

"We have a— a hurt—"

"Creature," Thor suggested.

Dr. Pedersen belted her housecoat more tightly around herself and then came across the lawn. Ethan saw the ferishers quickly tumble out the front end of the trailer and go scurrying into nearby woods, with Cinquefoil close behind, as if they could sense that Dr. Pedersen believed in fairies, and had decided it would be better not to distract her.

"Well?" said Dr. Pedersen. She looked, a little impatiently, from Mr. Feld to the three children he had apparently decided to drag out into the middle of the night. Then she looked at the tarp-covered trailer. She was a very tall, large-framed woman with a pinched mouth and wide, pale eyes. She wore her hair in a crew cut. It was the haircut, and that warm, exasperated voice, that made you want to trust her to heal a broken Sasquatch. Mr. Feld hesitated a moment longer, then pulled back the tarp in a single jerk. Taffy sat up, gasping, as if wakened suddenly from a startling dream. She and Dr. Pedersen stared at each other for a moment.

Dr. Peggy Pedersen, as they would later learn, had been awakened in the middle of the night many times in the past. As the only veterinarian on Clam Island, with her office in a trailer behind her house, she was accustomed to having people, often hysterically upset, show up at three in the morning because driving home from the bars of Clam

Centre they had struck or run over some dog. It was not even unheard of – after the Urgent Care Centre was forced to eliminate twenty-four-hour care – for late-night visitors to show up with *humans* needing some kind of emergency help. But this was definitely her first Sasquatch. She closed her eyes, and opened them again, then glanced helplessly at Mr. Feld, with an expression on her face that seemed to invite him to tell her the whole thing was a joke. Mr. Feld nodded, very solemn. Then Dr. Pedersen looked down, and saw the ragged stumps of Taffy's legs, and all trace of doubt and late-night bafflement vanished from her face.

"Oh, poor thing," she said.

THE DAY AFTER their return was a practice day, and when Ethan, Thor, and Jennifer T. showed up at Jock MacDougal they had missed only one game, another loss, 8–2 to the Bigfoot Tavern Bigfoots.

"Well," said Mr. Perry Olafssen, as they came across the parking lot towards the ball field. He put on his stern face, which was really just a variation of his disappointed face. "Well, well. Missed a game, you three. And we needed you." He said this last part to Jennifer T. "Can't do that, kids. Can't just not show up for a game. Not without calling first. Would never fly in the bigs. If you were paid, I'd have to dock you." He looked at Mr. Feld. "Not good, Bruce."

Though nothing was more important to Mr. Feld, as we know, than showing up for a game, he was too tired even to blush. For the last two nights he had worked feverishly to mould a pair of enormous prosthetic feet for Taffy out of his remarkable picofibre polymer, hoping to arrive at something that would be light and flexible and yet stand up to all the punishment that a Sasquatch's life inflicted on her feet. When he was not working on the feet, he was visiting Taffy over at Dr. Pedersen's, in the doctor's back bedroom. He was also, Ethan had begun to suspect, visiting Dr. Pedersen, who turned out to be a lifelong Phillies fan.

"Sorry, Perry," Mr. Feld said. "Won't happen again." And indeed it did not.

When that day's practice was over, Mr. Olafssen, who had been watching Ethan through narrowed eyes, called him over.

"Funny bat," he said. "Where'd you get it?"

Ethan handed Splinter to Mr. Olafssen. He had known this moment would eventually come.

"Made it," he said, neatly leaving out the pronoun. He did not want to lie – what if people started asking him to make bats for *them*? – but he did not care to get into the whole Grim-the-Giant thing with his coach, either.

"You missed a spot." Mr. Olafssen pointed to the Knot. "Must chafe a bit."

Ethan held out the palm of his hand. The blister had long since hardened into a thick yellowish callus. He shrugged.

"I'm used to it," he said.

After practice, the children cut through the woods to see what had become of Hotel Beach. The bulldozers were gone, the earthmovers and backhoes, all the warning signs that had been thrown up by the minions of TransForm Properties. But that was not all. The birch trees had grown back, to very nearly their former stature, or else they had simply been replacced, in the flood of healing. Standing there, now, looking out at the silent white trees, Ethan could *feel* the Summerlands, nearer than ever before. He felt that he could have leapt there himself, without any help from Cutbelly or Thor.

"I wonder how they're doing?" he said, and the others knew whom he meant right away.

"It takes a hundred years to build a ferisher knoll," Thor said. "They're going to be living in tents for a long, long time."

They saw less and less of Thor after that day; he began to spend more of his time leaping from this World to the Summerlands, scampering here and there across the World of his birth, travelling often in the company of Taffy the Sasquatch. Everywhere he went he inquired after a reuben baby who had been taken by a mob of ferishers outside of Cle Ellum, Washington, eleven Middling years before. The last time Ethan saw him, he had shrunk down until he was only a few inches taller than Cinquefoil, and invisible to 98.3 percent of the general population. But that was a while ago, and who knows where in the Worlds he and Taffy may have ventured, searching for the changeling whose place Thor had taken, looking for a homewood of their own.

Even without Thor, the Roosters posted what was always afterwards recalled as one of the most amazing comeback seasons in the history of Clam Island baseball. One lover of baseball cannot get a team out of the cellar, but two can turn a season around. Shortly after the return of Rideout and Feld, the Roosters started to win games. They had always placed great stock in Jennifer T., but now they very quickly, if somewhat to their surprise, learned to trust their catcher, too. Once they managed this, it was a very short step to trusting each other. They noticed that there was more to baseball than hitting the ball as hard as you could, than waving your glove in the general direction of the ball and hoping for the best. They took pitches, turned double plays, and hit the cutoff man, and instead of trying to cream it every time they got up, they just did their best to advance the runner. They played like ferishers, with careful abandon. Finally, they started to believe. They won their last twelve games in a row, and finished tied with the Shopway Angels for first place in the Mustang League.

A one-game playoff for the championship ensued. They had seen less of the Angels over the second half of the season than of the Reds and Bigfoots, and it took the Angels a while to realise that the boy behind home plate with a mask over his face and armoured pads on his shins, knees, and chest was their old pal, Dog Boy.

The realisation finally hit when Ethan, mask thrown off, mouth open in a hopeful O, killed an Angel rally by snagging a tricky pop fly at the backstop.

"Nice catch," said the hitter, Tommy Bluefield, who was also the Angels catcher.

"That's nothing," Ethan said. "Josh Gibson, the Negro Leagues star who was perhaps the finest catcher ever to play this great game of baseball, once got his pie plate around a ball dropped from the top of the Washington Monument."

Tommy Bluefield scratched his head.

"What happened to *him*?" he asked Jennifer T., as she came in from the mound.

"He read Peavine's book," she said. "Maybe you should, too."

"Tell him about it, J.T.," said Albert Rideout, holding out his hand for a high five. He was a regular attendee of Roosters games now, as well as of dinners at the Rideout table, and he had gone to work doing odd jobs for Ethan's father. The change in him, abrupt and apparently genuine, was universally remarked. Nobody knew the reason for it, though some whispered darkly, around the Clam Island Tavern, that he had gotten some kind of a bad scare, from some Hell's Angels up in Blaine, or from some gangsters down in Tacoma, or from some neo-Nazis out by Flathead Lake.

"Shut up, Albert," said Jennifer T.

She had not yet forgiven her father, and she was not sure that she was going to do so anytime soon. He had caused her too much embarrassment and shame over the years. He had missed too many ball games, recitals, doctor's visits, and school plays. Those which he had attended, he had too often spoilt. But he was trying, and though she doubted it would last, she was too pure a ballplayer not to give credit to the other side for trying. As she trotted past him, she slapped his outstretched hand.

"Way to pitch 'em, J.T.," he said, watching her go by.

"OK, Dad," she said, and then felt her cheeks burning. It had been a very long time since she had called her father "Dad."

As for Ethan, he was kept busy all through the game. There was a broken double-steal in the second inning that led to a rundown between third base and home. There was a foul-tipped third strike that Ethan bobbled but caught for an out. In the fifth, Jennifer T. got a certain itchy look that Ethan recognised. She wrinkled up her nose, and her sock seemed to be bothering her. She walked two batters in a row. Ethan went out to talk to her.

"You can do it," he said.

"I know I can," said Jennifer T. "Thank you. Now get off my mound, Feld."

Ethan nodded. Peavine warns, in his book, that pitchers do not like to be visited by their catchers, no matter how badly they may need the visit.

After that, Jennifer T.'s sock seemed to be all right. She struck out the next two batters to retire the side.

In the bottom of the seventh, with the score tied, the Angels runner at third came charging home. Ethan took the throw from short. He came out from behind the plate. He planted his feet. He lowered his shoulder. He remembered that you must hold on to the ball, in the words of the great Peavine, "as if you are holding on to the love of your very truest friend". He imagined that he was holding on to the love of Jennifer T. Rideout, and to the great adventure they had just lived through together. He had been so busy in the game, until now, that he had forgotten to remember that this would be the very last game of the season. The Angels baserunner, head down, fists pumping, came at him.

Ethan took a deep breath. He smelled the tar-and-butter smell of the oil Jennifer T. had used to soften up his glove. He smelled cut grass, and Kool-Aid, and hot dogs with ketchup. He could see the green ribbon of the outfield and the long shadow of the bleachers. He heard the scrape of the oncoming cleats in the dirt of the base path. He heard his heart beating behind his chest protector. Without even looking, he could see the Angels running wild on the bases. He could see his team-mates standing and jumping and yelling and staring in at home with their hands on top of their caps as if to hold them on. He could hear the ragged, hoarse cheering of his father, in his XXL Ruth's Fluff 'n' Fold Roosters jersey. He could see Jennifer T. coming halfway down the hill, glove on her hip, believing in him.

Ethan got knocked down. When he stood up again, his mouth was full of dirt, he had taken a knee in the eye, and his nose was bleeding. But he was still holding on to the ball.

PRAISE FOR MICHAEL CHABON

The Amazing Adventures of Kavalier and Clay, (winner of the Pulitzer Prize for Fiction 2001):

'Perfection' *Daily Telegraph*

'Dazzling. Chabon has not so much attempted the great American novel as brought to life the idea that it has already been written – week by week, in the humble heroism of the comic book' *Independent*

'An adventure story that keeps you up until 4am with the bedside light on...' *Observer*

'...proof of the abiding power of Chabon's complex, serious, engaged but above all entertaining story-telling' *Times Literary Supplement*

Wonder Boys:

'A superb creation...' *Sunday Times*

'The natural exuberance and extravagance of Chabon's writing is matched by dazzling wit' *Sunday Telegraph*